CRITICS PRAISE THE CHILLING PROSE OF GORD ROLLO AND *THE JIGSAW MAN!*

"Does not let up until the final page. A superb excursion into modern horror."
— Edward Lee, Author of *Brides of the Impaler*

"Gord Rollo is a writer of amazing—and dark—talent. Guaranteed to keep you turning the pages!"
— Brian Keene, Author of *Castaways*

"A suspense-thriller, pain-filled page turner that will surprise you right to the end. I nominate it for best horror novel of the year."
— Horror World

"In *The Jigsaw Man* Gord Rollo edges closer to his early promise as a northern Stephen King."
— Gene O'Neill, Author of *The Burden of Indigo*

"*The Jigsaw Man*...will break readers' hearts, and continue to haunt them long after the last page is turned. With this novel, Rollo establishes himself as a name to watch on the horror fiction landscape."
— *Rue Morgue*

"This novel's unforgettable payoff is what horror fans yearn for, and you won't be disappointed. If this one isn't at least nominated for a few awards, horror may be headed to a very sorry state. Yep—this sucker's that good."
— The Horror Fiction Review

"Gord Rollo is a talent of horrific proportions."

"Guaranteed to thrill yo style."

IN THE CREATURE'S DOMAIN

Tom, David, and Johnny didn't even look at their fallen friend. They couldn't take their eyes off the hideous, red-eyed beast blocking their path.

"So you pathetic worms are the fearless Knights of the Round Room?" said the creature, with a grin on its grotesque face. "Does that mean you're going to fight me?"

The three remaining "knights" still standing could do nothing but tremble.

"I thought not," it continued. "You boys should never have come down here. This is *my* domain... and I don't like uninvited pissants invading it."

The laughter had stopped now and the creature's eyes shone a brighter red as it stood to its full height with a cold scowl on its shredded face. A growl escaped from between its lipless mouth as it drew nearer to the boys....

CRIMSON

GORD
ROLLO

LEISURE BOOKS NEW YORK CITY

*This book is dedicated to my wife and friend, Deborah Rollo.
Only seems fair. After all, she has the horrific task of putting
up with me every day...*

A LEISURE BOOK®

March 2009

Published by

Dorchester Publishing Co., Inc.
200 Madison Avenue
New York, NY 10016

ISBN 10: 0-8439-6195-3
ISBN 13: 978-0-8439-6195-9
E-ISBN: 1-4285-0613-6

Visit us on the web at www.dorchesterpub.com.

ACKNOWLEDGMENTS

I want to send out a special shout to all my readers and fans. Thank you for helping me spread the word. I appreciate it more than these few words can express. Mind you, our job has only begun...

CRIMSON

IN THE BEGINNING . . .

The Genesis of a Small Town's Fear
Dunnville, Ontario, June 21, 1955

A tall, heavyset old man walks along a desolate country road by the cloud-filtered light of the full summer moon. In his wake he leaves a dotted crimson trail dripping from the blood-smeared head of the axe casually slung over his left shoulder. He is oblivious to the cool north wind blowing the thin branches of the willow trees around him into a lashing frenzy. His feverish mind a jumble of broken thoughts: *Get home, Jacob, before the police . . . That fucking bastard, Sanderson. How dare he try . . . Get hold of yourself. You've gotta . . . The blood, oh how I love that sweet coppery taste. . . .*

Jacob stops at the end of a narrow gravel driveway, not entirely sure where—or for that matter, who—he is, until he glances at the battered metal mailbox with the crudely painted HARRISON scrawled on both sides. *Ah yes . . . ,* he thinks, shambling over to smear a big red X over his family name with the sticky liquid covering his trembling hands.

Home sweet home . . .

Vivid images of his family flash helter-skelter through his confused mind, rapid-fire snapshots of recent days and years long past. Emma and him smiling on their wedding day, her white dress badly wrinkled from their sneaking off from the party for a quickie in the barn loft . . . Holding little Emily in his arms last year, joy etched onto his face at having fathered such a beautiful child so late in life . . . His older son, Josh, spitting out a mouthful of thick, syrupy blood after Jacob smashed his face against the dining room wall, two front teeth still stuck in the otherwise-smooth plaster surface . . . Proudly walking hand in hand with the two boys when they are little, heading to their favorite fishing hole in the woods . . . Christmas day five or six years ago and Jacob dressed in a red Santa's hat, merrily dancing around the brightly lit tree . . . Plunging a fork into Jack's throat to shut his younger son up and finally stop the whiny little bastard screaming . . . Using his body to hold Emma down as he saws through the wrist bones of her left arm with a rusty hacksaw . . .

These images and more swirl out of the dark abyss his consciousness has become. Part of him is sickened by these vivid memories, making him long for better days, but part of him also rejoices, reveling in the blood, torture, and pain. Death has come to the small Canadian town of Dunnville, and madness is Jacob's only companion now.

The shrill blare of a distant police siren brings Jacob out of his reverie. *The cops.* He knows they'll be coming for him soon, once they realize what he's done to Danny Sanderson back at the textile factory.

He turns from the mailbox to gaze toward the house at the end of the gravel drive. The Harrison farmhouse is a large two-story wooden box with a covered porch tacked on the side facing the road. There's a floodlight on the porch, but it's unlit. In fact, none of the lights in the house are burning, the visible windows as black as Jacob's murderous mood. Devoid of life now, but not empty of occupants. Jacob's family is still there—most parts of them, anyway—keeping a quiet vigil along with the gathering flies, waiting patiently for his return.

"They're all . . ."

Dead, Jacob is about to say, a smile forming on his bloody lips, but before he can spit the word out, over the noise of the howling wind he hears a sound from within his home.

A baby crying.

Emily?

He's forgotten about Emily. Sweet little Emily, who until recently has been the light of his life. How long has she been left alone, laying in darkness, in filth, amid the slowly rotting bits and pieces of the family she'd never know? Jacob doesn't know the answer to this question, and the weight of the shame that washes over him brings him to his knees. His mind is clear for the first time in months, crystal clear, but the dementia returns almost immediately, clamping down on him like a steel-toothed bear trap. A war rages within him, an internal battle between good and evil, sanity and oblivion, life and death.

Thirty seconds later, Jacob Harrison regains his feet and begins walking toward the porch. He's dragging the axe behind him, cleaving a thin groove in the gravel as he approaches the stairs. There is no emotion on his face, no pictures race through his thoughts. He's a man on a mission now, his decision unalterable. He knows exactly what must be done.

Inside the house, Jacob heads straight for the child, homing in on the infant in the dark by her high-pitched squeals. He finds her underneath an end table in the living room, wrapped in a blood-, urine-, and feces-soaked bath towel, half-hidden by an old newspaper. Emily is disgustingly dirty and screaming loud enough to shatter glass, but she's unhurt. Jacob hurries her to the large country kitchen, where he gently places her in the sink and washes her soiled body with soapy warm water. After she is thoroughly clean, Jacob gets her a bottle filled with apple juice from the refrigerator. Emily, starving and dehydrated from neglect, greedily slurps it down. After the bottle is drained, Jacob finds her pacifier, and soon little Emily is fast asleep in her father's powerful arms.

Jacob quietly searches for what he needs, careful not to make any noise that might wake the child. He finds the large metal pan on the floor in the walk-in pantry. He places Emily inside the deep pan, and then Jacob—without thought, without emotion, without remorse—carries the pan back into the kitchen, pops it into the oven, and cranks the cooking dial up to its highest setting.

Jacob then turns away from the kitchen and heads up the staircase to Jack and Josh's bedroom at the rear of the house. He retrieves a thick rope from the boys' closet, skillfully fashions a perfect hangman's noose, and slings the rope over an exposed rafter in the ceiling. He takes a moment to scribble a quick suicide note for the police, then gets up on Josh's bed to put his neck through the noose. Stone-faced and completely out of his mind, Jacob Harrison steps off the bed and into urban legend—his legacy of evil to influence the nightmares of the people of this small town for generations to come.

PRELUDE

Present Day

I was only a kid when it started, when we released the evil that would destroy our lives. Four of us—Tom, Peter, Johnny, and me, David. We set free a nightmare that warm Saturday in June of 1977, cursing our lives from that moment on.

We were only ten years old.

We lived in the small Canadian town of Dunnville, a rural Ontario farming community on the banks of the Grand River, near where its murky waters empty into Lake Erie. The madness began on the day we released the creature, but everything was set in motion the day before, on Friday, the day Tom, Pete, and I met Johnny for the first time. He was the new kid in town, and fate saw to it that he became our grade-five classmate.

Our whole class was shocked to find out Johnny and his mother had moved into the abandoned Harrison farmhouse out on Logan Road. It was common knowledge to everyone in Dunnville that the farm was haunted. In 1955, twenty-two years earlier, Jacob Harrison had done something so vile, so terribly evil in that dilapidated farmhouse, no one ever considered moving there. Everyone wanted it burned to the ground. So it sat empty, waiting for Johnny . . . and eventually, the rest of us.

We were stupid enough to agree to go play at Johnny's

house the next day, Saturday morning. We couldn't find a way of telling him about Old Man Harrison or the legacy of the house he was living in, so we didn't bother. Why should we have? Sure, Tom, Pete, and I were terrified of Old Man Harrison, but he was just a legend, a scary ghost story told around a roaring campfire. It was our buddy's place now, and nothing bad would happen to us there.

We were fools. The evil was waiting for us.

The line between imagination and reality is thin, my friend. Very thin indeed. Our tale begins at Johnny's farmhouse, on that Friday night in June of 1977, the night before we stepped over that line . . . and all hell broke loose.

BOOK ONE

Scared Little Boys
The Late Spring of 1977

CHAPTER ONE

Johnathan Page had a good life. He was poor, but had everything he needed. He'd dreaded moving out of the big city of Hamilton to come to a tiny town like Dunnville, but he already knew he loved it here. He'd met some decent friends and no longer felt like an outsider, a nobody, as he had in the city. Here, he felt he belonged.

Since he had arrived home from school, his mother had been lecturing him endlessly about how careful he should be. Mary Page was a huge woman with bleached blonde hair who proudly admitted weighing two hundred and sixty pounds.

"You're not familiar with this place yet," she warned.

"I hear you, Ma," Johnny said. "I promise I'll be careful. Okay? I'm real tired. Think I'll hit the sheets."

Before his mother had a chance to drown him in her arms for her nightly kiss, Johnny hurried up the creaky old staircase, off to bed.

Mary exhaled deeply, wondering again if moving to this farm had been a good idea. Not that they'd had any choice. Johnny's father, George, had disappeared about eight years ago. Johnny had just turned two. One rainy night George had failed to come home from work. The police didn't consider foul play, even though Mary stubbornly refused to believe George had simply walked out on her. Listening to Mrs.

Page droning on about how good a wife she was convinced the police that running away was exactly what he *had* done.

Mary and Johnny had lived on the best they could with a quickly declining bank account. How was she going to look after her poor son without an income?

Her salvation had come in the form of a piece of paper. Mary's lawyer had been collecting the necessary paperwork for her to claim bankruptcy, when he'd found the deed to a house George had purchased before his disappearance. The Dunnville property had cost next to nothing, was fully paid, and Mary legally owned it. George had even rented the land to a local farmer, so suddenly Mary found herself with a new bank account with sixteen thousand dollars accrued from the land rental. She tried to sell the property and stay in Hamilton, but no matter how low she dropped the price, nobody was interested. Eventually she packed up and brought her ten-year-old son to Dunnville to begin a new life.

Mary popped a dusty record onto an even dustier record player and settled into her favorite brown chair. She always promised herself that someday she'd get up and exercise a little, move to the rhythm of the big-band music she loved, but she never worked up the energy to follow through with it. She did, however, imagine dancing to the music and losing weight. She'd get up and exercise for real, soon—but not tonight. Tonight she'd just reach for a doughnut from the box on the table beside her and chew along with the beat.

Upstairs in his bedroom, Johnny undressed in front of his window, the darkness outside turning the glass into a mirror. He was a good-looking kid with short-cropped blond hair and clear blue eyes. His tall, athletic body already showed signs of natural muscle. Still too young for vanity, he pulled on his pajamas and jumped into bed.

It made him happy that his mother seemed content here. He loved her very much, he just wished she'd cut him a little slack, stop being so overprotective. Johnny figured she secretly feared he'd abandon her as his father had. She'd never admit he left, but Johnny could see the truth reflected in her sad eyes. Personally, Johnny never hated his father for running out on them. He often wondered about his father and where he was now, but that was all.

He could hear the record player downstairs, but it didn't stop his eyelids from drooping. Even the scratching of the weeping willow's branches against his dirt-smeared window couldn't bring him back from the brink of sleep. In fact, the sound of the branches lulled him closer, the same way the endless roar of waves at a beach do. The record downstairs finished and the old farmhouse on Logan Road returned to the quiet it had enjoyed for the past twenty-two years. One final soft brush from the willow's branch pulled him over the brink of consciousness into the dark chasm below.

The moment Johnny fell asleep, the wind abruptly stopped blowing. Having lost their partner, the willows along Logan Road swayed gently until they finally stood still, awaiting the next dance.

About seventy yards south from Johnny's bedroom window was an old, abandoned well. Twenty feet down into the murky, stagnant water lay a decomposing body. It had been there a long time and would have been totally decomposed, if not for the water staying cold during the summer and frozen in winter.

At exactly the same time Johnny fell asleep and the wind stopped blowing, the long-dead body at the bottom of the well slowly opened its eyes. From lifeless gray ovals, tiny pinholes of crimson began to form, which grew into bulging red orbs illuminating the dead man's face in the deep water's blackness. In that piercing red glow, it slowly examined itself to see how it had fared in its long and lonely sleep. Its skin was almost gone, but everything else seemed to have survived—the rest of its body thriving in its watery grave.

It felt incredibly strong as it flexed its massive chest muscles around an unbeating heart. It had somehow become bigger. Uncurled and standing, it would tower well over seven feet. Its hands had changed also. At the tip of each heavily muscled digit was a six-inch spear of bone that protruded out the end of the finger. The spears were razor sharp, and as an experiment, the creature brutally sunk its index finger deep into its left knee. It sliced through the bone and tendons as easy as a wood sliver stabs into the tender flesh underneath a fingernail. The creature removed its finger with a sickening plop that echoed under the well's foul water. The kneecap was left with a gaping wound that spilled blue blood that threatened to cloud up the already murky water. The blood only flowed for a moment before the wound began to heal. Within seconds the knee looked as old and rotted as it had before.

Everything I hoped is coming true, the creature thought.

If the creature had still possessed a full set of lips, it would have smiled. However, the smile would quickly have disappeared when the creature remembered it was still a prisoner of the well. Not for long, though, because someone must have moved into the farmhouse—otherwise it wouldn't have awakened tonight.

Its body was trapped in a watery grave, but that didn't mean the creature couldn't find out what was going on. Up through the murky depths its mind's eye traveled, slithering along the cool grass, and immediately sensed two occupants within the house. It moved in for a closer look.

Mary Page awoke with a start, the phonograph player crackling with static. The record had ended and was skipping continually at the end of its groove. While putting the record away, an overpowering feeling of being watched came over her. She spun quickly to see if anyone was there, but moved too fast. Her hefty body wasn't used to sudden movements, and she lost her balance, crashing down hard on the coffee table, pieces of wood flying everywhere. All thoughts of being watched forgotten, she picked herself up and hobbled off to bed.

* * *

Upstairs, Johnny slept on. He dreamed of his friends and the fun things they could do tomorrow. He also dreamed an angel was outside his window protecting him and his mother. Again, he heard the scraping of the branch against his window. This time however, the sound didn't soothe him into deeper sleep. The scratching sounded like long claws scraping against bone. In his dream, the angel morphed into a sickening beast with long talons for fingers, trying desperately to get into his room to tear him to shreds. What terrified him most about the dream were the creature's eyes. Johnny sat up to get a closer look, and when the creature made eye contact with him, its eyes glowed blood red.

Outside his window, the creature's mind's eye dreamed along with Johnny and was finally satisfied. It slipped back toward the well where its decaying body waited.

You might be the one. I've been waiting a long time for you, my friend. Don't worry about anything, Johnny. I'll take good care of you . . . and your friends.

The abomination reared back and howled with laughter, releasing great torrents of black water from its lungs. The well literally churned with evil laughter for a moment, but soon the monster settled down to wait for its new "friends."

Contented, the creature closed its fiery eyes and plunged back into restful blackness. The moment its eyes closed, the wind outside began to blow again, and the trees along Logan Road slowly resumed their dance.

CHAPTER TWO

David Winter reluctantly crawled out of bed at 6:34 A.M. and began getting dressed. He was feeling depressed. His large hazel eyes stared blankly off into some far-off imaginary world, while he unconsciously fiddled his pudgy fingers through his tangled mop of dark curly hair. He was so preoccupied with other thoughts, he failed to notice the outfit he threw on didn't match. One white athletic sock had been lying next to a gray one, so he pulled them on. His blue sweatpants didn't coordinate with his pumpkin orange T-shirt either, but fashion was the last thing on his mind today.

David sat for a few minutes with his hands in his pockets and his mind in the clouds, delaying his trip to Johnny's for as long as possible. David truly believed Old Man Harrison would be waiting for him and his friends today. No matter how often he told himself he was being stupid, that Jacob Harrison had died over twenty years ago, the feelings of dread simply wouldn't go away. He finally made his way downstairs. Rice Krispies didn't sound very appetizing, and the thought of runny eggs was even worse, so he headed out the back door, deciding against breakfast.

The slam of the door closing startled Steven Winter out of a pleasant dream in which he and Donna were rich and didn't need to work for a living. The booming noise brought him back to reality, and he jumped out of bed to see what had caused the racket. Out of his window, he could see his son wandering aimlessly in the back yard.

Steven and Donna worked on their three-hundred-acre tomato farm, left to Steven by his father ten years back. Steven was a big, powerful man with thinning dark brown hair, while Donna was his mirror opposite, a tiny wisp of a woman with long, blonde hair flowing down to her waist. They toiled hard to eke out an existence from the soil, and the last thing either of them needed was a son startling them out of a restful sleep.

Donna entered the bedroom and surprised Steven when she wrapped her arms around his midsection. He had thought she was still curled up in bed.

"Whoa big guy . . . it's only me," she said. "Didn't mean to sneak up on you, I just wanted to say good morning."

"Sorry, Donna, I didn't mean to jump. I just got a bit of a fright when the back door slammed. I've told that boy a thousand times not to bang it on his way out."

"David seems a little weird today, actually," Donna said. "I got up to go to the bathroom and saw him with this really sad look on his face, like he was scared or worried about something."

"I think I know something that might cheer him up."

Without another word to his wife, Steven quickly dressed and was outside talking to David in the backyard. From the bedroom window, Donna watched their brief conversation and noticed a big smile light up David's face. Moments later, David was racing out of sight, and her husband was coming back upstairs.

"What did you say to get a smile like that?"

"I asked him if he'd help me out this afternoon. I told him it was time to crucify Rodney again."

Johnny Page woke with the shocking thought that he'd peed the bed. His legs and feet were wet and he could feel the embarrassing and unpleasant way his Captain America pajamas clung to his skinny legs. When he opened his eyes, he received an even bigger shock. He hadn't wet the bed after all. In fact, he wasn't even *in* bed. Johnny was outside in the backyard, his legs dangling down into the old well.

He was soaked from the waist down, the cold water causing him to shiver uncontrollably, his legs numb as he dragged them out of the stinking black water. Waking up to discover he'd been sleepwalking was one thing, but to pull his legs out of the water and discover they were covered in huge, black, pulsating bloodsuckers—well, that was quite another.

Johnny began screaming, a high-pitched wail of shock and horror he couldn't contain. No wonder his legs were numb. Countless leeches had been feeding on his legs for who knew how long. The areas of his legs not affected were pale and pasty white.

Johnny began frantically picking and clawing at the slimy beasts, desperate to get them off. He'd heard stories that you could only get them off by burning them, but thankfully they detached from his legs easily, dropping into the filthy water with a sickening plop.

Mary Page thundered out the back door and charged over to him. Johnny removed the last of the leeches just before his mother reached the well. His relief was so great, he did something he hadn't willingly done in over two years. He stumbled to his feet and gratefully hugged his mother, who'd come to the rescue with open arms.

"What the dickens is going on here?" she asked, noticing her son's pale, blood-smeared legs.

Johnny had many answers flash through his head. He desperately wanted to cry in his mother's arms and tell her how horrible it had been to wake up covered in leeches, but he couldn't. He knew how overprotective she was. She'd probably send him to his room and forbid him from playing with his new friends.

"Johnny, what's wrong? I wake up hearing you screaming loud enough to scare the Devil, and then I find you soaking wet with blood on your legs."

"Nothing's wrong, Ma," he said. "I was dangling my feet

in the well and I slipped and scraped my legs on the sides. Sorry. I just scared myself a little."

Johnny could see a fat, juicy leech squirming on the ground a few inches from his mother's brightly painted big toenail. Johnny didn't want her to see the sucker and possibly make the connection with the blood on his legs. It wouldn't take a genius to find a few other leeches and notice the suction marks on his legs. Thankfully, just before the leech reached his mother's toe she wheeled away, dragging him toward the house.

"You'll be the death of me yet, boy. I told you yesterday about being careful, didn't I? You never listen to your old mom, even though all I ever do is try to take care of you. Maybe if your father were still here, you'd listen to him. He wouldn't put up with your silliness, I can assure you. There had better not be any trouble with those kids here today, either, or I'll send them straight home and you to your bed. Understand?"

Johnny nodded, his solemn expression breaking into a grin the second his mother turned her great, expansive rear toward him. Happy again, he quickly headed up the stairs and into the bath. He wanted to be ready when his friends arrived.

The creature at the bottom of the well was happy, too. As the blood-bloated leeches drifted down through the murky water, it snatched them out of the darkness and stuffed its mouth. Its razor-tipped fangs easily sliced into the soft, tender flesh of the leeches, sending gushes of blood into and down its rotting throat as if it were eating ripe, juicy orange slices.

Johnny's blood, it thought evilly, stuffing another blood-sucker into its already-filled mouth. *You taste delicious. I can hardly wait to taste your friends.*

As the creature enjoyed its "breakfast," it sent its mind's eye up into the house again. It was pleased to find out Johnny's friends were still coming over. It was even happier when it found out that Johnny, who was undressing to take his bath, was only now discovering that one repulsively fat leech had crawled up his shorts and attached itself to the bottom of his scrotum.

"Hurry up Pete . . . Tom's here," shouted Ken Myers, peering up the stairs in hope of catching his younger brother's attention. "What's taking you so long?" he asked, trying one last time before disgustedly returning to the living room to tell Tom what kind of an idiot he'd chosen for a friend. Deep down, Ken loved his younger brother, but you'd have a hard time getting him to admit it.

"I'll be right down . . . keep your shirt on," garbled Pete over the railing, his mouth still full of peppermint toothpaste. He returned to the bathroom to rinse his mouth, then bolted for the staircase.

"Hold it, mister," said his father.

Mark Myers was a handsome man in his early forties, a single father who had raised his sons to listen. He had a steely voice that commanded respect. Lately, a touch of gray had started invading his dark, curly locks, but this distinguished look only added to his authority. Skidding to a stop at the top of the stairway, Peter apprehensively walked back to his father's bedroom, but relief flooded through him when he found out his father only wanted him to switch off the bathroom light.

"I've told you a thousand times to remember to turn off the lights, but you never listen. Everyone forgets from time to time Pete, but you always do. You really want me to ground you over something so stupid? Promise you'll at least try and remember."

Pete promised he'd try, then hurried back to the bathroom. He paused to gaze at his reflection in the mirror, trying once more to wet down a stubborn cowlick at the back of his head. Pete had the same dark, curly hair as his father, and could never keep his wild locks in check. No matter how much spit he put on it, the cowlick sprang right back up.

"Great," he muttered to his small, freckled reflection. "Not only do I have to go to a haunted house today, I have to go there looking like Alfalfa." That thought brought a grin to his face, but his smile vanished as he thought about the Harrison farm. He really liked Johnny, but he wasn't sure he liked him enough to spend time there.

Pete didn't actually know the whole story of what had happened on Old Man Harrison's farm all those years ago. He'd heard the start countless times, but just as the story began to reach its gory conclusion, Pete would always get scared and leave. Jacob Harrison had done something ghastly to his family, but Pete didn't know what. He didn't want to know, either. He was more into making people laugh than trying to scare anyone.

Another yell from his brother brought Pete back from his daydreams. He reluctantly accepted that all the spit in the world wasn't going to make his hair look any better, so he flipped off the light switch and headed downstairs.

Through all of this, Tom Baker sat on the couch watching Saturday-morning cartoons. He normally laughed himself sick watching Bugs Bunny and the rest of the crew, but today he barely cracked a smile. He sat rigid and tense, managing to look far bigger and older than his age. He had dark brown hair too—the same as Pete's—but his was straight and fell down to his shoulders.

His thoughts were also centered on the Harrison Farm, but they were different than Pete's. Pete had a naive fear of the farm, whereas Tom had firsthand experience. He'd been there once on a stupid dare and had suffered nightmares ever since.

Last year, Tom had joined up with a few older kids from his neighborhood who'd formed a club called the Adventurers. The leader had been a tough eleven-year-old with slicked-back blond hair by the name of Boots. His real name was Lawrence, but pity the kid foolish enough to call him that. He was Central Public School's toughest kid, and he enjoyed his "bully" label to the fullest. He was big for his age, loved to start fights, and the boys in the Adventurers listened more to him than to their parents or teachers.

Anyone wanting to join their club had to perform a dare, set up by Boots. These dares usually involved shoplifting or drinking alcohol or some other stupid thing that showed your worth to the members. Tom had been asked to spend one hour inside the Harrison farmhouse all by himself. Most kids were terrified of that place, but spending an hour inside the old house hadn't bothered Tom in the least. He wasn't a coward like Pete and didn't have the imagination of David, so he wasn't scared of ghosts.

He'd pretended to be scared as Boots and the boys in the club crowded around him and reminded him of what supposedly had happened there. If he seemed scared going into the house, he would look braver and stronger once it was over and he hadn't chickened out.

Once inside the house, which he'd entered through a broken window, Tom felt much better. He could still hear the guys in the club out front on the road making what they thought were scary noises. "Idiots," muttered Tom under his breath as he checked his watch, which he had synchronized with one of the members outside.

"One hour, now, and not one second less, or you're not in the club," Boots had warned with a big grin on his face.

I'll give you an hour, Tom had said to himself. *In fact, just to show them I'm not scared, I think I'll stay an extra fifteen minutes.*

With his bravado fully pumped up, he decided he might as well look around, since he had nothing better to do. In twenty minutes Tom Baker had accomplished two things. He'd completely searched the house and found out that he'd been right all along—there was nothing there. He had also hurt his left leg rather badly. He'd been searching the upstairs bedrooms when, staring at a ceiling strewn with cobwebs, he'd stepped on a dusty toy train that had been left on the floor.

If there was anything in this world that truly scared Tom, it was spiders. He despised them. As a small child, he'd awakened to find his brother Roger's pet tarantula trying to crawl into his mouth, and Roger above him, laughing his guts out. The trauma of that event had stayed with him. He knew the Harrison house had been vacant for many years and had expected to find spiderwebs here and there, but he hadn't anticipated anything like this. The upstairs of the house was swathed in webs.

The one thing Tom couldn't find anywhere was a spider. Not that this was a particularly unpleasant thing. In fact, it was a blessing. If those webs had been filled with furry crawling nightmares, Tom would probably have hightailed it out of the house faster than if he'd come face-to-face with Jacob Harrison himself.

As he was staring up at one particularly nasty web, he'd stepped onto the toy train, flying ass-over-teakettle onto his back, wrenching his knee in the process. He had slightly twisted his left ankle too, and the scream he'd let out greatly improved the mood of the boys outside, who were beginning to get bored.

Hobbling downstairs on a sore ankle and puffed-up knee wasn't exactly his idea of a great afternoon, but he was still determined not to give in. He decided to pick a relatively clean room and sit down to read the paperback western he'd brought with him. In a few minutes he was riding along the range with Billy the Kid and was so engrossed in his book, he almost forgot where he was.

Then the scratching noises started.

Long, slow, scratching noises, like sharp claws dragging across a hardwood floor, quickly threw Tom off his imaginary horse and back to reality.

"What the heck . . . ?" he began, but stopped. The house was again silent. "Get a hold of yourself, Tommy boy. You're starting to spook yourself like you promised you wouldn't. It's probably just a mouse."

He began reading some more, but the scratching started again. This time it was accompanied by a series of long, slow growls. No, more like deep breaths, like someone gasping for air. Tom bolted upright, causing needles of pain to shoot down his injured left leg. He could no longer ignore the noise and pretend it was a mouse. It sounded like a person, and the noise had come from the basement.

He hadn't checked the basement on his first search, because the staircase leading into the cellar had crumbled away and was lying in a heap at the bottom.

An old tramp might have sneaked into the deserted farmhouse during the storm a few nights ago. Probably stumbled in blind drunk and tumbled into the basement without noticing the staircase was gone. Tom knew he should help, but what if the person was dangerous?

Quitting and going home was very much on Tom's mind, and he went as far as turning toward the window he'd entered. Just before deciding to exit, the noise came again, only this time the moan seemed weaker and more pain filled.

Who the heck is down there?

Tom had to hang from the second step down, the last one still intact, and then drop the rest of the way to the basement floor. The second his feet connected with the hard concrete floor, firecrackers of pain shot off in his left leg. The impact was excruciating. It was as if his knee had exploded inside and only his bruised and swelling skin was keeping it from leaking down his leg.

The scratching and the moaning cracked through Tom's wall of pain, and he dragged himself into a sitting position to look around. There was no sign of whoever had been making all the noise. A deadly silence now filled the lower floor. For the life of him, he couldn't decide why. They obviously knew he was here. Even someone almost stone-deaf would have been able to hear his scream when he'd hit the concrete. Maybe whoever was down here had passed out from their own injuries.

The only place where a body (which wasn't how Tom wanted to refer to it, since it brought up another idea as to why the moans had stopped) could be out of view was behind the furnace. It stood in the farthest corner away, and in the shadows cast by the fading light, he could just make out a large shape and some movement.

"Well at least the old bugger isn't dead yet," Tom said.

He attempted to stand up and go over to the furnace but only made it to his knees before falling back onto his rear end. He'd hurt himself worse than he wanted to admit, and suddenly the idea of climbing up and out of the basement didn't seem that easy. With the way his leg was feeling, standing up was going to be hard enough.

A sudden movement distracted Tom from his thoughts. He spun around, thinking the person behind the furnace was trying to catch his attention. Well, his attention was certainly caught, because sitting beside the furnace was a spider—a large spider.

Its body was about the size of a man's fist and was covered in thick black and red bristles. Tom froze. It was as if quick-setting concrete now ran in his veins instead of blood. A scream rose in Tom's throat, but before it could squeeze its way out, a leg emerged from behind the furnace and crushed the spider into a mushy, convulsing pulp. Tom watched the spider's death spasms with glee and was about to thank the person behind the furnace, when he noticed something odd. The leg grinding the dead spider into the ground didn't appear to have any pants on. The closer Tom looked, the more it appeared to be covered in thick black hair.

Black hair, like that of a . . . spider.

The scratching noises started up again, and this time Tom heard them for what they really were. They were the scratching and clawing of a colossal-sized spider trying to free itself from behind the furnace where it was tightly wedged. The human-sounding moans he'd heard upstairs turned to high-pitched laughter as he struggled to get to his feet. Tom knew he had to get out of this basement, and get out fast.

"You shouldn't have come here, Tommy," said the spider, having managed to scratch and claw half its bloated body clear of the furnace. "You've been a bad boy, Tommy, and you know what happens to bad boys, don't you?"

The hideous spider ground its hairy foot into the mushy remains of the dead spider again, just to emphasize its point. Tom got the message loud and clear and frantically began climbing out of the basement, oblivious to the volcano of white-hot pain that had once been his knee.

There were still small blocks of wood attached to the wall where the stairs had been anchored to reinforce each step. Now they functioned as his only means of escape. The King Spider (a name his frightened mind had for some reason latched onto) would be on top of him before then. Such a thought brought all his early childhood fears racing back, spurring him onward.

He reached the wall and began to climb the wooden blocks as fast as his injured leg would allow. The doorway to the kitchen and freedom was only a few feet away but it seemed so out of reach. Behind him, the scratching had stopped, and except for his own exertions, the basement was silent.

The joy of freedom was dashed in an instant as his injured left knee gave out on the last block. The damaged knee couldn't support his weight any longer, and he crashed back to the basement floor in a fall that seemed to last forever.

It only took a moment for Tom to shake off the pain and spin around to see what had happened to the spider. It was sitting, silently staring at him from three feet away. The King Spider was every arachnophobe's worst nightmare come true. Long black legs tapered to a bloated red body that measured about a foot and a half across. Its spittle-drooling mandibles worked endlessly, revealing a sticky pink tunnel outlined with razor-sharp fangs. Everything about the spider's appearance was ghastly, but its eyes terrified Tom more then anything else. Six large, rotating orbs the size of golf balls fixed unwaveringly upon Tom's own terror-stricken eyes. They all glowed red—the shade of freshly spilled blood—each casting an ominous crimson beacon over the basement, which was quickly losing whatever meager sunlight it had been getting.

"You almost made it out, Tommy, my boy." Seeing the look of despair on Tom's face, the monster mockingly said, "What's the matter? Scared of a little spider? Well, you're not gonna like this very much, then."

The grotesque spider opened its mouth wide, and Tom was sure it meant to bite him. It wasn't until he saw the first of the small spiders scampering out of the large spider's glistening throat *that he realized he was wrong. One spider dropped wetly to the floor, and soon others followed, until hundreds of creepy crawlers were teeming out of the King's gullet in a stream of gooey blackness. All the little spiders' eyes glowed red, and Tom realized, just before he ran for the wall again, that these must be all the spiders from the rest of the house. No wonder he hadn't seen any upstairs—they had all been swallowed and stored away inside the rotting stomach of the King Spider.*

With an army of spiders on his tail, Tom tried to scale the wall again. Thousands of red eyes locked on him as the tiny horde clawed over each other in pursuit. His terror gave him the strength to overcome the pain in his leg. He leapt at the wall like an Olympic high jumper and clung to a pair of blocks halfway up. The army of spiders wasn't far behind; they too hit the wall and started to climb. One glance was enough to panic Tom up and out of the cellar, and soon he was sprawling onto the kitchen floor. Relief spread through him, but he wasn't safe yet. The spiders had also gained the kitchen, a swiftly moving river of black and red pouring out of the basement doorway toward him.

That was the last thing Tom saw before he dove out the same window he'd entered just over forty minutes earlier.

"You come back and see us anytime you want, Tommy, my boy . . . anytime at all," was all he heard as he raced around the side of the house and right past the members of the Adventurers club.

Boots and the gang had laughed themselves sick at how scared Tom had looked, and unanimously voted to not let him into their club.

Somebody else had been laughing that day. Somebody with an active part in what had happened. Unknowingly, Tom had awakened the creature at the bottom of the well simply by setting foot inside the house. Twenty minutes of wandering around in there, and he'd certainly gained the creature's interest.

It had sent its underdeveloped mind's eye up into the house and had been furious to find out it was just some dumb kid on a dare. The creature needed rest, as it was still in the process of transforming. It still basically resembled the human being it had once been. There was no way the creature could have gotten back to sleep with Tom in the house. The boy had to be forced into leaving.

The creature hadn't been completely transformed, but it could make its presence felt—it could play with little Tom's mind and make him see and hear things that weren't really there. With a big smile that had caused the last of its human upper lip to fall off, the creature had put its plan into action. It had learned Tom's worst fear by probing his subconscious mind, and from there it had been easy to make Tom see the giant spider.

It will be a long time before that boy comes snooping around my house again, I'll bet, the creature had thought. It had been pleased and content with its developing powers. One more quick scan of the house to make sure it was empty, and the creature had settled back down to sleep, and to change.

Back in Peter's living room, Pete was trying to rouse Tom from the semitrance he'd fallen into.

"Hey Tom . . . wake up, bonehead. You're going to make us late."

Startled, Tom snapped back to reality looking glassy-eyed and perplexed.

"I thought I'd lost you there for a moment," said Pete with a grin. "Come on, let's get going, okay? We're supposed to meet up with David, remember?"

"Sure . . . I'm ready," replied Tom, unsteadily rising to his feet, still thinking about his last trip to the basement of the Harrison farmhouse.

He had later learned Boots and his buddies had slipped a little whiskey into a Coke he'd drunk before going into the house. He'd reassured himself it had been the alcohol that had caused him to hallucinate that day and see the spiders. Reassured though he was, he followed Pete very slowly and reluctantly out the door.

David Winter ran along Cedar Street with a wide grin on his face. All bad thoughts about today had vanished when his father had told him it was time to crucify Rodney. Every year around this time, for as long as he could remember, he and his father had performed the crucifixion, and every year he enjoyed it more.

The act of crucifying Rodney wasn't as sinister as it sounded. Rodney was just a big stuffed scarecrow his dad had put together to scare away the birds from their tomatoes. Actually, the scarecrow didn't do much of anything, since there weren't many crows in the area. There were lots of sea gulls that flew in from the lake, but they were more interested in heading toward the Grand Island Bar-B-Q and getting french fries from the tourists than they were in the Winters' tomato fields. The only reason his father went to the trouble of putting the scarecrow up was because David enjoyed it so much. With his wild imagination, David would talk to the scarecrow all summer, and considered it his best friend.

The term *crucifying* had come from a botched attempt to intertwine religion with something David enjoyed; Steven had hoped that David might take more interest if he could associate religion with things he liked. The lesson never really worked out, but the crucifixion label had stuck.

"This gives me the perfect excuse to go home early today," David said as he turned onto Logan Road.

His good mood diminished and his fears began to rise looking over at the Harrison farmhouse, until he noticed Tom and Pete laughing and running his way. Tom was covered in mud. His blue denim cutoff shorts were now black and most of his faded yellow T-shirt was the same.

"What happened to you, Tom?" asked David.

Pete was bent over holding his stomach from laughing so

much. "The goof was in a daze on the way over here. We get to the corner and he walks straight into the ditch. I made the turn and he didn't. It was the funniest thing I ever saw."

"Ha, ha, ha," mocked Tom who was grinning in spite of himself. "I suppose you've never done anything stupid before?"

Pete gave him the *Who, me?* shrug as they laughed and noticed Johnny bolting out of his front door to join them.

Seeing the look on Johnny's face as he skidded to a halt, Tom said, "Before you ask . . . I fell in the ditch. I had other things on my mind and I wasn't paying attention."

Pete piped in with one of his usual quick comebacks. "Yeah, Johnny, Tom was thinking about Becki Sullivan again, and he sort of lost his brain for a while."

Tom, who knew it was common knowledge he had a crush on Becki, and knew better than to try outjoking Pete, simply turned beet red and began chasing him around Johnny's lawn.

The wrestling match ended with Tom pinning Pete to the ground and making him take his last comment back. Pete did, and Tom rolled off of him onto the grass. All four boys lay down to catch their breath. The common act of scrapping around in the grass had helped everyone relax and dispelled most of David, Tom, and Pete's fear. This wasn't Jacob Harrison's farm—it was Johnny's. Nothing bad was going to happen to them here. This unspoken thought seemed to pass between them, and together they laughed away the rest of their doubts and fears.

Pete eventually asked, "Well, what are we going to do? I'm not gonna have to rough you guys up all day, am I?"

"You better hope not," said Tom.

Pete considered restarting the fight, but realized Tom was probably right. Instead he turned to Johnny and said, "It's your house, kiddo. You make the call."

All eyes turned toward Johnny, and for the first time he realized he had no idea what they would do. He had so much else on his mind this morning, it never occurred to him to make plans. An idea surfaced in his head that seemed to come from nowhere. One second his mind was completely blank; the next, he knew exactly what to do. It was very strange.

"I've got a great idea. There's something I want to show you, and I think you're really gonna like it."

He turned and led the small troop around the side of the weather-beaten farmhouse and past the large willow tree that grew outside his bedroom window. Without really knowing why, Johnny led his new friends out into the backyard. He was marching them straight out toward the deep, murky well.

CHAPTER THREE

Steven Winter had everything ready for the crucifixion. The large sturdy cross, which was actually an old railway tie, stood year-round on the side lawn nearest the fields. The rest of the materials, including the great Rodney himself, were stored in a metal shed behind the garage. Steven had dragged Rodney and all the other essentials out and strewn them on the grass at the base of the "cross."

Steven was always amazed at how heavy the scarecrow was. He assumed a pile of straw stuffed into some old rags would be as light as a feather. Wrong. Rodney was big. The clothes were originally Steven's old farm clothes, and he was a large man. The straw required to fill those clothes was enough to bed a couple of horses for a week.

Rodney's faded blue coveralls were ragged, but they'd hold up for a couple more years before needing replacement. His chest of straw was hanging out of his red and white–checkered shirt and needed to be stuffed back inside. The rest of the scarecrow had survived the winter quite well. His New York Yankees hat still sat, although lopsided, on the rather pointed head fashioned from a semicrushed Styrofoam wig holder. Rodney had even inherited the wig for a few years, until it became too ratty looking. Big green rubber boots with holes in the soles rounded out Rodney's stylish outfit.

Everything was ready to go except for one key ingredient:

David. He hadn't come home from Johnny's house yet. Steven glanced again at his watch to see that it was 4:35 P.M. It wasn't like David to be late, especially on the day they were to hang Rodney up.

David didn't come home until six o'clock that evening. His parents had finished hanging Rodney and were on the verge of calling the police, when Donna spotted him running across the yard at full speed with a look on his face that could only be described as one of sheer terror. All premade speeches about being on time and responsible were forgotten the second David entered the kitchen. He was shaking badly and looked far too pitiful to scold.

Donna rushed to get a large towel when she realized that he was shaking because he was cold and wet. He was soaked from head to toe and smelled like a dead animal.

Steven finally broke the silence. "What have you been up to, mister?"

David didn't answer the question, or any of the others that followed. He simply stared back at his parents with large, hollow eyes and held his empty left hand out in front of him as if in explanation. The tips of his fingers and the palm of his hand were blistered and bloody. His parents tried hard to find out what happened, but try as they might, David still wouldn't talk. He simply stared, his mouth open like that of a fish on a hook.

"I think that he's gone into shock, Steven. What do we do? Should we take him to the hospital?"

"Easy, Donna," said her much-calmer husband. "Let's get him into a nice hot bath and clean up his hand. There's no need to panic. He's just had a good scare."

After a hot bubble bath, David felt much better, and his mother had calmed down, but he still refused to talk about what had happened. All he would say was that he and his friends hadn't done anything wrong and they weren't in trouble.

David had gone up to bed without supper, partly because

he was being punished for scaring his mother half to death, but mostly because he couldn't stomach the thought of eating. He could hear his mother and father talking about him downstairs, and he overheard his father saying they shouldn't force him. His father was sure David would tell them all about it in the morning.

David didn't think he'd ever feel better and was positive he would never tell anyone what had happened to him and his pals. He tried not to think about it, already convincing himself it hadn't happened, that he'd imagined the whole thing. He couldn't keep the memories out of his head, though. They rushed in like an icy January wind, blocking out all other thoughts. As he rubbed his shaking left hand, David reluctantly began to go over the events of the day. . . .

"So what's so interesting out here?" David asked. "All I see is an empty field and a stinky old well."

Johnny walked around to the opposite side of the well, his arms dramatically outstretched. "This is no ordinary well. It has things in it, and they're what I want you to see."

"What kind of things?" asked David, his interest piqued.

Johnny whispered in his best scary voice. "Little monsters. Little vampire monsters. They attacked me this morning, but I got away." A shiver ran down Johnny's back as he remembered his horrible experience that morning.

Pete was already scared. "What do you mean, monsters?" he asked, noticing Johnny shivering.

Johnny looked on the ground by their feet and screamed, "I mean them! There's one right there between Tom's feet."

The three other boys jumped back. "Where? Where?" shouted Tom, until he spotted the tiny black leech. "Vampire monsters? Are you talking about bloodsuckers? You drag us all the way back here to show us a tiny bloodsucker?"

"No way, Tom," said Johnny. "Not one bloodsucker. Thousands!"

He proceeded to tell them about how he had sleepwalked out to the well and of his battle with the leeches, which he managed to

*exaggerate a bit. It was David who first noticed the marks on
Johnny's legs, and after they checked them out, they couldn't help
but believe. They looked on in awe, picturing their friend fighting
a horde of bloodthirsty creatures.*

*"You mean it really happened? You're not making it up?" asked
Pete, searching the ground for signs of the next attack.*

*Johnny gave the scout's-honor sign and was about to suggest
they dig around in the water to find more leeches, when his mother
screamed from an upstairs window.*

*"Get away from that well. What did I tell you this morning?
I'm not telling you again—now go play in the field. You can't get
into much trouble out there."*

*Embarrassed, Johnny led the others out into the large dirt field
behind the house. "That's my mother, guys. She's all right; she just
worries too much. Anyway, she's right, we should play out here.
The well stinks too much."*

*The field hadn't been used for farming in years. The farmer
who had leased the farmland from Johnny's father hadn't used
this section because it was too hilly and rough. Grass and weeds
grew wild among the large dirt clumps and rotted tree stumps
scattered about the field.*

*To an adult, the field would have seemed ugly and a waste,
but to a kid it was glorious. David had never seen such a perfect
place to play war games. This field was exactly how his overactive
mind imagined World War II battlefields must have looked. The
rest of the gang agreed, and Johnny ran to get his supply of toy ri-
fles and water pistols.*

*The boys played for hours, having a blast, and by the time
Johnny's mother came out to give them a late lunch, they were glistening with sweat and smiling from ear to ear.*

*Mary Page didn't have the heart to chastise them about the
noise they were making. The look of joy on her son's dirty face
more than compensated for the headache she'd developed. Johnny
hadn't had many friends in the city, so she wasn't about to ruin
his day. Leaving a platter of peanut-butter sandwiches on the pic-
nic table, she said, "It's good to see a smile on that face, love. If
only your father could have been here to see it."*

The boys dove into the sandwiches, amazed at how hungry they were. Johnny marveled at how well they were all getting along. Apparently the feeling was mutual, because just as Johnny was about to mention it, Tom motioned for everyone to be quiet.

"Hold it down, fellas. I'd like to welcome our new friend Johnny to Dunnville. We should form a club, so we can be together forever. We always wanted one, but three people weren't much of a club. Now that Johnny's here, though, I think we can do it. What do you guys think?"

Everyone thought it was a great idea.

"Yeah," said Pete, "we could build a clubhouse and have secret code words and everything. We'd have to come up with a cool name. What were those jerks you almost hung out with called, Tom?"

"The Adventurers, but we need something better than that." Tom glanced around, but nobody seemed able to think of a good name for the club.

"Forget it," said Johnny. "First we'll build our clubhouse. That'll give us plenty of time to find a name."

Everyone agreed, so they began gathering wood. After searching around the farm for an hour, it was obvious they didn't have enough wood to build anything. All they had was a few rotted pieces of two-by-four and some tree branches.

"Why don't we call ourselves the Club With No Clubhouse?" Pete joked, but nobody laughed. "My, aren't you guys fun? I might as well tell jokes to that pile of dirt over there."

David's eyes opened wide. "That's it, Pete. The dirt. We'll build our clubhouse underground, like they did in the war. I can't believe we didn't think of it sooner."

"Great idea," said Tom. "That way, nobody but us will know where it is."

Pete smiled triumphantly. "In that case, we'll call ourselves the Dirty Old Groundhog Club." This time everyone cracked up laughing.

Johnny ran to the metal shed and returned with two shovels. He kept one himself and handed the other to Pete. "Anyone who tells bad jokes deserves to be the first to dig."

"All right with me, Johnny, but where should I start?"

They looked around to see if they could find a good spot. "Anywhere is fine," said Tom. "A field is a field, right?"

Johnny was about to agree when he said, "Wait—I know the perfect place."

That strange feeling came over him again. He started walking into the field without really knowing where he was taking them. Somehow he just knew it was the way to go. He led them around a large dirt hill that completely hid their position from the house and the road, walked two steps farther, and stopped. "This is the spot, right here."

Turning around, he realized it actually was a good spot. He just wasn't sure how he'd picked it. It didn't really matter—they were here, and Pete had already started digging. With a shrug of his thin shoulders, he began digging himself.

The work was hard and tedious. For every few shovel's worth of dirt they threw out of the hole, a shovelful would erode off the walls and cascade down over their filthy running shoes. They took turns. Sweat and fatigue, mixed with the realization of the enormous task they faced, started to strip away their enthusiasm. Even Pete wasn't cracking jokes. As they dug on in sweaty silence, their smiles were fading fast.

By 4:30 P.M. the boys had managed to excavate a hole five feet deep and about six feet square. They had envisioned a huge clubhouse with three or four big rooms joined by secret passageways, but that was out of the question. David was about to say they should finish it tomorrow, when Tom's shovel made a loud grating noise like a cat hissing shrilly in anger.

"Hey, don't blame me," said Tom, noticing the looks he was getting. "I must have hit a rock or something."

"Sounds more like metal," said Johnny, jumping into the hole to relieve Tom.

David began to dig again and he hit it too. "Wow, whatever it is, it sure is big. Hurry, Johnny . . . let's uncover this thing and see what we've found."

Their excitement grew, the image of a buried chest of gold and jewels dancing in their minds, and soon all four were digging as *fast as they could. The two without a shovel used their hands, and before long they'd uncovered the whole thing.*

It was only a rusty piece of metal sheeting, like those used on barn roofs, measuring about three by five feet. They gathered around it in quiet disappointment.

"Don't be upset guys," said Johnny. "We can use this to help build the roof. Give me a hand getting it out of the hole."

David bent down with the rest of them, and together they started to lift the piece of metal. It was heavier than he'd expected, but they managed to lift it and toss it out. He watched it slide back down the bank toward them, but it stopped well back from the edge.

"We could always call our club the Treasure Hunters," laughed David, turning to face his friends. None of them laughed. None of them even looked up to meet his eyes. He glanced down to see what had caught their attention, and his laughter abruptly ceased. Directly in front of him, a cement staircase led down into the silent blackness of the earth.

Johnny immediately started heading down the stairs, but Tom raced forward and grabbed his shirt. "Wait a minute, for God's sake. You can't just go running down there."

"Why not?" Johnny asked, and tried to continue down the stairs.

This time David came over and helped restrain him. "Hold it, you don't know what's down there. What if it's a crypt with dead bodies stacked up all over the place?"

The mention of dead bodies in a hidden room hit Pete like a ton of bricks. His face turned white and his legs almost gave out as he said, "What if Old Man Harrison's down there?"

Tom and David let go of Johnny and glared at one another. Both of them knew something Pete didn't—that the Dunnville police never had found Old Man Harrison after that gruesome night long ago.

Tom and David looked into each other's frightened eyes, each silently wondering if Pete might be right. Maybe the police hadn't found him because he had this secret room to hide in, and maybe, just maybe . . . he was still down there waiting.

"Who's Old Man Harrison?" asked Johnny, taking a step back up out of the hole when he registered the frightened looks on his friend's faces.

"Nobody," David said, a bit too quickly. "Don't worry about it. What if this room has"—an insane old man with an axe—"poisonous gas in it or something?"

"What if it has piles of gold and silver and expensive paintings and things?" Johnny was a little peeved at his friends, who suddenly seemed scared of their own shadows. "You just said we should call our club the Treasure Hunters. Here we are with a chance to maybe find some treasure, or at least a perfect clubhouse, and you guys are scared to check it out. Maybe the Chicken Club would be a better name."

"Who you calling chicken, Johnny?" said Tom, regaining his confidence quickly.

"Easy," said David, who saw a fight developing. "He's only kidding, Tom. Look, Johnny, we're not scared to go down there, but look how dark it is. One of us could fall and break our neck. We need lights."

Johnny was about to run to his house for flashlights when, for some reason, he turned and took another couple of steps down. He wasn't even sure what he was looking for until his hand found it on the right-hand wall.

"I found it," Johnny said. "A light switch. I just knew this place would have electricity." He hadn't known any such thing, but it felt like the right thing to say.

"You don't really think it's going to work, do you? The electricity has probably been disconnected for years," said Pete.

"Only one way to find out," Johnny answered, flipping the switch.

For a split second they thought Pete might be right, but then the bulb at the bottom of the staircase flickered once, twice . . . then stayed on. The bulb was thickly caked in dust, but the gloomy light that filtered through was just enough to illuminate the sixteen cracked cement stairs that led to the bottom. Beyond the staircase, a narrow hallway, also made entirely of concrete, led off in the direction of Johnny's house.

They peered down at the bottom of the staircase in silence until Johnny said, "Can we finally go look at our new clubhouse?"

Nobody could think of anything to say—after all, maybe treasure was hidden down there. With more than a little apprehension, one by one they followed Johnny down into the cold earth.

They gathered at the bottom of the stairs and gazed down the gloomy corridor that led toward the back of Johnny's house. The dull bulb above their heads didn't emit enough light to reach the far end of the passageway. They could envision a great number of sickening beasts waiting just out of the area of light, not the least of which was Old Man Harrison with his cruel eyes and bloodstained axe. If it hadn't been for Johnny, they'd have bolted back up the stairs. None of them wanted to be labeled a chicken, so they huddled together, staring into the darkness ahead.

Johnny started down the hall, with the others reluctantly following close behind. Their eyes got better accustomed to the lighting as they crept along the chilly corridor. Long before they reached the end of the hall, they were able to see that the passageway opened into a circular room.

It was set up like a typical family room with a large sofa and a couple of beat-up armchairs. The floor, ceiling, and rounded walls had been built with the same ugly gray concrete as the rest of the place. No effort had been made to try cheer the place up. No pictures, no carpet, nothing at all.

A chill that wasn't caused by the cool underground temperature started to crawl up David's spine as he realized what this room reminded him of. It reminded him of the small, cramped submarine his father had taken him on at Disneyland on a family vacation. The ride was supposed to be all fun and games, but David had freaked out and started screaming to get off. He wasn't claustrophobic—well, maybe a little—but that feeling of being trapped underwater in a small sub had just been too much.

This room gave him the same uneasy feeling. The rounded gray walls and the way that footsteps echoed around the room reminded him exactly of that submarine. Even the cold, clammy floor helped give him the image that somehow his friends had led him down into a sub hundreds of feet below the surface of some cold black ocean.

Most of these feelings came and went within a few seconds of entering the room—the same time it took Johnny to reach up and flick on another light switch. This bulb cast a friendly and appreciated bright light on the surroundings. Relief registered on David's, Tom's, and Pete's faces as the light illuminated the entire room, casting out any lingering fears that monsters might be lying in wait.

"Say . . . this place is all right, isn't it?" said Johnny, pleased to see they had found an excellent clubhouse.

They all agreed this was probably the best clubhouse any kids had in the whole world. They launched themselves onto the dusty sofa and chairs and were pleased to find they were in decent shape. They would need to be cleaned, but so would the rest of the place.

Even David had to admit how wonderfully lucky they were to stumble onto a place like this. They could have dug a thousand holes in the field and never hit the secret staircase. Instead of feeling claustrophobic, with thoughts about drowning in black oceans, he should be excited like the others. They could all pitch in and clean, and maybe he could talk his dad into buying them some paint so they could brighten the place up. That thought caused him to bolt upright on the sofa.

"Dad!" he said. "I'm supposed to help my dad today at home. He'll be smokin' mad if I don't make it."

Tom pulled David back down into his seat. "If you're already late, a few extra minutes isn't going to hurt. You wouldn't want us to think you didn't want to be part of our club, would you?"

David sighed, settling back down on the couch.

They discussed plans for fixing up the clubhouse, and about all the fun things they could do in it. This was every kid's dream—a place where unwanted parents and grown-ups didn't belong. Heck, they could even have television down here, and radios, since they had electricity. They could watch and listen to anything they wanted without anybody telling them to turn it off or turn it down.

"This reminds me of a book," said David. "Not exactly, but this feeling of being free and not having to answer to anyone is the same. It's about King Arthur and the Knights of the Round Table. These knights were really cool. Sort of like soldiers, except they used swords instead of guns."

"I know that story," said Johnny. "They wore armor and had secret codes and huge castles to live in. They fought dragons and monsters to save the weaker people."

Both Tom and Pete were familiar with the story, too. In a flash of inspiration, a thought struck Pete. "Our clubhouse is round . . . like their table." The others turned toward him bewildered, but slowly it dawned on them what he was trying to say. "They were the Knights of the Round Table . . . " continued Pete, "but we could be the Knights of the Round Room."

A hush fell over the room as the boys slowly turned the idea over in their heads. "The Knights of the Round Room." They all repeated it to themselves and to each other. It was perfect. Without having to say it, they knew they'd just found their club name.

A new discussion opened up—talking about secret codes and decorating the place to look like a castle. They had gradually hyped themselves into a loud frenzy, when Pete asked, "Hey guys, what is this place, anyway? I mean, why is it here in the first place?"

The room fell silent again, but this time it was a grim, cold silence. David, Tom, and Pete all knew this chamber had to be connected with Old Man Harrison. Nobody had lived at this farm after him. Until that moment, they'd pushed that knowledge into the dark recesses of their minds, succeeded in chaining it down, and had almost forgotten the bad stories and the fear associated with them.

David could feel the restraining chains being snapped by powerful hands and those fears slowly rising to the surface again like a balloon filled with poisonous gas. The grandiose vision of their being powerful knights began to fade, and soon David was back in that cold damp submarine again. He could imagine Jacob Harrison was the captain of this death sub, standing at the helm still covered in the sticky fluids of his family, an insane smile on his bloody lips, as he began to steer the small sub farther and farther down into the icy depths of the black ocean.

Johnny broke them out of their dark thoughts. He knew nothing about Jacob Harrison, so he'd pondered Pete's question seriously. "Must have been some kind of fruit cellar, although I don't know why it wouldn't be attached to the house."

Pete was about to agree—any explanation was better than the ghastly ones racing through his head—when he heard a small ping. It was hard to tell where it was coming from so he decided to let it go. "That's probably right, Johnny, it's cool enough down—" But then he heard the noise again and stopped midsentence.

They could all hear it now. They looked around the small room trying to pin down the location of the noise. Ping . . . ping . . . ping! It seemed to be growing louder.

Tom found it. The noise was coming from behind the sofa. Together they hauled the heavy couch away from the wall to reveal an old and rusty water faucet about two feet from the floor. A small drip of water was coming out of it. The bubblelike drip momentarily defied gravity before falling to the cement floor.

Why hadn't they noticed this earlier? The noise was certainly loud enough to have caught their attention. The only logical explanation was that it hadn't been dripping. In fact, it couldn't have been, or there would have been water everywhere. Instead, only a few spattered drops mingled on the dusty floor. This brought on a chilling thought. If the faucet had just started to drip, who had turned it on?

Ping . . . ping . . . ping, it continued, as all four of the brave new "knights" gathered to investigate. All of a sudden it came to Johnny: the underground water supply, the solid concrete walls—this place was a bomb shelter. It made perfect sense. Canada had never been close to being bombed or attacked during World War II, but a lot of people had been convinced that it would happen.

David, Tom, and Pete had to admit Johnny could be right, and that made them less nervous. No ghost had turned this tap on. Most likely they'd bumped up against the faucet with the back of the sofa while they were jumping around.

"This is great," said Tom, "We've even got water down here.

*All the comforts of home, huh? I'd better shut it off before we
have a mess to clean up."*

Tom gripped the rusty faucet handle and gave it a crank. Water
began to gush out all over his running shoes, the stink hitting them
immediately. Tom had never smelled anything so foul.

Johnny agreed the smell was awful. It was rotten, like something
dead. It smelled like . . . like the well this morning. Of course! The
bomb shelter ran toward his house from out in the field and came
up to the well in his backyard. He thought about the well and the
bloodsuckers. Could they come through the faucet? He had a fleeting image of thousands of slimy leeches pouring out of the tap and
scurrying across the floor to envelop them.

"Turn it the other way," Johnny screamed.

The rusty handle wasn't accustomed to being forced, and it
snapped off into Tom's right hand with a noise remarkably similar
to the earlier ping noise—only louder.

They froze on the increasingly wet floor, staring at the broken
handle. Tom held it out with a bewildered look on his face, a look
that said, What are we going to do now?

Water freely gushed out, and a stream of water sprayed out of the
top now, splattering the ceiling. David was close to panic. He was
back inside Jacob Harrison's death sub and the torrent of water was
filling the sub. The water was black, like the ocean he'd imagined.
His worst fears were coming true. He knew he was being silly, but
just as at Disneyland, he couldn't help it. He stood rooted to the
floor, helpless from fear, as the stinking water ran over his feet.

Tom removed his T-shirt and was trying to wrap it around the
broken faucet, but it was like trying to stop Niagara Falls with a
sponge. The pressure seemed to be increasing in force and the noise
of the water was steadily building. Now that it had found an out-
let, it was scratching and clawing to get out.

A crack appeared in the concrete wall over the faucet and
quickly spiderwebbed up to the ceiling. Small chunks of concrete
began to chip off, and the boys backed up to the opposite wall.
Their path to the hallway and outside wasn't blocked, but they
would have to walk past the crumbling wall to get there. They
stayed where they were and watched wide-eyed as the wall began

to bulge. The concrete began to smear black, as the water leaked out of the ever-widening crack. The wall bulged, then finally exploded.

Remarkably, none of the concrete projectiles made it across the room to where the four boys cowered. The water was quite another thing. The collapse of the wall created a small tidal wave, sending a rush of black, icy water across to swamp them. For a minute, the noise was deafening, but the room began to quiet as the pressure dropped. Once the water had washed down the hallway to the stairs and drained itself to the level of the hole in the wall, all was silent.

Quiet, that is, until the boys realized they were covered in bloodsuckers. It wasn't the thousands Johnny had imagined, but enough to scare the heck out of them. They raked at the small beasts attached to their exposed skin, desperate to get rid of them. There must have been a drain somewhere, because while they struggled with the leeches, the smelly water slowly trickled away.

They were so concerned with ridding themselves of the leeches, none of the boys noticed the large shape lying just clear of the collapsed wall, its huge form slowly emerging from the receding water, its bloodred eyes opening, gazing in their direction.

With a grin on its large, rotted face, the creature stared at the frantic boys as they finally succeeded in removing the bloodsuckers. The boys had just started to breathe again when they looked up and realized they were no longer alone.

With glazed eyes they watched something that couldn't possibly be human laughing at them from the wet floor. They were even more shocked when the thing slowly began to rise to its feet. It was a living nightmare.

The creature was over seven feet tall and towered over the small children, its head almost brushing the ceiling. Its body and face were an unrecognizable, rotting mess. Huge chunks of flesh were missing, and the boys could see greasy muscles and entrails. A mass of squirming bloodsuckers wrestled around in a feeding frenzy inside the revealed cavity of the creature's stomach. The leg and arm muscles were massive and its incredible strength obvious, though it looked as if its body were torn and damaged beyond repair. Crimson *eyes burned holes into the boys, who stared back with an unavoidable feeling of fascination and repulsion.*

The creature was enjoying this immensely. It opened and closed its huge hands so the frightened boys could get a good look at the razor-sharp talons of bone that extended out of its ruined fingers. They were terrified, but they couldn't look away.

The thing continued to laugh, its glowing eyes protruding obscenely out of gleaming white sockets, illuminating and highlighting the other prominent feature on the creature's face—teeth. There appeared to be an incredible number of jagged teeth under its empty nose cavity, and all of them tapered to a needlepoint like the fangs of a cobra.

The creature finally stopped laughing and hobbled awkwardly to one of the armchairs nearby. It then sat down and stared at the boys in silence.

David found his thoughts sluggish, like an old tractor stuck in first gear. A sliver of icy terror was being driven deep into his heart, and it seemed to be freezing his thoughts. He was thinking clearly enough to realize that the creature had conveniently positioned itself between them and the only escape route, its bulky frame almost hiding the spacious armchair. David knew that he and his friends were going to die. He also felt certain he knew the creature.

"Old Man Harrison," he whispered. That thought got his mind working again. It was like a nitrous-oxide boost, and soon his thoughts were racing. Could it be true? Could it? His original idea that Jacob Harrison had hidden from the police down here might have been correct. He had no idea how Jacob Harrison's body had been turned into this monstrosity, but he was sure he was right.

"No one asked you to speak, boy," the creature hissed in a gravelly voice.

Pete watched the abomination stick one of its long, bony talons inside its own stomach cavity and impale a bloody leech feeding there. It writhed on the razor-sharp finger and was still squirming when it disappeared down the creature's rotting throat. That was it for Pete: his wide eyes rolled and he crumbled to the floor. No one made a move to catch or aid him in any way. His legs began to spasm as if his body were trying to run away, and then he lay still.

Tom, David, and Johnny didn't even look at their fallen friend. They couldn't take their eyes off the hideous red-eyed beast blocking their path.

"So you pathetic worms are the fearless Knights of the Round Room?" asked the creature, with a grin on its grotesque face. "Does that mean you're going to fight me?"

The three "knights" still standing could do nothing but tremble.

"I thought not," it continued. "You boys should never have come down here. This is my domain . . . and I don't like uninvited pissants invading it."

The laughter had stopped now, and the creature's eyes shone a brighter red as it stood to its full height with a cold scowl on its shredded face. A growl escaped from between its lipless mouth as it drew nearer to the boys.

"I have to be going now, but hear me well. You've trespassed against me, and there's a price to be paid that you won't enjoy paying."

"But we—we don't have any money," Tom managed to say.

"Silence, boy. I don't want any of your pathetic possessions. I've endured years of agony you couldn't imagine. I've paid the price for my crimes. Now it's your turn . . . and believe me, you'll pay."

The creature glared at them for what seemed like an eternity and then did a strange thing. It took off a large golden ring from its left hand and threw it at the boys. David acted without even thinking, snagging the ring in midair. The creature nodded its deformed head a few times, and then without a glance back ran out of the room, along the concrete corridor leading toward the stairs out of the bunker.

The impossibility of what they had just witnessed overrode their fear and broke their paralysis. Just to be sure, Tom and Johnny crept to the edge of the hallway to double-check that the hideous creature was really gone, not laying in ambush.

"Do you think he's gone?" Tom asked.

"Don't know," Johnny whispered, fear trying to steal his voice. "I think so."

"Help me wake Pete up. We've gotta get out of here, Johnny. We don't wanna be here if that thing comes back."

Pete was still out cold, a mass of leeches having their fill on his exposed arms and legs as he lay in the center of the room. Tom and Johnny rushed to his aid, tearing the disgusting pests from his helpless body and stomping them to a mushy paste beneath their wet sneakers.

As Pete started to come around, no one was paying any attention to David, who was lost in his own little world, examining the elaborate ring the creature had tossed him. The ring looked like it was worth a fortune. It was made of solid gold and studded with glittering diamonds. At the top of the ring was the most beautiful ruby David had ever seen. It was so deep a red it appeared to glow. It was beyond David's comprehension why Old Man Harrison would give him something so beautiful and valuable.

And then an unimaginable pain engulfed David, striking him with lightning speed. It began in his left hand where he held the ring. Instantly, his hand contorted into a twisted fist, the worst arthritic attack imaginable. From there, the pain raced up his left arm to devour his entire body. White-hot flashes of agony exploded over the tender membranes within his brain in a display of horrific internal fireworks. The skin on his left palm began to burn where it tightly gripped the ruby ring. David could feel the intense inferno that had once been his hand, smell the strong, pungent odor of burning flesh, but he was incapable of doing anything about it. The pain was completely shutting down his bodily functions.

David tried with all his might to unclench his smoldering, white-knuckled hand and throw away the unholy ring, but it was impossible. He wasn't even allowed the luxury of screaming. Just as suddenly, the pain stopped. Red-hot knives of agony one second, ice-cold release the next. Blissfully slipping into unconsciousness, David sagged to the ground, his still-smoldering left hand finally opening up as he hit the wet floor. The creature's ruby ring rolled out of his charred palm and settled in a shallow puddle amid a hiss of steam.

Johnny and Tom heard the loud thump behind them. They had been oblivious to David's painful ordeal and were surprised to see him passed out on the floor.

"What happened to him?" they both asked Pete, who was just stumbling to his feet, rubbing his eyes.

"Huh . . . I don't know." Pete was still trying to clear the cobwebs from his own head, and hadn't seen a thing. "Look at his hand."

David's hand was swollen, and large open sores covered his palm. The blisters were cracked and broken, with threads of bright red blood trickling between his slowly twitching fingers.

"What happened?" asked Pete.

"Beats me," said Tom, shrugging his shoulders. "Help me wake him up. We gotta get out of here."

While they were busy trying to revive David, Johnny's attention was caught by a faint red glow in a small puddle near his sneaker. He bent over and saw the creature's ruby ring. In the back of Johnny's mind, he somehow understood that this ring was the cause of David's anguish. That understanding was pushed away by a strange, angry voice in his head urging him, commanding him, to take the ring.

Johnny was soon cradling the ruby ring in his hands and didn't remember picking it up. His fear of the ring vanished when he saw how beautiful it was. He'd never seen anything like it. A feeling of greed crept through him, making him realize he wanted it for himself. Just because David had grabbed it first, didn't mean it was his.

That's right, Johnny, the voice inside his head whispered. It wasn't meant to go like this, but now that it has . . . why don't you try it on for size?

Johnny slipped the heavy ring onto the second finger of his left hand and was amazed at how perfectly it fit. That the creature's fingers were five times his size, that the ring should have been much too big, never entered his mind. A feeling of peace overcame

him as he stared in fascination at the soft glow. He didn't even notice David waking up.

David looked up at the relieved faces of Tom and Pete and
for a minute didn't know where he was. His throbbing left hand
quickly reminded him, and he had to get out of this evil place immediately; he didn't want to stay in this hellhole a second longer.
Pushing past his friends without looking back or saying a word,
David flew up the stairs and into the blessed, late-afternoon sun.

Tom and Pete couldn't have agreed more. They followed David
out of the clubhouse and watched their friend run across Johnny's
yard, heading for home.

"Do you really think that monster could have been Old Man
Harrison?"

Pete turned and looked into Tom's large, frightened eyes. "I . . .
I don't really know, but whatever it was, I thought we were goners
for sure."

"Me too, buddy . . . me too."

They walked slowly away from the hidden staircase, but picked
up the pace as they thought about the creature. They paused at
the well in Johnny's backyard and could clearly tell the water level
was way down. Peering down the stinking pit, they could see light
from the round room through the gaping hole in the wall far below.

"Hey Tom, you know that story David and Johnny were talking about? The . . . the one about the knights and all that?"

"Yeah, what about it?"

"Johnny said the knights were supposed to fight dragons and
monsters, right?"

"Something like that. Why?"

"Well, we seem to have a monster to fight, and I was just wondering if the knights in the book always killed the monsters . . . or
if maybe . . ."

Tom understood what Pete was saying, but couldn't come up
with an answer that would remove the terrified look from his
friend's face. "Come on Pete . . . let's go home. We'll be okay,
you'll see." Together they walked out of Johnny's yard, but before
long they were running toward home too.

Still belowground, Johnny sat down on the damp cement floor

and admired his new ring. No lightning bolts of pain hit Johnny the way they'd hit David—just the opposite. The ring made him feel fantastic, made him feel invincible, as if he could do anything he wanted.

After an hour on the cold floor, Johnny rose up and walked to the house in a daze. He didn't hear his mother yelling at him, or feel the dozen leeches attached to and feasting on his body. He walked past his mother and up to his bedroom, climbing into bed without even bothering to remove his wet, stinking clothes. He simply curled up in a ball and went to sleep with a big smile on his face.

That evening, David hadn't been able to fall asleep quite so easily—or so happily. He lay under his thick comforter and shook uncontrollably for a long time. Had they really found Jacob Harrison? Could that seven-foot monstrosity actually be him? Their nightmarish experience seemed unbelievable. Maybe they'd had some kind of group hallucination. Maybe the air down there *had* been bad, and after they'd breathed it for a while, it had affected their minds.

He almost started to believe himself until he rolled over and banged his damaged hand on the wall. Pain flared up his arm, reminding him how real things had been. David hugged himself as tightly as his sore hand would allow, rocking back and forth under the covers until exhaustion finally overtook him and he fell into a restless sleep.

The creature stood silently in David Winter's bedroom, not three feet from where he lay sleeping. It had been standing there for about half an hour, probing into the young boy's mind and rocking back and forth along with him.

You messed up today Davey, messed up bad. I had everything figured out, but you had to change things, didn't you? You had to drop the ring. You've forced me to change my plans . . . but no matter. In the end, it will all work out just fine.

The creature chuckled silently as it watched David finally

fall into a deep sleep. *I should rest, myself. It's going to get mighty hectic around here soon.* The creature let out another quiet giggle and disappeared into David's closet.

"Home sweet home," it whispered, taking one last look at the small huddled figure curled up under the covers. "You should have held onto that ring, Davey."

The creature closed the closet door quietly, and the house became deadly silent. David's parents had gone to bed early, so the entire house was in darkness, except for the light coming from under the door to David's closet.

It wasn't much of a light.

Not really . . . it was actually more of a glow.

A red glow.

CHAPTER FOUR

David never heard from his friends the next day, which was exactly how he wanted it. He needed a quiet day to himself without having to deal with the insanity of yesterday. He would deal with them tomorrow. Today was just for him.

He'd slept until almost noon, and the rest of the day was reserved for sulking around the house. His parents desperately wanted to confront him about yesterday, but fearing a casual conversation would end in an inquisition, they decided not to pursue the matter. This surprised David, and the unexpected relief from the inevitable onslaught of questions was exactly what he needed. By the time night had fallen, a cheery calmness had settled over the family. David excused himself early and put his tired body to bed.

Monday mornings meant school, and no matter how hard David tried to fake that he was sick, his mother had him out the door before he knew what hit him. She just didn't understand what he was going through. No grown-ups would, but luckily David knew someone who might. One person understood his feelings and had always been there for him, no matter how big the problem—Rodney the Scarecrow. David headed around the side of the house to where Rodney hung on his cross.

David and Rodney had been best friends for years. Being an only child, David had to rely on his imagination when he was lonely. When his father had first introduced him to their new scarecrow, David had instantly known Rodney and he were going to be buddies. Since that day, he'd spent countless hours talking to the scarecrow. Rodney knew things about him that nobody else in the whole world knew.

Today, Rodney looked rough. Last winter had been hard on him. David knew exactly how he felt; he was feeling rough himself. His body and nerves were still shot, despite yesterday's rest.

David could tell by the tired look in Rodney's Styrofoam eyes that he understood. David slumped down on the grass below his friend, ignoring the cool sensation of dew soaking through his blue jeans. He looked up into his friend's understanding face and released his pent-up feelings.

"I'm scared Rodney, I—I'm really scared. This time I've got a real problem and I don't know what to do. Old Man Harrison is after me. Not only me . . . he's after my friends too. I don't understand how, but he really is. What the heck are we gonna do?"

David gazed into his friend's eyes, partially concealed under his dirty New York Yankees cap, and searched long and hard for a response. Rodney didn't have any answers today; he just continued to stare back at David with his steadfast gaze. David let out a sigh and rose to his feet. Dusting himself off, he said, "Well, you think about it, big guy. I've got to get to school. I'll see you later, okay?"

He turned away from Rodney, walking across the field toward school. About halfway, David was certain he was being watched. He spun around quickly, but couldn't see anybody. Everything looked normal. *I'm getting paranoid*, he thought. He headed off to school at a quicker pace, determined not to let it get to him. He had to stay in control. Still, he couldn't push aside the fleeting image he thought he'd seen when he'd looked back at his house. For an instant, he could have sworn he'd seen Rodney's head swivel around, his small, beady eyes transfixed on him as he walked away.

The rest of the walk to school was uneventful. David pre-

CRIMSON   53

sumed none of his friends would show up today, but he was wrong. He found Johnny, Tom, and Pete sitting under a large, sprawling oak tree in the corner of the schoolyard.

David decided he wasn't up to pussyfooting around. If Old Man Harrison was really after them, they didn't have time for small talk. When he got to within ten feet of his pale-looking friends, he said the same thing he had said to Rodney half an hour before.

"What are we going to do?"

"About what?" replied Pete.

One scolding look from Tom, and Pete shut up and resumed staring at the ground.

"Look guys," continued David, "we have to come up with a plan, or Old Man Harrison will tear us apart."

Johnny sprang to his feet. "Hold on a minute, will you?"

He looked the worst of all of them. His skin was jaundiced and his eyes looked glassy and shallow. He obviously hadn't slept much last night. The feeling of euphoria that had overtaken him on Saturday night had quickly disappeared on Sunday morning. The memories of the hideous creature in the bomb shelter had still been with him when he opened his eyes. The putrid smell from his clothes had jerked him awake, and he'd had to sprint to the bathroom to throw up. A steamy shower and fresh clothes had helped a little, but the memory of the day before haunted him all night.

Unlike David's parents, Johnny's mother had questioned him endlessly, ranting and raving all day. All Johnny could do was endure her. He'd gone to bed a very scared and confused little boy.

"Will somebody let me in on what's going on around here? You three all seem to know something I don't. Two or three times I've heard you guys mention Old Man Harrison—now what gives? I want to know right now."

David, Pete, and Tom took turns looking around at each other until Tom finally found his voice. "Johnny's right, guys. We shouldn't have secrets. If we're going to help each other, we have to stick together."

Pete and David thought it over and nodded their heads in agreement.

"You tell him, Tom," said Pete, already trembling at the thought of having to sit through the awful story again.

"No, not me. David's the one to tell it. He knows it better than either of us."

David started to complain but realized Tom was right. It should be him. In fact, he should have told Johnny on Saturday, when they released the Jacob Harrison creature from its watery grave, but fear had taken over and made him run. The truth about Johnny's home couldn't be hidden any longer. Johnny had to know. David glanced around the playground to see if anyone else was listening, but they were alone. Slowly, reluctantly, he began to tell his three silent friends the tale that had haunted every person in Dunnville for the past twenty-two years—the tale of Old Man Harrison.

CHAPTER FIVE

The story had been told in many different ways. Each variation was similar, but individual storytellers would spice up a portion here or there, depending on their own particular sensibilities. David had no wish to spice anything up. He just wanted to tell Johnny the truth. . . .

On the corner of Cedar and Forrest streets, smack-dab in the heart of town, stands an old abandoned three-story brick building. Almost all of the windows in the old building are smashed out as a result of time and the ageless vandal's rock. The building houses nothing, save for the spiders and the rats—but things weren't always that way.

Twenty-two years ago, the building was the industrial lifeblood of Dunnville, a state-of-the-art textile mill that produced some of the finest towels and linens in the entire country. Wabasso, the name of the company, had a fine reputation as a leader in the textile industry. Jacob Harrison worked there as a foreman on the night shift. The mill shut down during the night, and Jacob's crew was in charge of all of the cleanup and maintenance required to get the place in shape for the morning whistle.

Jacob Harrison was one of the finest men you'd ever have the pleasure of meeting. He was a gentle, soft-spoken man—a family man. He had a loving wife and three adorable children. His coworkers admired him because he was such a hard worker. He had just turned sixty-three in the spring of 1955. They all bugged him about retiring, but Jacob would always answer that if he was still young enough to keep a younger wife happy—Emma was forty—and father a baby, which he had done just one year earlier, then he was still young enough to work. The men he worked with and his bosses knew that this was true. Jacob was a valuable employee who could always be counted on and trusted. That was why it was such a shock to the community when it finally happened.

Almost overnight Jacob seemed to change. He had always been full of fun and easy to get along with, but he suddenly started yelling and nagging all the time. No matter how hard his coworkers tried, Jacob would find some small fault as an excuse to dock their wages. The workers quickly grew bitter and resentful. Eventually, they stopped even trying to please him.

Rumors started to fly (as they're apt to do in a small town) that Jacob was getting senile or that he was hitting the bottle too hard. People even reported seeing his wife Emma at the grocery store with a painful-looking black eye, and his two older kids were missing an awful lot of school.

By the middle of July, Jacob became withdrawn and stopped nagging his men. The workers couldn't decide what was worse, his screaming or his silent, accusing glares. He started spending more time in his office, and the workers on the night shift seldom saw or heard from him. He would come in and head straight for his dimly lit office in the maintenance basement and stay there until he crept silently out the door in the morning.

The rumors were really flying by then, and Jacob's coworkers desperately wanted to know what he did all night. He didn't sleep, because they would hear him crashing around and laughing. They were thoroughly convinced that he was going insane, but they didn't know just how far gone he was until their curiosity got the better of them, and they decided to check out his office.

It was 2:00 A.M. when they made their move. A young

man by the name of Danny Sanderson was chosen. The rest of the gang lured old Jacob out of his office on the false pretense that the boss was at the back door. The minute Jacob was out of sight, Sanderson crept down the basement stairs and into the office. Danny knew he didn't have much time. He sure didn't want Jacob coming back to find him poking around.

Jacob had been in the middle of eating his lunch. On a plate on his desk sat a half-eaten piece of fried chicken, a hard-boiled egg, and a greasy sandwich. Danny bent over to examine the drawers in the desk, the most likely place he could think of for someone to hide something they didn't want seen. Danny had already checked two of them, when something bright flashed in his eyes from the top of the desk. As he straightened to see what it was, it glinted again.

The flash had come from the piece of fried chicken. The full impact of Jacob Harrison's insanity hit Danny like a punch in the stomach as he took a closer look at the lunch plate in front of him. It was a hand . . . a half eaten, human hand that had been roasted like a plump, juicy piece of chicken. The glint caught his eye again as he bent to examine the crispy severed hand. A wedding ring still clung to the blistered and bloated third finger.

Danny knew this hand must have belonged to Emma, Jacob's wife, and he also knew he had to get out of that office—fast. He was about to run when he noticed the hard-boiled egg on the plate had a dark circle on it. What he'd thought was a small egg was actually an eyeball. The eye stared blankly toward him with a large, dark, dilated pupil, watching as he regurgitated onto his boots.

Danny Sanderson finally got his stomach under control and realized he had to get away. It didn't matter where—anywhere away from the sight of the sickening feast. He took one unsteady step forward, but the doorway was blocked. Old Man Harrison stood before the only exit from the room, staring at him with demented eyes.

Jacob glanced back and forth between his lunch on the

desk and the quivering boy in front of him, and he knew his
secret had been discovered. His hands clenched and un-
clenched. Every fiber in his body began to tense, and the
veins in his arms and throat rose into dark purple rivers that
throbbed in rhythmic frenzy.

Danny tried to scream for help, but fear constricted his
throat and would only allow him to whisper. He dropped to
his knees and started begging for his life.

Jacob put a long, bony finger to his lips and gave Danny
the quiet sign. He then reached outside his office door and
grabbed something large and heavy. Danny found his ability
to scream when Jacob brought the object into full view. Held
tightly in his hands was a large fireman's axe that had hung
on the wall beside the extinguisher. Jacob slowly closed his
office door and walked toward the screaming young man.

Danny's coworkers contacted the police as soon as they
heard the screams, but by the time they arrived, Danny was
no more than a large heap of ground beef on the bloody floor.
Jacob was nowhere to be found. Neither was the bloody axe.

The police quickly headed to the Harrison farmhouse on
Logan Road. When they arrived, only one light was burning
in an upstairs bedroom, and the police cautiously entered.
What they found was a scene straight out of hell. It was a human slaughterhouse. Bits and pieces of half-eaten corpses lay
scattered about filthy floors. The smell of carnage was so overpowering that three of the policemen were unable to stay inside. Five others swallowed down their rising gorge and began
searching for Jacob.

They found him in the upstairs bedroom. He'd hung himself: his heavy body was swaying back and forth on a rope
slung over a sturdy rafter. The rope dug tightly into the tender skin of his neck. One look into his strained, bulging eyes
was enough to tell the police he was dead, but they still went
through the formality of checking for a pulse.

A note was found pinned to Jacob's chest. It was a basic
suicide note stating how horrible a life he'd had and that he
didn't regret anything he'd done. Jacob had signed the note

and at the bottom had written in an extra line. It said that if the police were hungry, he had left them something delicious, downstairs in the oven.

In the oven waited the most sickening and disturbing sight of all. In a large open roasting pan lay the charred and still-steaming body of Jacob's one-year-old daughter, Emily, her melted pacifier still sticking out of her tiny, burned mouth like an apple in a roasted pig.

As the police stood around in horrified silence, they heard a heavy thump from upstairs. A deafening crash reached them as they raced back up the stairs.

Jacob Harrison was gone.

The police could only find an empty noose swinging in the breeze from the shattered window. The glass was all over the lawn outside, the window definitely broken from inside—but by whom? Jacob was dead; five policemen could attest to that. How could a dead body climb out of a noose, leap out a second-story window, then run off into the night?

Nobody ever found out how Old Man Harrison had disappeared, and his body was never found. He simply vanished without a trace. The town was good enough to bury the Harrison family—whatever uneaten parts they found—and after a while everything returned back to normal.

"You're living in Jacob Harrison's house, Johnny," said David. "No one else has lived there in all those years. I guess everybody was scared. Most people won't even talk about it anymore, but don't let them kid you, they're still scared. Nobody will ever forget what happened, and deep down they all wonder if Old Man Harrison is still out there somewhere. Unfortunately . . . we know he is."

The school bell clanged explosively, breaking the silence that followed David's story, startling the high-strung group. Tom and Peter stood up and began walking toward the school entrance. David could tell that they were both physically and emotionally shaken. This had been the first time

Pete had heard the entire story. Tom was tough, but not tough enough to deal with the thought of an insane monster on the loose.

"Any questions?" David asked Johnny, who looked as if he might throw up.

"Can we beat Old Man Harrison? I mean . . . how do you kill a monster that's already dead?"

David couldn't offer any comfort. "I don't know, Johnny. I really don't know."

They followed Tom and Pete to the school entrance, David's arm slung protectively around Johnny's quivering shoulder.

"Any other questions?"

"Well . . . " he nervously replied, "can I maybe sleep over at your place tonight?"

"Sure, buddy," said David, smiling as they stepped into the school. "Anytime."

School seemed extremely long and boring that day, but the routine helped calm the four young boys. By the end of the day, Pete was back to telling jokes and cracking up the class. The laughter made them all feel better. After school they joined a baseball game, which helped dispel the rest of their lingering fears. Maybe Old Man Harrison wasn't really after them. Maybe things would be just fine.

The game had been an excellent way to forget their weekend. What problems could they possibly have on such a beautiful, sunny day? When they split up to head home, they were grinning from ear to ear and laughing hysterically. Little did they know that by midnight that night, one of them would be dead.

CHAPTER SIX

The warm breeze of the afternoon had slowly metamorphosed into a brisk, chilly wind by nightfall. The storm howling through the trees, accompanied by a full moon hanging low in the darkening sky, created the perfect atmosphere for telling scary stories, but the boys who sat around the Winters' dining-room table had heard enough ghost stories for one day.

David Winter and Johnathan Page sat quietly across from each other, feigning interest in the comic books they were holding. Johnny's mother had agreed to let him stay over only after she brought him fresh clothes and a warm sweater. She had kissed Johnny good-bye as if he were going off to war. David's parents were at the back of the house, in the living room, watching an old Errol Flynn movie.

Unable to concentrate on his Superman comic any longer, Johnny broke the silence. "What if it was my room, David?"

"What if *what* was your room?" asked David over the rim of his unopened comic.

"You know . . . Old Man Harrison? You said he hung himself in a second-story bedroom. What if it was my bedroom? I don't think I'll ever be able to sleep there again."

"Don't get excited, Johnny. Your house doesn't have anything to do with it. Old Man Harrison was evil, not the house."

"Then why have you always been scared to go near it?"

"Not all that scared," said David defiantly.

"Yeah, then how about we pack up our things and go sleep at my place tonight?"

The color on David's face drained away at such a thought, but before he could come up with a valid excuse to say no, a loud crash outside startled them.

They stared across the table at each other, wide-eyed, rooted to their chairs.

"What was that?" asked Johnny.

"Nothing, it's just the . . ." The noise returned before David could say it was only the wind.

They looked out the window, but their heavy breathing made the glass too steamy to see through.

"Maybe we should check it out," David said. "Think I should get my dad?"

"No way. If we cause a fuss and start bugging them, they'll send me home."

"Maybe. You wanna check it out *ourselves*?"

Not wanting to, but unable to think of an alternative plan, they headed out the kitchen door. The night was cold and their breath cut through the air like an eerie mist. The banging noise stopped as they rounded the corner of the house, but not before they realized it had come from the small metal utility shed. The rusty door stood open, swinging back and forth in the wind.

"Something's in there," David whispered. "My dad never leaves that door open."

The frightened boys inched closer. Inside the shed, a pair of glowing eyes fixed on their cautious approach.

Being out late wasn't exactly Tom Baker's idea of a good time, especially after all the things that had happened lately. Tom's father had sent him to the store to get something to settle his stomach. His father figured it was something he'd eaten. Tom figured it had more to do with the empty bottle of vodka on the kitchen counter, but kept his thoughts to himself. He only had ten minutes before the store closed at 11:00 P.M., but it was nearby, and he made it with plenty of time to spare.

Walking back home alone on a cold dark night began playing havoc with Tom's imagination. He began to think he was being followed. He could hear someone walking behind him—he was sure of it. Every few steps he would stop and turn, but the footsteps behind him would stop as well.

The night got darker and the shadows longer as Tom's fear took over. He saw monsters in the trees and ghosts in the bushes, his imagination racing as he quickened his pace. The footsteps behind him also sped up. He was about to break into a run when something stopped him dead in his tracks.

A circle of moonlight filtering through a gap in a large maple tree revealed Tom's worst nightmare. It was the grotesque King Spider, bigger and more hideous than he remembered.

"How ya doing, Tommy?" hissed the immense spider. "Long time no see."

The bag of medicine dropped from Tom's weak grasp, its contents breaking as it hit the sidewalk. Tom didn't notice. He remained still, but trembling, as his adrenaline kicked into high gear, every nerve screaming for him to run.

This can't be happening. His mind reeled.

He knew he should be running, but was unable to break eye contact with the beast. Its glowing eyes burned into his with a strange, hypnotic effect. He would have stayed rooted to that spot forever, but the King Spider suddenly scurried forward on its eight powerful legs, and Tom quickly decided this was not the place to be. He turned his back on the multilegged ghoul and ran for his life.

Peter Myers, still exhausted from the weekend, had gone to bed early, hoping for a restful sleep. He was angry, then, to find himself standing in the bathroom at 11:12 P.M. He'd gone to the toilet two hours ago, but here he was again. He knew better than to drink tea before bedtime.

His father and brother must also have retired for the night, because the house was dark and silent, save for the wind rattling against the windows. When Pete finished his

business—remembering his father's lecture—he hit the
light switch before sleepily walking toward his room. At the
end of the hall, a small table with a pink ceramic vase sat
under an elaborately framed mirror. Pete stopped to look at
his reflection and realized he shouldn't have been able to.
The hallway should have been too dark. Then he figured
out why—he'd left the light on in the bathroom, illuminating the hall.

"That's strange. I thought I just . . ." The sentence went
unfinished as Pete turned to head back to the bathroom. His
eyes widened and his mouth dropped open in disbelief. The
hallway and bathroom were in darkness. Pete rubbed his
tired eyes and returned his gaze to the mirror. In its reflection, Pete could undeniably see the bathroom light still illuminating the hallway.

"No way," he said, glancing back and forth between the
mirrored hallway and the real one. One was lit up brightly,
the other in darkness. "What's going on?"

A movement in the mirror caught his attention. Someone
slowly stepped into the light cast from the "mirror" bathroom.
Pete's bewilderment turned to horror as he recognized the
grotesque image coming into view.

It was the creature from the well. In its rotted, powerful
hands was something that would have emptied Peter's blad-
der, if he hadn't just done so. The creature was holding a
large, bloodstained fireman's axe. Pete instinctively knew this
was the same axe that had tasted blood in Jacob Harrison's office over twenty years back.

It was hard to pry his eyes from the mirror, but Pete was
compelled to look behind him. The hallway was still dark, but
he could see enough to reassure himself that he was alone.
Pete turned to look in the mirror again. The massive creature
with the axe was still standing in the brightly lit, mirrored
hall, only now it was much closer.

David and Johnny moved slowly to the open door of the
utility shed and the darkness within. Their fear building,

the boys paused outside and tried to peer beyond the gloom, but it was impossible to make anything out. They needed to get closer, and to do that, they had to go inside.

Before they reached the door, something lightning quick tore out and knocked them on their rear ends. Johnny let loose a deafening scream, muffled only by the surging wind. Both boys spun quickly to see David's cat, Fluffer, tearing off into the high grass. Relieved, the boys noticed its translucent eyes glowing in the moonlight as it disappeared around the side of the house.

Steven Winter came flying outside, followed closely by his wife, her housecoat billowing in the wind. Johnny's scream had startled them away from their movie.

"What are you doing outside?" Steven shouted. "I thought you guys had gone to bed hours ago. This is a school night, you know?"

David's mother gently grabbed Steven's arm and turned him toward the back door. Over her shoulder she said, "I suggest you two night owls hit the sheets. Okay?"

David nodded his head and followed his parents into the house. The small clock on the kitchen wall read 11:25 P.M. He'd had no idea it was that late.

"Sorry for getting you in trouble, David," said Johnny, embarrassed.

"Don't worry about it. My parents are used to me staying up late. We better not push it, though. Why don't we go upstairs and play a game in my room? If we're quiet, they'll think we've gone to bed."

"Sounds good. Do you have checkers?"

"Sure do. I have a whole mess of games in my closet. Go pick one out. I'll get us some pop and be up in a minute."

Upstairs in David's closet, the creature stood up. It was enjoying its fantastic powers, now being displayed. It was monitoring the conjured situations presently haunting Pete and Tom, but it was also very aware of Johnny bounding up the stairs toward it.

The creature waited behind the closet door for Johnny, running its black, bloated tongue across its razor fangs. The teeth sliced into the tender muscle, sending blood gushing out and dribbling down its chin. Johnny was nearing the top of the stairs and approaching David's bedroom. The rotting monster stood motionless in the closet, waiting, tasting its own blood and liking it.

Tom ran as fast as he could, leaving his father's medicine— and hopefully, the King Spider—far behind. The spider was fast. Every time he glanced back, it was closer. With only one block left before his street and the safety of home, Tom prayed the diminishing distance between them would be enough. It slowed him down, but he couldn't help himself— he had to turn around for another look. He was alone. The spider was gone.

Tom rounded the corner and looked longingly toward his brightly lit house. The spider had cut the corner by going through some backyards and was now sitting in the middle of the road between Tom and his house. There was no way Tom could elude the spider and reach the house, so he did the only thing he could. He turned and ran the opposite way.

Maybe he could catch the man at the corner store before he locked up. By the time he ran back to the store, his legs ached and his lungs were on fire. He was too late. The store lights were shut off. Tom tried the door anyway, but it was locked.

A light was on in the apartment above the store, so Johnny yelled and banged on the door until his throat was hoarse. Behind him, the King Spider lurched closer. Desperate, Tom continued to scream and pound on the door. Someone in the apartment moved the curtain a fraction, peered out, and then turned off the lights, pretending no one was home. Tom's heart sank, knowing there was no help coming from within. He slumped down against the door in defeat.

"Hey," a voice down the street shouted. "Are you okay?"

A tall man with his dog on a long leash was walking briskly

toward him. Tom ran toward his savior, cool relief calming his
red-hot fear.

"Over here, mister. I've never been so happy to see someone in my life," he said, bending down to pet the fluffy ears
of the cocker spaniel. The dog was appreciative of the rub-
down and rolled over so Tom could scratch its belly.

The man was strangely silent. Tom looked up to see the
rotting face of the creature, its two bulging red eyes glaring
back. The towering monster started to laugh.

"Why Tom," it said in mock surprise. "Fancy meeting you
here at this time of night. I was out walking my pet, when I
heard you shouting."

Pet?

Tom looked down at the dog he'd been scratching and
jumped back at the sight of the King Spider rolled over on
its back, letting him rub its squirming, bloated belly. Vomit
began to rise in Tom's throat. Carried on the wings of terror,
with no destination in mind, Tom sprinted into the night,
away from the madness behind him.

He could hear the creature's evil laughter as the leash was
removed from the King Spider's neck, and the inevitable noise
of its eight-legged pursuit. This time he didn't think about
looking back. Only one frantic thought was in his head.

Run!

Pete was overwhelmed. He stood frozen, silently denying
what his eyes were seeing. The hallway in which he stood
was completely empty, yet in the mirror, the hideous creature still kept coming. It barely moved, taking its time, enjoying the fear in Pete's eyes.

"This isn't real. It can't be happening," Pete spoke, as he
backed down the hall toward the mirror. It was crazy to retreat down an empty hallway, but every step he took toward
the mirror, his reflection took a step away from the creature.
He checked the hallway floor to see if something invisible
was making indentations in the carpet as it stalked him. He

saw nothing, but that did little to ease his mind. He turned back to the mirror, and screamed.

The creature stood only two feet away. Pete looked up into the grinning face of death and found himself unable to move as he watched the creature slowly raise its axe. Pete tried with all his might to run, lash out, to do something to defend himself, but he was powerless. He couldn't even find the strength to scream as the creature started to swing the bloody axe in a powerful arc toward the tender flesh of his throat.

Johnny vaulted the blue-carpeted stairs two at a time to the second-floor hall and entered David's bedroom. The room was unusually cold compared to the rest of the house. Freezing. Goose bumps rose on his arms the instant he entered.

Strangely, the cold seemed to emanate from the closet. Johnny could feel the chill blowing under the door and through the keyhole. He walked over and gripped the doorknob, quickly releasing it again when he discovered it was ice cold. "Something weird is happening here," he muttered, the short hairs on the back of his neck prickling to attention. He turned the frigid doorknob all the way and slowly opened the squeaky door.

David had finished pouring two glasses of Coke and turned to put the bottle into the refrigerator when he heard a scream from upstairs. Startled, he dropped the bottle onto the kitchen floor. It shattered, spraying the floor with sticky liquid and broken glass, but David ignored it. He rushed up the stairs ahead of his parents, fear squeezing his stomach like a fat woman's corset. His apprehension tripled when he found his bedroom door closed. Behind the door, Johnny had stopped screaming. The bedroom was draped in silence.

Tom exerted himself harder than he thought possible. They say kids have limitless amounts of energy, but that isn't true. Tom was tiring quickly. He was also lost, but didn't really care—his single concern was to stay ahead of the relentless spider.

Tom turned left between a hardware store and a bank. Seconds later, he realized his mistake. It was a dead end, an alley with high brick walls in front and on both sides.

He turned to flee, but it was too late.

The King Spider squatted twelve feet from him. Tom was boxed in. He begged the giant spider to leave him alone, but it sat watching him with unblinking red eyes, motionless, its mandibles continually snapping, making an eerie ringing noise as they crunched together. The spider dripped thick ribbons of drool from its mouth as its salivary glands responded to the noise, like one of Pavlov's dogs anticipating an imminent feast.

Pete's mind unlocked and he ducked just in time. The axe missed his head and buried itself deeply into the wall. There was a gaping hole beside his head, confirming that this craziness was real. He'd hoped the entire mirror scene was a hallucination, but the damaged wall was proof he was in mortal danger. The edges of the hole moved back and forth in front of his eyes, the axe wedged in the wall, and the creature was trying feverishly to work it free.

Pete's brief reprieve evaporated as the creature yanked the weapon free. Staring down at Pete, its fiery eyes blazed with an expression of joy as it moved in for the kill. The hallway wasn't long, and the creature would be on top of Pete shortly if he didn't do something. He backed as far away from the creature as he could by moving closer to the mirror. Pete cried out when he smacked into the table underneath the mirror. The ceramic vase overbalanced, tumbling off the side of the table, and would have shattered, if not for Pete's quick reflexes. He caught the vase just before it smashed on the floor.

"Smashed," Pete whispered, quickly realizing he might accidentally have figured a way out of this mess. "That's it. Smash the mirror and the creature can't get me."

With clenched teeth, the creature raised the axe above its head and swung down toward Pete's unprotected skull.

Pete hurled the ceramic vase at the mirror as hard as he could.

Time moved in slow motion as he watched the vase move closer to the mirror and the axe closer to his skull. All Pete could do was pray the vase shattered the mirror before the axe opened up his head. A few seconds felt like a lifetime as he crouched down, fully expecting the blinding pain of steel cleaving him apart. The vase struck the fragile, silver surface just as he felt the axe move through his thick brown hair. The mirror exploded, scattering thousands of pieces of glass like shrapnel from a grenade.

Pete slumped to the ground in trembling relief, putting his hands to his head to check for damage. His left hand came away dripping with blood—the axe had cut a thin groove in his scalp. He shuddered at the thought of what might have happened if the vase had taken a second longer to find its target.

Pete leaned against the cool plaster wall, relaxing, but something was still bothering him. Something didn't seem right. Where were the broken pieces from the vase? They were nowhere to be seen, and most of the mirror glass was missing too. Puzzled, Pete glanced at the mirror and his blood ran cold again.

There was no wall behind the frame. He stared at a black opening.

His mind reeled. There had to be a wall behind the mirror. Didn't there? Pete's curiosity got the better of him—he had to take a closer look. He reached unsteadily toward the frame with his left arm. He spread his fingers open as wide as he could, expecting—maybe hoping—his hand would come into contact with the cool plaster wall. His eyes opened in amazement as his hand passed through the picture frame into the darkness beyond.

A huge, rotted hand shot up from the darkness and locked painfully onto Pete's skinny wrist. The creature stood up from below the mirror frame and stared down at Pete with a look of victory. Pete was so close to the beast he could smell its pungent odor and feel the heat from its glowing eyes.

The creature grinned savagely and produced the axe, still gripped in its other powerful hand. The axe had a thin stream of fresh blood dripping off of it.

My blood, Pete thought.

He desperately tried to pull his hand free, but the creature's grasp was like a vise. Before Pete could scream, the creature raised the cruel axe and slammed it down hard. Pete was helpless to do anything as the razor-sharp blade descended toward the fragile skeletal framework of his face. . . .

Pete woke up screaming in his small, sweat-stained bed, his mind still frantic from the fiercely realistic nightmare. He pulled the pillow over his head, trembling and crying like a baby. When his tears dried up, he emerged from under his pillow and realized he wasn't alone.

The creature was sitting four feet away in an old chair, its twin orbs sending beams of red light around the dark room as it surveyed its surroundings. Finally the creature's eyes locked on Pete, who shrank back against the wall.

"Ah Petey . . . you've come out of hibernation. Good." The red beams moved up and down as the creature talked while nodding agreeably. "I know how you feel. Bad dreams can really suck, can't they? Sometimes, however, being awake isn't much better."

Pete wasn't sure what the creature meant until it stood up. In the crimson glow of its eyes, Pete could see the creature's outstretched right hand was still holding the bloody axe.

David listened outside his bedroom door for any noise that might tell him Johnny was all right. He knew he should open the door, but he couldn't. His mind was ready to go, but his body just wouldn't do it, the fear overpowering. Steven Winter didn't hesitate at all before he rushed in, followed by his wife. David wanted to run the other way, but his friend, and now his parents, might need help. Bracing himself, he followed them inside.

Johnny was lying, dazed but unhurt, in a jumble of games and puzzles that had collapsed on him when he'd opened the closet door. The wall of games crashing down had scared him, causing him to scream. David's father didn't say a word. He simply stared at Johnny and then glared a final warning at David before leaving the room.

Donna whispered to David on her way out, "Get into bed, young man. Now!" She closed the bedroom door and was gone.

"You scared the heck out of me, idiot," David said, turning toward Johnny.

"It wasn't my fault, Dave, all I did was open the door and everything came crashing down. I scared myself too."

David wasn't really mad, and in a minute they were laughing as they gathered the games up and closed the closet door.

"Why is it so cold in here, Dave?"

David hadn't noticed, but it was true. His room was ice cold, almost like a meat freezer. "That's why. The window's wide open."

David pulled the window shut before climbing into bed. "It'll warm up soon. We better get to sleep. I think my dad's pretty mad."

Johnny climbed into the sheets beside his new friend and was soon listening to David quietly snore.

Sleep was a long time coming for Johnny. He was absolutely sure the window was closed when he'd opened the closet door. How had it suddenly opened? Maybe a better question was, who had opened it?

The clock ticked over to 11:45. Johnny huddled down into the thick blankets and stared out the window at the darkness. The bed was warm, but still he lay there shivering.

Tom could tell the King Spider was getting ready to pounce. He could see it in its eyes and in the way its leg muscles were tensing. Tom was certainly frightened, but through his fear shone a fierce anger. Damned if he would give up without a fight.

He found a broken broom handle lying on the ground outside the hardware store. He quickly picked it up and was pleased at how good the heavy wood felt in his hands. Even better, the broken broom had splintered down the center of the shaft to form a crude but relatively sharp point. With a weapon firmly in his grasp, he confidently faced his adversary.

"Why, Tommy, my boy, I didn't think that you had the balls for this. Do you seriously think you can kill me using that little toothpick?"

Tom mustered as much false bravado as possible. "Come over and let's find out. I've been squashing your cousins for years. Why stop now?"

The King Spider's expression changed; a look of hatred now masked its hideous features. Its glowing eyes turned a noticeably darker shade of red and its bulky shoulders hunched and tensed in much the same way a predatory cat would before delivering its lethal strike. Tom shivered, gazing at the grotesque freak of evolution, but stood his ground.

Tom was a picture of concentration. When the spider scurried to the right, he moved with it. When the spider scurried left, Tom matched it. Every time the spider tried to get into a better attacking position, Tom countered to maintain his defense, his spear always aimed directly at the spider's massive midsection.

The giant arachnid let out a sigh of resignation. It lowered its head in hungry disappointment and took two steps back. Hope flooded through Tom as he watched the spider slink away. He lowered the makeshift spear and flexed his aching muscles, and that was when the spider attacked.

Finally succeeding in getting Tom to drop his guard, the spider saw its opportunity and struck with the speed and power of a coiled viper. Its surprise attack left Tom with little time to maneuver; his only chance was to fake one way and jump the other. The King Spider took the fake, and Tom plunged the broken broom deep into its side with as much brute force as he could muster.

The spider collapsed, grunting once in surprised pain. A thick river of gore spewed from the wound in its side, and each time the spider attempted to stand up, another spray of blood would shoot out. Eerily silent, almost worse than if it had been screaming, the King Spider convulsed for a few painful minutes, and then lay still.

Tom knew he should run, but he couldn't leave. Not yet, anyway. He had to find out for sure if the beast was dead. He walked as close as he dared. The spider remained still, showing no evidence of life. Was it really dead? Had he actually beaten it? Just to be sure, he took the bloody broom handle and repeatedly bludgeoned the immobile hulk. The spear sank again and again into the bloated mess with a sickening sound, like a shovel plunging into wet sand.

His anger and fear finally abated, Tom staggered backward feeling empty and sick, his mind whirling with the impossible events that had transpired. Then he noticed something strange about the sack of dead meat. There was no blood flowing out of it. He had speared the spider at least twenty times, and somehow none of the wounds had produced any blood. The original wound on the monster's side had even stopped bleeding.

Tom leaned down to take a closer look and something hit him in the throat. He swiped at it, and a small spider fell to the ground. It had come from one of the puncture wounds. Tom remembered that terrible day in Old Man Harrison's basement a year ago and quickly took a few steps back. He was just in time, as thousands of small spiders started pouring out of the wounds.

Tom turned to run, but the spiders didn't seem to be coming after him. Instead, they started fighting each other. Tom paused, shocked to see them greedily eating each other, the larger spiders devouring the smaller ones as the battle intensified. Every time a spider devoured one of its own, it increased in size and strength. Hundreds of increasingly larger spiders were whipped into a frenzy, pouring over each other, biting and tearing at everything in sight.

Hundreds turned to dozens, and the number continually decreased as the bloodlust raged on. Finally only two huge, stuffed, but still-hungry predators stood facing each other. The battle was too much for Tom, and he closed his eyes to shut out the horror. Unfortunately he could still hear them, clashing again and again until the final snarl of triumph sounded, accompanied by a unbearable screech of pain.

Only one spider remained in the blood-smeared alleyway. It sat motionless, its eyes closed as if it was sleeping. Tom knew he should be long gone from here, but he was too fascinated to move. He realized he was witnessing something amazing. This monstrosity had somehow changed the evolutionary process, emerging into the world, being born as the victor of the most brutal survival-of-the-fittest contest ever. Tom had just witnessed the birth of the new King Spider.

Tom finally turned and ran. He thought he could hear the sound of pursuit, but he didn't turn around. Two glaring beams of light struck him in the face as he approached the entrance to the alley, and he wondered how the spider had managed to get in front of him again. He was about to turn back when he realized they were headlights.

The automobile turned out to be a police cruiser. He burst into the arms of one of the two officers who had stepped quickly from their car.

"Hey kid, what are you doing out here at"—he glanced at his watch—"holy cow, 11:55?"

All Tom could do was point in the direction of the alley. The first policeman motioned for his partner to go check it out, but he came back to report the alleyway was empty.

"Figures," said the first policeman. "These damn kids think we've got nothing better to do than run around babysitting them all night."

Tom was shuffled into the front seat of the cruiser

between the two irritated police officers. As they pulled away from the alley, Tom was sure he saw two shiny red eyes watching him from the shadows. Maybe it was just his imagination, but he could have sworn he heard the King Spider whispering inside his head, *Tommy, don't go thinking this is over. You and me, Tommy, my boy . . . we'll be meeting again. Count on it.*

Moonlight coming through the bedroom window glinted off the razor edge of the fire axe as the rotting creature moved toward Pete. Pete didn't have a lot of time to think, so he reacted on instinct, dashing out of bed and running for the closet. If he'd been thinking clearer, he would have fled out the door.

Slamming the closet shut, he held it closed with all his might, screaming at the top of his lungs for his father or brother. With an icy shiver Pete realized maybe the creature had already butchered his family and he was alone in the house. His mind whirled with sickening images of his father and brother lying on blood-splattered sheets, hacked into unrecognizable lumps.

These images were replaced by visions of his own mutilated body. The visions became more vivid as the blade of the creature's axe crashed through the closet door, inches from his face. He released the door handle and cowered in the darkness, too frightened to move.

The axe head was pulled back, allowing moonlight to flood into the closet and clearly reveal Pete's pitiful hiding spot. The golden moonlight changed suddenly to crimson, and Pete knew the creature was looking through the axe hole. He prayed the remaining shadows in the closet would hide him from its gaze.

His prayers went unanswered.

"I can see you," the rotting corpse whispered. "I'm going to kill you, Petey. I told you you'd pay for trespassing, didn't I? Well, like it or not, tonight's your turn."

The creature laughed and started furiously attacking the door. *Thunk . . . thunk*, the axe crashed, wood splintering in all directions, the thundering sound of the blows echoing off the closet walls. Pete's world closed in on him. There was nowhere left to run. The walls seemed to shrink around him, and he had no trouble imagining he was already inside a small wooden coffin.

Thunk . . . thunk . . . thunk, the axe slammed against the door, more moonlight illuminating Pete's sadly inadequate hiding place. In his terrified brain, the sound of the axe was like someone hammering the nails into his coffin.

Thunk . . . Thunk . . . Crack. The closet door finally surrendered to the onslaught and split down the middle, falling in chunks to the floor. The coffin lid had almost been sealed; now it was suddenly removed. Pete's shattered nerves reacted instantly to his sudden release, and he bolted out of the closet like an Olympic sprinter reacting to the sound of a starter's gun.

The quick exit almost caught the creature off guard. Pete ran by the monster and had nearly reached the door, when a long-taloned hand cut painfully into his shoulder. Before he could struggle free, the creature wrapped him in its massive, rotting arms. It spun Pete around and moved its powerful hands around his tender neck. It began to squeeze, softly at first, but increasingly harder.

Spots appeared in his blurred vision, and deep down, Pete knew death was near. He felt the creature's grip tighten as he gazed at its grotesque, smiling face, and barely heard the sickening, snapping sound of his neck shattering as he . . .

He woke up screaming again: a nightmare inside of a nightmare. He stopped screaming, but no matter how hard he tried, he couldn't stop shaking. He didn't think he would ever stop shaking again.

He sat up from his sweat-drenched bed and looked around his room. Everything looked normal; this time his bedside chair was empty, as was the rest of the room. He let out a sigh of relief and took a few deep breaths.

He heard noises in the hallway outside his bedroom door.

Pete froze in the middle of a half-drawn breath and listened to the sound of approaching heavy footsteps. They stopped just outside, and paused.

"Please God, not again . . . I can't take anymore."

The doorknob began to turn. Pete sprang from bed and screamed at the top of his voice. "Leave me alone! I didn't do anything. I didn't do anything wrong."

His screams turned to racking sobs as he backed away. The door began to slowly swing inward and a large dark shape stepped into the room.

"Please," Pete whimpered, retreating from the shape. The bedroom light came on at the same instant Pete's knees hit the bottom sill of the window, knocking him off balance. As he crashed backward through the thick windowpane, he noticed the large dark shape was that of his father.

Mark Myers had come to check on Pete when he'd heard his son screaming. He rushed across the room to his son, who was pinwheeling his arms for balance.

Pete felt himself going over the edge, out the window, so he reached out with one final effort to grab his father's hand. Their fingers actually touched, but Pete's backward momentum was too great. All he could do was stare into his father's wide eyes as he plummeted fifteen feet to the cold ground below.

The thick shards of shattered windowpane rained down to the ground ahead of Pete. One large piece stuck upright in the ground, a cold, cruel spike awaiting him. He landed back first, the glass shard scraping along his spine and traveling mercilessly up through his pulsing heart. He was dead before he hit the ground.

His disbelieving father ran as fast as he could in the futile hope his young son might still be okay. When he reached the crumpled body, he fell to his knees in anguish. Somewhere in the distance, carried by the wind, the sound of a grandfather clock chimed twelve times.

Mark did the only thing his cloudy mind would let him do. He lay down beside his dead son in the red sticky grass, and wept.

CHAPTER SEVEN

"He can't be gone," David cried.

He sat in the cool grass in an emotional state of shock. It had been two days since he'd learned the awful fate of his friend Peter, and still David found himself not believing. His trip earlier that evening with his parents to the Hart Funeral Home and the ghostly, somehow plastic appearance of his friend lying in a blue steel coffin should have been ample evidence Pete was gone, but David couldn't accept it.

He'd found out the following morning, when Pete hadn't showed up at school. Tom, Johnny, and he had felt something bad had happened, but they weren't prepared for the horrible news relayed by the school principal. He obviously hadn't gone into the nasty details in front of the class, so they had gone to see Peter's brother. Through noticeable pain, Ken had told them all he knew. It wasn't much, but more than enough to confirm the boys' worst fears. Everyone was saying it had been a terrible accident, but David and his friends knew better.

Knowing the truth and being able to do something about it were two different things. David had tried his best to explain all the events of the previous week to his bewildered parents, but he was ignored. They had pretended to listen, they had even pretended to agree with him, but David was smart enough to see his words were falling on deaf ears.

After returning from the funeral home, David's anger at

his parents for not believing him had cooled to frustration, and now he sat in the grass thinking dark thoughts about his own mortality. The world outside didn't believe him, so he turned inside himself and went to talk to his lifelong friend, Rodney.

It had been raining from the moment he'd found out about Peter's death and had just stopped an hour ago. The farmer's fields were swamped, but where David sat, things were relatively dry. Rodney hung majestically in the brilliant after-storm twilight. The sun was a sliver of fire in the western sky as it prepared to tuck North America to bed. The smell of fresh grass after a rainstorm was one of David's favorite things, but tonight it was overpowered by the musty smell of Rodney's wet, rotting hay. That was okay. Stinky or not, Rodney was still the best friend David had, and the only grown-up who would understand the danger he was in.

"We have to talk, Rodney," he said. "Have you thought about my problem? You know . . . about Old Man Harrison? Things are getting worse, and we don't know what's going to happen next." David let out a choked sob and continued. "I'm scared, big guy. We've got to stop him, Rodney . . . we've just got to, before he strikes again."

David hung his head low and finally let the tears come. Huge racking sobs escaped from his lungs and tears ran in abundance like the nearby overflowing stream.

"We . . . ?"

David stopped crying, turning toward the house, instantly alert. The voice had been very quiet and had come from somewhere close by.

"We . . . ?"

It was much louder this time, almost demanding a response, and this time David knew it had been spoken from behind him. He slowly turned back to the fields, but couldn't see anyone. David scratched his head, bewildered for a second. And then he looked up.

Rodney was staring directly into his eyes.

A mask of seething fury replaced Rodney's soft, gentle

face. Huge, overengorged blue veins pulsed and twitched, where moments before had been smooth white Styrofoam. A dark, gaping mouth filled with razor-tipped fangs snapped open and closed, where before had been a calm, thin crayon smile. There were large weeping sores covering the scarecrow's once-unblemished forehead, oozing a greenish-yellow afterbirth of slime that ran down Rodney's ruined cheeks into his cavernous mouth. As repulsive as those changes were, the worst by far were Rodney's new eyes. Gone were the doelike crayon eyes that were always so loving and understanding. In their place, two fiery-red cauldrons blazed from the deep recesses of his face.

When the transformed scarecrow spoke again, there was no more whispering. His voice boomed out in the night, rough, like the sound of churning broken glass.

"What do you mean . . . *we?*"

He continued in a gravely mocking voice. "We have to stop him Rodney, old buddy. You have to help me. Whine, whine, whine.

"We"—back to his commanding growl—"don't have to do anything, you whimpering nuisance. It's you . . . *you* that's got the problem, not *we.* For years I've hung here and listened to your petty problems, and frankly I'm sick of it. Sick of you, Davey boy!"

"No," David said, his mind whirling. "Don't say those things. You're . . . you're supposed to be my friend. I need you, Rodney."

This caused Rodney to laugh all the more, his body shaking in demented glee.

"Friend? *Friend* you say? You hang me in a field and nail me to a pole and have the nerve to call me a friend. You're no friend of mine, you little asshole. You need me? Bah. I know exactly what it is you *need.*"

Inside, David's heart was hammering like an industrial jackhammer. "Please," he tried once more. "You're all I've got."

"All right, Davey," Rodney seemed to ponder. "I'll help

you out with one thing. Come a little closer and I'll tell you something."

David knew he shouldn't go any nearer, but he just couldn't accept that his best friend had turned against him. The thought that an inanimate scarecrow had suddenly sprung to life didn't seem strange to him at all. He'd always believed Rodney was real, he just couldn't accept that he'd turned bad. He needed him to be good, as David had always imagined, and now that Rodney was offering help, he found it hard to refuse.

He inched closer to the hideous parody of Jesus nailed to the cross, fighting the urge to back off, but at the same time wanting to get closer.

Rodney gazed down at the small, tearstained boy in front of him and whispered, "You said you didn't know what was going to happen next. I'll tell you, if you'd like. Old man Harrison is going to kill again, Davey. He's going to kill again, soon."

David had to ask, "Who's he going to kill?"

"You, you interfering little brat. *You!*"

David's mouth dropped open in astonishment. Rodney's body began to shake violently as if in an epileptic seizure. Almost too late David realized what was happening. Rodney was struggling with the metal spikes that held him. He was trying to break free.

David stepped backward just as one of Rodney's arms tore free of his bonds and whisked through the air, narrowly missing his head. Six-inch talons of blackened bone sprang into view as Rodney's large straw hands strained to reach out and grab him. David backed away and narrowly avoided being impaled on the scarecrow's newly formed "fingers."

"Miss your dear old friend Petey, do ya? Don't worry, Davey, you'll be meeting him again real soon."

Rodney was clearly enjoying the hopeless look on David's face, and the more his fear showed, the greater was Rodney's lust for blood. He thrashed his body back and forth working the huge spikes loose, relishing the degree of agony he was inflicting upon himself. Slowly the spikes on the other arm and the legs began to give, and Rodney howled in eager anticipation. Within seconds, he tore the rest of his massive limbs free and dropped clumsily to the ground.

Terrified, David stared at the towering beast, whose blood freely poured from its self-inflicted wounds. David didn't waste any more time—he was off and running into his father's fields, wondering how something made of straw could possibly bleed.

Behind him he heard the loud, uncertain stumbling of a seven-foot-tall fledgling killer learning to walk. David didn't take time to stop and look, but from the frustrated cursing sounds, the big "baby" wasn't making out too well.

Run, David urged himself. *Get as much of a lead as you can, before . . .*

Before what?

He pushed that awful thought from his mind before it had a chance to sink its cancerous tentacles. Instead, he tried to concentrate on finding a place to hide. Circling back to the house would mean having to get around Rodney, who was rapidly mastering the art of walking, covering an amazingly long distance with each awkward stride. Going back was out of the question, so David decided to keep running deeper into the tomato field, fully aware it wouldn't take Rodney more than a few minutes to cover the distance. To make matters worse, the wet, muddy condition of the field was making running increasingly difficult.

As the ground became sloppier, one of David's sneakers was sucked off his foot. Three sluggish strides later, he lost the other one, and this time his sock went with it. He didn't realize his shoes were gone until he felt the soft goo squishing through his toes.

Slugging through the muddy terrain made it impossible to run with any degree of speed. David turned, fully expecting to be pummeled to the ground by the much larger and faster scarecrow. He was taken aback by what he saw.

It was undeniable that Rodney was larger and faster, but what David had forgotten was he was also much heavier. In fact, Rodney was about two hundred pounds of wet soggy straw heavier. If David thought he'd been having trouble, it was nothing compared to the problems Rodney faced.

About a hundred yards away, David's once-upon-a-time friend was mired in slop to his knees. The scarecrow was livid, beating his fists on his chest and releasing the foulest deluge of obscenities David had ever heard. The more the massive creature struggled, the deeper he sank.

David decided to take advantage of Rodney's predicament while he could. He turned and moved away in haste, still not quite sure where he was heading. Behind him he heard a low guttural rumble that, at first, resembled approaching thunder.

The noise didn't trail off, as a thunderclap usually does. Instead, it increased to a high-pitched, resonating sound more like that of a tuning fork. David turned to discover the strange, almost-hypnotic sound was emanating from Rodney.

Rodney's face was a mask of concentration, his muscles flexing as if to burst. His massive arms extended out perpendicular to his body in a strange reenactment of his former position nailed to the cross. Rodney threw his head back as far as he could and stared up at the dark, murky black sky, still projecting that eerie resonating noise.

And then he started rising.

David thought his eyes were playing tricks on him, but no, it was really happening. Rodney was slowly rising out of his muddy bondage without moving a muscle or even batting an eye. It was the most amazing thing David had ever seen. This was pure, unrestrained evil happening in front of him, and he could feel the enormous magnitude of it radiating all the way across the field. And behind it all, that steady, hypnotic chant building and falling, building and falling . . .

David watched helplessly as the entranced scarecrow pulled itself to the surface, and beyond. Rodney was levitating. First one inch, then two, then more, until the monstrous demon was hovering a foot above the wet earth. The guttural chant abruptly ended and the silence of the night crept back in.

Rodney started drifting toward David, silently moving across the muddy field, covering half the distance between them before David turned and ran.

Now it was only David who had to worry about the soggy field, and it was clear by his slow, panic-driven progress that he would never outrun the gravity-defying monstrosity. He had to do something quick or he was finished.

"Think, David," he muttered, looking wildly around for a hiding place.

Then he spotted it: a drainage culvert that ran under a road his father used for entering and leaving the fields with heavy machinery. The culvert was simply a hollow pipe that ran under the makeshift road to allow for drainage. It was fairly small, but David knew it was big enough to crawl through, because he'd done it last summer. If only he could get to the pipe in time. A quick glance back told him it was going to be close.

It was like running through cement: the more tired he became the stickier things seemed to get. Rodney was close now. David didn't need to look. He sensed the evil seeping around him, chilling his skin. At any second he expected to feel Rodney's deadly talons skewering him like a fish on a hook. He could even picture his body, convulsing with pain, being lifted off the ground and whisked silently away into the black night.

David was so close to the drainpipe now, he brushed his morbid thoughts aside. He was going to make it. Just a few more steps and . . .

Rodney grabbed hold of his head, his bony claws tightly gripping his hair.

David instinctively dove for the ground, crying out in pain as some of his hair was torn out by the roots. He scampered the final few feet to the drainpipe sure he wasn't going to make it, but he did. Amazed at his good luck, he moved deeper into the pipe to ensure he was well out of Rodney's long reach.

Rodney was lying stretched out on the ground in front of

the pipe opening, staring silently in. The scarecrow's hideous eyes radiated their crimson hate, and David shivered in spite of his safe position. It was obvious the pipe was far too small for the massive scarecrow to follow, but Rodney still frantically tried to wedge himself in.

Even madness will eventually succumb to reason. After a few futile minutes of trying to get in, Rodney gave up and simply stared at David from the muddy entrance.

"Where do we go from here, Davey? It looks like the hunter has the poor little rabbit trapped in its hole."

"Yeah," spoke David with more confidence than he really felt, "but the rabbit is safe, because the hunter is too fat to get in."

"You shouldn't be so sure of yourself, little boy. Remember, there's more than one way to skin a rabbit."

"What do you mean? There's no way I'm coming out."

"Well, we'll just have to see about that, won't we?"

David watched Rodney get up and step out of his circle of vision. Everything was silent except for the thud of his heart inside his chest. From outside the pipe came a cry of unbearable agony. When Rodney popped his head back into view, he was obviously in severe pain. Sweat poured down his ruined face, soaking the collar of his coveralls, his teeth gnashed together in suffering.

"If the hunter can't get to the rabbit, Davey, he must make the rabbit come to him. Some hunters might use a trained dog to flush out their prey, but sadly I don't have one."

The huge straw man pulled back out of sight again, gasping in misery. There was no doubt he was hurting badly. Without showing himself, David heard Rodney whisper.

"No flea-ridden mutt . . . so I had to improvise, that's all."

Rodney threw something long and thin into the pipe. It bounced and rolled and came to a stop six feet from where David lay. In the darkness of the small pipe, it took him a minute to recognize the object. When he did, his screams carried along the inside of the pipe and echoed out across the deserted fields.

It was Rodney's severed left arm.

Rodney had torn his own arm off at the shoulder. It lay in a shallow, gory puddle with blood still squirting from the severed veins and arteries. David was appalled at such a demented show of self-mutilation, but he didn't understand how Rodney hoped this would somehow entice him out of the pipe.

Then the arm started to move.

Rodney peeked in and let out a pained laugh. "How do you like my *dog*, David? Think I'll call him Goliath, get it?"

The amputated arm twitched a few times, its powerful bone fingers pulling itself toward David. Its sharp talons scratching the metal pipe as it moved, creating a spine-tingling sound. Inch by inch it moved closer, leaving behind a slimy trail of blood and gore. Rodney lay at the entrance, cheering it on.

There was nothing David could do except retreat farther into the pipe. Just the thought of that bloody arm touching his pant leg and clamping down on his bare foot was enough to give him palpitations. He clambered along the pipe on his belly, moving farther into the darkness. Behind him, the scratching noises drew closer.

David's plan was to crawl to the far side of the road, shoot out the other end of the pipe, and run like hell. It wasn't brilliant, but the only other option was staying in the pipe and arm-wrestling with Goliath. *No thanks.*

He should have reached the other opening by now, yet he still couldn't see anything. A little farther on, he discovered the problem by running headfirst into a wall of dirt. The heavy rains had washed muddy soil into the drainpipe, piling it up and blocking the end of the pipe.

He tried to dig himself out, but it was impossible. There was too much dirt, and no place to put it. David turned back to face the oncoming arm but couldn't see where it was. He could still hear its steady approach, but this section of the pipe was in darkness. He tried to determine how close the crawling horror was, but everything echoed inside the pipe, and panic was clouding his judgment. He found it increasingly difficult to breathe; his rapid heartbeat and panicky breathing were making him feel dizzy. The scratching noises suddenly stopped, cranking David's fear up another notch. For a minute, the whole world was quiet—dead calm.

Then the bloody arm grabbed his ankle.

David was too frightened to scream. He felt himself losing his grip on reality, spiraling down into the realm of dreams, as the monster arm started dragging him toward its evil master.

"That's a good boy. Bring the little rabbit to Daddy," were the last hazy words that drifted through David's foggy mind as he slipped into the deep, dark abyss of unconsciousness.

"Wake up, sleepyhead," David's mother said. "Time to get up."

David opened his eyes to find his mother drawing back the curtains in his bedroom. He was curled up in his own warm bed.

"I know going to Peter's funeral today is going to be hard on you, but I think it's for the best."

Donna leaned over and gave her son a kiss, leaving the room with the promise of a big country breakfast waiting for him downstairs

A dream? It couldn't have been, could it?

There was no other explanation. Here he was in his own bed with daylight streaming in through the window. He must have dreamed the whole thing. He let out a big yawn and stretched. Man, his body was sore. Best thing to do was get up and get moving.

Shock, horror, and panic struck him simultaneously as he untangled himself from the sheets. His entire body was filthy. Caked-on dry mud splattered his legs and feet. On one foot he still wore a mud-encrusted sock.

Like in my dream, David thought, and then the horrible truth lit up his mind like an eerie full moon crossing the midnight sky.

Slowly he slid out of bed and crept closer to his bedroom window. Every fiber of his being fought against it, trying to convince him not to look, but he had to—he simply had to.

You would think things couldn't get any worse for someone about to bury his best friend, but unfortunately for David, things could. When he finally found the strength and courage to look out his bedroom window and across the yard at his father's field, Rodney the Scarecrow was gone.

CHAPTER EIGHT

By early afternoon, the rain returned with a fury. It was Thursday, the first day of June, and it was hard to believe summer was just around the corner. Gusting winds surged through the abandoned streets, with lashing rain that increased in strength with each passing hour. It was definitely one of those times to sit in front of a roaring fire and let the storm have its day.

For the forty residents of Dunnville who'd gathered at the cemetery, their rain-soaked clothing did little to keep out the cold. Collars had been turned up and shoulders were hunched against the wind. Bluish hands were thrust deep into damp pockets in an effort to keep warm. Nothing they did seemed to help much, but then again funerals were always chilling occasions, regardless of the weather.

Peter Andrew Myers had been far too young to die. A funeral is never a pleasant experience at any time, but at least if the deceased has had a full life, it's easier to accept. When such a young boy is taken, the pain and loss are multiplied a thousandfold.

The tragedy that ended Pete's life affected different people in different ways. Obviously, for the family, the grief was absolute. Shock and pain at their profound loss could clearly be seen in their swollen eyes. Nothing could have prepared them for this. For most of the members of the congregation who listened quietly to Pastor Raycroft's somber "Ashes to ashes, dust to dust" sermon, expressions of sadness and disbelief showed on their sullen faces. David, Tom, and Johnny were also affected greatly by the loss of their friend, with feelings that ran deeper than most onlookers realized.

David was unable even to look at his friends without shaking, the memories of last night's encounter with near death still fresh in his thoughts. In his mind he could clearly see a second hole in the ground beside Pete's, reserved for him. That image left him drained and quite speechless. Tom and Johnny shared these feelings. It could easily have been one of them in that coffin. All three friends knew what really happened, but today wasn't the day to talk about it. Today was a day to stare at the ground and pay their last respects to a friend.

From the back of the cemetery, fifty yards behind the small gathering, one other person—unseen—was saying good-bye to Peter.

"Good-bye, Petey . . . and good riddance," the creature said. It was tickled pink by all the suffering going on. The stormy weather helped make things even better.

The creature was bundled up in a huge overcoat and hat it had stolen, and had crept as close as it dared to the small group of mourners. Everyone was too caught up with his or her private grief to notice the presence of a stranger. The creature kept stealing glances at David, Tom, and Johnny throughout the brief ceremony and had to fight hard to stifle the laughter building within.

"If only they knew I was here. Now that would *really* make things interesting."

Unfortunately, that was something it couldn't let happen. Being this close was probably a mistake, but it couldn't resist the temptation. To get up close to the suffering it had caused was exhilarating.

The creature was tired. It would soon be time to sleep again, to rest and evolve some more. The last week had been extremely taxing. It wasn't strong enough yet to move to the next stage of its plan. Creating the image of itself and the King Spider to Peter and Tom a few nights ago had been relatively easy, but last night with David had been another story. Rodney the Scarecrow was far more than just an image. The power involved to make him come to life had been enormous and had almost destroyed the creature. It would have to rest and reenergize, building its power back up again.

Before it would allow itself to rest, there was one more enjoyable task to perform. The creature peered through the crowd and noticed Johnny staring silently at the ground.

"You and me, Johnny . . . We have to have a little chat, and today might be a good day for it."

As the ceremony ended and people quickly scurried away, a new onslaught of wind and rain battered the departing assembly.

"Yeah. Today would be perfect."

CHAPTER NINE

Johnathan Page wasn't feeling very well by the time he arrived home. The rain began to taper off, but the sky was still murky gray, without the hint of a warming sun. Strong winds still raged, whipping the thin branches of the surrounding weeping willows into their frenzied dance. The weather had nothing to do with Johnny's health, unfortunately. He barely noticed the environment as his mother quickly shuffled him into the house.

"Hurry along, love. You'll catch your death in this dampness."

His mother's outburst caused him to bolt for the door and dash upstairs to his bedroom. Mary Page, not realizing what she had just said, waddled quickly behind.

Johnny tried to lie down and rest for a while, but he couldn't relax. It was too dark and quiet in his bedroom—his nerves were jumpy and his thoughts too haunted. He had to get out of there.

Johnny decided he would go for a walk. Maybe exercise would keep him from drifting into that beckoning pit of depression. It wasn't just the depression: ever since they'd released the creature, he'd been experiencing brief periods of amnesia. Two or three hours would slip away, and he wouldn't be able to account for that time. What had he done during those blackouts? Where had he gone?

Pete's funeral had made him feel worse, and his mother

was no help. She was fine doing her motherly thing, but she wouldn't be able to handle the truth. Johnny loved her, but she would worry too much, and he wasn't prepared to put her through that. No, this time he was on his own.

Johnny made it outside, but only after his mother had bundled him up in enough clothes to survive an Arctic blizzard. Bundled up or not, it felt good to be outside. Even the chilly wind felt good against his flushed face. He'd been too close to death lately. During the last week he'd felt it reaching for him. With every step he took, he distanced himself from the dark, gloomy house and the reaching hand of death. On and on he walked, the rain and wind sweeping away time and haunted memories. He willed himself to stop thinking, to feel no pain, to concentrate on nothing but the song of the wind and the squishing of his boots. . . .

Trailing behind, unnoticed by Johnny, the creature brooded. It had plugged into Johnny's thoughts and had listened to his internal struggle for peace. At first the creature had been amused by what it perceived as a futile struggle. It believed Johnny was no match for its awesome power.

Experimenting with that power, the creature had caused Johnny's recent blackouts. It was convinced its hold on Johnny couldn't be broken, but it was also aware the boy was regaining some control.

The more calm and peaceful Johnny became, the more tense and furious the creature felt. It knew it had to regain control, which would probably take all of its remaining strength, but that was a necessary evil, since Johnny was a key ingredient in the events to come.

Johnny finally decided to have a break and spotted a park bench across the street. He had been sitting there for five minutes before he realized someone had quietly joined him. When he looked up and saw the creature staring passively down at him, his heart almost exploded. Adrenaline shot through him, and he tried to bolt.

The creature was tired, but its reflexes were lightning fast. Before Johnny could get his rear end off the damp bench, the creature had clamped onto him and easily held him still.

"Not so fast, boy. We need to talk."

"Please, Mr. Harrison, don't kill me. I don't wanna die. Let me go. . . ."

The onslaught of begging caught the creature off guard. It was *Please, Mr. Harrison* this, and *Please, Mr. Harrison* that, until the creature couldn't take it anymore. It had a good mind to kill the little whiner so it wouldn't have to listen to his monotonous tirade. Instead, the creature put its huge rotting hand over Johnny's mouth, effectively stifling his pleas.

"Now shut up . . . or I'm going to rip that flapping tongue of yours out and eat it right in front of you."

Tears ran freely down Johnny's face as he started to mumble something from behind the creature's hand.

"I mean it, Johnny. *Not . . . one . . . word.* Understand?" The creature carefully removed his stinking hand. "That's more like it—now listen up. Like I said before, we need to talk. I've got big plans for us, boy. I'd like to think we can be friends."

Johnny started to say something, but one deep growl from his would-be friend convinced him to hold his tongue. Johnny looked around for some help, but the streets were empty. The awful weather was keeping everyone inside. His roving eyes reluctantly found their way back to the creature. Its firelike eyes seemed dimmer than he remembered, but they still sent a sliver of fear through his body. After looking into the evil creature's eyes for a moment, Johnny tried to look away, but found he couldn't. No matter how hard he tried, he was stuck. Trapped like a fly on glue. Eventually the power in those fiery eyes triumphed, and he stopped fighting. He sat passively on the bench, waiting for the inevitable. He was finally, completely, at the creature's mercy.

"That's better. You have to get a few things straight, Johnny. I'm not your enemy. I promise here and now I'm not going to kill you. You're perfectly safe with me. In fact, I'm going to go out of my way to see that you stay safe. I won't let *anybody* hurt you."

Johnny listened intently to the creature as it spoke, but he still couldn't understand what was happening. Why on earth would Old Man Harrison want to protect him?

The creature picked up on his skeptical thoughts. "You have me figured all wrong, Johnny. You and your friends are even wrong about who I am."

The creature paused to let everything sink in before dropping the bombshell it had been saving all week.

"My name's not Jacob Harrison, Johnny, it's George Page. Don't you understand, boy? I'm not that crazy bugger Old Man Harrison. . . . I'm your father."

INTERLUDE: A FEW WORDS OF WISDOM

Time waits for no man, or so the saying goes. The years just sort of blurred by, like being on a superfast roller coaster. Up and down, up and down, such was my life. Up and down, spin me around. It was pathetic.

I can't really speak for Tom and Johnny, since we kind of parted ways for a while, but my childhood basically evaporated. I turned into a loner, fear my only constant companion. I lived life day after day, year after year, never quite sure what was going to happen next. The only consistent thing I could count on were the nightmares. Oh God, such *horrible* nightmares. How many times can one guy get butchered in his dreams and still retain his sanity? A butcher's knife one night, a razor blade the next, strong bloody hands around my neck the night after that.

After a while I was so empty, even the bad dreams became unimportant. I'd slump off to bed, get mutilated two or three times, then wake up and eat a well-balanced breakfast. That was life—always tired, always scared.

I never let myself forget about the creature. I always remained on guard. I knew it was still around somewhere. Something that evil doesn't just go away. Deep down I knew it was responsible for my nightmares. My killers were different shapes and sizes, but I knew it was the creature, tormenting me in various guises. It enjoyed inflicting torture and pain, keeping me in anguish, no peace for the damned and all that jazz.

There were times during my teenage years when I was sure I was going to have to kill myself. I thought about it every day, but I was a coward. I just didn't have the guts, and to end your life, no matter how miserable, takes more balls than you might think.

Like I said, I never let myself stop believing in the creature. The trouble was, time has a way of screwing around with even the firmest of beliefs. When I was thirteen, I was positive it would be coming back to get me. When I turned sixteen, I still knew it was coming, but by the time I hit nineteen, things had started to change. It had been nine years since I'd last seen that rotting abomination, and after millions of nightmares, things have a way of blurring together. Maybe the creature had just been another dream, an early version that had triggered the rest.

I don't think I ever truly believed that crap, but I sure hoped it was true. After all, I was getting too old to believe in scary monsters. I was nineteen, a man. Yeah right. I still pissed the bed on occasion, depending on how bad my dreams were. Pretty sad, huh? Eventually, the nightmares stopped. One night of solid rest, then two. Before I knew it, a month had gone by, and for the first time, I started to believe things were actually going to be okay. Another few restful weeks and I was sure I was finally out of danger. There would be no more bad dreams, and I had finally seen the last of the dreaded creature.

Like most other times in my life . . . I would be wrong.

BOOK TWO

Scared Little Teenagers
December of 1986

CHAPTER TEN

For years David had harbored a crush on a girl by the name of Linda Heatherton. She was about the closest thing to perfection he'd ever seen. She was one year younger than he was, and everything about her was wonderful, from her swirling golden locks to her long, athletic legs—and all those delightful places in between. In short, Linda could have been anyone's dream girl, but tonight she would be his.

Until recently, Linda had paid about as much attention to David as a cat does to a swimming pool. It wasn't that David was homely—he'd grown up into a fine-looking young man—but he never seemed to look after himself. He always had a cigarette butt sticking out of his mouth, and his dark hair was a tangled mess. For reasons unknown, David had recently caught Linda looking at him. The looks were innocent enough, but they melted his heart. Eventually he worked up the nerve to ask her out and was flabbergasted when she agreed.

The night had gone fabulously so far, and before David had time to thank his lucky stars, he found himself in the backseat of his father's '84 Mustang.

"God, you're beautiful, Linda," was all David could say, as he desperately tried to think of some excuse to fondle her breasts. Linda, sensing his timidness, grabbed his sweaty hand and placed it herself. That was all the encouragement David needed.

Their clothes were discarded as fast as their inhibitions. Once they were naked, things escalated, heating up considerably until both clumsily, yet eagerly, merged as one. It was fast and furious and certainly far from romance-novel perfect, but David couldn't have cared less. He was on top of the world.

Afterward, mixed feelings raced through David's mind: peace, satisfaction, tenderness, desire, love.

Love? Had that been one of them?

He lay comfortably on top of Linda, still inside her, reluctant to move. They lay together in a state of mutual bliss and shared their own sleepy thoughts. David wondered about love. Could he really be that lucky? To be with a girl like this a week ago would have seemed ridiculous, but here she was in his arms. He held her tight, not wanting her to slip away.

Linda nuzzled closer to his neck, gently kissing his ear. In that moment, he knew he was in love with her. He could feel himself harden inside her again. A scary, yet wonderful question came to him: was there any hope Linda felt the same way?

"Linda, I need to ask you something," he started, lifting up to gaze into her beautiful deep red eyes.

Red?

David pulled back, shocked at the sight in front of him. Linda's face was still as beautiful as ever, but her blue eyes now shone crimson, like . . . like . . .

"No, it can't be," he stammered, trying to get up. The Linda-thing grabbed his waist and pulled him back down.

"What's the matter, Davey?" she said in Linda's sweet voice, but then changed to the gravelly deep growl of his worst nightmare. "Don't you like me anymore? Don't you want to fuck me again?"

David was horrified beyond words, trying with all his might to break free. The Linda-thing clamped down on his manhood with ironlike muscles. The she-devil howled with insane laughter as David struggled to free himself.

Her laughter was abruptly cut off as David watched a knife push up from inside her throat and stick out her neck, severing her vocal cords in the process. No, it wasn't a knife, it was a finger, the creature's six-inch bone finger. It twisted and turned in her throat for a few seconds, sticky blood shooting everywhere. Slowly, the finger began cutting down toward her stomach, slicing muscle and bone as it went.

As the muscles and bones parted, great streams of entrails burst out of the widening gash, twisting and unwinding in front of David's petrified eyes. The morbid sight of her insides and the unimaginable stench accompanying them had his stomach doing cartwheels.

Nine more fingers of bone joined the one already protruding from the steamy pile of gore, and soon two massive rotting hands were tearing the wound open wider. Within seconds the head of the creature emerged, followed by its powerful shoulders. In the most brutal and sickening C-section imaginable, one where the "baby" was delivering itself, the creature was returning to this world, being born again right in front of David's eyes.

David tripled his efforts at freeing himself from the dead Linda-thing, but he was still held fast. The more he struggled, the more her muscles tightened.

The creature propped his bony elbows up on Linda's ruined body, with its head resting in its bloody hands. It was enjoying David's struggle immensely, gasping for breath from its strenuous laughter.

"Boy, oh boy, Davey, it seems like you sure got yourself into a heap of trouble," it roared. "Didn't your Mama ever teach you to keep that thing in your pants?"

"Please . . ." whispered David, tears starting to flow, "Let me go."

"I'd be happy to, my boy . . . but unfortunately it's not me that's got you. You're gonna have to talk to young Linda here and . . . Oh, I forgot. She's not with us anymore? Well, that does create a problem, doesn't it?"

David didn't answer, deciding instead to renew his struggle

to get away. The creature watched David squirm, but then held one bloody finger up as if it had suddenly been struck with a brilliant idea.

"I've got it. It's just the thing, you'll see."

David watched as the creature took one of its razor fingers and inch by inch moved slowly toward his manhood.

"I'll have you free in a jiffy."

Horror like no other engulfed him as he realized what the creature intended. It was going to cut him free, leaving his severed penis inside the dead girl. Panic welled up in him as the bone finger drew closer, until David could feel it touching his pubic hair. Totally frantic, he let out a primal scream of such intensity that . . .

That he woke up screaming.

Just another dream. It had been six weeks since the last nightmare, and David had been sure they were finished forever.

"Just another dream," he kept telling himself, rocking back and forth cupping his groin gently. "Just a dream, that's all. Another silly dream."

While he rocked back and forth, consoling himself, he failed to notice the faint red glow emanating from under his closet door. He had no way of knowing that tonight, dream or no dream, the creature had returned for real. Soon enough he would find out it was back—but not tonight. David was in a state of anguished shock, and for tonight at least, he had been through enough.

CHAPTER ELEVEN

Tom Baker also woke from the grip of a nightmare. For the life of him, he couldn't quite remember what had scared him. It was one of those dreams that lay barely out of reach behind his subconscious curtain. He sensed it had been more than just a silly nightmare, that this particular dream was quite important, though he had no idea why.

Tom still looked like he had as a kid. His hair was long, and he was taller and more muscular than most of his friends. He lay back down and closed his eyes, trying desperately to hold onto the fading fragments of his dream. If he could fake his subconscious into thinking he was falling asleep, that thick, black curtain in his mind might draw back just enough to allow him a glimpse. And it worked, almost. Tom found himself slipping gently back to slumberland, and as he did, the fog clouds began to dissipate. Soon, hidden memories began to emerge from the mist.

The memories were incomplete and fragmented. A bloody hand floated by on the swirling mist and a tortured scream rang out somewhere to his left. A butcher knife whizzed by his face, so close he could see strands of brown hair matted to its crimson edge. He strained to peer deeper into his foggy dreamscape, until suddenly a torrent of objects came flying past. There was a muddy cowboy boot with the sole half–ripped off, followed by a broken pair of dark green sunglasses. A beat-up typewriter floated by, its keys still typing out some invisible message, chased by a long stick sharpened to a point, like something out of a cheap vampire movie. An assortment of other strange objects also streamed by at too high a speed for him to identify them.

Tom had a feeling these things were trivial memories. They'd all been connected to his nightmare, but weren't at the heart of it. Whatever had scared him was still out there, hiding in the mist. He sensed its presence, convinced that this ghoulish apparition was watching him.

He could hear it creeping slowly along without the slightest effort to mask its approach. *It wants me to know it's coming*, Tom thought, a familiar chill brushing the hair on the back of his neck. *It wants me to be scared.*

And he was.

Something about the way this thing moved didn't sound right. He probably would have run if he could, but sometimes dreams have a funny way of not letting you do those things. The more Tom tried to back away from the mist, the closer the dream seemed to push him forward. A few struggling moments later, Tom found himself being pushed to the edge of the swirling wall of fog. He was so close, he could have reached out and touched it, but chose not to.

So the dream took over and did it for him.

To Tom's rising horror, his arm began to lift up and reach out toward the fog. His left hand moved closer until it broke through and disappeared from view.

The fog was so dense, he couldn't see anything. His left arm seemed to end at his wrist, and he had to wiggle his fingers to reassure himself his hand was still attached. The image of the severed bloody hand that had floated by at the start of his dream returned, and his heart began to pound fast. Tom was sure something was about to grab his hand.

Why had he reached into the fog? He could distinctly remember choosing not to. It was as if his direct thought not to reach into the mist had somehow triggered his arm to do it. Tom realized it was the same when he'd wanted to back up and had inadvertently moved forward instead. Somehow his thoughts and actions were being turned around.

Okay, he thought, *I'd like to run fast, straight into the mist.*

The dream hesitated for a split second, then quickly obliged. Tom's eyes swelled to about the size of watermelons as he found himself running forward into the swirling fog. This wasn't part of his plan—the opposite should have happened.

Stop! I want to go back. The dream ignored his demand, and he continued to run forward. He finally realized that whoever—or whatever—was controlling his dream obviously didn't give the slightest fuck what he wanted, so he turned his thoughts to more important matters.

Where was the thing that had been creeping toward him?

He was terrified of running straight into it, so he willed himself to stop running. To his amazement, he actually did. It wasn't until he'd come to a full stop that he noticed how quiet it was. Inside the swirling mists of the dream, it was deadly silent. Off to his right he heard a footstep, and another. He couldn't see whatever stalked him, but it could probably see him just fine. Or smell his fear.

From the sound, Tom figured it was fifteen feet away, and closing. He tried to back away, but the dream took over again and he couldn't move. A scratchy foot landed three feet away, causing him to cry out. His scream seemed to dissipate the mist around him, and inch by agonizing inch the thing at the heart of his nightmare began to emerge. . . .

Tom bolted upright in his bed, practically jumping out of his dream. A puff of steamy mist caused him to jump again, until he realized it was only condensation from his warm breath in the chilly bedroom.

He hadn't remembered his first nightmare, but he clearly recalled this one. He could visualize the thick fog being whisked away and the emergence of the ghoul. He hadn't seen much before he awoke, but he'd seen enough to be glad he'd left his dream behind. In the few seconds he had glimpsed his stalker, he observed a long leg covered in thick black hair. He had also seen another just like it through the thinning mist, and the hint of maybe others, but he couldn't be sure. It had reminded him of . . .

No! His mind shut that thought out.

He wouldn't allow himself to think about the past. For the last nine years he'd pushed his fears into the far recesses of his mind and was determined not to let them resurface. Still, there was something about those hairy legs and the awful lurching way the stalker had walked. It reminded him of the way the . . .

Stop it. Those bad memories are just childhood dreams. None of that stuff really happened. None of it!

He almost convinced himself, until he remembered Peter's funeral. That part had happened, but it had been an accident. Even the newspaper had said so.

Tom wasn't convinced. Tonight's dreams had really rocked the foundations of his memory walls. He'd built the walls thick and high over the years, but apparently he hadn't used very good mortar, because they were starting to crumble a few bricks at a time. He tried with all his will to hold the walls together. He looked around his bedroom desperately seeking something to concentrate on, something to help clear his mind of the horrible memories that threatened to breach the wall.

His eyes locked on something sitting on his desk. Instead of helping, however, it made things worse, because the object was something out of his dream. It was the old typewriter that had floated past him near the start of his second nightmare. The cover was gone.

Just like in the dream.

A few more interior bricks fell. Tom never left the cover off his typewriter. The old machine was beat-up and had seen better days, but he took great care of it. He longed to be a writer someday, and the typewriter was one of his prized possessions. He had typed out a silly, but effective, science-fiction story about intelligent talking fish just before going to sleep last night. After he finished the story, he was positive he'd wiped the machine clean and had replaced the cover to keep the dust out.

A sheet of white typing paper was still scrolled into the machine. No matter how tired he'd been, he knew for a fact he'd finished the story and put it into a folder on his nightstand. Tom sat up and checked. He flipped open the wrinkled folder to confirm it was all there. It was—every last word of it.

If the story's here in the folder . . . why is there still paper in the machine?

Another few feet of his memory wall crumbled as he remembered that in the dream, someone had been typing out a message on the keys as it drifted by.

Was it possible the invisible hand had typed a message on his typewriter?

Tom didn't want to do it, but knew he had to go check the typewriter. If he didn't, he might go crazy. Then again, if he did check, and something was written on the sheet, that might drive him loony too. Either way, he had to find out.

He tiptoed across the floor, not exactly sure why he was trying to be quiet. The carpeted floor was cold against his bare feet, but it didn't feel nearly as icy as the blood racing through his veins. When he finally found the courage to look down at the typewriter, Tom saw . . . nothing.

The paper was blank. He let out a nervous laugh. What had he been thinking? It all seemed silly now. Some of the bricks in his memory wall reassembled, giving him some peace of mind.

Tom lay back down in bed and was almost asleep when he realized he was missing something. He sat up, looking over at the typewriter again. The part of the paper he'd looked at had been blank, but only a quarter of the sheet was exposed to him. The rest was still hidden in the machine.

The rebuilding of his memory wall stopped at that thought. It didn't start to crumble again; it just held its own and waited.

Tom rushed back to the desk and, without hesitating, began to scroll the sheet of paper. He knew he was acting a bit irrational, but he couldn't help it. Fear had crept back into him and he had to know for sure. The first covered line was blank, and the same for the one after that. A sigh of relief began to escape from between his lips until one more crank of the handle cut the sigh off permanently. On the next line was a short six-word sentence that sent Tom's carefully ordered universe into total chaos. In bold capital letters, it said,

I'M COMING TO GET YOU, TOM

He tore the rest of the sheet out by hand. It was signed,

AN OLD EIGHT-LEGGED FRIEND

The wall of suppressed memories inside him didn't just crumble, it exploded into millions of razor-sharp needles that pierced and fragmented his memory bank. He dropped to the floor at the foot of the desk, still tightly gripping the sheet of paper. The weight of his suppressed memories pinned him to the carpet, and he lay there for the rest of the night in a quivering fetal-like heap. He remembered.

He remembered *everything*.

CHAPTER TWELVE

The same night that David and Tom were experiencing such distressing nightmares, Johnathan Page was up very late. He was thinking about how wonderful life was. His memories of childhood were pleasant, aside from his father's splitting, but that was no big deal. Up to now, his maturing years had been fantastic.

His marks in class were brilliant, the best in school. He'd been elected president of the student council the previous year and captain of the debating team, not to mention being made quarterback of the championship football team. His life seemed truly blessed. He was developing movie-star looks, and his smile and shiny blond hair brought sighs from the young ladies. Everybody loved him and tried to be part of his "in" crowd.

Yeah, Johnny thought. *I've got it made.*

The future looked no less bright. He was going to breeze through college and then take on the world. Most students said the same thing, but he meant it. Somehow he knew he was destined for greatness, and nothing was going to stop him—ever.

Having let his thoughts run full circle, Johnny climbed under the covers. He was asleep almost before his head hit the pillow. He never had trouble getting a good night's sleep, which was no real surprise—he never had much trouble with anything. Johnny slept soundly, a small smile gracing his face.

The creature's cerebral eye kept watch over Johnny, as it always did. It sat inside David's closet, smiling along with Johnny. It was very happy. It was enjoying the suffering it was causing David and Tom, but was also enjoying watching Johnny.

"Don't you worry, kiddo," it lovingly cooed. "I won't let anything bad happen to you. You see, I've got awfully big plans for you. Big, *big* plans."

Finally the creature dozed too, sucking on its razor-sharp thumb.

Back in Johnny's bedroom, the sleeping young man curled up on his side and put his thumb into his mouth. He slept on, blissfully unaware of the massive internal wall that had been built inside his mind. It was a veritable fortress and made Tom's suppressed memory bank look like a dollhouse. Tom had built his own wall as high as he could, but Johnny had help. He also had a guard to make sure that nothing could break through his wall—a guard with fiery, crimson eyes.

CHAPTER THIRTEEN

It was a beautiful early December evening—December 3, to be exact. David was out for a walk. He couldn't remember making a conscious decision to go outside, or when he'd left the house, but he'd had a lot on his mind lately. It had been only two days since the "Linda-thing" nightmare, so it was understandable his mind was wandering a bit. In truth, his mind had been wandering a lot.

No matter how hard he tried to convince himself his dream had been nothing but an extremely graphic nightmare, he found it difficult to ignore. Deep inside, he knew it had been much more. The creature had returned to Dunnville, and that dream had been its morbid way of saying hello.

David knew the creature would be coming after him again—probably after Tom and Johnny also—so yesterday he'd spent the entire day in hiding. He'd tried to contact his old friends to warn them, but Tom's mother had said he was sick in bed, and Johnny had simply laughed, told him to fuck off, and hung up. David spent the rest of the day locked away, smoking incessantly.

Dusk had begun settling over the land, but the bright orange rays of the sun still peeked through the fluffy gray cloud cover. More clouds loomed in the distance, carrying with them the dark promise of snow, but for now the western sky was picture-perfect.

David walked along Pine Street heading in the direction of
the river, which he knew would be glazed with a thin covering
of ice. The street wasn't named Pine for nothing: both sides of
the tarmac were lined with towering coniferous trees stretch-
ing to the river's edge. This time of year, when most trees had
long since dropped their summer dress, it was pleasant to see
the pine needles still resiliently swaying in the breeze.

The crisp December air wafting through the trees was
cold, yet exhilarating. For the first time in ages, he felt good.
Somehow, he felt free. Hiding in the house had been a waste
of time. If the creature was really after him, hiding wasn't
going to make it go away. No matter where he hid, the creature would eventually find him.

When David reached the intersection of Pine and Broad,
he thought, *I think I'll hang a left and head uptown.*

Instead of rounding the corner, his feet kept walking south
on Pine toward the river. The first alarm bell registered in his
head that something wasn't right. The second alarm went off
when he tried to stop and head back to Broad Street. As before, his legs continued on as if they had a mind of their own.
By the time he crossed over the Lock Street intersection and
had made a dozen more unsuccessful attempts to control his
body, every damn bell in the cathedral was clanging.

He'd lost control. He couldn't even blink on command,
never mind use his arms or legs. He felt violated, like a mar-
ionette being manipulated by an unseen puppeteer. He soon
came to a T-shaped intersection where Pine ended at Main.
Beyond Main Street was the icy water of the Grand River.

*What if I can't turn the corner or stop, and I keep walking into
the river?*

From this close he could see the murky river was indeed
coated with a layer of ice, as he'd imagined, but it was veneer
thin and offered no hope of holding his weight. If he stepped
onto the thin ice, it wouldn't matter if he regained control of
his body or not—the frigid temperature of the water would
quickly seal his fate.

As he stepped off the curb onto Main, David concentrated every ounce of willpower he could summon, willing himself to turn left toward downtown Dunnville. His body decided to turn right and head away from town.

What the hell is happening?

He tried to scream, but found he had no voice.

Main Street followed the contours of the river, flowing northwest toward the town of Cayuga. On David's right sat a row of family homes, and on his left ran the mighty Grand River, with Wingfield Park nestling along the shore and separating the river from the road. The park was apparently David's destination, as he found himself crossing the road and sitting down on a park bench.

It was an incredibly strange feeling to lose control, and stranger still to sit motionless on a splintery old bench. At least walking, he'd sensed motion and felt the cooling breeze brushing his face. His body was in fact moving, but it was controlled by some unknown power operating on a frequency alien to his mind. David's head looked left, so he had no choice but to look at what lay in that direction. A group of young girls pedaled past the park, heading down Main Street. His eyes were forced to watch as they rode out of sight. After a few more minutes gazing around, the most frightening thing yet happened.

He unwillingly closed his eyes.

Nothing could have been worse. He'd lost control of his body, but at least he could still survey his surroundings. Now he was in a dark, uncontrollable world, trapped in some dark abyss with no one around to hear his cries for help. David tried again to scream, but his efforts were futile.

Something was jabbing him painfully in the ribs, something in his coat pocket digging into his side. The more he thought about it, the more it irritated him, yet he was powerless to move to a more comfortable position. He lost all sense of time in his trapped, darkened world.

Eventually, he realized he was able to see again. He might

have had his eyes open for some time, but night had fallen—it was just as dark with his eyes open as shut. Something was falling on his face, chilling his heat-flushed cheeks.

Snow. It's starting to snow.

Why am I sitting, freezing my ass off in the park this late?

It didn't make sense. What was he waiting for? Or better yet . . . whom?

The answer came faster than expected. Emerging from the hedges at the west end, a burly, older man quietly whistled as he walked. David easily recognized him as Bert Cooper, the town mayor, by his huge, distinctive girth.

David's body jumped up off the bench and quickly scampered behind a nearby tree. He peeked around the trunk, eyeing up the mayor and the rest of the park. They were alone.

Why hide from the mayor? Mr. Cooper's a pretty cool guy.

David continued to try to break the invisible bonds controlling him, willing himself to step out from behind the tree, but it wasn't happening. The mayor would be passing very near his hiding spot. For some reason, that thought filled him with dread. He felt his hand reach into his coat pocket and grab something inside. His mind whirled back to the object that had been poking him in the ribs earlier, his fear turning to terror as his hand emerged.

He was holding a knife.

Not just any knife, the blade was a filleting knife—long, thin, and razor sharp. David had no idea where such a thing had come from. He sure as hell had never owned a fishing knife.

David decided it didn't matter where the knife had come from, he was more concerned with what he intended to do with it. The mayor's good-humored whistling drifted closer to his hiding spot and blinding white fear began to flood his mind.

No way. There's absolutely no way I'm going to . . .

He couldn't say it. It wasn't possible. Was it? Had he come here to . . . kill?

The mayor approached. Behind the tree David felt himself unwillingly tensing, like an animal about to pounce on unsuspecting prey. He waited in eager anticipation, as if enjoying the hunt. He tried to convince himself he was only imagining the feeling, but he couldn't. There was no denying it. Deep down, he felt good. Great, in fact. Never in his life had he ever felt so powerful, so alive.

His mind screamed *Stop!* but his body acted independently. As Mr. Cooper walked past the tree, David silenced his whistling by plunging the knife deep between his shoulder blades. The long, thin blade pierced through muscle and bone, slicing down into the mayor's tender heart, killing him almost instantly. The mayor's overweight body sagged down David's leg and dropped heavily to the grass.

Through a haze of conflicting emotions, David was amazed at how quickly and easily the mayor had died. There'd been no struggle, or even a scream. He was also surprised—and strangely disappointed—by the lack of blood.

You murdered him, David. Cold-blooded MURDER.

He tried to justify that it hadn't been his fault. He had no control over his body. His body had killed the mayor, not him. That sure made a lot of sense. He could visualize himself explaining that to the cops. He knew he should run away as fast as he could, but still his body was not his to control. He continued to stare at the sprawled body.

And then he started to cut again.

He hacked away the mayor's clothing and began repeatedly stabbing the cooling corpse. As the snow began falling heavier, he was swept into a crazed frenzy. He butchered the mayor, slicing and dicing every area of his body, spattering blood everywhere—on the tree, on the grass, on his clothes, in his hair, in his mouth. Still he hacked away, oblivious to the blood and the snow and the cold and . . .

And his alarm clock began ringing, waking him up.

David surfaced from his nightmare into bright daylight with the coppery taste of blood still fresh in his mouth. He spit twice into his wastepaper basket to get rid of the taste and then stared with disbelieving, blurred eyes at the clock.

"You've got to be kidding," David said, sitting up, realizing how nice it was to have control of his body again.

He was sick and tired of these damn dreams. Sometimes it seemed like his life revolved around them. He wasn't sure he even *had* a life anymore. Dreams had been the central issue in his life for so long, he had a hard time differentiating between the two.

"Another stupid dream. Relax," he told himself, shutting off the annoying buzzer.

He couldn't just push it away that easily, though. This feeling was too powerful, just like the dream about the creature returning. They were different than the run-of-the-mill nightmares he so often had. Both were too prophetic . . . too real.

David was sure the mayor had been murdered. Maybe he hadn't done it, or—God forbid—maybe he *had*, but the feeling that Bert Cooper was dead continued to haunt him. He had to find out.

The clock beside him showed 8:32 A.M., and he knew the town hall wouldn't be open until 9:00. He decided to take a hot shower before making a call. He scrubbed his body repeatedly in the scalding water, desperate to clean the imaginary blood he could feel still sticking to him everywhere.

After his shower, David dressed and left the house to find the nearest pay phone. He could have called from home, but he wanted complete privacy to make this call. It was 9:30 A.M. when David finally dialed the mayor's number. The efficient secretary answered before he had time to consider what he wanted to say. He couldn't just ask if anyone had murdered the mayor. This had to be approached with more tact.

"Hello," the secretary cheerily said, "Is anybody there?"

"Yes," David finally said, "I was just wondering if . . . ahh, if I could talk to the mayor, please?"

"May I ask why you want to speak with Mr. Cooper, sir?"

Now that was a good question. David tried to come up with an equally good answer, but couldn't. "Ahh . . . I'd rather explain it to him personally if you don't mind. Could you just put him on the phone?"

"No," she said.

No? What the hell did that mean? No she wouldn't put him on the phone, or no he wasn't there? David's forehead began to break out in a cold sweat. Maybe the mayor really had been murdered last night.

"What do you mean by no, miss?"

"I mean . . . no, Mr. Cooper can't come to the phone right now. He's currently indisposed, sir, but I'd be happy to take a message."

Currently indisposed?

David was getting frustrated. Currently indisposed? Yeah, nothing like a few thousand stab wounds to keep you busy. Last night the mayor had looked a lot more like someone *permanently* indisposed.

This tap dancing around wasn't getting David anywhere. He came right out with it. "Listen, all I want to know is if the mayor is alive. I don't want to hear any other runaround bullshit. Just tell me in a plain yes or no. Is the mayor still alive?"

It was the secretary's turn to be speechless now, and it took her thirty seconds to find a response. To David, the silence on the line was agonizing, and all but confirmed his dream.

"What kind of question is that?" she finally asked. "I've already told you . . ."

"You've told me dick-all, lady," interrupted David. "Cut the bullshit." David was screaming now, out of control. "*Yes* or *no*. Is the mayor *alive*?"

"Of course Mr. Cooper is alive. What are you, some kind of a fruitcake? He's in a meeting. I just talked to him five minutes ago. Who is this anyway? There should be a law against nuts like you. . . ."

David hung up. Part of him registered tremendous relief that his vision had turned out to be nothing but a dream after all. The other part of him remembered how much he had en-joyed the kill and was sad it hadn't actually happened. That part had him really scared. As sickening as the murder had been, underneath the disgust was a definite sensation of eu-phoria. Never before had he felt that much excitement and power.

David fiddled the rest of the day away smoking far more cigarettes than he should, and accomplishing nothing. He had missed work, but didn't care. It was a shitty part-timer anyway, down at the Esso gas station on Concession Street. He hated pumping gas and disliked the owner even more. If they fired him, big deal, there were always other shitty jobs he could find and hate equally as much.

He tried to keep his mind off of all the nasty dreams that had become the cornerstone of his existence lately, but as nightfall returned, so too did the memories. By the time he climbed into bed, he was more than a little anxious about what tonight's dream might have in store for him. As it turned out, he slept undisturbed.

David was shocked to hear his alarm ringing and see the sun shining. Was it morning already? He'd slept like a rock all night from the time his head had hit the pillow. It was a per-fect night's rest, totally unbroken, totally peaceful. David couldn't believe it.

Outside his window, he could see it had snowed during the night. The sparkling whiteness of the snowy ground reflect-ing the brilliant glow of the morning sunlight was a truly magnificent spectacle.

What an incredible morning.

He sang his way through a quick shower and headed down-stairs for breakfast in a better-than-usual mood. He and his mother exchanged pleasantries throughout David's slightly burnt French toast. He was heading for the front door when his father stumbled into the kitchen looking pale and shaken.

"Sit down," Steven said. "The mayor's been murdered."

David certainly didn't need to be told to sit; on hearing

the news, his legs crumbled out from under him. He sat on a nearby stool to hear the rest of the story, but with every sentence his body sought the floor.

"Rita McBride found the body. You remember Rita, don't you? Jake McBride's daughter? Anyway . . . she found Mr. Cooper's body in Wingfield Park, alongside the river. It was really nasty, I guess. She'd been out walking this morning, and she thought it was some kid's snowman that had been knocked over. With all the snow last night, I guess the body was completely covered."

David's numb mind whirled back to his dream two nights ago and how it had been snowing then. He could also remember the snow starting to fall harder as the dream went on. *As you butchered him?* his mind screamed.

"No," he shouted out loud, accidentally answering his conscience.

"Yes," his father continued, thinking David had been speaking to him. "I'm serious, David. I wouldn't make up something like this. I guess whoever did it really made a mess. They weren't satisfied with just killing him; they mutilated his body. From what I hear, the murderer must have stabbed Bert a hundred times."

More like two or three hundred, his mind whispered. "Shut up," he said but this time in a weaker voice. His parents were beyond listening anyway, babbling on about the shocking crime. David slipped by them unnoticed.

Back upstairs in his bedroom, having decided he wasn't going to work again, David lay down to try and clear his head. A real cracker of a migraine was beginning to settle in. Instead of taking something for the headache, he lay still and welcomed the pain, hoping it would block out all other thoughts. Unfortunately, the pain leveled off and did little to ease the guilt raking David's conscience.

The mayor was murdered, David. Worse yet, he was murdered exactly like in your dream . . . Exactly. The same person, the same location, the same savageness . . . everything. And the snow, David. Remember the snow?

He didn't want to remember, but he did. He remembered the murder and, yes, even the snow, but he also remembered one other disturbing part of the dream. He remembered the sweet coppery taste of the mayor's warm blood splattering inside his mouth . . . and how much he had liked the taste.

CHAPTER FOURTEEN

Someone once described Dennis Walker with the simple yet precise sentence, *He looks like an oak tree.*

While, on its own, that statement might sound derogatory, if describing Mr. Walker, it would be clear the statement was not only correct, but also entirely complimentary. At six foot seven, he towered over most men. His arms and legs were thick with muscle, like huge, knotted tree limbs. His hard-chiseled face and close-cropped hair rounded off his envied features. He was huge, hard, and as tough as they come. In short, he was an oak tree.

Dennis was known to be fearless, yet calm in dangerous situations—the kind of man you liked on your side if trouble came calling. That went double today when the shit hit the fan, because Dennis Walker wasn't just a big powerful man, he was Dunnville's chief of police.

As Chief Walker strode down the jade-colored hallway to his office, he did so with a strong, confident stride appropriate to a man in his position. His quick military stride never faltered, not even when he walked past the large front windows and noticed a steadily growing mob gathering on the front lawn. Dennis noticed out of the corner of his eye the flag flying at half-mast. He was aware it was the proper thing to do, yet he hated doing it. In his opinion, flags at half-mast didn't show respect. All they did was depress people. The black armbands didn't help much either. Not everyone he passed had one on, but the majority did. With a sigh, Chief Walker produced his own black band, which his wife had insisted he bring, reluctantly tying it around his ample right bicep.

"Black," he muttered. At least that part felt right. It was a black day all over Dunnville, blacker then any since the final days of World War II. By the time the United States atomic bombs had ironically blasted peace back into the world, Dunnville had lost a total of four taxpayers to the war effort. That loss, trivial as it may seem, had caused quite a shock to this small farming community, but at least those men had died fighting for a just cause.

The murder of Bert Cooper last night couldn't be explained quite so easily. Least of all by Chief Walker, who came to a halt outside his office door and just couldn't find it in himself to open the door and walk in. He knew all eight of his patrolmen were inside anxiously awaiting a pep talk, but there lay the problem. He wasn't sure what he could say to them. No idea at all.

If only Chief Adams were still in charge. He'd know what to say.

With that thought came the real problem. Chief Walker had been plain old Patrolman Walker up until two months ago. Phil Adams had been the chief of police in Dunnville for over twenty years and was held in high regard by everyone. For reasons unknown to Dennis, the departing chief had recommended he be elected his successor. Dennis had been shocked when they actually did it. He knew he was a damn good cop, and at forty years of age had more than enough experience for the job, but he still wasn't fully sold on the idea.

Why did his first real case as chief have to be a murder? Why couldn't it have been car theft or arson? Hell, even armed robbery. He knew it shouldn't bother him as much as it did; murder was something society had learned to accept. Television and radio were filled with violence, and it was very much a part of the twentieth-century lifestyle. Chief Walker and the rest of the good people of Dunnville were no exception. They fully understood that their normally quiet town was not immune from such antisocial behavior, but in reality they never actually thought that it would happen here. Murder in Detroit . . . absolutely. Murder in Toronto . . . sure. But murder in the peaceful little community of Dunnville? . . . never.

But it *had* happened here.

Murder had reared its ugly head, and the citizens were already hitting the panic button. It was up to Dennis to allay their fears and catch this killer. Catch him in a hurry.

Standing outside his office, he took a deep breath and sauntered through the open door. The small, drab office fell silent the second he entered. All eyes riveted on him as he slid behind his desk. A quick count confirmed all his men were present. Acting Mayor Alan Thorpe was also in attendance.

"Well," Chief Walker started and was immediately sure that would be all he would say. Dennis began to slide down into his seat, but then quickly regained his composure. He'd never been a quitter in his entire life, and he wasn't about to start now.

"Well," he started again, "Let's catch this son of a bitch. What do we know?"

This was the piss-and-vinegar attitude that was really Dennis Walker, even if he didn't realize it himself. This no-nonsense, get-the-job-done attitude had been what had caught Chief Adams's eye.

"Very little, sir," Constable Barnes said. "Well . . . we have the mutilated corpse of our mayor, Bert Cooper. It was obviously a homicide, the weapon being a very sharp object, probably a knife or a straight razor. Forensics is checking and will get back to us if they come up with something. The county coroner is autopsying as we speak, but probably won't tell us much more than we already know."

"Any fingerprints, footprints, anything?" Chief Walker inquired, although he already knew the answer. He had checked in with forensics prior to the meeting.

"No sir. They figure the killer was wearing gloves or didn't touch the body . . . except with the blade, of course. The ground was too cold for footprints, and besides, the snow covered everything."

"Okay, men, let's recap." Dennis stood and walked around to lean on the front of his desk. "We have a homicide with no motive, no clues, and no suspects. That's *great*."

He let his men and the rather nervous new mayor digest what he'd just said, before springing his ace in the hole. "Don't worry, men. We'll get him. There's something I just found out a few minutes ago that you guys haven't heard. We do have a suspect." He let this information settle and saw the hope he'd been waiting for.

"I just took a call from Cindy Bedford, the mayor's secretary, over at town hall, and she's pretty hysterical. She told me some nutcase called her yesterday around nine thirty in the morning and demanded to know if the mayor was dead."

Chief Walker saw the shock register on each face, the importance of his words sinking home.

"But that call happened before the mayor was killed," Alan Thorpe said.

"That's right . . . which could mean someone knew the mayor was going to die. Better yet, it could mean Miss Bedford was talking directly to the killer. She didn't get a name. The call was made from the pay phone outside the Avondale convenience store on Niagara Street. Whoever it was, Miss Bedford said he sounded awfully upset. Maybe upset enough to kill."

Silence had fallen on the small, crowded office while everyone chewed on this new scrap of information. It wasn't much to go on, but it was a hell of a lot more than they'd had when they'd come in.

"Okay, men, here's what I want to see happen. Get out there and scour the streets. Talk to anybody and everybody who might have seen something. No information is stupid or too small. If anyone knows anything, get them in here. Got it?"

They nodded enthusiastically and almost ran for the door. It was great to see them that eager. Chief Walker also knew it would be good for public morale to see such a strong police presence on the streets. They might even get lucky. Somebody out there knew something. That was always the way it worked. They would first have to find that someone, and then they'd have to make him talk.

CHAPTER FIFTEEN

Saturday night, December 5, David Winter found himself walking down Pine Street again. This time, there was no grace period to admire his surroundings; he knew he had re-entered his dream world. Even before he tried, he knew he'd lost control of his body again. He tried anyway, willing his feet to stop walking, but as in his last dreamwalk, his legs kept trudging along.

As he walked, he felt a bulky object in his pocket digging painfully into his ribs. *The knife*, his mind screamed. *Oh my God. I've got the knife again.*

There was no denying it. If he had the knife, it surely meant he intended to use it. Like it or not, this little walk was going to end in bloodshed. Eventually, David found himself sitting down on the same splintery old bench in the middle of Wingfield Park. He prepared himself for his eyes to shut and plunge him into that awful dark world again, but this time it didn't happen. He just sat there and watched the world go by.

And the people.

Yes, it was the people his body was watching, and tonight there seemed to be a fair number of them wandering about. This in itself seemed odd. He would have thought people would stay home and keep a low profile, but small minds in small towns think differently about this kind of thing. Everyone seemed to think the mayor's death had been some outrageous fluke that couldn't possibly happen again. Dunnville was a safe town, far away from the escalating violence found in the bigger cities. David felt the knife jab into him again and realized what fools they all were. No one should ever assume such drivel, no matter where they live—danger lurks everywhere.

Dusk ran away, pulling closed the curtain of night in its wake. Light snow drifted lazily toward the ground, but from the look of the sky, it wouldn't fall for long. Only a few stragglers remained. Most were young punks without anything better to do. David supposed it was cool for them to hang around and prove they were brave enough to spend time where the murder had taken place. It was crazy how kids got their jollies. Sadly, one of them might be getting a little more than their jollies by the time this night was over.

David watched them come and go—not that he had any choice—and began to wonder which one was going to be the unlucky one. Would it be the tall, skinny kid in the leather jacket, or maybe the pencil-thin girl with the long, greasy black hair? As time drifted by, he started to hope that maybe none of the young punks were in danger. That thought vanished as David realized his hand had slipped into his pocket and tightly grasped the hidden blade.

Somebody was going to die all right. The feel of the sharp blade in his hand was ample proof. David felt that sickening emotion welling up in him, that feeling of desirable power. Part of him wanted to slice and rip again. It made him feel sick, but there was no kidding himself—the desire was there.

It was getting late now, and some of the punks started to leave. After another half hour, only a few diehards remained. David supposed each of them wanted to be the last to leave, guaranteeing them chief bragging rights in the morning.

Again David wondered which person would be chosen for tonight's sacrifice.

"That's exactly what I was wondering," said a loud booming voice—a voice that originated from inside his head and, without a doubt, had not been spoken by him.

Fear froze his mind. His body had never been his to control, but he'd at least enjoyed freedom of thought. Now fear took that away too. He sat speechless, waiting for the voice again.

He didn't have to wait long. "Which one, David?" someone in his head said. "You decide this time, my friend. Which one do we kill tonight?"

And then it all came clear. The loss of independence, and that helpless feeling of not being in control. He understood it all. He didn't have control of his body for the simple reason that this wasn't *his* body. That voice wasn't a stranger in his head—David himself was the stranger. He was inside someone else, traveling along inside *their* mind. It all made perfect sense now. He still had no idea what was going on or how it was happening, but he knew he was right.

He must link up with this person when he falls asleep. He then, as near as he could figure, slips into this madman's mind—a madman who is fully awake and sitting in the park. If David could wake up, he could probably run to the park and see them sitting on the splintery old bench. No, that wasn't right either, because he had dreamed about the mayor's death a full night before it happened.

Somehow, I'm dreaming my way into this other person's mind a full day before that person is doing the things I'm dreaming about tonight.

Now there was some fucked-up thought, huh? It sounded straight out of *The Twilight Zone*, but it did make some sort of sense. He was inside someone's mind, seeing through their eyes and feeling through their body. But who?

What had the killer said to him, anyway? Something about him choosing the next victim? That didn't make a heck of a lot of sense, since he had no way of choosing anything. He couldn't control the killer's body in any . . .

Wait a minute.

David realized he could control the killer's eyes. This must have happened within the last minute, because he hadn't been able to look where he pleased earlier. He'd only been able to see where the stranger had looked, and had seen only what the stranger had wanted him to see. Then the magnitude of what was happening hit him like a slap on the face.

He's letting me control the eyes so I can choose the next victim.

David's gaze naturally began to drift toward the group of punks that were still hanging around. *Don't look at anyone,* he warned himself. *That's what he wants you to do. Stare at someone, and you'll have made your choice.*

Making a conscious effort to not look at anyone was harder to do than it sounded. Two or three times, David caught himself just in time and stopped his gaze a few feet away from one of the remaining punks. He tried to close his eyes, but apparently his control didn't reach as far as the eyelids. He tried to think about waking up, but that wasn't possible either.

He was looking directly at an uninteresting tree when something caught his attention out of the corner of his eye. It was a sight so unusual, he couldn't restrain himself in time. He found himself staring wide-eyed at a little old lady shuffling along Main Street, headed toward town. This lady had to be at least eighty years of age and was stumbling back and forth across the street.

Why would a tiny old lady be wandering around by herself this late? Don't tell me she's drunk too?

David had no way of knowing this lady had never drunk an ounce of alcohol in her life. Her name was Olivia Stanton and she was seventy-nine years young. The real reason she was staggering around was shock. Only two hours earlier, she had become a widow. Her husband of sixty years, Bradford J. Stanton, had just succumbed to a fatal heart attack. Bradford's eighty-three-year-old ticker had been ready to blow a fuse for twenty years, but it had still shocked Olivia when it happened. They'd been enjoying dinner, when Bradford had clutched his chest and fallen face-first into his apple dumplings.

Before Olivia knew what was happening, she was alone in this world, and the hospital staff had sent her home. Nobody had even bothered to ask if she needed a ride. Olivia had never obtained a driver's permit. Bradford had always been around. Even tonight, with his heart doing cartwheels, he'd driven to the emergency room.

So Olivia simply passed right by their old Ford and started walking home. With her aged mind confused with grief, she had quickly gotten lost and disoriented.

It was while she was in this state of confusion that David spotted her. No one could blame David for thinking she was drunk. He had no way of knowing about her loss, or how she was going to cope without her husband. Not that she needed to worry, since she'd be reunited with her beloved Bradford sooner than she expected.

David lost control of the killer's vision.

Oh my God, he thought. *I've made my choice.*

The killer began to slowly stalk the old lady, again speaking to David. "It'll all be your fault too. This is the one you wanted, David, not me. I would've chosen the blonde with big tits."

No, David tried to scream, hoping the killer would listen. *I didn't mean to look.*

The killer's voice boomed out like a thunderclap. "But you did look, David. Snuck a little peek at the old bitch, didn't you? Sorry, Davey, my boy, but you made your choice. Now the wrinkled old bag is going to die. She's going to die hard!"

Davey, my boy? Only one person had ever addressed him like that. It was the creature. The creature was the killer. Of course. Now that he thought about it, who else could it be? He couldn't believe he hadn't recognized the voice earlier. Maybe he'd been too disoriented and frightened to think straight.

David and the creature followed the old woman until she ducked into a small house on the left side of Main Street.

David noticed the mailbox at the house—or rather, the killer noticed it as he walked by. It read, BRADFORD AND OLIVIA STANTON.

"Olivia . . . now isn't that sweet?" the creature said.

The killer confidently strode to the front door and knocked as loud as he could. Olivia Stanton opened the door, a large grin filling her face.

"Bradford? Is that you?"

Before she could ask anything else, they plunged the long fillet knife deep into her throat. She died quickly and easily. Olivia Stanton seemed still to be smiling as they dragged her limp body inside and shut the door.

Another easy murder, but just like last time, the slaughter was far from finished. David tried not to look at the grotesque things they did to the old woman, but it was impossible. What the killer looked at—so did he. By the time they finished, all David could see was a tangled mess of juicy red meat that used to be an nice old lady.

Please let it end. Get me out of here and just let it end.

There was only so much a person could take, and David felt close to his breaking point. Unfortunately, things were about to get worse. They began removing their clothes.

NoNoNoNo! David screamed as he stared down at the ghastly mess that had once been a woman. He felt the killer's growing erection and as if in some hypnotic trance, he laid down with the killer on top of the dead lady. Together they kissed the bloody lips on her ruined face, and . . .

And then David woke up.

That last act of utter madness had been too much. Whatever unimaginable connections were holding him to the creature, he had torn free of those bonds at the thought of raping the mutilated corpse. The creature was truly a sick bastard. When David thought about what it was doing right at this . . .

"No, not this minute," he corrected himself. "It won't be killing and raping her until tonight."

This was all too crazy. Why was this happening? Had he suddenly turned into some powerful psychic that could predict future events?

"Think David. Think."

The creature had murdered the mayor yesterday, and tonight it was going to murder some old woman named Olivia Stanton.

Can I stop it from happening?

Good question. David went over what he knew. He knew the creature would wait for her while sitting in the shadows of Wingfield Park. He would follow her to her house on Main Street and then mutilate her just inside her front door. David knew what the creature looked like. He also knew what Olivia Stanton looked like and where she lived. The only thing he didn't know was what time it would happen. Still, the information he had was more than sufficient.

He could tip off the police, and they would put a stop to it. They might think he was some kind of crackpot, but he was willing to bet they would at least check it out. If the creature noticed a few cops snooping around, maybe it would call the whole nasty business off. David picked up the phone and dialed the police station. Nothing happened. No ring, no operator, nothing.

He disengaged the cradle bar to clear the line. He was about to dial again when he heard a soft voice coming from the phone. David put the receiver to his ear.

"Operator?" David asked.

Insane laughter drifted back to him. "No, Davey my boy, this isn't the goddamned operator."

David felt as if he'd been run over by a tractor. It was the creature.

"Listen good, little man. Listen *real* good. If you ever try calling the police again, Davey, I'm going to bring down a world of hurt on you. Understand? If you so much as dial one number, I'll be over to practice on you before I hit that old bag tonight . . . and I don't mean the part with the knife."

Then the line went dead.

That couldn't have happened. That couldn't have been real.

But it had been. The creature not only had the power to control his dreams, but was able to listen in on his thoughts too. A chill ran all the way down David's tailbone to the place the creature had threatened to visit if he called the police again.

The police were out. He might be stupid, but he wasn't *that* stupid. He knew he was no match for the creature and deep down realized the police probably wouldn't be either. Again he wondered why this was happening. If it wanted to kill him, it could have done it a thousand times over the years. What did it want?

If David couldn't turn to the police, than where could he get help? Certainly not his parents. "Tom," he yelled out, practically scaring himself with the half-crazed sound of his voice. "And maybe Johnny," although he knew that was a long shot. Johnny never talked to him anymore. Johnny ran with the A-crowd—in fact, he *was* the A-crowd. Everyone else at school was grouped behind him. In alphabetical terms, David was barely part of the Y-crowd. The last time he'd tried to say hi to Johnny, he had looked at David as if he were a total stranger. No, Johnny wouldn't be any help.

Tom might be, though. He and Tom had kept up a distant relationship. They had been best friends for years, but the creature had torn them apart. Tom had been unable to handle the death of their friend Peter and pulled farther away each time David wanted to discuss the creature. The last time they'd talked about it was when they were fifteen, but by then Tom was convinced it had all been their imagination. To this day Tom refused to talk about that long-lost summer.

That would be the tricky part. Tom would gladly spend time with him, but not if David wanted to stir up bad memories. They were friends, but the creature topic was taboo.

I have to try anyway. I don't have a choice. Tom's the only person, other than Johnny, who might understand.

David got dressed in a hurry. Somehow he would make

Tom listen to him and make him understand. He simply had to, or a lot of innocent people were going to die.

He ran all the way to Alder Street where Tom still lived. Tom's father was no longer alive—he'd drunk himself into the grave three years earlier—but Tom and his mother still shared the same old house. Their relationship was strained, but tolerable. Tom was all she had left.

Although it was early, Tom was up and sitting quietly at the kitchen table when David showed up at the back door. Tom invited him in, but clearly wasn't thrilled to see him. David ignored the cold-shoulder treatment and jumped straight to the point, telling him about the creature's return and how it had killed the mayor. He never stopped long enough to let Tom object, or to dismiss anything he had to say. He even revealed how he was seeing the murders in his dreams through the creature's eyes.

"Look, Tom. I know you don't believe me, but—"

"Oh I believe you, David," interrupted Tom, who all of a sudden looked frightfully pale.

"What?" asked David, who'd envisaged dozens of possible responses from Tom, but none of them close to that one. "You really believe me? You're serious?"

"Of course I believe you, David. I don't want to, but I don't have a choice anymore. A few nights ago I had a real weird dream. It scared the crap out of me, but it also brought back a lot of memories I'd conveniently forgotten. Things about the creature and stuff . . . you know, from that summer when we were ten."

This was music to David's ears. *Tom believes me. He remembers.*

"This is great, Tom. I can't tell you how good it feels to have someone who understands. You remembered everything that happened that awful summer, and now you believe all this weird shit I'm saying. Great."

David was excited that he had a brother-in-arms, but the withered, haunted look on Tom's face soon sobered up his mood.

"What's the matter, Tom? You don't look so swell."

Tom looked downright ill. He took a huge breath before answering. "Well, Dave, I haven't exactly told you everything. It wasn't the memories that made me believe your story about the creature killing the mayor."

What Tom said next caught David completely off guard. "The real reason I believe you is that I'm having those exact same dreams you are. The walks down Pine Street, the loss of body control, the knife digging into my ribs as I sit on the bench in the park, the mutilations . . . all of it."

David was shocked. Tom was dreaming out of the creature's eyes too? This was getting freakier by the moment. "You mean you were dreaming along with me last night, and two nights before that? You saw the mayor get killed in the park and that Olivia Stanton woman last night?"

Tom had been nodding along with David's questions until the mention of Olivia Stanton. Her name brought a frown to his face. "Who's Olivia Stanson? I never dreamed about her."

"Stanton," David corrected him. "Olivia Stanton."

"Stanton . . . Stanson. Either way, I've never heard of her."

David was confused. "Are you saying you didn't follow a little old lady home from the park last night?"

Tom was shaking his head. "No, I followed some young, dark-haired girl. I think I heard one of the guys call her Yvonne. We followed her across the bridge over the river and killed her in the ditch beside that place where you buy fishing tackle. I never even saw an old lady."

David was about to say that he didn't know what Tom was talking about, but suddenly he did. "Wait a minute. Did the creature talk to you in your dream last night and let you choose the next victim?"

The look of understanding on Tom's face was answer enough for David, and he hurried on. "That's what I thought. The creature made us both choose a victim. I was stupid enough to look at the old woman and you must have looked at this Yvonne girl. From there, our dreams split and went their own direction."

They sat quietly, absorbing what they knew was the truth. Tom finally spoke, putting words to the question both had been silently wondering. "Well . . . which one of our dreams is going to come true? Which one of them is going to die?"

Neither knew the answer. They just sat staring into each other's haunted eyes. David briefly considered telling Tom about his idea to tip off the cops, but he didn't dare. Tom also sat quietly and thought his own private thoughts about the police. He didn't dare mention them to David, either. He'd been warned too.

CHAPTER SIXTEEN

That night, the creature mutilated Olivia Stanton. The police found her the following day exactly as David had dreamed—in her living room and messy.

Two days later, the police discovered another horribly slashed corpse in the drainage ditch beside the bait shop. It had once been the pretty young body of Yvonne Dupont. She had died exactly as Tom had said she would.

Both dreams had come true. Each boy felt quite a bit of guilt, since neither had informed the authorities. Both knew that tonight they would dream again, and another body would be found. Both also knew things were going to get a whole lot worse before they got better.

They shared one other feeling. Both were utterly terrified.

CHAPTER SEVENTEEN

It was only eight o'clock in the morning, and Chief Walker already had a hell of a headache, literally and figuratively. His swollen temples throbbed to the beat of some marching band, but this headache was merely a tickle compared to his other one. His other headache wouldn't go away by chewing a couple aspirins.

And it had killed again.

Six innocent people had now been butchered. Irene Sharp had been the latest to join the list. Her mutilated and partially dismembered body had been found early yesterday morning. Irene had been murdered sometime the night before, which fitted the pattern perfectly. So far, all six murders had been committed every even day of the month, starting on the fourth with the mayor. Likewise, each corpse had been found the following morning on the odd days.

The newspapers were having a heyday. For over a week they'd been calling for the chief's head, each new body swaying the citizens toward agreeing with the papers. The people of Dunnville were starting to panic. The town council was aware of this and had obtained the assistance of eight extra patrolmen from nearby districts. The chief began to wonder when his replacement would be showing up, as well. Things weren't that desperate yet, but they were getting close. If he didn't get some answers soon, he would have a full-scale panic on his hands.

The headlines splashing the newspapers sure didn't help. Reporters sniffed around the station trying to get any scrap of information. The police and town officials did their utmost to prevent details of the slayings from reaching the press, but for the most part they'd failed miserably. The papers told the public everything. Well, almost everything.

The police had managed to keep one fact out of the papers longer than they'd thought possible. Everyone had missed a vital bit of evidence. They all saw how brutally hacked and mutilated the corpses were, and obviously noticed the blood and guts, but there was one thing the reporters had missed. To the chief's amazement, nobody had noticed that all of the victims, including the new name on the list, were missing their ears.

Apparently the killer had some type of fetish. Why would he take their ears? Some sort of gruesome trophy? A sick memento, perhaps? Lunch? From the similarities in the murders, the police had been able to put together the modus operandi of the killer.

Someone strong: two of the victims had been big men. Someone extremely unstable, with a possible long list of violent arrests: this wasn't merely someone confused, this guy was way off the deep end. Someone who was probably abused as a child: somebody had to have fucked this guy up somewhere. Someone with a strange ear fetish. Someone with delusions of grandeur. Someone who . . .

On and on it went. Helpful, but basically useless. The MO really didn't tell anybody anything they didn't already know. The most upsetting thing about it was that it so closely resembled one other lunatic killer from the past— the viciousness of the attacks, the time involved to complete such brutality, but most of all the missing body parts. If someone were to search back through police files, one madman's name would pop up with the exact same MO. That infamous murderer of the past with the same killing style was quite well known. He'd called himself . . . Jack the Ripper.

By five o'clock that afternoon, Walker's headache had become considerably worse. The source of his increased anguish lay in front of him. It was the *Dunnville Chronicle*. The chief hadn't seen a copy of it until two hours earlier. The paper had hit the streets late, and Dennis had known they must have gotten hold of a big story and were holding off to reprint today's edition. He reread the front-page headline for the umpteenth time.

RIPPER KILLER STRIKES AGAIN
IS JACK THE RIPPER LOOSE IN DUNNVILLE?

They knew. Somehow the bastards had found out the police were hunting a Jack the Ripper copycat and they were spreading the word. Just what the police needed.

"How the hell did they find out?" the chief spoke to himself. "I told those idiots to shut their big mouths."

He was furious. The information about the missing ears and the similarities to the Ripper killings of 1888 were all the secrets the police had. He had forbidden any of his men to breathe a word about it. Obviously, someone had talked. It wasn't all that surprising. In a small town, it was impossible to keep a secret. The hows and whys didn't really matter now. Now they had to worry about repairing the damage.

Having a serial killer in your community was bad enough, but now the people of Dunnville were being told someone who thought they were Jack the Ripper had moved in. That made things much worse. Fear had an awful way of overcoming logic, and before Chief Walker could do anything about it, the town would be in a panic.

Dennis tossed the newspaper wearily into the wastebasket. "We have to catch this bastard. We have to catch him quick."

It was 5:15 P.M., December 16. Dennis should have been thinking happy thoughts of Christmas. Instead he gazed again at the list of victims. His heart went out to the families. What kind of a Christmas were they going to have? Worse yet, today was an even calendar day, which meant the newly dubbed Ripper Killer would strike again. Through his office window, Dennis watched the sun sink slowly out of sight. Nightfall was approaching, and with it, darkness. A darkness that would hide a madman determined to kill again and again until someone stopped him. Chief Walker knew he was supposed to be that someone. His large, powerful hands trembled as he retrieved his newspaper and reread the headline.

RIPPER KILLER STRIKES AGAIN
IS JACK THE RIPPER LOOSE IN DUNNVILLE?

Would tomorrow's paper say the same thing? Chief Walker thought so, but wasn't certain. Outside, the sun sank a little lower, and somewhere a killer began to prepare for the approach of the blessed dark.

Chapter Eighteen

As it has since the dawn of time, night passed into day. The morning of the seventeenth brought with it more tragedy and pain. The Ripper Killer had struck again. The seventh victim was a poor old bag lady by the name of Susanna Hobbs. Everyone in town knew her and referred to her simply as Susie. Who would ever dream of killing little Susie? She'd never harmed a soul in her life.

Susie was found slaughtered inside three side-by-side-by-side garbage cans at the end of Church Street, near the railway tracks.

The pain and tension stood out on Chief Walker's face like a flashing neon billboard. He had just returned from inspecting Susie's remains. It hadn't been pretty. The morgue was still digging through the cans trying to piece her back together. Her ears were missing, of course, and so possibly were a few more parts. It was too early to tell. Dennis lay his head in his hands and shut his eyes.

"Er . . . I'm sorry, sir," a voice said from the doorway, causing the chief to snap back to attention.

Police Constable Davis continued to apologize from the doorway. "I only wanted to tell you something. If this is a bad time I could . . ."

"No, Martin, come in. Shut the damn door behind you and sit down." Constable Martin Davis was one of the new reinforcements who had been sent to help out. "What do you need, Davis? It's been a rough day."

Davis sat down across the desk from Chief Walker with a huge, pearly-white smile plastered on his face. Walker considered chewing him a new asshole for being so happy. *Susie Hobbs hadn't been smiling when her head rolled out of the trashcan.*

Constable Davis's next words put a stop to such thoughts and even managed to put a small grin on Dennis's hardened features. "This time he messed up, Chief. We've found some evidence this time. Old Hopkins and I were going over the scene, and we think we've found an article of clothing belonging to the killer. It's a New York Yankees baseball cap. We found it covered in blood, behind a bush. Maybe old Susie put up a fight and knocked the cap off the killer's head. Maybe it was too dark for him to find it, or maybe he was disturbed or something. Either way we have our first clue."

With this new information, the gears inside Chief Walker's head started turning. It was great news, but still unlikely to help much. Lots of people wear baseball caps. The killer could still be anybody.

"There's more, Chief. I can tell what you're thinking, but I haven't told you the best part. Inside the cap we found a couple of initials. Hopefully the killer's initials."

"What are they, Davis? The initials?"

"Well, they're smudged with blood and years of sweat and dirt, but we're almost positive the initials are . . . DW. Forensics has the cap and are making sure."

One quick call to forensics confirmed that indeed, DW were the correct initials.

"DW, DW, DW," the chief repeated over and over like some mystical mantra. "Okay, first of all, get over to town hall and get me a list of every male DW we have living in Dunnville and the immediate area. Second . . . No, make this first. Get in touch with every available cop and let them all know. Tell them if one single word of this gets out to those bloody reporters, I'll fire every one of you. Now move!"

Davis was gone in a flash.

It took him an hour to arrive back at the chief's office, and by the look on the chief's face, he knew he'd taken too long. Davis simply handed over the sheet of paper and said nothing.

Walker had spent the last hour ready to eat rocks. He could finally start to imagine they were getting close to nailing this son of a bitch. It was always possible the baseball cap belonged to some other person, but the chief didn't think so. His gut instinct told him it belonged to the killer. He yanked the offered sheet of paper out of Constable Davis's hand and scanned it furiously. There were more names on the list than he'd hoped. Thirty-nine of them. Dunnville being as small as it was, Dennis had hoped there would only be a few people with the initials DW.

"Those are only the males in town over the age of fourteen and under sixty-five," Davis said, seeing the concerned look on his chief's face. "I figured that age group would be good enough."

"Yeah, should be. Get some men working on these lists, and hurry them up."

Davis took his leave and went about his duty. Dennis sat down and scoured the list again. He was sure one of those names would turn out to be their man.

"I'm going to find you, you sick bastard. I promise you that. You better run while you can, 'cause come hell or high water, I'm gonna find you."

Thirty-nine potential killers on the list to check out. The chief chewed his fingernails down to the quick, trying to guess which name would end up being the one.

The thirty-first name on the list belonged to a lonely, scared, nineteen-year-old boy named David Winter. Still just another faceless DW to the police . . . but not for long.

CHAPTER NINETEEN

The morning of the twenty-third could only be described as ugly. The clouds were shaded a grayish black, hanging heavy in the sky, almost low enough to touch. At forty-one degrees, it was too mild for snow, yet cold enough to chill to the bone. The milder temperatures in the last few days had melted away any hope of a white Christmas. The little snow left lay slushy and dirty, adding to the ugliness of the day.

The incessant wind howled through the streets again, unimpeded by the bare trees. There would be no Christmas cheer in Dunnville this year—they hadn't even set up the huge Christmas tree in the center of town. The festive season didn't seem important, losing its priority to the Ripper. The residents had moved past the panic stage, and paranoia was rampant. People kept to themselves, having lost each other's trust. The streets were practically deserted.

David Winter was deep into one of his blackout sleeps, which always happened on murder night. It never changed. One night he'd be forced to witness the murders, the next, nothing. No dreams, no restless stirring. As soon as his head hit the pillow, bang, he was gone until morning.

A ringing noise brought him out of the darkness, causing him to repeatedly strike the alarm clock in an effort to silence it. The ringing continued until he realized it was the telephone and not the alarm at all. Down the hall, the phone continued to ring. David's parents had gone to visit his grandmother in Sarnia for a week, so he was the only one who could answer the call. Two rings later he picked up the receiver, holding it to his ear, prepared for the worst.

"Hello?"

A pause, then, "David, you're there. It's me, Tom. I knew you were home, but I thought you weren't gonna answer."

"I wasn't going to. Usually these days, it's bad news, and I've had enough of that."

"Yeah, I hear ya. Sorry, but I've got more bad news."

David sighed and already figured out what the news was going to be. "It's killed again, right?"

"Yeah. It was that woman we saw. I just found out her name was Rhonda Tate. I guess she worked over at the boat marina, in the restaurant."

David didn't know what to say. Both young men were racked with guilt about what was happening to their friends and neighbors. They knew exactly who was doing the murders and even knew a day ahead who the next victim was going to be, but were too afraid to say anything to the police.

"No dreams last night?" David asked.

"Of course not. Same old routine. You wake up from a good night's sleep, totally refreshed, but then crash back into depression because you know what's happened."

David knew exactly what his friend meant. He was crashing at this very minute.

Tom continued, "The worst part is trying to pretend you don't know someone's been killed. Someone asks if you heard what happened, and what can you say? I always feel like screaming, 'Of course I do asshole, I was there helping hold the fucking knife.'"

Silence. Neither knowing what to say.

"I can't take it anymore," Tom whispered. "I can't find any more excuses for myself. It's partly my fault these people are dead."

"Partly *our* fault you mean," David said. "Don't lay all the guilt on yourself."

"I know . . . but what are we going to do about it?"

"What *can* we do? The creature will kill us if we go to the cops."

"We have to do something, David. They're dead because of us. The creature doesn't care about them. It's playing with us. The only reason it's killing them is to fuck us up. I don't know why, but I'm right."

"I know, Tom. We have to put an end to this. Somehow."

"Stay put then. I'll come over and we can talk about it, okay?"

David agreed and said good-bye. He went downstairs to have breakfast. Food was a good way to keep his mind off things. Ten minutes and two bowls of cornflakes later, he heard a knock at the back door and rushed to let Tom in.

"Get in here, Tom, we . . ." he cut the greeting off abruptly. Standing at the door were two people, and neither one of them was his friend Tom.

Both were policemen.

David quickly wiped the shocked look off of his face, but not before the cops had noticed. They exchanged a suspicious glance, and then the taller policeman spoke. "Sorry to bother you, young man, but are you David Winter?"

They were here looking for him? His mind raced, but couldn't come up with anything to say.

"My name is Constable Davis, and this here"—he pointed to the shorter cop beside him—"is Constable Barnes. We were just wondering if we could ask a few questions."

"Questions? About what?"

Constable Barnes talked this time. "Just a few questions . . . about the murders."

David had almost handled his shock at first seeing the policemen, but this time he didn't come close. He started shaking, his nerves were rocked so badly.

"Murders? What could I possibly know about them?"

Both policemen, trained to know when people were hiding something, immediately went on the defensive. "Probably nothing, sir," said Constable Davis. "This is just routine. We found a certain article of clothing at one of the murder scenes recently that had the initials DW on it. We're just doing a door-to-door of every citizen in Dunnville with those initials. The computer spit out your name along with all the others."

"Does this mean I'm a suspect?" David asked, trying to sound light and jocular.

Constables Davis and Barnes again exchanged glances before Barnes answered. "No, no, just a few simple questions and that'll be it. It's routine, David."

When David nodded understandingly, Constable Davis continued. "Would you mind coming down to the station?"

He knows I know something, David thought, but accepted their offer to drive him downtown. Not that he had much choice in the matter. To refuse would have made them even more suspicious.

"Just routine," they said to the young man in the backseat of the cruiser, but both patrolmen had a funny feeling about this one. All the others had been routinely questioned at their homes, but Davis and Barnes wanted the chief to meet Mr. Winter.

In the backseat of the cruiser, David's nerves were getting worse. The two cops said they'd found an article of clothing at one of the murders. That had to be the baseball cap Tom and he had seen fall to the ground during the dream murder of the bag lady. Why would the creature make such a stupid mistake? And why did it have his initials?

It's trying to frame me, David's mind exploded, everything clicking together. *Holy shit, it wants them to think I'm the Ripper!*

He had to get out of there—fast. He was losing control at the worst possible time. If he acted as scared and nervous as he felt, he'd be in a whole heap of trouble. He had to get control of himself and calm down before they made it uptown.

He felt better by the time he was escorted into Chief Walker's office. After all, they didn't have anything on him. If he just stayed cool, everything should be fine.

"Thanks for coming," Chief Walker began, as he poured

David a glass of ice water. "Have a drink, son, you look a little hot under the collar."

"No thanks, I'm fine," David said, wondering if his nervousness was that obvious. He started to sweat under the intense stare of the chief.

"You know why you're here, don't you, David?"

"Constable Davis and Barnes said you were questioning everyone in town with the initials DW in connection with the Ripper murders."

"Not exactly," the chief said. "We're only questioning a small selection of the people on our lists. Only the people we feel know something about the homicides."

Dennis leaned over David, staring like a vulture waiting for its meal. "We happen to think that you"—he accentuated with a finger pointed at David's face—"know something you're not telling us."

David sunk back into the intentionally uncomfortable chair he was seated on and tried his best to disappear. He had no immediate response to give the chief. He had enough wits about him to know the chief was blindly probing. The trouble was, the chief had unknowingly hit the nail right on the head. David *was* hiding information. He *did* know a hell of a lot about the murders. He just couldn't say anything.

To stall for time, he took a deep swig out of the water glass. *They probably think I'm some long-haired drug addict or something.* Maybe that held the answer to his predicament. If they believed he was just a punk, he might get out of there. Not having the luxury to think up a better plan, he went with it. He would give the cops the tough-guy, rebel routine and see what happened.

"Okay, boss man," David started, slipping into his tough-guy voice. "You're right. I do know something."

The three policemen in attendance leaned closer in unison as if performing some sort of bizarre synchronized maneuver. *Synchronized interrogation.* That thought brought a smile to David's shaking lips and helped build his confidence to go on.

"Yeah, I know you three dickheads and the rest of the clowns around here are grasping at straws. You don't have the slightest clue who the murderer is, so you waste time harassing innocent people like myself."

Chief Walker tried to control his temper. Inside, he wanted to grab this little arrogant asshole and throttle him. Dennis was under enough criticism from town hall without this snot-nosed prick shooting his mouth off.

"Listen, Mr. Winter, nobody is harassing you. You came here willingly, and all we're trying to do is ask a few simple questions . . . okay?"

"Sure boss, it's your dime."

"Okay, good. Now I'm sure that Constables Davis and Barnes informed you that you were brought here as part of a routine survey—"

"Routine?" David interrupted. "Isn't it sometimes considered *routine* for cops to actually *catch* the criminal? I doubt you jerks could *routinely* catch a cold."

David laughed as if this were the funniest thing he'd ever heard and could tell his plan was working. The chief was struggling to control his rage. If David could just push him a little more, he was sure the chief would completely lose it.

"Listen, David," Constable Davis tried to get things back on track. "Where were you on the night of December 16, when Susie Hobbs was killed?"

"Oh, that's an easy one. The same place I've been every other night this month—the backseat of my dad's car with the chief's sexy daughter."

That was the straw that broke the camel's back. "Get this punk out of here," was all the chief could manage to say through clenched teeth.

"Hey, no need for the escort, Chiefy. I'll find the way."

David felt quite proud he'd thrown the chief off his trail so easily, but he also wanted to cover his tracks and make sure they didn't bother him again.

"I told you to get the hell out, boy."

"I'll leave when I'm ready. I have something else to say."

"Well, we're finished listening, smart-ass, so get out . . . now." Together Constables Davis and Barnes started dragging David toward the door.

"Police brutality, police brutality!" David began screaming. "Keep these big apes away from me, Chiefy."

David was dragged down the hallway, one cop holding each arm. He spoke louder so the chief could still hear him. "You'll hear from my lawyer, Chiefy. You can't harass someone for no reason, badge or no badge. Just because you found my initials in some ragged old baseball cap . . . that doesn't mean squat. I don't know nothing about your damn case. You hear me? Nothing."

Constables Davis and Barnes dragged David outside the police station and dumped him in the parking lot. They watched him long enough to make sure he was headed away from the station. Returning to the chief's office, they prepared for the chief to chew them out for wasting his time. It was a shocking sight, to say the least, when they walked in to find Dennis smiling from ear to ear.

"What are you so happy about?" they asked at the same time.

Chief Walker didn't answer them, but started issuing orders. "Get that drinking glass down to the boys at forensics. I need fingerprints, fast." He also pulled the tape recorder out from its hiding place in his top drawer where it had recorded their meeting with David. "Get that secretary from the mayor's office down here too. I want her to listen to this tape and see if the voice sounds like the guy who called her."

Davis and Barnes looked questioningly at each other. "What for?" Davis asked. "You just had us throw the punk out."

"Oh, he's a punk all right, but I think he's also a killer."

"I don't get it. What gives?"

"What gives, Constable Davis, is that all we ever said to the little bastard was that we found an article of clothing with his initials in it. Right?"

"Yeah, so?"

Chief Walker leaned back in his chair with his hands clasped together. He looked like he was trying to shake his own hand, congratulating himself. "Well, you tell me. If that kid isn't the Ripper, how come he knows that the article of clothing we found just happens to be a baseball cap?"

CHAPTER TWENTY

Of all the stupid, moronic plays, David cursed as he headed home from the police station. He'd only taken five steps across the parking lot before realizing what he'd done. There was no way he should have known it was a baseball cap they'd found at the scene, no way at all. Only an idiot would miss the obvious connection that somehow he was involved in the murders, and Chief Walker was far from being an idiot.

And to think I pissed him off too.

He should have known when to stop. He had accomplished his objective but, through sheer stupidity, had placed himself at the crime scene. They were sure to think he was the Ripper. His tough-guy act would only reinforce that conclusion. He continued to glance behind, convinced a cruiser would be fast on his tail, but it never happened.

Fifteen minutes later he arrived home, where Tom was waiting for him. David sat down beside his friend, nervously puffing on a newly lit cigarette. For several minutes, neither of them spoke.

"So, what did the cops want?" Tom asked.

David almost swallowed his cigarette, "How do you know about the cops?"

"I saw them put you in the cruiser just as I was getting here. Figured they were taking you to the station. I take it you've got bad news? Well, let me in on it. We're in this together, right? Don't tell me you've forgotten about the Knights of the

Round Room? We promised there'd never be secrets between us. That still holds good."

David told Tom everything that had happened.

"Oh my God, David. Do you realize what you've done?"

"Of course I do. I'm not an idiot."

"You could have fooled me. They're going to think you're the one. They'll throw you in jail until you rot."

"Not if I can hand them the real killer first."

"What does *that* mean? If you go to the cops and try telling them it's really a seven-foot, rotting creature that—"

"No, no. We physically turn him in. That way there'll be no doubt I'm innocent."

"And just how do you intend to pull that miracle off? A couple dozen cops have been after him for weeks and come up with squat, but somehow you alone are going to find him. Good luck."

"I'm not gonna be alone. You're going to help."

"Oh, no. That sounds too crazy for me, man."

"Come on, Tom, a few hours ago you called and said you couldn't take things the way they were anymore. Hell, this is your chance to turn it around. Our chance to finally get rid of this bastard once and for all."

"I don't know, David."

"Remember the Knights of the Round Room?" David slyly added.

"Okay, okay, but how do we pull this off if all those cops can't?"

"We have an advantage the rest of them don't. Today is the twenty-third . . . an odd day, which means tonight we're going to dream about the creature's next victim."

"So?"

"So, we pay close attention and try to figure out where the next murder is going to happen. Its location, I mean. Then all we—"

"Then all we have to do is go there tomorrow night when the creature shows up," Tom interrupted, leaping to his feet. "When it shows up, we jump it, right?"

"You got it, buddy. Simple really."

"Hold on. It'll be easy to find the creature, you know, from our dreams, but how do we capture it so the police can see it? That isn't going to be easy."

David grin faded and was replaced by a hard, determined grimace. "I don't think you quite understand, Tom. I don't intend to capture the creature . . . I intend to kill it."

CHAPTER TWENTY-ONE

David slipped swiftly into his dream, feeling his mind connecting with the creature instantly. That same awful feeling of helplessness and loss of bodily control hit again, but he was getting used to it and didn't put up a fight.

The creature could listen in on his thoughts if it desired, so he would have to be careful. Before going to sleep Tom had also agreed not to think about anything that might alert their adversary. Neither wanted to let the creature know what they were planning. Surprise would be their only chance.

Unfortunately, the plan was falling apart. When David entered the dream, he couldn't see very well. Everything was foggy, as if he were viewing things through a dirty window. The tall trees along the roadside told him he was wandering down Pine Street. Something didn't feel right. A barely distinguishable car would rumble by hardly moving, while David himself seemed to be walking extraordinarily fast. The next moment things would change, and the car would speed off, while his pace slackened.

The hazy view, accompanied by the crazy speed fluctuations, was confusing. It was like trying to watch a movie through a stained-glass window while sitting in a room with a flickering strobe light. It was nearly impossible to follow what was happening, never mind where, but he tried to concentrate in spite of things. Maybe he had a bad connection with the creature. He hoped Tom's dream was clearer.

After fifteen minutes and an unknown number of turns, David was completely lost. The only thing he had recognized was the Wabasso building on Cedar Street, and that was only because of its size. It was the only building in Dunnville that large within walking distance of Pine Street. The creature had stopped briefly to caress the knife in its pocket, before moving on.

A few minutes later the creature stopped again. It had turned down a gravel roadway, hidden behind what looked like a bush, and sat very still. David knew this was going to be the spot, if only he could figure out where he was.

And then the smell hit him.

A rotten stench assaulted him, something that reeked of dead fish and stinking . . . *Garbage!* That was it. The creature was at the dump. The smell was unmistakable—as a kid he'd played there and came home reeking of the same smell.

Okay, he cautiously thought, *now what?*

It didn't take long to get an answer. The creature sprang up from behind the bush and ran. David still couldn't see where they were running and again hoped Tom was having better luck. The blood started to fly even before David was aware the creature had a victim. The fresh, coppery smell of spilled blood replaced the pungent garbage odors, and he sensed the creature's excitement increase with his own.

The shadow-shrouded image of the knife flashed again and again into a crouching, unidentifiable victim. Or was it victims? The fog seemed to be thickening by the minute. The crimson-smeared knife was cutting through the mist, followed by a crescendo of horrible screams. An incredible amount of blood seemed to be carpeting the ground, running over his sneakers and . . .

And then he woke up. To his surprise, it was still dark. Usually he slept through until morning. The clock by his bed said 4:12 A.M. The unearthly hour didn't stop him calling Tom, who answered on the first ring.

David explained his rather blurred dream, predicting the

murder was going to take place at the town dump. Tom confirmed it, having also experienced his dream through a misty haze. He also hadn't seen the victim, but had clearly seen the heaps of garbage and the pits where they disposed of the trash.

"All right then," David said. "Here's what we do. Meet me tonight at ten o'clock at the entrance to the dump. Okay?"

"Sure, but what then? Maybe you don't realize it, but the creature isn't going to lie down and play dead. It's savage, David. If we screw up, it'll tear us to shreds."

"Relax. I have it figured out. Ten o'clock, on the dot. Don't you dare stiff me."

"I'll be there. Your plan better be a good one, though, or they'll be burying something other than garbage tomorrow night."

David hung up and went back to bed. In spite of his racing thoughts, he was soon fast asleep.

Outside David's window, the creature's mind's eye returned to its body standing in the shadows below. "That's it, Davey. Get some rest. Tonight you're going to need it."

The monster wandered off into the night, roaring with laughter. Its plan was working perfectly. It would have to go into hiding to rest again soon, but tonight it felt great. The two young fools were so ignorant. The whole reason it had made them witness the murders was just to give them this opportunity to implement their feeble plan. Their ambush was exactly what it wanted.

"I knew you two were cowards, but I still figured you'd have tried taking me on long ago. No matter, things are working out fine . . . just fine indeed."

Tonight had been perfect. The creature had, of course, carefully planned the dream, but had been concerned in case the young men caught on. Its worrying had all been for nothing. Tonight David and Tom believed they had witnessed just another random killing, like all the rest. They were wrong.

The creature did intend to kill again tonight, but what Tom and David weren't aware of was that the blurry victims in their dreams had actually been themselves, and that all the spilled blood they had seen would end up being their own.

CHAPTER TWENTY-TWO

It was the most miserable Christmas Eve in recent history. The night sky was black as coal, with only a hint of the moon grimly peeking through the cloud cover. It wouldn't have been so bad if those storm clouds had held a promise of snow, but with the temperature unseasonably high at forty degrees, snow wasn't likely. Even the frozen ground had begun to thaw, producing a slushy, dirty landscape that everyone despised. All dreams of a last-minute white Christmas had long been abandoned.

Tom Baker waited outside the Tamarac Street entrance to the town dump, not caring if Christmas was white, green, purple, or orange, just as long as he was still alive to see it. He'd arrived early, at a quarter to ten, and had nervously checked his watch each minute since. David finally arrived late at 10:17, strolling along the deserted street puffing on a cigarette.

"Where the hell have you been?" Tom asked, shaking with tension. "For Christ's sake, what if the creature showed up before you?"

"Relax, everything's under control."

"Under control? We're standing out in the wide open when we know at any minute a sadistic killer is going to show up. We have to hide, man."

"I know, Tom. Quiet down, you're *way* too loud." David pointed to where an old lady was nosily poking her head out her front door to see what the commotion was.

David led Tom by the arm down the long gravel lane into the dump, which sat back off Tamarac Street surrounded by dense woods. They remained silent until they were sure they were out of listening range.

"What took you so long?" asked Tom.

"I had to stop and pick up something, and it took me longer than I thought."

"*Tonight?* What could be so important you had to get it tonight?"

"How about this . . . ?" said David, as he held out his right hand under Tom's nose. In it, he was holding a gun.

"Holy shit," said Tom. "Where did you get that?"

"I bought it off Boots, your old gang buddy from way back. Don't have a clue where he got it, but it doesn't matter. I have it, and I'm gonna use it. Here's the plan. We find somewhere to hide, and when—"

"Stop, David. Watch out."

Tom pointed to the ground in front of where his friend had been walking. Two feet in front of David lay a deep hole in the ground. He'd almost walked right into it. As his eyes adjusted to his dark surroundings, he could see more holes scattered around.

"What are they?" he asked.

"They're garbage pits. Don't you know anything? They use that excavator over by the fence to dig the pits, and then they dump the garbage in. After that, it's either buried or burned. What did you think they did with the garbage, eat it? Best watch where you're stepping, there are holes all over."

They skirted the deep pit and ducked down behind some half-filled oil drums. From where they were, they had a perfect view of the entrance. The town dump was completely fenced in, and this was the only way in or out.

"So the plan is to simply jump out and blast away, right?" whispered Tom.

"Right. It'll be dead before it knows we're here."

"What if it doesn't work? What if bullets don't stop it?"

"Why wouldn't bullets stop it? Of course it'll work."

"Aren't you forgetting the creature is already dead, or un-dead, or some other weird thing? Is it possible to kill something like that?"

"Don't worry, Tom, the gun will work just fine," David said, not sounding quite as confident as he had a minute earlier.

"Still, you have a backup plan, right?"

"Uhh . . ."

"You mean that's it?" Tom said, pointing at the gun. "Maybe the gun *will* work, but can we afford to take the chance?"

David had spent the day building his confidence that his plan would work. Now he wasn't sure. "Maybe we should get out of here and rethink things. We can try again later. We'll watch our next dream and take it from there."

Tom didn't hesitate. "You said it. Let's go before it's too late."

But it already was.

They heard the distinct noise of approaching footsteps moving down the gravel lane. "It can't be the creature already, can it?" Tom asked. "There isn't anyone else here yet to be its next victim."

And then it all fell horribly into place for David. The foggy, obscure dream made perfect sense now. This out-of-the-way, deserted killing ground too.

"I don't think anyone else will be joining us tonight, Tom."

"You mean *us*? The creature is after us?"

"I'm afraid so. It set us up. It used that weird dream to lure us here. It's coming in through the only exit, which means we're trapped."

"But why now? It could have killed us anytime. Why's tonight so special?"

"I don't know. Maybe it's tired of playing games."

Strangely, David felt the same way. He actually felt quite calm crouching behind the drums. The fact he might die soon really didn't faze him. He was so sick of living in fear every day, the thought of dying was almost peaceful. He'd known someday it would come down to this, so it might as well be tonight.

Tom wasn't taking the possibility of impending doom quite so well. "What are we gonna do? I don't want to . . . I mean I'm not ready to . . ."

Tom couldn't even bring himself to say it.

"Don't give up yet, Tom. We've still got the gun. Shut up and stay low. We have to try to surprise this thing."

They crouched in silence, watching the semilit patch of gravel at the mouth of the lane. The footsteps were close now.

Be patient, aim straight, kill the bastard, David thought. *No mistakes, no fear.*

But fear did strike David. A small gasp seeped between his clenched teeth when he realized who was stepping into view. David and Tom were taken by surprise. It wasn't the creature. It was worse. Lurching out of the darkness was Rodney the Scarecrow, and beside him, the hideous King Spider—both young men's worst childhood fears.

David had never seen the giant spider before, but Rodney looked exactly as he remembered, only bigger. Rodney was huge, towering well over seven feet. The old coveralls containing his massive straw muscles were stretched to the max. Rodney's left arm was still missing, severed at the shoulder. In its place, a handful of matted straws were haphazardly sticking out. Rodney's New York Yankees hat was missing, answering David's question as to where the creature had obtained a ball cap with his initials in it. His head looked weird without it, but the same demented look was etched on the scarecrow's once-placid Styrofoam face. His piercing eyes still blazed a fiery red.

Those same glowing eyes now focused on the friends' hiding spot, leaving little hope for a surprise attack. Rodney and the massive spider seemed to know exactly where they were hiding and started walking toward them.

Tom, by now, was a complete mess. The sight of the King Spider stepping out of the darkness accompanied by a huge, bodybuilding, one-armed scarecrow was too much for him. Tom's blood raced as the King Spider's multiple red eyes zeroed in on them. An enormous beast, it was hairier and infinitely more frightening than he remembered.

The spider worked its giant mandibles open and closed, leaving a trail of thick, dripping saliva. Nine years ago, it had done the same thing in front of Tom in the uptown alley. That time he'd barely escaped. An image flashed before his eyes of the cryptic message left in his typewriter on the night he'd dreamed about the swirling mists.

I'M COMING TO GET YOU, TOM
AN OLD EIGHT-LEGGED FRIEND

"I have to get out of here," Tom said, almost begging, tugging on David's arm.

"No way," David shot back, "Stay down. Our only hope is the gun, but they're not close enough yet. Just control yourself."

Unfortunately, Tom couldn't. He couldn't bear the thought of letting that spider crawl up to him. He could picture it reaching behind the oil drums, its long, knobby arachnid legs inching toward his face. Letting the spider get that close was insufferable.

So he ran.

David tried to snag the back of his collar, but Tom was off and running like a man possessed, fear coursing through his veins, providing a boost for his heavy legs. The King Spider immediately sprang after him. With its eight legs much more powerful than Tom's two, it was rapidly closing the gap.

Tom only had to look over his shoulder once to know he was a goner. He tried to run faster, but his legs had little left to give. He stumbled and nearly fell on the uneven ground. Regaining his stride, he noticed the spider had closed to within fifteen feet. It was salivating even more now, hungrily anticipating the kill.

From where David sat, still in hiding, he thought Tom might make it. The fence by the woods was only twenty feet away. David glanced at Rodney, but he'd also stopped to watch the chase. There wasn't much sense hiding, now that Tom had given them away, so he stood up to cheer his friend on.

"Climb the fence, Tom. It won't be able to follow you. Run, damn it." ·

From somewhere deep inside, Tom found an extra burst of speed. Adrenaline pumped through his weakening limbs, building his strength and bringing renewed hope. The fence was only ten feet away. *I'm gonna make it,* he thought, leaping for the fence. He gripped about halfway up and frantically began climbing for the top and the safety of the woods on the far side.

And then the spider struck.

The King Spider had also reached the fence and, in one cruel efficient swing of its claws, reached up and slashed across the back of Tom's ankles, severing his Achilles tendons. Blood poured out of the gaping wounds, drenching the spider beneath. The hairy ghoul paused for a moment to lap up the warm fluid.

The pain was excruciating, blanketing Tom in a cloud of agony. Just as quickly, it was gone. His legs went completely numb, which was a blessing in disguise, as it spared him the feel of the spider's slimy tongue.

He tried to climb on, aware of the severity of his wounds. Tom's will to survive was so great, he continued to pull upward using only the strength in his arms. He almost made it, struggling clumsily up to the top rail. The King Spider, sensing he just might get away, stopped its feeding and jumped up at its prey. For all its bulk and awkwardness, the spider was powerful. It leapt high onto Tom's back, wrapping all eight of its legs around his midsection.

Tom's arms were young and strong, but not strong enough. His weight, plus the spider's considerable bulk, combined to sap his last remaining strength. Gravity took care of the rest as he lost his grip, dropping heavily to the ground.

* * *

David watched helplessly, hoping Tom would fall on his back and crush the bloated spider, but it wasn't to be. Instead, he slammed hard onto the semifrozen dirt. Even from a distance, David heard the sickening snapping of Tom's ribs and had to cover his ears to drown out Tom's screams.

The King Spider quickly pounced once more. Tom had somehow managed to regain his feet, only to topple again under its savage attack. David watched in horror as the monster straddled Tom's chest and began clawing and slashing.

Nobody deserved to die that way . . . *nobody*. Bolting from his hiding spot, David ran at breakneck speed toward the unguarded back of the predator. As he ran into range, he pulled out his gun and began to shoot. The first shot went wide; the second just barely skimmed the spider's bulging head. David lowered his sights and fired again. The bullet flew low this time and struck Tom in the middle of his chest. Tom had to already be dead, but David still felt a sickening guilt.

Oh God. I shot him, David chided himself, still advancing on the spider, his anger soaring with each step.

The victorious beast never even noticed the gunfire, so great was its hunger. It was now slitting open Tom's throat and greedily drinking the warm liquid. David didn't bother wasting more shots while running. He waited until he was right behind the spider and pressed the revolver into the spongy back of its grotesque, bloated head.

Only then did the spider realize it had company. Its many eyes swiveled round to take in the young man with the crazed look on his sweaty face. As it turned, David rammed the gun into its bloody mouth. "Payback's a bitch, motherfucker," he screamed, pulling the trigger.

The explosion knocked him off his feet. The bullet had smashed its way down the King Spider's throat, somehow causing it to explode. It was as if the beast had swallowed a grenade, rather than a small-caliber bullet. There was nothing left on the ground to identify the once-massive animal.

Seconds later, tiny fragments started raining down, and David had to shield his face from the downpour of sticky flesh.

The most incredible thing happened next. All the tiny pieces started moving. In fact, they were sprouting tiny legs, the fleshy chunks turning into little spiders. David watched closely for signs of attack, but none of the hundreds of new spiders had the slightest interest in him. Almost as if by silent command, the tiny army skittered through the holes in the fence and disappeared into the darkness of the woods beyond.

David lit a cigarette and shakily inhaled the calming nicotine.

"Fucking weird, man."

David could not find any trace of the giant spider. Even its blood appeared to have been used in the bizarre transformation. That left David alone in the dump with . . .

Rodney!

He'd been so preoccupied with avenging Tom's death, he'd forgotten about the evil scarecrow. Unfortunately, Rodney hadn't forgotten about him. When David turned from the fence, Rodney was standing ten feet away, his one remaining arm perched defiantly on his right hip.

"Nice work, Davey . . . impressive. My multilegged buddy made quite a bang, didn't he? Blew up *real* good."

"Hopefully not half as 'good' as you do," David said, rising to his feet and pointing the blood and saliva-stained gun at the scarecrow's heart. He pulled the sticky trigger twice, both bullets finding their mark perfectly. Two small holes appeared on the upper-left-hand pocket of Rodney's coveralls.

This time there was no explosion. The bullets passed harmlessly through Rodney's thick straw chest and exited out his back, causing little or no damage.

"Come now, Davey. Did you really think it was going to be *that* easy? Just show up, pop off a few shots, then head on home? How naive can you be?"

David could feel his newfound courage seep away. Part of him wanted to give up and let Rodney put an end to his miserable existence. He was so sick of running scared, of always looking over his shoulder. He'd seen far too much pain and suffering, far too much death. First his friend Peter, then all the Ripper killings, and now poor Tom. He just wanted it all to end.

He glanced over at what was left of Tom. It made his stomach turn a little, but part of him was actually envious. Tom had died violently, but at least his suffering was over.

"I won't let you do that to me, Rodney," said David, pointing at Tom's corpse.

"You don't have much choice, Davey. I'll tear you apart any old way I want."

"No, Rodney, you won't," David whispered, raising the revolver to his own head and pulling the trigger.

Click . . . Click . . . Click . . .

Nothing. The damn gun was empty. A quick mental recount of his shots confirmed he'd indeed fired all six bullets.

Dismay welled up inside David. He couldn't even commit suicide right. More out of frustration than anger, David drew back and hurled the gun at the hulking scarecrow. Rodney ducked it easily and it crashed harmlessly into a pile of garbage bags.

"Playtime is over?" Rodney growled. "Time to die, David."

David slumped down onto his knees as Rodney moved in for the kill. He was too damn tired to fight anymore. Closing his eyes, he waited for death. He hoped, Rodney would finish him quickly, without too much pain. He'd suffered enough.

Half a minute passed and nothing happened. What was Rodney waiting for? David opened his eyes and gasped when he saw Rodney almost on top of him. He cowered back against the fence, more out of instinct than actual fear.

Rodney charged forward, but again halted his attack. His face was a cauldron of hatred, but David could sense something else there too. Could it be . . . *fear*? He followed Rodney's gaze and realized the massive scarecrow wasn't looking at his eyes, but lower, concentrating on his mouth. Then it dawned on him. It wasn't his mouth Rodney was looking at. It was his cigarette.

Fire, David thought. *Rodney is made of straw and he's afraid of fire.*

David couldn't help but laugh. The powerful demon above him was terrified of a little cigarette. "If you don't like my cigarette, Rodney," David said, reaching into his pocket, "you're really gonna be impressed with this." He flicked on his lighter and held it toward Rodney's exposed chest.

Retreating backward a few more feet, the beast screamed like a frightened child. Fear made him stay away, but hunger kept him close. Raw terror and confusion registered on his face.

Perhaps David didn't need to die tonight after all. With renewed hope, he leapt to his feet. By the time David cranked up the flame to its highest setting, Rodney was shaking. To him, the lighter probably looked like a flamethrower. The scarecrow backed up another few steps, not sure what to do.

"How do *you* like being scared, Rodney?" David said, stepping boldly forward. "You're shaking, Rodney. Are you cold? Hold still, and maybe I can warm you up a tad."

Realizing it was better to go hungry than fry, Rodney turned tail and fled. He was an awkward runner, but fear aided him along. David took up the chase, seeing Rodney nervously checking over his shoulder as he ran for the exit gate leading to Tamarac Street. All of a sudden, he disappeared.

David was astonished until he remembered the garbage pits. Rodney must have fallen into one of them. Sure enough, when he jogged to the spot where Rodney had vanished, there he was, about fourteen feet belowground.

Rodney was cursing loudly and clawing frantically at the sides of the deep pit, desperate to climb out. When he noticed David peering down, he tried even harder, but it was no use. The pit was too deep, with no handholds. Having only one arm, no matter how strong, Rodney wasn't going anywhere. He stalked around and around like a caged animal, eventually resigning himself to the fact he was trapped.

Fearfully, he gazed up at David, unsure of what would happen next.

David simply grinned at the scarecrow, lit another cigarette, and walked away without saying a word. He was going to make Rodney pay for all the misery he'd caused.

Rodney's fear increased tenfold with each passing minute. He could hear things being rattled around, but from the bottom of the pit he couldn't see anything at all. His evil mind conjured up all sorts of things David might be planning.

He had to find a way to get out of here, but how? The dirt sides of the pit crumbled when he clawed at them. A thought suddenly hit him, something he'd forgotten about. A small ray of hope crept into his black heart. He cupped his hand to his mouth and let out a high-pitched noise that sounded like something between a whistle and a scream. Smiling, Rodney sat down on the dirt floor and waited.

David appeared back at the rim of the pit, carrying two large, rusty buckets. He sat them on the ground beside the edge of the hole. "No need to whistle Rodney, I'm right here. You didn't think I'd gone off and left you, did ya?"

Rodney didn't reply. He just sat there with a smug look about him that David found disturbing. David looked around, but the dump was silent and deserted.

"Anyway, pal, all that running must have tuckered you out, so I decided to get you a nice cool drink." David picked up one of the rusty buckets and dumped it into the pit. Rodney wasn't alert enough to dodge out of the way, and was drenched in the black, slimy liquid.

Rodney, a little puzzled, looked questioningly up toward David.

"Oil and gasoline," David said, his smile changing to a leer. "Got some more for you too." He threw the second bucket.

Rodney moved faster this time and avoided the majority of the falling fuels. The remainder splashed on the pit floor, washing over his boots. The scarecrow looked desperate now, his eyes wide and savage. He began whistling again in that same high-pitched frequency that reverberated through the still night air.

Why is he doing that? David wondered. *Nobody's here to help him . . . is there?*

David heard a small noise, a scratchy sound coming from behind him. He spun around just in time to see something fly off the ground toward his face. Instinctively, he caught hold of the long object, stopping its forward progress inches from his face.

It was Rodney's severed left arm.

The same arm Rodney had torn off to drag David out of the pipe in his father's field nine years ago. It was still around and obviously very much alive. Its claws snapped inches shy of David's widening eyes.

"Get him, boy," Rodney shouted with glee at the arrival of his "pet." "Claw the little bastard's eyes out." The scarecrow had whistled and his disembodied arm had obediently answered.

How can it push without having anything on the ground for leverage?

But it *was* pushing, slowly inching its way forward, regardless of how much effort David used to try and hold it at bay. From this close, he could clearly see how long and razor sharp its nails were. He knew the powerful limb would soon be close enough to rip his face off. He had to do something, quick.

He couldn't overpower the possessed arm, so he decided to use its own brute strength against it. He pulled instead of pushed, ducking his head down at the same time. It worked. Rodney's "pet" flew over his head, almost snagging his hair, and dropped behind him into the pit beside its master.

That had been close—too close. David's heart was hammering inside his chest again. He lit a fresh cigarette to help calm his nerves. He promised to give up his nasty habit if he made it through this hair-raising night.

When he'd sufficiently calmed down, he peered down at the trapped, oil-stained scarecrow. It didn't look scary anymore. Gone was the ferocious monster of his nightmares. Gone was Rodney's evil grin. He looked more like a little boy who'd just been caught with his fingers in the cookie jar.

"Please, Davey," Rodney begged, realizing all other options were gone. "Don't hurt me. I never intended to kill you. I was just going to scare you a bit."

"Sure you were, Rodney. You sent your little pet to try take my head off, but that was just to scare me, right? Just for fun."

"That's right, Davey. I was only fooling around. I wouldn't have really let it hurt you. Like last time in that drainage pipe, remember? Who do you think carried you home that night and tucked you safely into your bed? It was me . . . your old buddy Rodney."

"Save it—I'm finished listening to your bull. I do remember that awful night in my father's field. I remember it well. I've had nightmares about it for years. Do you remember how you told me there was more than one way for a hunter to catch a rabbit? Well, now I'm the hunter, you're the rabbit, and I'm going to smoke you out."

"*Smoke?*" Rodney asked, somewhat puzzled. "That won't bother me. Smoke won't bother me at all."

"Oh yeah?" David cruelly grinned, tossing his glowing cigarette end over end into the garbage pit. "Then smoke *this*, you son of a bitch."

"*Nooooooooooo,*" Rodney screamed, instinctively moving to catch the falling cigarette. If he could have caught it, he might have been able to snuff it out, and would have been all right. In the end, he just couldn't bring himself to let the cigarette touch him, and he pulled his hand away.

The cigarette landed on the floor of the pit in a shallow pool of dirty fuel. The oil and gas mixture immediately burst into flames, and the fire spread quickly. Rodney tried to get out of the way, but there was nowhere to run. The blazing oil soon found his legs, and within seconds Rodney was an inferno. His screams of agony echoed throughout the dump and probably well into the neighboring area. A tower of flames shot out of the garbage pit, causing David to back up. The intensity of the heat was incredible. Rodney didn't stand a chance. Slowly his screams gurgled off.

David sat down and watched until the fire began to die. It didn't take long—straw burns quickly. The small pool of oil might burn for a while, but all traces of Rodney were now gone. Not even his severed arm had escaped the wrath of the blaze.

David felt no sense of victory. More than anything, he felt drained. Empty. Tom was dead, the King Spider was dead, Rodney the Scarecrow was dead, and he was alone. He let out a deep sigh and rose to his feet. He knew he should get away from here. The cops must surely be on their way, what with the fire, the gunshots, and all the screaming. Chief Walker already suspected him of being the Ripper Killer; all he needed was to get caught red-handed out here.

David turned his back on the dump and headed toward Tamarac Street. He was almost to the street when he heard a noise behind him. *Tom?* He'd never actually checked to see if he was dead. Maybe somehow he'd survived the spider's attack. David spun around in hopeful anticipation.

It wasn't Tom.

The creature stood tall in all its hideous glory, flesh literally dripping from its rotting frame. Despite the creature's disgusting condition, it looked more powerful than ever. From head to toe, it was dressed in black leather. Black shirt, black pants, black biker boots, with a silver-studded, black, full-length overcoat draped over its massive, rotting shoulders. Its crimson eyes flared, contrasting sharply with the dark outfit. A steely grimace formed on its ruined face. It looked pissed off.

David hadn't thought the creature was here, believing it had sent the spider and the scarecrow to do its dirty work tonight. Obviously, he'd been wrong. He stared into the creature's eyes and found he was unable to look away, its riveting eyes holding him transfixed. David thought he could feel heat radiating off of its hateful stare.

"How *dare* you murder my servants," it said. "I had no intention of letting Rodney kill you, fool. It was Tommy I wanted, not you. I could have forgiven you killing the spider, but not Rodney. I still needed him. You'll pay for the damage you've done, boy."

David trembled like a leaf in a hurricane as the creature continued its tirade. Its piercing voice seared into his tender nerves like a white-hot poker. He watched as the creature took a step closer and started removing something from the folds in its overcoat.

"No more games, Davey. It's time you paid for your meddling."

The creature took another step, and David could see what it held in its hand. It was the razor-sharp filleting knife used in the recent killings.

Words could not describing the fear David felt. He'd seen firsthand what the creature could do with that knife. It could keep him alive for hours suffering immeasurably. He wanted none of that. Before the creature took its third step toward him, David forced his limbs to move and was soon running as if the Devil himself gave chase.

The creature watched as David turned and ran. It started to grin, extremely happy with tonight's outcome. It didn't give a damn that David had killed the King Spider and Rodney. After tonight they would have been useless anyway. It had only pretended to be furious, to scare him into running. David didn't know it yet, but he was already running toward the next step in the creature's plan.

The creature stifled a yawn behind its massive fist. It was getting sleepy. The last few weeks had really taxed its powers, and soon it would have to lay low and rest again.

"But not yet. There's still a few things to take care of. . . ."

It walked back to the dump to survey the area. The creature wanted to make sure no traces of the spider or scarecrow remained for the cops to find. The only things it wanted the cops to see were the gun David had thrown away with his fingerprints all over it and Tom's dead body. It was remarkable how the spider's claw marks would look to the police—exactly like the knife marks left by the Ripper Killer on previous victims. It was the creature's guess that after tonight, David would have a lot of questions to answer.

The creature turned to leave, but then remembered it had always cut the victims' ears off and taken them away. It bent down and used the filleting knife to quickly remove Tom's ears. It casually tossed them into its gaping mouth, swallowing them whole.

Everything was working out exactly as it had planned, not that the creature had ever doubted otherwise. It started heading for Tamarac Street. In the distance, police sirens were beginning to wail as the cops raced toward the dump. The creature intended on being long gone by the time they arrived. David had already been through a lot for one night, but unfortunately, the creature wasn't finished with him quite yet.

CHAPTER TWENTY-THREE

Chief Walker relentlessly paced the floor of his cramped office like a caged animal futilely searching for a way out. Conflicting emotions flashed through his mind and across his unshaven face. He felt nervous, angry, excited, and pissed off all at the same time, shifting constantly between moods. Nervousness and anger tormented him because he had learned that the killer had struck yet again. Excitement sent adrenaline pumping through his body, because this time his men had a witness to the crime and had also located another piece of evidence from the scene. The pissed-off sensations stemmed from the fact the guys in forensics seemed to be taking an eternity to get the results back to him.

Dennis glanced at the clock on his office wall and his watch to see what time it was. Both showed it was 11:27 P.M.

"What the hell is taking so long?"

Dennis forced himself to sit down and try to relax. He was still positive that smart-ass kid David Winter was his man, a feeling he'd had ever since questioning him. Unfortunately, gut feelings don't win convictions. So far, the Chief's list of hard evidence was painfully inadequate. Out of his top left drawer, he removed the case file and quickly scanned its contents. From start to finish, their evidence was sparse.

They had an untraced phone call to the mayor's office on the morning of the first murder. The secretary who answered the call had said the caller was male and sounded emotionally unstable. She had been unable to obtain a name from the caller before he'd hung up.

They also recovered an important piece of evidence from the murder site of the seventh victim, Susie Hobbs. It was a baseball cap believed to have been worn by the killer. Inside the cap, the initials DW had been etched into the sweat-stained band.

A search had been initiated to question all possible male subjects in Dunnville having those initials. Out of the residents interviewed, only one subject was considered a possible suspect, a nineteen-year-old punk by the name of David Winter. Winter had appeared nervous and uncooperative during routine questioning and had slipped up by revealing his knowledge of the baseball cap displaying his initials. Obviously, the suspect knew more than he was telling. No prints had been found on the cap, but Winter's fingerprints had been obtained from a water glass during questioning and were now on file.

A tape recording had also been used during the questioning session and subsequently played to the mayor's secretary. She believed that the voice on the tape and the voice of the person who had called the morning before the mayor's death were similar and could possibly be the same person. None of this information would stand up in court, since the interview was recorded without the suspect's knowledge or consent.

Dennis closed the file and sat back in his chair, more frustrated than ever. Everything they had pointed toward David Winter's being the killer, but none of it was enough to warrant his arrest. The Crown attorney would not proceed based on such inconclusive evidence.

But tonight, things might be different. Tonight, they had a witness.

Her name was Edith Krantz, a seventy-one-year-old widow who lived at 48 Tamarac Street, just two houses down from the entrance to the town dump. She hadn't actually witnessed the murder, but had information that might prove valuable.

Apparently Mrs. Krantz had been sitting in her favorite

chair on her front porch a little after ten o'clock in the evening. She'd overheard two people arguing and had peered out of her front door to get a better look. She had seen two young men standing near the entrance to the dump. She was sure the young men had spotted her before hurriedly walking down the gravel lane into the dump.

Fifteen minutes had passed before Mrs. Krantz heard screaming, followed by the crisp, unmistakable explosions of gunfire, and she had later observed a raging fire flaring over the treetops. Minutes after that, one of the young men she'd spotted earlier came running out of the dump. Mrs. Krantz could clearly see splashes of blood on the young man and said he looked terrified. The other man never emerged. It had been then that Mrs. Krantz had called the police. Two patrol cars had responded immediately.

The first patrol car arrived at the town dump at 10:55 P.M. and found everything quiet. A small oil fire flickered in one of the deep garbage pits, but the constable had considered it harmless and hadn't contacted the volunteer fire department.

The mutilated corpse of a young man named Thomas James Baker—according to information found in the deceased's wallet—was discovered near the back fence of the property. The multiple injuries to the victim's body were consistent with the injuries incurred by the previous victims. And as in each earlier case, the young man's ears were also missing. There had been little doubt: the Ripper had struck again.

For some reason the killer, in addition to his normal method of mutilation, had also used a gun. A small-caliber bullet wound had been located in the victim's chest. A search of the area had turned up a Smith & Wesson revolver, which was immediately sent to forensics for testing. If their luck held, the gun would yield fingerprints.

Chief Walker reopened the case file and thumbed through it to the set of prints they had from David Winter. Silently, he prayed the prints on the Smith & Wesson—if in fact there were any—would be a match. It would give the chief great pleasure to throw that young punk into the slammer and toss away the key. Maybe then he'd be able to sleep at night again.

"What's taking those forensic guys so long?"

His patience was at an end. He grabbed the phone, ready to chew somebody a new asshole, but before he could make the call, Constable Barnes burst through the door, out of breath and wiggling a sheet of paper in front of him.

"I got it, Chief . . . the forensics report on the gun." Barnes paused to catch his breath, but the look he received from his boss convinced him to go on. There would be time to breathe later. "The prints were good ones, Chief, clear as a bell. They match Winter's prints from the water glass. He's our boy, Chief. We got him!"

"We haven't caught the little psycho yet. Radio every available man . . . Christmas Eve be damned. I want a sweep made of the town starting from the dump out. Find out from Mrs. Krantz which way she saw Winter running. Get a few men over to his parents' house too. Move, Barnes . . . *move!*"

Barnes took off like a shotgun blast, and the Dunnville Police Department sparked to life. Chief Walker also sprang into action. Grabbing his gun and coat, he quickly followed Barnes to the door.

"You're smart, Winter," Dennis whispered as he threw on his coat. "But like every other madman who thinks he's above the law . . . you're just not smart enough."

Dennis hit the lights and raced out of his office to rally his men. Within minutes they were assembled and ready. David didn't know it yet, but both the police department and the creature were closing in on him. The race to find him first was on.

CHAPTER TWENTY-FOUR

David ran until his gut felt like bursting open, and then he ran some more. Fear pushed him beyond his normal limits, into the adrenaline-aided realm of the truly panic-stricken. His only concrete thought was to make it home. The creature could kill him there just as easily as anywhere, but for some reason, dying at home had a better feel to it.

Police sirens screaming down Tamarac Street caused him to take cover behind a parked car. He was tempted to jump out and flag the cruiser down, but he knew they would never believe his account of what had happened. The patrol car screamed past without slowing. As soon as it disappeared from view, David was back up and running.

David made the corner onto Forrest Street, his insides cramping up. Twice more he had to hide from the screaming red police beacons as he headed toward Pine Street. All hell must be breaking out back at the dump, and he secretly prayed the cops had found the creature and disposed of it. That was just a pipe dream, though, and he knew it. The police would *never* find the creature, much less kill it. He'd been a fool to think he could triumph over the monster, and now Tom was dead because of his stupidity.

About three-quarters of the way down Forrest Street, a shadowy figure stepped off the sidewalk right in front of him. His heart leapt from surprise, and they crashed together heavily, sending both of them to the ground. When

David looked up, he was shocked to see whom he'd run into. Beside him was Johnny Page, the only other surviving member of the Knights of the Round Room.

"*Johnny?* What are you doing here?"

Johnny looked over, glassy-eyed. "I've been looking for you, actually. I know the creature's after you and I'm here to help."

"I don't get it, Johnny. I thought you didn't believe in the creature. The last time I tried to talk to you about it, you told me to fuck off. What changed?"

"I'm sorry, David. I had this awful dream that you and Tom were in trouble, and I could clearly see the creature in the dream. A whole pile of memories flooded back from when we were kids, and I just knew my dream was real and I had to try and help."

It sounded good to David, but didn't feel right. Johnny had avoided him for years—then one dream and he's running to the rescue? Something just didn't click.

"We have to hide," Johnny said. "Follow me, I know just the place."

He dashed off without waiting for David to object. David wasn't sure what he should do. His head was telling him to forget Johnny and continue home, but his heart was saying, remain with his friend. After all, Johnny was the only person left who knew about the creature and what it was capable of. His heart won the battle, and he ran to catch up to his old friend.

Johnny hurried down Forrest Street to where it crossed Cedar. This was the corner where the old Wabasso building stood, run-down and abandoned since shortly after the bloody fiasco involving Old Man Harrison. For years the neighboring residents had been trying to get it knocked down, but still it stood, dilapidated and sinister.

Johnny headed off the road and waited for David in the factory's weed-infested parking lot. "Hurry, we can hide in here."

"I don't know," said David. "This place is condemned. It's not safe in there."

"You think it's safer to stand here and wait for the creature to rip your lungs out?"

"No. It's just I'd rather run home, that's all. I'm already—"

"There's no time for that . . . look!"

David spun around to follow Johnny's finger. The creature
was practically flying down Forrest Street, running, but at
an inhumanly fast pace. Its long black overcoat billowed out
like a gigantic bat. It was still a long way off, but Johnny was
right. There was no way he'd make it all the way back to
his parents' house. The creature would catch him within a
block.

"Come on, David. I don't think it's spotted us yet." He led
David around the side of the building out of the creature's
sight. David helped him tug off some boards blocking a first-
floor window, the glass long since gone.

"You first," Johnny said. "I'll be right behind you."

David half climbed and was half pushed through the opening. He received two sore knees and a sliver in the hand for his
effort, clumsily sprawling onto the dusty wooden floorboards
three feet below. He expected to see Johnny clambering in behind him. Thirty seconds passed, and Johnny still hadn't
climbed through the window. David stuck his head back outside to see what was taking him so long.

"Hurry up, man, what's taking . . ." But Johnny wasn't there
anymore. Puzzled, David leaned farther out and looked both
ways. He choked back a scream when he saw Johnny standing
back out on Forrest Street. Beside him stood the creature.

David almost yelled for Johnny to run, but noticed that
Johnny didn't look scared. In fact, he looked incredibly
pleased at the sight of the creature, smiling with that same
glassy-eyed, faraway look he'd shown earlier.

What's he doing?

The creature raised its massive taloned right hand, and
David was sure Johnny was done for. Those claws would rip
him to pieces. Instead, the creature patted Johnny tenderly
on the back, as if they were long-lost pals.

David's confusion multiplied tenfold as Johnny spun

around and pointed his finger toward the building. The creature turned too and smiled as it saw David leaning out of the window.

The son of a bitch sold me out! Why?

The monster patted Johnny lovingly on top of his head and handed him the long, thin filleting knife. Johnny tucked the razor-sharp weapon into his jacket without even looking at it. The creature bent down and whispered something into Johnny's ear and gently nudged him away. Johnny immediately turned and walked off into the darkness.

David couldn't believe what was happening. His last friend in the world had just given his hiding spot away and then walked off without even looking back.

The creature was halfway across the weedy parking lot before a nearby police car's siren snapped David back to reality. Running home was no longer an option, so he retreated into the shadows of the Wabasso building as quickly and quietly as possible. He had to find a hiding spot . . . fast.

The interior of the abandoned textile mill wasn't as dark as David had imagined it would be. Light shone freely in through the window he'd just entered and also filtered in through the hundreds of cracks in the boarded-up windows. In the filtered light, he could see that the large room he stood in was completely empty. The owners of the company must have hauled all the machinery and workstations away when they closed the factory. On the right-hand side of the room, he spotted a staircase heading up to the second floor. He bolted for the stairs and took them two at a time. The ancient wooden stairs, riddled from decades of neglect and termites, groaned painfully under his weight, but held.

The second floor, much to his relief, was jammed full of old junk. Everything from large machines and huge piles of old rotted linen to mountains of liquor bottles covered the floor. It must have been too much of a bother for the owners to haul this stuff out. Either that, or they couldn't get it down the stairwells. David didn't really care; he was just happy to have someplace to hide.

Downstairs, he could hear the creature smashing its way into the factory.

Hide, man. Hurry!

The floorboards sagged with every step, but David made it across to the far side of the factory. Beside him, a pile of old mildewed towels held together by a greasy thread of twine leaned against what looked like an industrial clothes-drying machine. The towels almost covered up the opening to the dryer, but he managed to cram his skinny body into the opening and pulled the bundle of stinking towels over a foot to completely conceal the opening. The inside of the dryer was actually quite large, but extremely uncomfortable. The metal ribs inside stuck painfully into his back and something was digging into his legs. It was also dusty. David barely contained the urge to sneeze, and willed himself to ignore the dust and pain. One tiny noise might be all it would take to give him away.

As quiet as he tried to stay, he still heard little noises. It was then he realized he wasn't alone in the dryer. He wasn't the one making the sounds. He almost screamed when he reached under his legs and felt his hand touch the grimy fur of something big. It was a large rat.

Luckily for him, he'd crushed the animal when he'd flopped into its home. The noises he'd heard were from its dying convulsions. Carefully, he slid the rodent out from under him. It was dead, silenced by a broken neck. David wanted to get rid of it, but couldn't risk having the creature spot him. He didn't know where the creature was, but it was safer for him to stay hidden, rat or no rat.

The minutes stretched into hours as he waited inside the dryer. The smell of rotting towels was overpowering, and the dead rat didn't help, either. Outside he could hear what seemed like dozens of police cars zooming by, presumably going to or returning from the town dump. Inside the factory, he couldn't hear anything. He wasn't even sure if the creature had ventured up onto the second floor or not. He hadn't heard the groaning of the stairs or the creaking of floorboards.

Where is it? he wondered. *Maybe the police cars whizzing around scared it off?*

Fifteen more painful minutes trickled by before David decided to vacate his hiding spot. He couldn't bear to wait another minute. The nauseous smell coming from the dead rat was starting to overtake the disgusting odor of the towels. David shoved the towels away from the doorway and flung the rat out as soon as he had a big enough opening. Dusty, stale air blew in, and David had never smelled anything so sweet.

Peering out of the dryer door, he scanned the second floor. The creature was nowhere in sight. Without waiting another second, he unfolded his cramped body out of his hiding spot. Once clear, he stretched his aching back and legs.

What an awful hiding place, David thought, *but at least the creature's gone.*

"I wouldn't be so sure of that, Davey, my boy," the creature's low, gravelly voice spoke from close behind.

David spun around to find the creature sitting cross-legged on top of the dryer he'd been hiding in. *How did it come up the stairs, cross the floor, and climb onto the dryer without making a sound? I didn't hear a thing.*

"Like this, Davey" the creature smiled, having read David's mind again. It spread its arms out and tossed its head back. A small gap appeared under the creature's legs, between it and the top of the dryer. The creature rose a few inches higher and then levitated slowly forward, toward him. It unfolded its long, powerful legs and silently lowered itself back down to a standing position on the floor.

David had seen that levitating trick before, with Rodney on the night the scarecrow had chased him through his father's muddy fields. No wonder the creature hadn't made the floorboards creak—it hadn't touched any of them.

The creature bent down and picked up the dead rat and bit its head off. The rest of the smelly rodent soon followed, until all that remained was its long curly tail. The creature threw that part away.

"Mustn't get *too* full. I'd better save room for the main course—right, Davey?"

When the creature started walking toward him, it left little to the imagination as to what the main course was going to be. David turned and fled, his heart threatening to give out at any moment, but it was the floor that gave out first.

He'd started to run for the staircase on the far side of the room, when the old rotted floorboards caved in. There hadn't been any warning sign it was about to let go. One second it was there, the next . . . nothing but air.

The drop to the first floor happened in slow motion. It seemed to take an eternity to fall the fifteen feet to the dusty floor below, but when David did hit bottom, he hit hard. Mind-numbing pain flared up his body as his legs jammed unbent on the wooden floor. His legs almost drove up through his hip bones, and probably would have, if his left knee hadn't snapped like a twig. The pain was unbearable. His leg felt as if it had received a blast from a flamethrower. He lay in a heap on the dusty floor for an unknown length of time, unable to do anything but grimace in pain. In his agony, he picked up the sound of someone approaching. His icy fear of the creature cooled some of the pain in his leg as he struggled to get to his feet. If he was about to die, he didn't plan on doing it lying down. He could at least go out with a struggle—maybe go for the creature's eyes.

Near the doorway, he spotted an old, rusty sledgehammer forgotten by the wrecking crews. Every painstaking move toward the hammer was grueling, each step as if he were running a marathon. The slightest movement caused the flamethrower to ignite on his ruined knee again. Two feet from the rusty hammer, he nearly passed out. He could feel the world slipping away, so he bit down hard on his tongue. The fresh pain washed over him like a cool bucket of water, clearing his clouding mind and keeping him awake.

After what seemed like forever, he finally held the heavy weapon in his sweaty hands, positioning himself at the edge of the doorway. The creature would enter the room through this doorway, and when it did, David was going to knock its bloody head off.

Footsteps confidently approached the doorway, the creature undoubtedly sure he was helpless. *Come on, you bastard*, he thought with a crazed grin on his face. *I'll show you how helpless I am.*

The footsteps came to the door and David swung the hammer as hard as he could. It connected solidly in the creature's face, teeth and blood flying everywhere. The loud thump of its body hitting the floor caused David to start laughing. Instead of trying to get away, he swung the hammer again and again . . . and again.

He didn't stop until he heard the creature's skull crack open and he'd spattered its gray matter all over the dusty room. He was covered in blood and brains from head to toe, and his knee screamed from all the movement, but still, he felt good inside. He'd killed the bastard. He'd actually won.

It was then David noticed the police hat.

His first blow had knocked it off the constable's head as he was entering the room. David stared wide-eyed at the corpse at his feet, seeing it now for the very first time. The face was completely gone, along with most of his head, but the badge on his chest clearly identified the body as Constable Davis.

"How . . . ? Where did he . . . ? I didn't know . . ." David mumbled as his legs gave out. He didn't feel the pain as his broken knee smashed into the floor. He couldn't do anything but look into the ruined face of the police officer he had just murdered.

The creature popped his head down through the hole in the second floor through which David had fallen. It had never followed him downstairs, having known the policeman had already entered the building. Constable Davis had been parked outside when David's crashing fall had brought him running to investigate.

"Well, Davey boy, you've sure done it now." the beast gloated. "They're really gonna nail your ass now, my boy. Really nail it hard."

David looked up through uncaring eyes. "Would you please go away?"

"Sure, Davey. I have to get out of here anyway. I have a feeling a few friends of ol' pasty face will be showing up soon."

The creature pulled its rotted head out of view but almost immediately looked back down. "Oh, I almost forgot to tell you, Davey. It's just after midnight. Merry Christmas, my boy. Have a happy New Year too. See ya."

Twenty minutes later, Constable Davis's abandoned cruiser led the rest of the police to David. He was sitting in the same spot, his hands still tightly clutching the blood- and brain-encrusted sledgehammer.

David was off in another world—a world that was fair and made sense. He didn't hear the police as they closed in on him with their guns cautiously drawn. If he *had* heard, and had had any idea of what horrors the future still held for him, he would have looked into the nearest policemen's eyes and begged him to pull the trigger.

ANOTHER INTERLUDE: A FEW MORE WORDS OF WISDOM

Again, time rolled on. Time waits for nobody. Especially nineteen-year-old accused murderers dangerously close to the edge of insanity. And I was close, my friend, real close to that edge. One more little push from the creature that night in the Wabasso building, and my mind would have taken a nosedive off the cliff. I couldn't let myself fall. Lord knows I wanted to, but some stubborn part of me held tight, refusing to let the creature destroy me.

By the time I resurfaced into that wonderful land of coherent thoughts, my murder trial was well under way. To make a long story short . . . it wasn't even close. They had me pegged for guilty long before I set foot into the courtroom. Not that I blame them—I would have done the same thing.

My lawyer didn't really even try to get me off. He probably thought I was guilty too. I don't hold it against him, either. The best damn lawyer in the world wouldn't have been able to argue against all the evidence the prosecution presented. They had eleven dead bodies and one bloodied suspect who had been captured at the scene with the twelfth. I had been caught with the brain-smeared sledgehammer still clasped in my hand, for God's sake. Apparently it had taken three police officers to pry it from my fingers. They had a gun with my fingerprints on it that matched a bullet removed from Tom's body. They also had the baseball cap with my initials, along with the testimonies of the mayor's secretary, the chief of police, and the old lady that lived by the dump.

All my poor lawyer had to counter with was the fact the murder weapon used in the first eleven murders, the filleting knife, had never been found. Not to mention the excellent testimony of myself—an incoherent, babbling fool who kept slipping in and out of la-la land.

What did it all add up to? I was fucked, that's what.

Like I said before, I didn't hold it against anyone. In many ways, I was grateful. That might sound weird, but it's true. My head was pretty spun out for a while, and prison was the perfect place for me to pull myself together. I'd have a long time to accomplish this, seeing as I'd been sentenced to twelve life sentences.

The prison facility was in Toronto. The Toronto Maximum Security Penitentiary, to be exact. Inside, most people thought it was Hell in a concrete and steel basket, but to tell you the honest truth, I kind of liked it there.

For the first time in my life, I actually felt like I belonged. In prison, nobody looked down on me. In fact, it was the opposite. My reputation as the Ripper Killer preceded me, and almost everyone showed immediate respect. I even tried to play the tough guy for a while, but found too many tougher screwballs and didn't see much merit in that approach. I decided to just lay low, and everyone simply left me alone . . . which was exactly how I wanted it.

From there, the years seemed to fly by. The eighties ended, and then all too quickly, the nineties were gone too. I didn't really care. One day was the same as the next. The year didn't really matter.

Then one night it just hit me. I realized I was happy. Seriously, I really was. I don't recall missing the outside world at all. The only things out there were my parents, and they had virtually abandoned me. When I heard they died in an automobile accident in 1998, I wept, but only for a short time. I hardly knew them by then.

After that I tried to ignore the outside world. For me, nothing but bad memories lay outside my prison walls. One thing still nagged at me, though. It was Johnny. No matter how much I tried, I was unable to eradicate him from my tormented mind. Why had he sold me out to the creature that night? It just didn't make sense. And worse, why didn't the creature kill Johnny when it had him that close? Something about that night still haunted me: I had an uneasy feeling that Johnny and the creature were in on my demise. Partners in crime, so to speak.

That was why I kept such a close eye on Johnny's life while I was in prison. I wanted to see what else I could find out about him and the creature. It was simple to do this by just picking up the newspapers, as Johnny was constantly in the public eye. Since my incarceration I had compiled a scrapbook on his life, adding to it whenever I found something in the papers. His bio was interesting and impressive.

Johnny graduated top of his college class in 1991. He immediately jumped into the computer-programming industry and rode the newly developing electronic highway for all it was worth. Within four years his company, Electronic Futures, hit the Fortune 500. Johnny made millions and was set for life.

A multimillionaire at age twenty-eight, Johnny cashed out and stormed onto the political scene. With his business connections, not to mention his abundance of disposable cash, he quickly kissed babies and asses up the ladder until he'd become one of the youngest members of Parliament in Canadian history. The newspapers, magazines, and television all over North America couldn't get enough of him. It was clear, even to a bum like me, Johnny was headed for greatness.

He shocked the political world in 2003 by completely dissolving his affiliation with the Liberals and announcing he would be starting his own independent party. Critics laughed at his arrogance and mocked him for trying the impossible, but they wouldn't be laughing long.

Johnny named his new political group the Evolutionary Party, and his slogan, "It's time for a change," was plastered everywhere. Evolution . . . Time for a change. Get it? Well the Canadian public sure did. His new party caught on like wildfire, with Johnny's riveting speeches turning thousands of voters' heads away from the established parties.

Public discontent with the current government and the fact that Johnny led by 60 percent in the weekly polls forced the ruling party, the Progressive Conservatives, into an election. Incredibly, Johnny won it in a landslide, and the Evolutionary Party was now in power. In 2006, at the tender age of thirty-nine, Johnathan H. Page was prime minister of Canada and on top of the world.

That's about it for Johnny. You might think I'd be angry or jealous about how successful he became, but to tell you the truth, that wasn't so. My life, although often boring and hard, was the only life I knew. I was content in my little cell with the small group of friends I had grown close to.

You're probably wondering about the creature. For years I did too. That was why I closely followed Johnny's career. I was sure the creature would surface somewhere—if not to me, then at least to Johnny. Yet, in all those years, not once did I see or hear a mention of the monster. Even the horrible nightmares that had always plagued me were gone.

It wasn't that I believed the creature was gone or dead, it was more like I figured it was finished tormenting me. It had framed me with all those terrible murders and stuck me behind bars for the rest of my life. Possibly that was enough. I can distinctly remember how my heart burst with joy at the thought I had finally seen the last of the hideous creature.

Unfortunately for me, I would once again end up being wrong. Oh, so horribly, horribly wrong . . .

BOOK THREE

Scared Little Men
The Fall of 2006

CHAPTER TWENTY-FIVE

October 2, 2006, was one of those glad-to-be-alive days. The day may have been crappy for some people, but that was their problem. For David, it was simply marvelous. Indian summer was checking in to kick October's unseasonably chilly ass out the door for a few more precious weeks of warmth. The heat had returned quite suddenly, and the frigid October weather had retreated without a fight. The frosty weather would be back soon enough to do some ass-kicking of its own, but until then Toronto, as well as the rest of Ontario, could look forward to more beautiful sunny days.

The warm breeze gently rushed through David's thick dark hair as he sat by himself on a dull gray bench alongside a tall, even-duller gray wall. Through the years, he'd managed to keep himself in relatively good shape. He'd been true to his word and stopped smoking, and even managed to exercise on a regular basis. He was a little skinny, but that was okay. Nobody's perfect.

He stretched out, leaning back against the wall, happily gazing over the courtyard at the magnificent display being put on by the setting sun. No matter how many times he sat on this bench and watched the sun going down, it never ceased to amaze him. Looking into that giant furnace in the sky as it slowly nosedived into tomorrow was David's favorite pastime. The day having been so perfect, he'd expected tonight's sunset to be fantastic—and it was. So glorious, in fact, David could almost forget he was locked up in prison.

If the sunset took his mind off where he was, the stone-faced guards patrolling the high wall were a constant reminder of his actual surroundings. That thought dampened his mood somewhat, but his smile reappeared on seeing his good friend Jack Goldsmith heading across the yard toward him. Jack had been his best friend for about twelve years now, and life would have been quite unbearable without him.

Everything about Jack's features could be described as ordinary. He was of average height and build, and his facial features were nondescript. He was the perfect nobody, a man who wouldn't normally attract attention, except for his having a thick, tangled shock of fiery red hair ablaze on the top of his head.

"How you doing today, Fingers?" David asked. Fingers was Jack's nickname in the joint. Most people probably didn't even know his real name. The "Fingers" label came from the fact he was the greatest thief the Toronto pen had ever housed. His reputation as a master thief on the outside was only topped by his reputation inside. If you wanted or needed anything while you served your time at the pen, Fingers was your man.

"Hey, Muddy, not too bad. Watching that damned sun again, weren't you?"

Muddy was David's nickname—whether he liked it or not, everybody got stuck with a nickname. Good or bad, once it circulated, it stuck. Muddy had been given to David in the first few months after he'd arrived, way back in 1987. His head had been pretty spun out from the creature and his subsequent arrest and trial. He hadn't made much sense for a while, and one inmate had casually remarked that it was easier to see the bottom of a muddy river than to try and understand some of the shit coming out of his confused head. Everyone got a kick out of that one, and the nickname Muddy had been born. David's cloudy mind had eventually cleared, but here it was nearly twenty years down the road, and still the name stuck.

"I wasn't watching the sun, I was watching the guard movement on the wall, so I can plan my escape. I think I have it figured out. You with me?"

"You know it, man. Just say the word and old Fingers will be right behind you."

It was an old joke between them, but it still hadn't become stale. Fingers had first brought it up years ago when someone had told him David knew a way to escape. For two years, Fingers had hounded him before finally figuring it wasn't true.

The truth was, David *did* know of a way to get out and had known for quite some time. You don't spend half your life caged inside a cement wall and ignore the cracks. The only trouble was that, by the time he'd found the way out, he was perfectly content to stay where he was. Life was good here, and life outside the wall held nothing for him anymore. He could have sold his knowledge to someone in the endless line of dreamers, but most people died trying to escape, and he couldn't risk imposing that guilt on himself. He didn't want anything or anyone to disturb the contentment he'd finally found after so much pain and anguish.

David was just about to ask Fingers if he could maybe swipe him an extra slice of bread at lunch tomorrow, when they were startled by a huge shadow. They spun around to see an absolute giant of a man towering above them. He was six eight, with huge muscles that rippled like ocean waves beneath his tight shirt. Below a massive, shaved-bald head that shone brightly in the twilight, his dark eyes locked onto David's. Instead of cowering, David broke into another big grin and jumped up to greet the new arrival.

"Mouse, buddy, good to see you," David said, grabbing the big man's hand.

How any man that large and powerful could end up with a nickname like Mouse was beyond David. Someone had apparently asked him once why they called him that, and he'd said it was because he enjoyed hearing the squeak bones made when he tore arms and legs out of their sockets. David wasn't sure if that was a true story or not, but to be on the safe side, he never raised the subject.

Once you broke through Mouse's tough exterior, he was just a big softy. One day Mouse had found a robin redbreast in the courtyard that had broken one of its tiny wings flying into the brick wall. He had tenderly loved and cared for that tiny bird for two months with medical supplies and food Fingers had somehow managed to get his hands on. The nest Mouse had constructed for the poor bird had been made from the shirt off his own back. Neither inmate nor guard went anywhere near that makeshift nest in the courtyard during the entire time it took to nurse the robin back to health. On the day David and Fingers helped Mouse release the healthy bird, the big man had shed a few tears. He'd said it was the best day of his life, seeing that beautiful bird flying high and strong over that awful gray wall.

David's smile disappeared when he noticed the worry lines on his large friend's face and the sadness in his eyes. "What's the matter, big guy?"

Mouse usually talked in a slow, deep voice that was quite soothing. Tonight, it was edged with pain and anger. "I just got told by one of the guards they're organizing the Game for later tonight. Bastards are making me fight again." Mouse sat down heavily beside them and cupped his huge head in his hands.

Not the Game. David shuddered. *Anything but that.*

The Game, as the guards liked to call it, was the one thing every inmate in the prison feared above all else. People died playing this game—the guards made sure of that. Out of the eighty or ninety Games David had witnessed, he'd only seen about five that hadn't ended in death for one of the fighters.

The Game was staged almost like an old-fashioned Roman gladiator match, updated slightly with whatever materials were readily found. The small group of cruel night-shift guards would choose two fighters from the prison population. To the guards, the inmates were nothing but human garbage, and they saw the Game as an effective way to keep troublemakers in line. If an inmate didn't toe the line, he could find himself playing the Game. That threat usually was enough to control the inmates.

Once chosen, the inmate had no choice in the matter. A first refusal meant a severe beating and still having to fight. Further refusal meant death inflicted either by some prison thugs hired by the guards or by the guards themselves. Once both players were confirmed, the word went out to the rest of the inmates, and the betting would begin. The guards looked after the money, paying out very little and keeping most. The winning fighter would get a cut of the winnings, but nothing compared to what the guards earned.

The Game was highly illegal, of course, but there wasn't a lot the prison inmates could do about it. Accidents could always be arranged. Inmates could die without turning too many heads. It was far better to maintain a low profile and pray you weren't chosen. Mind your own business and the guards will leave you alone; talk and you're dead. It was as simple as that.

Once all the betting ended, the competitors would be brought to the prison gymnasium. It usually didn't happen until about one o'clock in the morning, long after the day shift was gone. Randomly chosen inmates were released to act as a cheering section and used later to clean up the mess. The Game itself, although brutal, was simple. As for the rules, there were none. All the competitors had to do was run across the gym floor, climb one of two exercise ropes to the ceiling, cross a steel-mesh heating grate, ring a small bell on the opposite edge of the grating, and then reverse their path back to the finish line. First inmate to cross the finish line was declared the winner. It sounded simple, but wasn't. If two men know that crossing the finishing line second almost always means death, they invariably try harder and dirtier *not* be that second-place guy.

A razor-sharp knife also added to the fun. One knife, and

one knife only, was taped to the suspended bell that had to be rung. The first player to reach the bell got the knife. In addition, the fact that most players were chosen because of their size, strength, and toughness usually made the Game a brutal bloodbath—a life-and-death struggle to the end. Sometimes, if the Game was unusually fierce and entertaining, the guards would spare the loser to fight another day.

When it was all over and the money divided, the mess was cleaned up and the prisoners returned to their cells. In the morning, the guards would report the death as the result of a dispute between the inmates, or simply cover it up as an accident. Prison life would then return to normal, until the next Game.

David eventually broke the silence. "Did they tell you who you're fighting? Is it someone we know?"

"I think it's some new guy," Mouse sighed. "They call him Shadowman."

A chill ran down David's neck at the mention of his friend's opponent. Maybe Mouse hadn't heard about him, but David sure had. Shadowman had been transferred to the Toronto penitentiary only three months ago from down the road in Kingston. Apparently, he'd killed five people with an axe a few years ago and three more while in Kingston Pen. Already he'd killed one inmate here in Toronto. Rumor had it he was totally insane, without a shred of conscience. He killed for the fun of it.

David had never actually seen Shadowman. He'd spent most of his first three months in solitary confinement, but it seemed they were prepared to let him out tonight. The thought of Mouse having to fight that animal sent a chill coursing through David's body. He wondered if he should tell his friend about what he'd heard, but decided not to. Mouse had to fight him tonight, whether he wanted to or not. He'd probably be all right, anyway. Mouse was a powerful man. He'd already played and won the Game twice. The last time, the guards promised it would be his last. Obviously, they were liars.

"You'll take him," Fingers said. "You took those last two guys easily . . . remember?"

"I remember it all too well, my friend. I still wake up shaking, imagining their blood all over me. Not all that fond of the memories, you know. I'd give anything if those guards would just leave me the fuck alone."

"Yeah, or at least let you play against one of them for a change," David said.

Mouse looked over at David with his gentle, big eyes and started to laugh. "Now *that* would be something to look forward to, wouldn't it? I'd volunteer to play, if it would let me get my hands on one of their scrawny necks."

"Do you want us to be there with you again, Mouse?" Fingers asked, wishing that the answer would be no. Every player was allowed to choose two cornermen. They couldn't do anything to help, but it was always nice to have friends around for support.

"Of course. That's what I came over to ask. Will you guys be there for me?"

What was there to say but yes? Their friend was putting his life on the line; the least they could do was stand beside him and let him know he wasn't alone. "Of course we'll be there, you big lug, as long as you don't mind if I throw down a few bucks on Shadowman." David joked.

"If you do and I find out about it . . . I'll break your bloody neck myself, Muddy."

"Kidding, big guy. Just be extra careful tonight. I've had enough of my friends die, and you better not be another one."

"I'll try my best, Muddy. Promise."

The whistle blew to signal it was time for the inmates to clear the courtyard and return to their cells. David knew that sometime around one o'clock, a guard would come to escort him to the gymnasium. He hoped Mouse would beat this Shadowman guy and everything would be fine. He glanced once more at the spot where the glorious sunset had been taking place, but found the sun had gone. Darkness was rapidly approaching. David hated nighttime and couldn't wait until tomorrow when he could see that wonderful sun once again. He just hoped Mouse would be there to watch it with him.

In what seemed like no time at all, two burly, gray-uniformed guards appeared at David's cell. He didn't have to worry about waking up his cellmate, because for the last week he'd had the cell all to himself. Old Benny, his roomy for years, had taken a turn for the worse and had finally been admitted to the hospital ward.

The guards led him quickly and silently through the darkened prison corridors, nudging him constantly with their nightsticks every time he slowed his pace. He was escorted into the gym, where a crowd of about seventy inmates and guards already waited. He spotted Fingers immediately in the large throng of people, the red bird's-nest hairdo drawing his eyes like a magnet. Most of the other inmates just stood around passively, but the guards laughed and joked in anticipation of the approaching battle.

Fingers's mood improved visibly when David arrived, but he still looked upset.

"What's wrong, Fingers?"

"I'm just worried about Mouse. Have you heard what the odds are? Mouse is a seven-to-one underdog. *Seven-to-one.* Do you believe that shit? I mean, I heard some nasty things about this Shadow dude, but he can't be that tough. Everybody inside this joint is scared of Mouse . . . *everybody*! So how can they all pick Shadowman?"

"I don't know, Fingers. The last time, the guards had Mouse an easy favorite."

"Yeah, I know. Shadowman must be one scary fuck, let me tell you."

Mouse was paraded through the crowd with all the hoopla of a boxing title fight. The sheer size and power of Mouse dwarfing those around him caused many a person to change their minds about betting against him. By the time he was ushered over to where David and Fingers waited, the odds had already dropped to four-to-one.

"How you feeling, big guy?" Fingers asked.

"Well, I'd rather be drinking rum in Jamaica, but that ain't gonna happen."

Overall, David thought Mouse looked confident. No trace of fear appeared on his large, gentle face. He'd had to fight for everything since he was an oversized kid. Fighting had been a way of life, and he'd always come out on top. Mouse probably didn't see why tonight should be any different. David hoped he was right.

The dull roar from the crowd all of a sudden hushed down to a silence that was almost palpable. Tension floated through the air like a thick, dark mist. Mouse, Fingers, and David spun around to see what had quieted the crowd, but deep down they already knew the answer.

Shadowman was coming.

All eyes turned to watch the dressing room door where a path was being cleared by the guards. The door opened, and all those watching eyes enlarged at the same moment, as they finally caught sight of the infamous Shadowman. David drew in a shallow, sharp breath. He'd expected Shadowman to be tough looking, but nothing had prepared him for what he was seeing.

Shadowman looked to be straight out of a nightmare. He was bigger than David had imagined, standing nearly as tall as Mouse, at six foot seven. His greasy hair was long and scraggly, the darkest jet black imaginable. It covered most of his face, with only his mouth exposed, which pulled back in a grimace revealing dark, disease-ridden teeth. The rest of his body had a sickening ghostlike tone, his skin marble white. Despite his deathly pallor, his body looked far from sick, every inch bulging with muscle. He looked like a vampire on steroids.

The guards brought both players together at the start/finish line. They stood face-to-face, staring each other down. This was the first time David had ever seen anybody look eye to eye with Mouse without having to tilt his head up. Mouse stared him down, without a trace of fear. Both men were equally huge, but Shadowman looked infinitely more frightening. This was the last opportunity for people to place their bets.

Just before the two players separated, Shadowman pulled his hair from his face and tied it back. His eyes were dark, crazed, and lifeless.

My God, David thought. *What kind of horrors does someone have to go through in life to end up with haunted eyes like that?*

There was nothing much David or Fingers could say to Mouse, except to wish him luck. Mouse didn't wait for words from them anyway. He just removed his shirt and took his place on the starting line. Shadowman didn't have any friends in his corner, so he just psyched himself with a few slaps across his face before joining Mouse on the line.

The distance was eighty feet to where the two ropes hung from the high ceiling. Above them was the heat grating, and beyond that, the bell. From where David stood, he could clearly see the light glinting off the sharpened edge of the single knife taped to the bell, and one glance confirmed both Mouse and Shadowman were noticing it too. It was usually the player who reached the knife first that ended up winning, so both men would try for a quick start.

The betting was over now, and the crowd quieted as Henderson, maybe the nastiest of the night-shift guards, happily strolled out to the starting line. He looked back and forth between the players, smiled greedily, and loudly brought his hands together.

Game on.

Mouse bolted off the starting line, adrenaline coursing through him, as he pumped hard for the left-hand side rope swaying slightly on the far side of the gymnasium. There would be time for fighting later. Right now his main concern was to be the first to get to that knife. From there, he'd do what he'd done both previous times he'd played. He would throw the knife as far away as he could, removing it from play. Mouse would fight his opponent hand to hand without either of them having the advantage of a weapon. Never in his life had anyone been able to manhandle him. In a straight fight, he felt unbeatable.

The removal of the knife would also mean he wouldn't be forced into killing anyone; when he busted back across the finish line first, his opponent would die at the guards' hands, not his. The guards could force him to play, but he'd be damned if he'd kill a man for their sadistic pleasure. None of these thoughts were more than a flicker across his mind as he let his body become the machine it really was. He tuned out the noise of the crowd and concentrated only on the distant rope.

Mouse should have reserved a small amount of concentration for his opponent. Shadowman also jumped out to a fast, catlike start, grinning savagely as if enjoying himself. Madness has never been a substitute for raw power and speed though, and before Shadowman had run twenty feet, Mouse was already pulling swiftly ahead. Sensing his opponent would reach the ropes first, Shadowman quickly changed his initial plan, which had been to get to the knife first. Unlike Mouse, he had no intention of casting the weapon away. He planned on using it. In fact, he was looking forward to it.

David watched from the sidelines as Mouse began to run steadily away from his ghostly looking adversary. His joy was short-lived as he helplessly watched the pale figure launch his body through the air and lock his arms around Mouse's feet. Mouse slammed heavily onto the hard, wooden gym floor. David could read the startled look on Mouse's face as he crashed facefirst. Very few men had ever knocked him down before, and this sudden maneuver had caught him completely by surprise.

Shadowman took advantage of his momentary confusion, pouncing quickly on top with his fists flying. The powerful blows hammered down on Mouse's kidneys and the back of his head. Mouse tried to throw his foe off his back, but Shadowman was too strong.

David and Fingers almost ran to their friend's aid, but two

guards stepped forward to restrain them. They could only watch as the long-haired freak grabbed Mouse's smooth head and began beating it viciously against the solid floorboards. The sickening thump echoed loudly throughout the gym above the roar of the crowd. The grin on Shadowman's face stretched wider with every thump.

David breathed a sigh of relief when Shadowman crawled off Mouse and dashed for the ropes. Those blows to the head must have hurt like hell, but David knew his powerful friend well enough to know it would take more than that to subdue him.

"Get up, Mouse, you son of a bitch. Don't let this bastard beat you," Fingers screamed at the top of his lungs.

Mouse groggily made it back to his feet. Through the din, Mouse seemed to hear Fingers, and a steely glare of determination swept across his gentle face. Within seconds he was back running, pursuing Shadowman with a vengeance.

Leaping for his rope, Mouse furiously began to haul himself skyward. The sheer power of his arms alone propelled him up the thick cord at an incredible rate. Shadowman had already reached the top and was beginning to cross the metal heating grate. He had to stick his fingers through the grating's metal mesh and move fingerhold by fingerhold over to the suspended bell, supporting his entire body weight from his fingertips. Should one of them fall, it was a forty-five-foot drop to the unforgiving floor waiting below.

When Mouse had made it to the top of the rope, he heard the tolling of the brass bell, telling him his adversary had successfully managed to cross the grating. The noise also told him his opponent now had the knife. The first sliver of fear slipped into Mouse, but he pushed it away. There was no time for fear, only action.

This was the situation Mouse had been hoping to avoid. Even though Shadowman was in the lead, the only way for him to win was to recross the grating and get down the rope. Mouse, on the other hand, still had to cross the grating himself and ring the bell. Somewhere in the middle, they were going to cross paths, and both knew that this was where the final fight would take place. Mouse was probably more powerful, but Shadowman would have the advantage of the knife.

The bloodthirsty crowd stirred themselves into a frenzy, anticipating the clash to follow. David and Fingers glanced nervously toward each other, but remained silent. Their friend's life hung in the balance, and their inability to help was utterly frustrating.

On the ceiling, both men stared each other down, searching for a sign of weakness or fear they both knew wasn't there. Shadowman, holding the sharp knife clenched between his teeth, growled fiercely like a cornered animal. A thin line of ruby liquid drooled down his chin where the blade sliced into his tender tongue. The madness shone bright in his haunted eyes, seemingly excited by the approaching confrontation. He moved swiftly to the center of the grate, awaiting his dancing partner.

Mouse moved quickly and decisively onto the grating. He had a major-league score to settle with this greasy-haired lunatic. He'd been hurt quite badly on the gymnasium floor and was now primed and ready to dish out a world of pain himself. Another three feet, and he would be close enough to strike.

Shadowman had no intention of allowing his powerful opponent to get close enough to get those huge paws on him. Instead, he pulled up his body, thrashed out with his feet, and connected solidly with a direct hit to Mouse's chest. A lesser man would have been torn off the grating by the blow, but Mouse had stubbornly hung on and braced himself for the impact. The double-footed kick rocked his body backward away from Shadowman, but he managed to keep his wits, and as his momentum carried him forward, he unleashed a savage right hook of his own. Mouse's thundering punch slammed crisply into Shadowman's teeth, causing the knife in his mouth to slice even deeper. A torrent of blood drained freely out his mouth and accompanied a few of his diseased teeth on the long drop to the gym floor.

Mouse unleashed his fist twice more in rapid succession, pounding into his opponent's exposed ribs. Even with the roar of the crowd, Mouse could detect the satisfying snap of one or more ribs breaking. There was a moment when he thought Shadowman was going to plummet to the ground, but he grimaced against the searing pain in his side and held on.

Mouse took advantage of the brief period in which the madman fought to overcome his pain, skirting around him to ring the bell. All that remained was for one of the fighters to get back down to the floor and be the first across the finish line. Shadowman was closest to the ropes, but it was clear to Mouse that he wasn't moving anywhere. His opponent intended to finish the fight up here and moved toward Mouse, away from the safety of the ropes.

So be it, Mouse thought. *Let's do it, motherfucker.*

As he closed in, Shadowman quickly grabbed the knife from his bloodied mouth and struck out with it. The blade flashed like lightning, and before Mouse could move, the knife slashed across his chest, cutting him deeply. Once more, his wounded opponent surprised him with his uncanny speed, and another deep cut appeared, this time raking across his belly. Blood ran thick from the wounds, cascading down to the floor to join the red splashes of his opponent.

Mouse could feel his strength, along with his blood, starting to flow out of him. His fingers ached from the continuous strain of holding up his massive weight, but there was nothing he could do about it except fight on. Shadowman had fooled him twice with his speed, but this time he was ready. When the knife flashed out again, Mouse let go with one hand and grabbed hold of his opponent's arm, deflecting the blow away. He pulled the arm close, and with all his strength, he bit into the maniac's muscular forearm. Mouse tasted copper, as fresh warm blood spilled over his teeth and down his throat.

Shadowman let out a scream of agony and rage, the scream of an animal caught in a jagged steel trap. The knife dropped from his spasmodic hand and Mouse let him go, believing he had him now. It was a terrible mistake, for as soon as his arm was free, his opponent drove his knee with all the strength he could muster up and into Mouse's unprotected groin.

He might have been okay, if he hadn't lost so much blood, or if he'd been hanging on with both hands, but only one arm supported his weakened body, and that last blow had been too savage. A starburst of pain needles shot through Mouse's body, working their way quickly from his crushed balls up his arm to his already-ravaged fingers. He tried with all his might to hang on to the grating, but his strength was used up. His blood-raw fingers released him into thin air and without a scream, he found himself falling.

Mouse fell for what seemed like an eternity, and when he finally landed on the hard floor amid a puddle of his own blood, he landed badly. He hit knees first and then buckled over onto his face. The crowd grew silent for a moment as he lay broken and still. David and Fingers tried to tear away from the restraining guards, desperately wanting to help their friend, but they were held fast, going nowhere.

"The Game's not over yet, little man," the guard whispered. "Look for yourself."

David looked, but he couldn't believe what he saw. He'd thought Mouse was dead. Nobody could survive a fall like that, but there he was, struggling to get to his feet.

The crowd started cheering wildly again as they realized that Mouse was trying to make it to the finish line. He was broken and bloodied, but was still trying to win. He had rung the bell, and back down on the floor now, he only had to succeed in hobbling over the finish line to be declared the winner. His opponent was still up on the grating and way behind.

Mouse didn't seem to be able to get to his feet—both his knees were probably shattered. Instead, he started dragging himself along using only his arms. It was the most incredible act of courage David had ever witnessed.

"Come on, Mouse, you can do it. Just keep moving, big guy," David cheered.

Some of the other inmates also began to cheer him on as he inched his broken body along, but after a few seconds, the crowd suddenly hushed. David glanced around at his fellow inmates to see what had silenced them. Almost everyone was staring openmouthed, up at the ceiling. He followed their gaze to Shadowman, and his mouth too dropped open.

Shadowman wasn't heading across the grate so he could climb down. Instead, he was moving the opposite way—away from the ropes.

"Where the hell is he going? There's no way for him . . ." David began, but then it dawned on him what was going to happen.

"He's going to jump," David screamed.

"He *can't* jump," Fingers responded, "He'll bust up too, when he lands on that hard floor."

"He's not planning on landing on the floor."

The whole crowd had noticed it by this time. The madman had moved away from the ropes so he could position himself directly over Mouse's slowly crawling body.

Without hesitation, the crazed Shadowman released himself and hurtled through the air toward Mouse. David and Fingers screamed for Mouse to speed up or roll out of the way, but he was beyond listening. He inched closer to the finish line, his body a vessel of pain, oblivious to everything except the finish line ten feet away.

David watched as the grinning Shadowman landed squarely on Mouse's back with a sickening *crack-thump*. The crack had been Mouse's spine fragmenting into several pieces, while the thump had been Shadowman's muscular frame pounding down mercilessly onto that shattered spine.

The crowd had been shrieking as Shadowman fell, but now that he'd landed, the crowd returned to silence. Only David was screaming, "Noooooooooo!"

Shadowman, who appeared to be unhurt from the fall, snapped his head up and looked directly over at David.

Their eyes met, locked for a moment, and to David it felt as if the temperature in the room had suddenly dropped twenty degrees. His knees felt weak, but he glared back defiantly. They may have gone on gazing at each other longer, had it not been for a flicker of movement that caught both their eyes. It was Mouse.

Unbelievably, he was still alive. His stomach and chest were slashed to ribbons, his fingers were worked raw, his kneecaps had exploded, and his spine was a twisted, broken ruin. Nobody could hope to survive the kind of injuries he'd sustained. David just prayed his friend would die quickly and put an end to his suffering.

Shadowman had no intention of letting him die peacefully. He reached down and grasped Mouse underneath his chin and then looked back into David's eyes. He wanted David to watch him, as if to say, *This one's for you.*

The deranged animal was smiling wickedly as he jerked Mouse's neck violently to the left. David averted his eyes in time, but his ears still picked up the snap of his gentle friend's neck. When he looked back, the victor was standing up and walking over to the finish line with his arms upraised in triumph.

The members of the crowd, who had watched the final indignity to Mouse quietly, were now building their cheers back up to a deafening level. It wasn't that they were cheering their new champion, it was more that they feared the madman so much, they were scared *not* to cheer. David remained silent. He had no intention of kissing this lunatic's ass. Mouse had been a good person and an even better friend, while this long-haired freak was nothing but an animal. All David wanted to do was get back to his cell and try to forget this awful night. He turned and sulked away toward the gymnasium exit.

"Hey, little man, where do you think you're going?" a screechy, high-pitched voice called out from behind him.

David knew it was Shadowman long before he turned around to face the fiend. He had felt the chill of those haunted eyes on his back. The crowd was gathering around to congratulate the winner, but for a moment no one stood between them. Even the husky guards stepped out of the way.

"Back to my cell," David replied in what he hoped was a calm, steady voice.

"You forgot to congratulate me. You should show more respect. You never know, next time, I might let you be *my* cornerman. Your friend won't need you anymore."

David should have backed down and let it lie, but he began to seethe at this madman's arrogance. He *should* have backed down, but he couldn't. Somehow it would be like betraying Mouse, and David wasn't prepared to do that for anybody.

"You've got all the congratulations from me you're ever getting, psycho. Mouse was ten times the man you'll ever be, so pick someone else to be your cornerman. I'm getting the hell out of here. Being in the same room with you is turning my stomach."

David spun on his heels and started walking away, leaving the rest of the crowd in shocked silence. Shadowman burst after him, grabbing him by the neck before he made it outside the gymnasium. The guards rushed over, but none of them intervened.

"Better keep your eyes and ears open, little man, because someday soon, I'm gonna be there to rip that tough-talking tongue of yours right out your throat."

He started to let David go, but quickly pulled him back to within inches of his face. It was like standing in front of an open freezer door. Shadowman gazed deep into David's frightened eyes and whispered in his ear.

"One other thing . . . Don't you *ever* turn your back on me again. You may not see me coming, till it's too late."

Two of the guards stepped in and separated them. All bets were settled and the inmates were escorted back to their cells, except for the few who had to stay behind to help clean up what was left of Mouse. For most, it was time to calm down and go to sleep.

Sleep, for David, wasn't something that came quickly that night. His cell seemed too cramped, and a bit colder than usual. He tossed and turned for hours thinking about Mouse and what a waste his death had been. Exhaustion finally won over, and he fell into a deep but troubled sleep. He dreamed he was running through dimly lit cement corridors, pursued relentlessly by a large black shadow. He wasn't aware of it, but as he dreamed, his back was pressed tightly to the wall.

Chapter Twenty-six

Like something out of his darkened dreams, a huge black shadow fell across David's face, startling him from slumber. He sprang off his small metal cot, his nerves taut and frayed, only to realize he was making a first-class fool out of himself in front of a prison guard who'd walked up to his cell.

It was Pearson, one of the day-shift guards. He was a short, stocky little man who treated the prisoners as fairly as possible. None of the guards were overly friendly, but at least he wasn't a total asshole. "Gee, Muddy, take it easy. What's the problem?"

"Nothing. Bad night, that's all."

"Oh, you must have already heard about Mouse. Damn shame. He was rough around the edges, but I liked the big guy. Never gave me any problems. Too bad he messed with those skinheads."

"Skinheads?" David asked, curious to hear what lie the night-shift guards had come up with to cover up Mouse's death.

"Henderson said Mouse was stealing cigarettes from the skins. Bad move."

The skinheads were a large gang of inmates who shaved their heads so they could easily be identified, and therefore protected, by the other members. Mouse was always assumed to be a member because of his shaved head, and it was well known the skins resented him for not joining. It had been smart for the guards to blame Mouse's death on those guys. Nobody would question it, and there were too many skins to pin the murder on any individual.

David considered telling Pearson the truth, but bit his tongue. What good would it do? Mouse wasn't coming back no matter what, and the only thing he'd accomplish would be to get himself killed. Hell, Pearson might even be in on it.

"Anyway, Pearson, what brings you here to bug me this early? You finally here to tell me I'm free to go home?"

"You wish. Actually, you've got a visitor. Some guy's waiting for you."

"Visitor?" David inquired. It had been years since anyone but his lawyer had come to see him, and his lawyer was a woman named Paula Lewis. "Who is it, some other lawyer?"

"Hey, how the fuck should I know? I'm just here to give you the tour. Doubt it—he's dirty and grubby. Looks like a bum. Says he's a friend of yours and wants to see you. If you'd rather I send him packing, I'd be happy to tell—"

"No, I'll see him." When you didn't get many visitors, you couldn't be choosy.

David was escorted into the visiting room. It was long and narrow, painted festive pink, with eight separate wooden cubicles lined up along the center. A thick wall of glass separated the inmates' side of the cubicles from their visitors. The cubicles had high walls for privacy, and conversation was carried on via matching telephones hanging on both sides of the glass.

"Which one?" David asked Pearson.

"Number eight, right at the end. I'll be back in ten minutes."

Pearson stepped out of the room, closing the heavy metal door behind him. David walked past the cubicles toward number eight. Numbers one and three were being used, but the rest were empty. A tinge of fear clenched his stomach as he approached number eight and his still-unseen visitor. Something inside him wanted to stop, turn around, and get

GORD ROLLO

out of there. He dismissed that thought and sat down across from his guest.

Through the glass sat a man that looked just as Pearson had described—a bum. His clothes were tattered and dirty, his hair long, greasy, and tangled. He had an unshaven face with eyes that looked . . . eyes that looked . . . *familiar.*

They were hidden by some of the man's greasy strands, but something about their glassy, spaced-out look was uncannily familiar. David sat back and took a harder, closer look and gasped as he realized who it was. Unbelievable as it seemed, this was none other than his old friend Johnny Page.

Johnny picked up the phone, and with much trepidation David did likewise, putting it to his ear as if it might explode. "Johnny?" David managed to whisper.

"Hello, Davey. It's been a *long* time. How you been doing?" Johnny was smiling, seemingly glad David had recognized him.

"Not quite as well as you, mister Prime Minister," David replied with much sarcasm. "You've done quite well for yourself. I'm surprised the powers that be allow you to go around so casually dressed."

"Just a little disguise, Davey. Fooled the guards admirably. They barely gave me a glance. We're not here to talk about me, though. I'm in Toronto for a meeting with the premier of Ontario, but I have a far more important agenda. I'm here to bring you a message from the individual you refer to—rather childishly—as the creature."

"The what? You *serious?* It can't possibly be still around. Can it?"

"Very much still around, as you're soon going to find out."

"What's that supposed to mean?"

"You and the creature are about to be reintroduced."

"Get lost. How the hell is the creature going to do that? I think the guards will give *it* more than a glance if it tries to get in here."

"No, Davey, as usual, you don't quite understand. It's not

going to be hard for the creature to get into the prison with you . . . because it's already here."

"Impossible," David said with conviction, but already his stomach was clenching with fear again.

"It's been inside the prison for quite some time now, actually, biding its time. It's been watching you. In fact, standing beside you at times."

"Why haven't I seen it, then?"

"You always were slow, weren't you? The creature is in disguise. You may not want to believe it, but you've stood beside the creature, Davey. You've even talked to it."

"Who is it? You have to tell me, Johnny . . . who the hell is it?"

"I don't have to tell you anything, Davey, and I won't. It will reveal itself to you in its own sweet time. Don't worry, you'll be the first to know. It's really looking forward to seeing you again. Together, you'll have a real blast of a reunion."

"Is this for real? It can't be!"

"I've said everything I was instructed to say, Davey boy, so now I'll be on my way. I've a country to run, you know?"

Johnny rose to leave.

"Wait," David cried, causing Johnny to pause and pick up the phone again. "You can't just leave me like this. Tell me who the creature is. Tell me what it is, and what it wants. Why are you doing all this? What's your connection to the creature? Please, Johnny, don't walk away. Tell me something. *Anything.*"

Johnny just tapped his finger against his forehead and smiled. He carefully hung up the phone on its plastic cradle and left without saying another word.

David sat in his chair somewhat bewildered and a tad nervous. It was enough of a shock to receive Johnny as a visitor, but to hear him say the creature was still around and lurking somewhere inside the prison . . . that really blew his mind.

Was it possible the creature had managed to disguise itself

and enter the prison undetected? Could David really have been talking to it without realizing who it was? Of course it was possible—deep down he knew it was true. The creature's powers were vast. David had no idea just how vast, but was positive it could pull off the things Johnny had said.

If he was willing to believe Johnny, he had to accept that sometime soon he was going to have to face the creature again. The small knot of apprehension clenching his gut supernovaed into a million white-hot fishhooks that tore ruthlessly into his soul. On the outside, he had at least been able to run away and try to hide, but in here he was locked up, trapped. There would be no running this time. This time he was going to have to look the creature right in its blazing crimson eyes and make his stand.

CHAPTER TWENTY-SEVEN

If David had felt scared after his visit with Johnny, it was nothing compared to how he felt later that evening in the prison courtyard. The fear had spread from his stomach to encompass his entire body like some deadly fever.

For years he'd tried to forget about the creature and the suffering it had caused. It was a difficult battle that had almost cost him his sanity. Ever so slowly, he'd managed to carve a life for himself here at the Toronto pen. It wasn't a dream life, perhaps, but he had a contented, acceptable existence. That was all he asked for, all he ever wanted. Now Johnny had come to see him and reopened his worst nightmare.

He'd been collecting information about Johnny since his arrival at the pen, but he'd never dreamed he'd actually see and talk to him again. Obviously, Johnny was still somehow connected to the creature, but for the life of him David couldn't figure out what it had to do with him. Why couldn't Johnny and the creature leave him alone? Hadn't they already ruined his life? What else could they possibly do?

He couldn't come up with those answers, so he concentrated on one that he might find. Since leaving the visitors' room, he'd been trying to figure out whose face the creature was hiding behind. There had to be some way of detecting it. He'd seen through Johnny's disguise, so if he took a closer look at the people around him, he might identify the creature in the same way. That had been his plan anyway, but it turned out to be a bad idea. After lunch he'd started out on his quest, riveting his attention on anyone he encountered, without success. All he'd accomplished was making himself extremely paranoid. After an hour of scrutinizing hundreds of people, he'd found himself spotting the creature in everyone he glanced at.

His fear was starting to escalate, increasingly consuming his rationality the more paranoid he became. He might have completely lost his mind if he hadn't fixated on one special thing—the sun. The glorious sunset happened to catch his eye as he raced in a delusional frenzy around the courtyard, running away from the creature he spotted in every face.

David stopped his futile search, reveling in the sun's amber brilliance. It was so warm and peaceful, so soothing. It was exactly what he needed to pull himself together, calming his nerves and allowing him to think rationally again. He realized it was idiotic, running around looking for something he was never going to find. The creature, as Johnny had said, would stay hidden until it was good and ready to reveal itself.

David forced himself to sit down and relax. He remained sitting, contentedly watching the painted sky, until the whistle blew, signaling the end of the day. The entire way back to his cell, he ignored the countless faces he passed, fearing he might see another glimpse of the creature.

Pearson, the guard who had earlier accompanied him to visit Johnny, met him in the hallway of the cellblock. "How come you're still here?" asked David.

"Thought I'd let you know old Benny died this afternoon."

David was shocked. Benny had been his cellmate for years. The old bugger had been a good companion, and they'd become quite close.

"Ah, shit. What happened? I thought he'd outlive us all."

"Don't know. Guess he just got tired of fighting all the time. Anyway, thought I'd let you know. I knew you two were close. Christ, losing two friends in twenty-four hours. That sucks, man."

"Fuck. Thanks for telling me. This mean I'll have the cell to myself for a while?"

"No such luck. In fact, they've already assigned you a new cellmate. He's waiting to meet you right now."

"Who is it?"

"Don't know, Muddy. Don't care. I'm sure you guys have some crazy nickname you might know him by, but I think his real name is Rodney something. Anyway, my shift is over and I'm out of here." Pearson disappeared around the corner and David continued on toward his cell at the far end of the gray corridor.

Rodney? As in Rodney the Scarecrow? No, that thought was crazy. Thinking about the creature and Johnny all day had jarred a screw loose. Still, ridiculous or not, his fear started to rise again as he walked down the corridor to meet his new cellmate. Try as he might, he couldn't shake the horrible image of Rodney the Scarecrow waiting in his cell, his left arm missing and his body black and charred. It took all the strength David possessed to take that last step to see who was waiting in his cell. It wasn't Rodney the Scarecrow, but believe it or not, it was worse. Much worse.

It was Shadowman.

CHAPTER TWENTY-EIGHT

The next two days were terrible for David. Shadowman hadn't said a single word to him since they'd become cellmates. His cold eyes gazed intensely at David, like those of a hungry vulture, and he smiled incessantly. His sinister grin unnerved David. It was more like a grimace than a smile—no lips, just twin rows of black, rotting teeth.

Once his initial fear subsided, David had tried several times to communicate with his cellmate. If he was going to have to share a tiny cell with this animal, he should at least start some kind of relationship. Friendship was out of the question, but some rapport would have to develop. Unfortunately, his efforts brought no success. All he ever got was that cold stare, and of course, those awful teeth.

The nights had been the worst. At least during the day David could wander around the pen facilities and happily avoid him. At lockup, he had no choice but to confront his unwelcome guest. Sleeping was a luxury he had to do without.

Shadowman appeared perfectly calm at night, snoring softly and seemingly at peace, but whenever David felt himself drifting to sleep, his cellmate's eyes would always be open and watching. It might have been just paranoia, but David was sure Shadowman was waiting for him to fall asleep so he could do something. What, he didn't care to imagine.

For two days he hadn't slept. He would get a few hours' nap during the day, but not enough. He badly needed a full night's sleep. His eyes itched and watered and felt like they'd been dipped in acid. He wanted so much to just let them close. His eyelids felt as heavy as bowling balls.

Just for ten seconds, he convinced himself. *Just ten little . . .* No! His eyes snapped open again. Ten seconds might spell disaster. On the other side of the cell, Shadowman winked at him and lay back down. He closed his eyes, but he was still smiling like a thirsty cat who'd just found a large bowl of cream.

That does it, David thought. *I'm not closing my eyes again tonight. I'll just get lots of sleep tomorrow, that's all.*

He winked back at his cellmate, even though his eyes were closed, just to spite him, smiling to himself now that he was fully awake and his resolve was built up again. Whatever game Shadowman was playing, David was going to play it by his rules.

Less than two minutes later, he was fast asleep. . . .

He dreamed he was being pursued by a large black shadow through dimly lit cement corridors again. This time he knew what the shadow was, and it scared him even more. He knew this shadow would have a face, and on that face would be two dark, cold eyes and a rotted smile.

He ran through his dream, aware that the presence behind him was closing the gap. Slowly the corridor narrowed until he could barely squeeze his body through. A little farther on, the cement corridor just stopped—a dead end. He could feel the shadowy thing close to him now, and having no other choice, turned to face it. The shadow began to take form in the dim light. David knew it had a face, but the shadow kept it tilted down to the floor and hidden. It drifted right up to him, and he could feel its chilly hands roaming over him. Finally it lifted its head and gazed into his eyes. David screamed. The face he was looking at was his own. . . .

* * *

He was still screaming when he woke up.

"Just another bad dream" he reassured himself. "Just a dream."

Realization burned into him then, like a hot dagger.

David snapped his neck around so fast it hurt. His unsociable roommate was awake, sitting up on the edge of his bed. He was staring straight at him, but even more frightening, Shadowman wasn't smiling anymore.

"Wanna know something?" asked his cellmate in a high-pitched, demented voice.

David had been trying to get him to talk for days. Now that he had, David wished he'd stayed silent. "Ahh . . . sure."

"I hate your name."

"I never liked being called Muddy, either. I got that nickname from—"

"Not Muddy," Shadowman broke in with a hiss. "David. I hate the name David."

David didn't know what to say to that. "How do you know my real name?"

"Oh, I know lots of things, Davey. *Lots* of things."

David didn't like the way Shadowman was looking at him, so he decided to humor him. "Well, it's just a name. I don't give a shit what you call me."

"Good. I think I'll call you, Diana."

Diana?

"Diana?" David repeated out loud. "What the hell are you talking about?"

"Diana is a pretty name, and I like all my girlfriends to have pretty names. Been in solitary for a long time, Diana. *Too* long."

David's eyes widened, as he understood what Shadowman was telling him. He watched in disgust and horror as the powerful freak stood up and took a few steps toward him. As he walked, he was unzipping his pants.

* * *

Paula Lewis sat in her high-backed, leather armchair and thought about David Winter. This wasn't unusual for her, as she had been his lawyer for three years. What was unusual was that she was starting to believe he might actually be innocent of the Ripper murders. David had been saying that all along, but she hadn't really listened. Everybody in prison says they are innocent. Paula hadn't really thrown her stubborn mind into David's case as much as she normally would have. After all, the case was over twenty years old.

Paula, at twenty-nine years of age, barely remembered the Ripper case, but knew it had been an open-and-shut case right from the start. It wasn't until she met David and got to know him better that she'd started to look into his case file and take his claims of innocence seriously. The more she dug around, the more she began to believe. Now, on October 5, 2006, she was finally convinced of her client's innocence. She just had to figure out what she was going to do about it.

She sat back in her chair and stared across the room at the big grandfather clock that, ironically, her grandmother had owned. It was 11:49 P.M. Paula decided she would get up early and drive to the prison. She wanted to tell David she believed him and was going to fight to get him released. She also needed to talk to the warden. Until she could get him out, maybe she could get him some special treatment or something, so that his stay at the pen would be a little more bearable. Probably would be best if she called the warden first. Paula much preferred to make first contact using the telephone. She'd learned from past experience that she was taken more seriously if she used the phone first. Paula Lewis was a beautiful woman, and that sometimes got in the way of her work. Men would melt at the sight of her silky golden-blonde hair cascading around her cover-girl face. She was fairly short, at five foot five, but her body was exquisite, curving in all the right directions.

She certainly wasn't complaining, but her looks sometimes

got in the way. It was tough to talk law with someone salivating and undressing her with their eyes. That was why she
called first. If she could let them hear her intellect first, her
body was less likely to steal the show later on.

She climbed into her soft bed and snuggled under the cool
sheets. She felt good about her decision to fight for her client's
freedom. She was fairly sure of his innocence and of her ability to convince a court of that fact. Sure, they'd caught David
with a bloody sledgehammer still in his hands, but he'd never
denied killing the policeman. What he'd said, and what Paula
believed to be true, was that he was temporarily insane at the
time and had no idea he was killing an officer. He'd thought
he was striking out against the real killer, the one framing him
so he'd take the fall. Paula had uncovered some new proof and
a lot of questions that weren't answered at David's first trial.
She intended to ask those questions this time, and—if luck
was on her side—win him his freedom.

Goose bumps spread across her body as she imagined a
jury deciding David could go free and the newspapers broad-
casting how brilliant she'd been. It was a good thought, and
she hung on to it as she fell asleep. By ten after twelve she
was sleeping peacefully, totally unaware that at that precise
moment David was screaming himself awake to find out that
Shadowman had lost his smile.

His disturbed roommate advanced on David, unzipping his
pants as he approached. David could see that his eyes didn't
look as dark and cold anymore. They seemed to tingle
slightly and dance in their sockets. It only took David a second to recognize that look: lust.

David was frightened, but he hadn't survived nineteen
years in the pen by being stupid. When men are locked
away with no female contact, homosexuality is inevitable.
He'd been attacked only once before in his entire stay and
had been able to fight the young man off rather easily, but it
had still been an upsetting experience. He'd learned from it,
fortunately. Ever since that attack, David always kept a

knife in his bed. Every now and then, a guard would find it and take it away, but he always got himself another.

Instinctively, he reached under his mattress and for a brief second thought his knife was no longer there. Fear squeezed his heart like a boa until his finger finally brushed across the homemade weapon, and he pulled it out from under the bed.

In the darkness, Shadowman didn't see him holding the shiv. His lust was so great, he probably wouldn't have noticed if David had been holding a bazooka. All he was thinking about was satisfying the growing interest in his pants, and he jumped hungrily toward his new "girlfriend." David tried to remain calm. When Shadowman pounced, there was no time to think about anything—all he could do was react.

And react he did, driving the knife upward with all his strength. It easily slid into his assailant's muscular stomach right to the hilt. His attacker screamed loud enough to wake everyone in the cellblock. His weight came down against David, and for a sickening second he could feel Shadowman's stiff erection rubbing against his arm. He exerted all his weight into rolling him off and onto the floor. As he did this, he savagely twisted the knife, causing more screams from his astonished attacker. People all over started yelling, causing a hell of a racket.

Finally the guards showed up. David tried to pull the blade out of Shadowman's stomach before the guards reached them. He intended to stab him again and again before they dragged him away. With any luck, he'd kill the bastard. Unfortunately the knife blade snapped off inside his bleeding stomach, and David was left holding the handle.

The guards quickly assessed what had happened. It wasn't too hard, what with Shadowman's penis still sticking proudly out of his pants. They realized David had only been protecting himself, so it was the assailant they grabbed, and they rushed him unceremoniously to the hospital ward for emergency treatment.

Thick ribbons of dark blood flowed freely out of the wound David had inflicted, and dropped to the cement floor beneath Shadowman's feet. David could still see the end of the broken blade barely sticking out of the open wound. Every movement must have been agony as the guards began to drag him away, but he'd stopped screaming.

"I'll be back, little man. Count on it. I didn't think you had the balls for this type of thing, but I guess you do. That doesn't scare me . . . it excites me. Sit tight, darlin'. When I get back, we'll have us a ball. Yeah, that's it, a real nice reunion."

David lay trembling on his blood-stained bed. He'd been lucky this time. If the pervert returned, he knew he'd be in deep trouble.

Reunion?

A vision of his old friend Johnny came to him, saying how the creature had said it was looking forward to their reunion. Coincidence? He didn't think so. As the guards struggled to drag Shadowman to the hospital, David tried to stop himself, but the words burst out of his mouth.

"Are you the creature? You've got to tell me. God damn it . . . *Tell me.*"

The guards looked at David like he was crazy, but he didn't care. "Please tell me if you're the creature," David begged, slouching off the bed onto his knees.

There was no response from Shadowman, no sign, no clue. All he did was stare at David with those cold, dark eyes. Worse still, he was smiling again.

CHAPTER TWENTY-NINE

Although tired, David still found it hard to fall asleep, even with Shadowman safely tucked away. He tossed and turned, thinking about what he was going to do if his cellmate really was the creature, but he had no answer for his dilemma, and eventually exhaustion overcame him. He dropped into a deep, dreamless sleep, like a small pebble sinking endlessly into the dark recesses of a bottomless pond.

He woke late, missing his call to breakfast, but didn't have much of an appetite anyway. His mind was still plagued with thoughts of Shadowman's return and their ensuing reunion.

Maybe I can avoid him, he thought, but shot that down immediately. It would be difficult—no, impossible—to avoid someone locked in the same small room. He might be able to ask for a change of cell, though, or find someone to switch with. He spotted the guard he was somewhat friendly with wandering around the courtyard, and rushed toward him.

"Pearson, wait up a second. I need to ask you something."

"Muddy, this is unreal. Every time I go out looking for you, you seem to find me first. What do you want?"

"I was wondering how difficult it is to change cells around here. If it's possible, I'd really like to do it."

"You kidding? What do you think we're running here . . . a fucking play school? Why? You having trouble with your new roomy?"

"You wouldn't believe the half of it. I've got to get out of that cell. What if my life depends on it? Will they move me?"

"Haven't a clue. Ask the warden when you see him today."

"The warden? Why would I see him today?"

"Because he *wants* to see you, that's why. Some lady lawyer called asking a shitload of questions. Guess the warden wants to talk to you about it. I was told to send your butt to his office. You know the way?"

"Sure, I know where I'm going. Did he say when?"

"Yeah, about an hour ago. Get moving."

BENJAMIN J. STEELE
CHIEF WARDEN
TORONTO MAXIMUM SECURITY PENITENTIARY

David couldn't help but notice the huge black letters, immaculately hand painted onto the thick oak door. They were impressive, and somehow imposing. The warden was a particularly tough customer to deal with, especially when he called you to his office. The chief screw had absolutely no fear of the inmates, wandering freely about the courtyard with complete disregard for his safety.

David and almost everyone else in the pen would straighten up and acknowledge him when he walked by. One didn't get a last name like Steele for nothing.

David knocked softly on the door, not wanting to damage the warden's sign in any way. He planned on asking the warden about getting his cell changed. If anyone could do it, he was the man.

"Come," the warden's voice commanded.

The office was filled with nothing but the essentials: four bare walls, an ordinary desk, two plain-looking chairs, an early-model telephone, a small box of pencils and pens, and one large, grumpy-looking warden. David was motioned to the chair in front of the desk and quickly took a seat, wondering if this meeting was over the stabbing incident.

Ben Steele was a big man, at least six six. He hunched over his desk, gazing intensely at David from over the oval-shaped reading glasses balanced on the tip of his crooked boxer's nose. His hair and moustache were dark brown, cropped military style, making David think he resembled a much younger Charles Bronson.

For the longest time, neither spoke. They just looked at each other, sizing each other up. David was the first to break down and respond.

"I heard my lawyer called you this morning?"

"Yes." Followed by more silence.

"What did she want?"

Finally the warden sat back and relaxed a little. He reached for his phone and immediately got his secretary. "Stella, it's Ben. Hold my calls and keep everyone from bugging me. And Stella, I do mean everyone. I don't want to be disturbed. Got it? Good."

The warden then returned his attention to David.

"She called me early—8:15, in fact. I had just arrived and I took the call in the outside office. She told me she thinks you're an innocent man, wrongly incarcerated. What do you think of that, Mr. Winter?"

David was stunned. He didn't know what to say. He'd been telling every lawyer handling his case he was innocent; he was tongue-tied one of them finally believed him.

"I don't really know what to say, sir. I wasn't expecting this sort of thing. Did she tell you *why* she thinks I'm innocent?"

"Sure. She rattled on about all these unanswered questions that never came up at your trial, and about some evidence she's got. I didn't really listen to most of it."

"Meaning, you didn't believe her?"

"No, Winter, not at all. I stopped listening to her because I didn't need to hear anything she had to say. I already knew you were innocent."

"You already knew . . . *what?*"

"That you were innocent. God, I've known that all along. I just couldn't let everyone else find out. You never had the brains to mastermind those murders . . . but I know someone that did."

"Who?" David asked, his mind spinning with confusion.

"Me, Davey, my boy. *Me!*"

And then the warden began to change.

David watched as the warden stretched his fingers out on the desk in front of him. The ends suddenly burst open and long shards of bone began growing out. He lifted his right hand up and pierced two of his bone fingers into his eyes. When he pulled his fingers back out, his gooey eyeballs came with them, popping out with the sound of champagne corks being released. Out of his gaping eye sockets, twin beams of fire flashed, leaving two glowing, crimson holes.

The creature!

It was the warden, not Shadowman. It had been disguising itself as Ben Steele.

David thought about running, but was held fast by the creature's hypnotic eyes. He was unable to do anything except watch as the thing continued its change. The warden's flesh began to bubble and slide away off his ruined face. Almost no skin at all remained on the creature's head, just a few strands of white hair matted on a darkened skull. When it tilted its head back to laugh, David could see its rotting brain pulsing through the hole where its nose had been. Its rows of teeth looked as razor sharp and lethal as ever.

At first, David thought the creature was starting to stand up, but it was just growing bigger. Its body swelled until it burst out of the warden's clothes. David could only see the top half of the beast, since it was still behind the desk, but that was more than enough to make him feel nauseous. The creature's diseased muscles and bones were covered in thick, weeping yellow sores. Maggots and worms crawled freely through its decayed entrails and stomach cavity.

"*Ta-da!*" it said when its metamorphosis was complete.

David vomited without warning.

"Nice, Davey. See . . . I told you this would be a reunion you'd never forget."

"How can—? Why—?" David tried to ask.

"Quiet down. You'll get your hows and whys in a minute. Shut up and listen."

David did as he was told.

"That's more like it. Long time no see. Twenty-one years, isn't it? That's a heck of a long time for two old friends to be apart."

"You're no friend of mine," David shot back. "What the hell do you want this time? Haven't you ruined my life enough?"

"Now, now, let's not get huffy. You might not believe this, but I don't want to be your enemy. The things that have happened between us have happened for a reason. Nothing you could have done would have changed anything. You have to believe that."

"Why should I? All you've ever done is screw me around."

"True. I see your point. That's why I've chosen to reveal myself today. I was going to wait a few more weeks to let you sweat it out, but I never figured on Shadowman trying to use you as his personal pincushion. Between that and your lawyer asking all kinds of stupid questions, I had to change plans."

"I thought you *were* Shadowman."

"Me? Shadowman? Don't make me laugh. That psycho is nothing more than an animal. An admirable animal, but an animal nonetheless."

David struggled to break the creature's mental bonds, but it was useless.

"Stop being such a fool, Davey. Where are you going to run to? You're a prisoner, locked behind bars for life. Settle down. I have a story for you."

"I'm not interested. Just leave me the fuck alone."

"Oh, you'll be interested in this one, because it's about you. I'll tell you everything, Davey. *Everything.* Who I really am. Where I came from. What plans I have for Johnny.

Most importantly, I'll tell you exactly what I have planned for you."

"Why tell me all those things now? You've always been a mystery."

"Yes . . . but until now, you might have been able to screw up my plans. Now everything has fallen into place, and nobody can do anything to stop me. Maybe you'll finally accept things as they are and stop being such a pain in the ass."

David resigned himself to the inevitable, his curiosity getting the better of him. "Tell me then. Everything. I wanna hear it all."

The creature sat back rubbing its bony chin with his bloody hand, pausing as if wondering how to begin. "I'm going to have to go back quite a ways to fill you in. Way, way back to the fifteenth century."

David's eyes widened, but he didn't say anything. He waited impatiently, but quietly, for the creature to continue.

"Have you ever heard of a man by the name of Zoltan Baltizar? No? How about Baron Baltizar or Baron Bloodshed?"

David shook his head to all of the names.

"You know, I wasn't always this . . . creature, as you refer to me in that feeble little mind of yours. I was once a man, Davey. A great man. My name was Zoltan Baltizar, and I was born in the year 1407 AD. Those damn fool historians cheated me out of my greatness. Those monks and Byzantine chroniclers couldn't get a story straight if their lives depended on it."

"I don't understand. Are you saying—"

"Shut up and I'll tell you what I'm saying.

"The feudal system was popular back in my heyday. It was simple, really. A wealthy landowner allowed peasants to live on his land in exchange for their working his fields and paying for protection. The feudal lord reigned supreme, and his authority was absolute. Whatever he said was law, and pity the poor bastard that disagreed with him.

"I became the Baron of Kranstatt, the owner of a thousand square miles of good land smack in the heart of Romania, at the age of twenty-one. I inherited my position from my father, who was one of the most feared, bloodthirsty animals in history, bless his rotting heart. His legacy of tyranny left me with some big shoes to fill, not to mention an incredible number of enemies. Fortunately, I was up for the challenge. More than that . . . I relished the opportunity.

"My father had been a cruel man, and I was a chip off the old block. I treated my peasants like filthy pigs, but being oppressive wasn't enough for me. I was young and strong and thought I could do as I pleased and get away with it.

"In the beginning, I satisfied my growing passions by simply mistreating everyone. I'd whip the men's backs raw for no other reason than that maybe they failed to address me with what I deemed an appropriate amount of reverence. I just enjoyed watching their pain. I raped the women too. Why wouldn't I? They were mine to use and abuse as I saw fit. But soon I tired of such petty games and required more pain and suffering to quench my desires. Soon I required blood.

"I committed murder for the first time on Christmas day, 1433. It was an event that would shape my destiny. I was having my way with both a mother and her daughter, raping the mother while the terrified daughter waited her turn. I decided to see what kind of response I could get out of the daughter if I started strangling her mother. I didn't mean to kill the old wench, but the look of sheer, helpless horror on her child turned a key in me that led into all kinds of interesting rooms.

"It had taken me twenty-six years to discover the joy of cold-blooded murder, but it didn't take me long for my next."

"The daughter?" David hesitantly asked.

"And after her, I killed three more that night. I couldn't stop. It was the most glorious night of my life. I was filled to the brim with unabated joy. Total euphoria."

"Total madness, you mean," David risked.

"Madness to you. Destiny to me. I realized that night what my goal in life was. My father had been hard and cruel, but I didn't have to live in anyone's shadow. There would be no more silly whippings handed out; no, now my punishments were truly severe. Hangings, stabbings, decapitations, and impalement. I burned them, I boiled them, and I bathed in their sticky, warm blood.

"The blood ran in torrents out of my torture chamber, and soon I heard whisperings the locals now called me Baron Bloodshed. It was a title I honored, but unfortunately, nothing lasts forever. The peasants turned on me. Revolted. It didn't bother me at the time—I was too busy enjoying myself—but later on, after my death, it would come to haunt me. I should never have been so stupid.

"Yes, David, I see that look in your eye. I did die. It was in the year 1454. I was out riding with a small battalion outside the city of Kranstatt when we were ambushed. To this day, I don't know if the attackers were peasants or traitors from my own army.

"I personally slew ten of the bastards before some coward drove the life out of me with a long sword through the back of my neck. Even then, I managed to gut one more before my lips kissed the soil for the last time."

David's interest was definitely aroused now, curiosity overriding his fear. If the creature's story was true, then the repulsive monster in front of him was almost six hundred years old. "So how the hell did you end up here, talking to me?"

"Exactly right, Davey. That's the answer—via Hell.

"After I died on that battlefield, things were confusing for a while. The first thing I remember is, oddly enough, swimming. I eventually found myself washed up on a dark, desolate beach. It was freezing. An icy wind howled constantly around me, chilling me to the bone. My body appeared to be unchanged. I went down to the water's edge and could see my reflection in the murky ocean clear enough to know

I still resembled my earthly form. I realized my real body was still sprawled in blood on the battlefield, so this form I was in now had to be my soul. Strange, I never really expected my soul to look like me. I had always pictured it as a thin mist, escaping out of a body on the dying breath. My shivering reflection in the dark water told me I had been wrong.

"Many people, in my time and yours, have wondered about what Hell is really like. None of them want to go there, but they'd sure like to see a postcard, know what I mean? The first thing that struck me was the vastness of the place, and how alone I felt there on that beach. The silence was deafening, if that makes any sense. No voices, no machinery, no screams, nothing. Just silence—except when the wind picked up and howled in my ears. The worst was the cold. Once the icy winds started pummeling me, I froze right to the core. There wasn't any driftwood to build a fire or any type of shelter.

"I'd never been the type to wallow in pity or cry about hardships, so I decided to start walking inland. Damned if I was going back into that water again. I picked a point on the horizon and walked toward it, and with every step, cold sand stung my face like wasp bites. I wandered for months in that seemingly endless desert, never encountering another living or unliving thing. I was alone with the blowing sand.

"Daylight was also something I longed to see. Even the pitch-black curtain of night would have been soothing, but no, not in this godforsaken place. Hell seemed to be stuck in perpetual twilight. Neither day nor night, light nor dark.

"When I finally stumbled over a great sand dune to see a walled city filling the horizon, I thought I was hallucinating. It seemed too good to be true. That was when I realized I was in Hell, and that Hell wasn't a landmass, like a region or a country. Hell was a city. A massive, spectacular, high-walled city.

"I hurried toward Hell's thick, ancient gateway. Most people on Earth had regarded me as evil through and through; surely there was a place for me in a city such as this. I thought they might even regard me as some sort of hero and treat me accordingly. Let's just say I received somewhat less than the hero's welcome I'd hoped for. I was tortured. Tortured for fifty years, all part of some macabre initiation or rite of passage into the city, if you will. Whatever the reason, it was savage.

"Every conceivable method to inflict pain on my soul was applied, then reapplied again and again, just to make sure they hadn't missed anything. Just like in the desert, I was unable to die, which I prayed for every second at their House of Pain. I was already dead, so they could continue my suffering forever. Eventually the torture ended, and I was loaded onto a wooden slab and carried away. From the House of Pain, I was taken to a magnificent marble cathedral in the heart of the city. I have no memories of my trip through the city or who carried me, but the next breath I remember drawing was from within the cathedral.

"Twelve men stood around me in a circle. They were dressed in beautiful scarlet red, silken robes, with hoods drawn up so I couldn't glimpse their features. From their powerful builds, I could tell they were all males. I remember thinking that finally I was going to meet somebody in authority. I followed the tilted heads of the men around me as they joined hands and turned their shadowy faces skyward. My heart would have surely stopped right then and there if it hadn't already done so back on that battlefield. There, suspended in midair, twenty feet above me, was the Master himself . . . *Satan*."

David, who had been fascinated by the creature's story, suddenly broke into laughter. "You expect me to believe all this? Next you'll be telling me the Devil was wearing a red jumpsuit, with horns and a pointed tail, right?"

"No, Davey, he wasn't. Laugh now, but believe me, every word I've told you is true. Shut up and listen. By the time

I'm finished, you'll believe. You might not want to, but you will.

"Where was I . . . ? Oh yes, the Master was above me in the cathedral. He didn't look anything like the cartoon devils, Davey. He was by far the most beautiful man I'd ever laid eyes upon. His eyes blazed bloodred, like twin blast furnaces illuminating the rest of his face. His facial features were flawless, and I remember thinking I had seen him before, or at least his likeness, in some ancient Greek statue. His muscular body was covered neck to toe in midnight black armor, and the Power that radiated off him was greater than the strength of a thousand trained armies.

"He was reading a scroll and glancing down at me periodically, nodding his head as if in approval. I realized he must have been reading an outline of my short but colorful life. Ten minutes later he descended to the floor and began to talk to me. His lips never moved, his silky voice coming to me through my mind.

"The Master explained how the city of Hell functions. It has a class structure similar to most cities. The degree of evil that a person shows back on Earth determines on which class level they spend their existence in Hell. First are the Nobodies, whom I had met during my stay at the House of Pain, faceless, nameless people who've been sent to Hell, but are of no use to the Master. Then there are the multi-leveled privileged classes, who work and take care of the inner city.

"*Yes*, Davey, people work in Hell. What did you think they do all day? Stand around in boiling tar and wait for the Master to come stick a pitchfork up their ass? Of course people have to work. The privileged classes enjoy hard, but decent lives in recognition of their evil on Earth. The greater your evil, the better job you are given.

"Above this large group of people comes Satan's inner circle. These are the red-robed twelve that stood around me that day. The inner circle helps the Master rule his people, and they also have great powers given to them by Satan, allowing them to control vast armies of spirits and ghosts that roam the earth. Above the inner circle is the Master himself, whose authority and power is absolute.

"I was positive, by the way Satan was praising my accomplishments, that he was going to appoint me to his inner circle. He especially liked my knack for impalement. I was shocked and bitterly disappointed when he finally told me he was placing me in the highest ranks of the privileged classes. I asked why I wasn't good enough for his inner circle, and he only laughed. He said that those twelve men had devoted their entire evil lives to serving only him. I on the other hand had served only myself and had never bowed to him at any time.

"I accepted the Master's decision, but that didn't mean I had to like it. I was outraged. I was put to work, and you'll never guess what they had me doing."

David took a wild guess. "I don't know. A blacksmith making weapons?"

"Of course not, fool. No weapons are allowed in Hell. There are too many murderers and psychos running around to be handing out weapons. The only weapons are those that permanently reside in the House of Pain."

"How was I supposed to know? What were you then?"

"I was a jewelry maker. If you laugh, I'll rip your lungs out right here and now. Can you believe that, me, a fucking *jewelry maker*? They kept going on about how my profession was the most prestigious position anyone in the privileged classes could ever hope to hold. They said I should be grateful. *Bah!*

"The reason jewelry was so important was that it was Hell's official and only form of currency. If you wanted to buy a magazine or a book, you had to fork over a golden earring; if you wanted a first-class whore for the night, you'd better have yourself a diamond. Even in Hell, diamonds are still a girl's best friend . . . to quote a bad afterlife joke. Anyway, you can see why my job was a respected one. Still, I hated it. I was a baron, damn it, and refused to humble my-self by doing menial labor. I wanted to make decisions . . . to have authority. I wanted *power*.

"I put up with it for much longer than I would ever have dreamed. Years went rushing by, hundreds of them. I became a master of my jewelry craft and could manufacture anything that was asked of me. Big deal. I didn't want to be praised for making intricate pieces of shiny crap. I wanted to be a mem-ber of the inner circle, and gain the Power I would have ac-cess to there.

"That was why I eventually found myself sneaking into the grand cathedral as the Master and his inner circle conducted a secret meeting. I thought maybe I could learn something that might help me to get some of the Power I so badly craved. I quietly slipped into the secret meeting, and it was there the seed of this plan that you're involved in first started to grow.

"I was hiding in the balcony, looking down through the oak slats. I counted thirteen red-robed figures kneeling around the Master, so obviously in the last three or four hundred years, only one new addition to the ranks of the inner circle had been added.

"Satan was going around the circle of kneeling men, painting an inverted cross on each man's forehead with a thick red liquid taken from a large golden chalice he was holding. While he painted each man, the Master repeated the same message. He said. "Remember, my son, my blood is the life. Without it, you are nothing. Without me, you are nothing." I listened to that message again and again as Sa-tan made his way from man to man, but all I ended up con-centrating on was part of it.

" 'My blood is the life. . . .'

"That was the important part. I knew that I'd blindly stum-bled onto a possible solution to my problem. My ears were hearing 'My blood is the life,' but my mind kept screaming back, *His blood is the Power.*

"My mind began to race. Of course the men of the inner circle were more powerful: the Master was giving them the Power through contact with small samples of his blood. The inner circle wasn't special—it was the blood.

"I began to wonder what might happen if I could get myself a small sample of the Master's blood? What if I could get hold of lots of it? If a tiny drip of it could give the inner circle such wonderful power over Hell and on Earth, what might I be able to accomplish with, say, an entire spoonful? Or maybe, an entire golden chalice full?

"I never stopped to consider what might have happened to me if I'd been caught, but I'm sure my punishment would have been long and severe. Entry to the grand cathedral was forbidden, let alone trying to steal the Master's blood. But I didn't get caught, not then anyway. I waited until the meeting was over and everyone had left the cathedral. I crept down and stole the entire golden chalice from off the sacred altar. Maybe if I hadn't been so greedy as to take all of the blood, the Master might not have noticed. But I was greedy . . . very greedy. It was the Power that fed my greed. From the first second my hands touched the chalice, the Power swept over me. It enveloped me in an aura of such intensity, that I felt almost invincible.

"My soul surged with excitement as I hurried back to my workshop, where I immediately began to use the machines at my disposal to change the form of the Master's blood. After all, it wasn't as if I could just leave it as it was. I used the machine I had for turning coal into diamonds. The machine was complex, but the principle of it was simple. It heated the coal, compressed it under hundreds of thousands of pounds of pressure, and crystallized it into various-size, top-quality diamonds. A little buffing and they'd be ready to go. The whole process only took about an hour.

"Instead of the coal, I carefully poured the Master's blood from the chalice into the pressurization chamber. While the blood was crystallizing, I took the golden chalice, which still harbored a certain amount of residual Power itself, and melted it down to form an elaborately decorative ring. Then I fancied it up with a few diamonds—"

"The ring. In Johnny's well," David suddenly cried out.

"Yes, Davey, the ring I threw to you that day in the bomb shelter. That's the one. You thought it was a ruby, didn't you? Everyone else did too. I made it to look like that. How would you have felt that day, if you'd known what you were really holding wasn't a ruby, but a cupful of Satan's crystallized blood?"

David turned white, extremely disturbed by this revelation.

Oh my God. I was touching that ring. Holding onto part of the Devil! David could still remember how touching the ring had sent intense pain raging up his arm, spreading over his entire body. It had burned his left palm too. His hand had blistered and bled the entire way home. The evil Power of the Devil had actually done those things. He wasn't sure if he really wanted to hear the rest of this story. It might be better for his sanity to just stop it right now. That wasn't an option, though, and soon the creature continued on.

"When the ring of Power was finished, I eagerly placed it on my finger. The rush was exquisite, to say the least. So exquisite that at first I was in agony. You know what I mean, don't you? After the pain came the true Power. Like nothing I had ever experienced. It wasn't just the strength it gave me, but also the knowledge. Doors and pathways leading to countless libraries of hidden knowledge were suddenly opened up. I realized I didn't just have the Power. . . I *was* the Power.

"I thought I'd gotten away with it too. Vanity always had been one of my downfalls. In my euphoria, I had forgotten about the Master, but believe me, Davey, the Master had not forgotten about me. He must have known right from the moment I snuck into the cathedral. I think he just let me have my way to see what I was up to. Thinking back, it had been a little bit too easy to sneak in and out without being caught.

"The Master was waiting for me when I stepped outside my workshop the following morning. His eyes shone like the sun itself, and he hadn't come to play games. He walked up to me and said, 'You have taken something that wasn't yours to take. Forgiving is a weakness, and not part of my nature. I admire your tenacity, but I'm afraid this has cost you *everything*.'

"I was sure I was in for an eternity of severe punishment, but the Master surprised me. All he did was cast me out of the city. I was ostracized from Hell, left to wander eternity in the icy desert. All in all, I was let off quite easy. The Master didn't even take back the ring I'd made. I suppose he figured having all that Power with nothing to use it on would drive me insane. That was where he went wrong. I was smarter than he thought.

"I made my way across the desert, back to the beach and the dark ocean. I ran to the water and played in it like a child for hours. I had just come back up onto the beach, when I was startled by a man and women swimming toward me from offshore. I tried to talk with them, but they ignored me and walked away. Soon they were over the first sand dunes and had disappeared. Obviously they were headed toward the city, which meant they must recently have died and crossed the dark ocean, as I had done long, long ago.

"That really got me thinking, Davey, and for a few days I sat there on the beach and watched as seventy other people swam their way to shore. Where were these people coming from? I kept asking myself. Obviously the answer was, from wherever they had finished their lives. That meant there had to be various entrance points connecting this underworld with Earth. The people were getting there somehow, right?

"These entrances to Hell had to be located somewhere out or beyond the dark ocean. I thought, hey, if there are entrances, there are probably exits too. If I could find one of them, I could get back to the real world. With the Power I possessed in the ring, anything might be possible. Maybe I could even *live* again.

"Without another second's delay, I jumped into the water and soon left the beach far behind. I didn't have a clue as to how far I was going to have to swim, but it didn't matter. I was determined to succeed at any cost. Days went by, and soon time blended into one continuous stretch of pain. My arms and legs ached with the effort of the swim, but still I pushed on. Being dead, it was impossible to drown, so when total exhaustion took over, I'd just let myself sink like a rock to the bottom of the ocean floor. I would rest there in that icy darkness until I regained the strength to carry on. In the murky ocean depths, numerous large shapes swam and slithered by me, but thankfully I never got a closeup look to see what they might possibly be. It was probably better not to know.

"Numerous swimmers passed me headed in the opposite direction, each of them oblivious to my presence. I remember thinking that maybe I should give up and turn around, but it was a good thing I didn't, because that very same day I finally found one of the portals into the real world.

"I was shocked when I found it. I'd been sort of expecting to find the end of the ocean, or another shoreline, perhaps. The ocean just seemed to carry on forever into the horizon, but not more than ten feet in front of me, the body of a man was emerging out of thin air along the surface of the water. I couldn't see any doorway or portal, just a slight shimmering of the air around him.

"I moved aside to let the new swimmer by, and then without a moment to reconsider, I swam as fast as I could toward the still-slightly-shimmering portal. I felt the Power in me surging, and I knew I was going to make it. Satan could travel into the real world using the Power, so why couldn't I? I hit the portal between worlds and felt only a slight resistance tugging at me. Hell tried to keep me, but it didn't try very hard. The next moment, I was completely through and back on Earth. I'd done it. I'd successfully escaped from Hell.

"My joy soon turned to fear. I had escaped Hell's dark ocean to find myself in water once again, this time at the bottom of a foul-smelling well. Yes, Davey . . . Johnny's well, where you later found me. I'll get to all that in a minute.

"I found myself with no shape . . . no *body*. It took me a scary moment to realize that this was what I should have expected. Of course I didn't have a body here in the real world; my flesh and blood had long ago turned to dust. The shape I'd occupied in Hell had just been my mind and soul. Back on Earth, I guess that made me a ghost, for lack of a better word. A spirit with nothing but mind and soul . . . and of course, a ring.

"Yes, I still had the ring. It had made it through the portal too. No obstacle could hold that much power at bay. My fear passed. I still had my mind, I still had my soul, and I still had my ring of Power. All I had to do now was find myself a new body.

"I knew that all I had to do was get people to put on or even just touch my ring, and I would be able to use the Power to jump into their unsuspecting bodies. I hoped it would be that simple, anyway, but it turned out to be a *bit* more complicated.

"In the well my Power continued to grow, but I still had much to learn. I developed a way to leave the confines of the well. Using my new ability, my *mind's eye*, I could send out a small portion of my consciousness to travel a short distance to spy on my surroundings. It was with this mind's eye I learned I had reentered the world in your miserable little town of Dunnville in the spring of the year 1955, and that a man by the name of Harrison owned the land and the well in which I was imprisoned."

David nearly fell off his chair. "Jacob Harrison? *The* Jacob Harrison?"

"I believe you knew him better as Old Man Harrison. Now listen up. I used the Power to lure Jacob out to the well. It wasn't difficult, seeing he was always walking right by it. He was making that bomb shelter you and your friends found. Anyway, I used the Power to get him to fish around in the water until he scooped up my ring. From there it was easy to jump into his body and push his mind and soul out of my way.

"I pushed too hard though. Instead of slipping into his mind unnoticed, like I had planned, I ram-charged my way in. His old mind snapped right then and there. He fought it for a while, but eventually his mind just couldn't accept having to share his body. It drove him helplessly and totally insane. I tried to help, but my control of the Power wasn't as good back then, and his mind had been too fragile.

"You already know what happened next, Davey. Old man Harrison slaughtered his entire family. He had them half eaten too, before that kid found out his secret that night at the Wabasso factory. Jacob killed him too, and then hung himself in the upstairs bedroom of his house before the police got there. He did all of those things with me inside him, and there wasn't a damn thing I could do about it. My Power seemed to have no effect against his insanity. It was only after Jacob died on the end of that rope that I was able to regain control. The police were searching the house, and I waited until I was alone before making my getaway. As soon as the police went downstairs, to find Jacob's daughter roasting in the oven, I tore myself down from the rafters and jumped out the second-floor window. I dashed back to the well on Jacob Harrison's shattered dead legs and jumped back into the cold, dark water before the police could spot me.

"I hung out down there as the police searched for me—or for Jacob, I should say. Within half an hour, a strange sensation began to overcome me. It was like a pulsing in the center of my stomach, a tugging. It only took me a moment to realize what was happening. Jacob Harrison had died, and the tugging I was feeling was one of the afterlife worlds— most likely, Hell—coming to claim his soul. Hell was calling Jacob. Seeing as I was still linked to Jacob's soul, I was scared.

I feared Hell was going to drag me back into that dark ocean, and that was a trip I didn't want to take. I kept thinking about the House of Pain as the tugging sensation increased, and I guess I panicked.

"I used the Power to jump back out of Jacob Harrison's body, and then I threw his body toward Hell's shimmering portal. I thought that only his soul would go through, but I was wrong. His entire body disappeared and was instantly gone. I was shocked. Only his soul would make the long swim to Hell's beach, so what would happen to his flesh? Most likely, Jacob's soul would swim away and leave his flesh to sink to the bottom of the dark ocean. Maybe it would eventually be found by one of those large, slithery shapes I'd sensed swimming around down there. Who knows?

"Whatever happened to Jacob's body, it was gone from this world. That was why the police—no one—ever found it. It wasn't there to find. Unfortunately, I was back at square one, but I'd gained some important knowledge. I'd learned that I'd have to be gentler the next time I entered someone's mind. I'd have to be more careful.

"It would be thirteen years before I had the chance to try again. The fiasco with Old Man Harrison, as you know, caused quite a stir around Dunnville. People believed the farmhouse was haunted, and nobody wanted to buy it. Eventually, an out-of-towner from Hamilton finally bought it. He was your friend Johnny's father, George Page. He never abandoned Johnny and his fat bitch of a wife, like most people thought. He never abandoned anybody; he just simply had the bad luck of meeting me.

"I used the growing Power in me to get George Page to wear the ring too. This time, I tried my best to ease into his mind real gently, so he wouldn't even know I was there. Again I failed. No matter how softly I trod, his soul still seemed to sense me, like a rooster instinctively knowing a fox had entered the hen house. As I quietly became a part of him, he also became part of me. He knew what I was and what I had caused Jacob Harrison to do to his family.

"Johnny's father was a devoted family man and couldn't bear the thought of ever bringing harm to his loved ones. At the first sign his mind was beginning to slip, he decided to put an end to his own life. He'd seen a glimpse of the future I was offering, and his moralistic soul couldn't accept it. George committed suicide by tying a heavy weight tightly around his neck and jumping into the well. I tried to stop what was happening, but his love for his family overcame his fear of me, and it was overpowering.

"When Hell came tugging for him—or maybe this time it was Heaven—I was better prepared. I didn't panic. I just calmly chucked his soul out through the portal, and was done with it. This time, I kept hold of the body.

"Did I tell you Johnny knew I was his father?"

David was too stunned by everything he was hearing to answer the creature's question. All he could manage was a brief shake of his head.

"Well I'm telling you now. Johnny's known for over thirty years. If you get right down to it, I guess technically I wasn't lying. Just manipulating the truth. You see, the rotted body you see today is still the body of Johnny's father. I've . . . how can I say it? . . . just enhanced things a bit, that's all.

"I haven't tried to take over anyone else's body since George Page's suicide. I don't mind spending my days in this dead carcass of a forgotten man, but it's not enough. I want to live, Davey, really *live*. I want to breathe with a healthy set of lungs, and feel real blood pumping through my heart again. I've been waiting a long time, Davey, biding my time, but my wait will soon be over.

"It took until 1977 before Johnny and his mother came to claim the farm as their own. From what I gathered with my mind's eye, they only came to Dunnville because they had run out of options. The second I laid eyes on Johnny, I saw the answer to all my problems. Johnny was just a child . . . a child, get it? I'd been trying to take over the bodies of fully grown adults. That had been my mistake. Once people reach adulthood, their minds are pretty much set in their ways. It's nearly impossible to change them, even if you do possess the Power of the ring.

"What I had to do was concentrate on a child. A child whose mind and soul was still flexible enough to handle my invasion, without snapping like Old Man Harrison and Johnny's father. An adult can't even begin to comprehend spirits and ghosts. Their lives are too ordered and structured—but not so a child's. A child believes in things that go bump in the night. Children can accept the existence of the boogey-man just as easily and unquestionably as they accept there's a Santa Claus. Well, I had gifts of my own to bring. All I needed was the proper child.

"So you, Johnny, Pete, and Tom eventually ended up down in Jacob Harrison's bomb shelter, but it was you, Davey, who ended up with the ring, wasn't it? Of course it was, but you let go of it. Couldn't handle the pain, could you? You made me sick. I was *furious*! You have no idea what you did to me that day. I'd used the Power to conjure up a spell on the ring, so that when you grabbed it, you would be the one that I'd merge souls with. I didn't care which one of the four of you it ended up being. I just tossed the spellbound ring toward all of you. Fate chose you to catch the ring, and the second you did, your body received the conjured-up spell. You let the ring fall and Johnny picked it up, but it was already too late. The spell was already cast.

"You've never known that the spell was on you, but it was, from that moment on. And still is today. Any time I wanted, even right now, I could use the Power to slide into your soul. I've always been able. I just never wanted to."

This new revelation was almost too much for David. His throat tightened up so badly, he could hardly breathe. His heart was pumping a mile a minute, and he thought he was going to pass out. "Why . . . Why haven't you then?" David managed to ask. "If you could have . . . entered me at any time. Why haven't you?"

"Why *would* I? What good would it do me? Without the ring, you're no use to me. If I were to enter you, I'd be stuck in a weak little man's body with no access to the Power. It's Johnny that I want now, not you. Johnny claimed the ring off the floor after you dropped it, and the ring subsequently claimed him. I want to merge with Johnny's soul, so I'll have control of the ring again."

"Then do it. Do it and leave me the hell alone. If I'm so useless . . . why do you keep fucking with *my* life?"

"Ahh . . . we come to the root of the problem. I don't enter Johnny, simply because I can't . . . yet. The spell I put on you is still in place. While you live, the spell lives. You're the only person I can enter and merge with. That was why I was so furious when you dropped the ring."

David thought all the information over for a minute before asking, "Why didn't you just kill me back in 1977?"

"I almost did, but I stopped myself. The more I thought about it, the more you dropping the ring seemed like a blessing in disguise. It would have been easy to kill you and conjure a new spell on Johnny, but by letting you live, it allowed me some time. If you would have kept the ring, even for as little as a few more minutes, the spell would have pulled me into your body to merge our souls. You dropped it, so that didn't happen. Dropping the ring was sort of like pulling the plug on the spell. Now the spell still lingers on you, waiting to be plugged back in so it can complete the circuit. The same thing would happen if I had killed you and put the spell on Johnny. He had the ring, so I would have been pulled into him. That would have been fine, but Johnny was still a kid. It was far smarter for me to allow you to live, keep the spell on you, and use my granted time to guide Johnny's life.

"Who do you think caused Johnny to grow up so healthy, good looking, and strong? Me, of course. I used the Power in the ring he was wearing to guide and shape every aspect of his life. Even politics was my idea. I stood outside the voting booths and broadcast the Power over the televisions and radios, to make sure Johnny won the election. I handed him the leadership of this country on a silver platter, but believe me, none of it was done to help him. The entire time I was shaping Johnny's life, I was also preparing his mind and soul for my arrival. By now, he's nothing more than a breathing husk. I have a small room built inside of Johnny where I keep his mind and soul. The door is still open to allow him to function, but the day I join him, I'll seal that door as tight as a drum. In effect, Johnny will cease to exist, leaving me in the driver's seat. When you die, and I eventually take over Johnny, I've made sure I'm in a favorable position to fully maximize my Power. First you, then Johnny, then Canada, and from there . . . the *world*!

"I also influenced you and your friends. How do you think Rodney the Scarecrow and the King Spider came to life? You already know it was me that framed you for the Ripper killings, but the only reason I did that was so it would be easier to keep an eye on you. I had to follow Johnny all over the place. I didn't feel like chasing you too. Prison was the perfect solution. When you die, I'll take over Johnny, and my plan will be complete. After all these unbearable years, I'll finally be alive . . . again."

The creature finished and spread its decaying arms out wide. It gave David another *"Ta-Da!"*

David found he wasn't as terrified of this hideous beast in front of him anymore. He was still scared, but something about the truth had set him free. He even managed a weak smile. "Aren't you forgetting something? Johnny and I are the same age. Has it occurred to you that, just maybe, Johnny will be the first to die? He's under all that political stress, while I'm relaxing here getting three squares a day. Even if I go first, he likely won't be far behind me. By the time you get the spell lifted off me, Johnny will be nothing more than a weak old man."

"Wrong again, Davey. When I take over Johnny, he'll still be young and running this country. You think I'm going to sit around and wait for you to die of old age? *Wrong.* I have a much shorter time frame than that in mind. Here . . . take a look at this." The creature produced a newspaper from under the desk and tossed it onto David's lap. David scanned the accompanying article. In large bold lettering, the headline read,

DEATH PENALTY REINSTATED: PRIME MINISTER DELIVERS ON PROMISE

Prime Minister Johnathan Page has made good on his campaign promise to take a harder stand against crime than his predecessors. In one of the most surprising political maneuvers in recent history, the PM has used his mass popularity and political savvy to rush the House of Commons into putting the death penalty back onto the books. Although surprising, the move wasn't all that shocking. The PM had been making his "tough justice" speeches all over the country for . . .

And farther down the article,

Prime Minister Page, in this morning's press conference, declared that electrocution will be the method of execution to be implemented, and that a total of five federal penitentiaries will eventually be equipped with the required facilities. The PM stated that the Toronto Maximum Security Penitentiary in Ontario has been chosen to house the controversial first chair. Spokesman for the prime minister, Lawrence Duncan, stated that construction of the facility would begin within the month. . . .

When David finished with the article, he looked up at the creature, which was watching him eagerly. David was more than a little confused. "You managed to get Johnny to reinstate the death penalty. What's that got to do with me?"

"My, you sure are thickheaded aren't you? That electric chair is coming here, Davey. Coming here for you, as my little going-away present. I could just kill you myself, but I have a bit of a flair for the dramatic, you might say. You're going to be the first person to sit in that chair, Davey, and when you get that nasty old shock, I'm gonna to be there to watch the steam roll out your ears. When you're dead, the spell will disappear, and I'll be able to overtake Johnny. I've already got the ball rolling. Johnny's body is all set. I've already got the ring set up to start my transformation when you die. I'll be in charge of Johnny's body before they even scrape you out of that chair."

David felt the familiar slimy fingers of fear starting to crawl up his well-traveled spine. Could it be true? Was it possible he was really going to be electrocuted for crimes he'd never committed? "Wait a minute. For the Ripper murders, I was given multiple life sentences. *Life* sentences. Not you, Johnny, or anyone can change that verdict now."

"Davey, Davey, Davey . . . Do you think I'm a fool? I know perfectly well how your pitiful justice system works. Who said anything about your old crimes? You're not going to get the chair because of the Ripper killings; you're going to get zapped for your latest murder. You'll fry for murdering the warden of this prison, Benjamin J. Steele."

"The warden? What do you mean? I didn't murder the warden."

The creature stood up and proudly walked over to a small door behind him. "Oh you killed him all right . . . you just don't know about it yet."

The door, leading to a closet, was yanked swiftly open as the creature spoke. From out of the shadows, a large figure slumped forward and dropped heavily at the creature's skeletal feet. On the floor, with a blue metal letter opener protruding out of his ruined left eye socket, was the obviously dead corpse of Warden Steele.

"You see, Davey, I've been playing with the warden's mind for quite some time now. I've had him sort of zoned out and locked in this closet while I was masquerading as him. It wasn't until early this morning, after your lawyer friend called, that I decided to finally get rid of him. I just put the idea in his head that it would be fun for him to ram his letter opener into his brain. He did it with a smile on his face, without hesitating. It was great. I must confess, though. I think I enjoyed it a little more than he did. Either way, it's over and done with, and you're left holding the bag once again.

"The secretary, some of the prison guards, and hundreds of the inmates all have seen him—or rather me, posing as him—this morning. Your own lawyer thinks she talked to him. The guards think he sent for you. His secretary let you into his office, and later, while you were with the warden, he called her and told her he didn't want to be disturbed. Remember? When they come in to find the warden dead, take a guess what's going to happen? The way I figure, sooner or later you're going to end up sitting in that lovely chair Johnny's sending here. You're going to die, Davey, and then I'll be able to live. Hell of a plan . . . huh?"

"You won't get away with it, you bastard. I'll tell them everything. No, better yet . . . *you'll* tell them. *Guards . . . get someone in here. Help!*"

"You're slicing your own throat, Davey. They won't be able to see me if I don't allow them to. So keep screaming, this might be fun."

David wasn't listening to the creature anymore. His mind had started to close up on him, his sanity already trying to crawl under that large rock again. He was losing it, but he was helpless to stop. When two burly guard burst into the warden's office, they found David curled up in a tight ball, still screaming his head off about some monster that had escaped from Hell and was trying to take over the world. Lying less than five feet away was the gory corpse of their boss, Mr. Steele. It didn't take them long to figure out what had happened and to drag David away to solitary confinement. He screamed the entire way, but put up no resistance.

In the next two hours, guards came and went in the warden's office. A doctor, and finally a coroner, was also summoned. Morgue attendants and various police detectives were also present. Even some low-level government officials poked their heads in to put in their two cents' worth. In total, over thirty men and women scoured the office, running in and out and all over. The cause of David's anguish hovered peacefully near the plastered ceiling, blissfully unseen by one and all. No one could hear it, but the creature was laughing hysterically.

CHAPTER THIRTY

It was February 10, 2009, just over two years and four months since David's fateful meeting with the creature in Warden Steele's office. Sometime during that interval, he'd managed to stop screaming. He had completely withdrawn and showed no signs of ever coming out of it. The world had been a strange and cruel place, and David found peace only when he let his mind drift.

This reclusive withdrawal of emotions, although blissful to David's soul, had made him a terrible witness in his own defense at his ensuing murder trial, a trial in which the cards had been unfairly stacked against him and his lawyer. Paula Lewis had shown up at the prison that awful day a few Octobers back, ready to do battle with the warden over the validity of the Ripper charges. When she learned of the warden's murder, her snappy my-client-is-innocent attitude wilted noticeably. Every scrap of evidence and information she had raked up— and she had raked deep—pointed toward David's being the warden's killer. She had no defense other than an insanity plea, but the province's chief psychiatrist had met with David and declared him mentally sound to stand trial. After that, everything went downhill fast.

David's emotional state left him a sitting duck on the witness stand. His detached and seemingly uncaring attitude made him appear guilty and without any feelings of remorse. The prosecution tore him to shreds.

To make matters worse, Johnathan Page, the prime minister himself, had shown up at a crucial point in the trial, making a remark that this case warranted the death penalty. If the members of the jury hadn't made up their minds by then, the prime minister put them over the top. They deliberated for about two hours, just to make it look good, before returning a verdict of guilty.

The judge, an obese little man in an oversized black robe, had promptly declared David guilty of murder in the first degree by a jury of his peers, and that in accordance with the law of the land, he would be sentenced to death by electrocution. The time and date for such execution would be determined later.

Five weeks later, at another hearing, David was scheduled to die in Toronto's newly constructed electric chair on September 12, 2007.

Paula Lewis had nearly blown a fuse when she heard how soon the judge had set the execution date. She complained that the date set was outrageous and offered her little or no time for the appeal process. The judge informed her that this wasn't the United States, and that the mandatory step-by-step appeal system was not the way things worked in Canada. Of course her client would be allowed the right to appeal his sentence, but he wouldn't be allowed myriad appeals, which served no other purpose than to delay implementation of the court's decision. The judge had advised Paula not to waste the court's time with appeals, unless she could come up with what he called "*extremely* convincing evidence" her client was innocent.

She hadn't uncovered anything "extremely convincing," but Paula had appealed the court's decision anyway, and had sworn to David she'd keep appealing until they ran out of options. She'd been true to her word, working like a bulldog to champion David's cause for the past twenty-eight months. She'd managed to get the execution pushed back from the original September 2007 date, but she wasn't a miracle worker. Now it was a frigid day in February 2009, and Paula was working on what she had informed David was their last realistic hope. If this appeal failed . . . well, David didn't even want to think about it.

Where the hell is she? he thought.

Paula was already an hour late, and he didn't have many fingernails left to chew on. It struck him as funny that he was so nervous. What did he care how the appeal went? He'd stopped caring about anything a long time ago. It had been the only way to hold onto his sanity throughout the bogus trial and subsequent appeals. If he *had* cared, he'd have gone completely over the edge long ago.

Now that life had calmed down again and he was left alone most days, he began to realize maybe he'd been wrong. The more he contemplated death, the more he wanted to carry on. His life sucked, but damn it, it was all he had. He wanted to live.

Twenty minutes later, Paula finally made an appearance. A guard named Featherstone rushed David to the visiting room. Hope surged momentarily, but it washed away with the first glance he had of his lawyer. Her shoulders were slumped, and she looked red-eyed and exhausted. He knew right away that she had bad news.

"Sorry, David, they rejected your appeal. Turned us down flat. They wouldn't listen. Their minds are made up on this and have been since day one. It's just not fair."

David thanked her for trying, then lapsed into silence.

"When is the . . . I mean, how much longer until . . . ?" David asked.

"July 29, David . . . at the stroke of midnight. I'm sorry"

Fear began to tighten its grip on David's throat, making it hard to breathe, but a moment of inspiration hit him, and he grasped it as a drowning man clings to a life preserver. He'd have to think it through, but maybe—just maybe—he wasn't finished quite yet. Maybe he could get out of this mess after all. He should have known nobody would be able to help him. If anything were to be done, he would have to do it himself.

Paula promised she wouldn't quit. She'd keep digging around and fighting right until the end. David wished her luck and thanked her again. He just wanted to go to his cell so he could think in peace.

Back in his cell, David was convinced the plan forming in his mind might work. It might not too, but what choice did he have? If he just sat on his ass and did nothing, he had less than six months left to live. He'd never been any kind of hero, but if he wanted to live, he couldn't give up. There was really only one thing he could do. He was going to have to get as far away from here as possible, where neither the law nor the creature could ever find him. To accomplish that, he would have to break out of prison. To live, David somehow had to escape.

CHAPTER THIRTY-ONE

"What do you mean, you've always known?" It was Fingers. He was pretty angry.

"Calm down." David whispered. "It's not like I was deliberately lying."

"What else would you call it? For years I've been asking if you knew a way out of this joint, and every time you denied it. Now you're telling me you did, but didn't want to tell me. That stinks, Muddy. Why couldn't you trust me?"

David couldn't think of anything to say. He'd lied to his friend, and sometimes in the pen, all a man had was his word. It had taken him a month to get this meeting, seeing as he was locked in Security Wing F—death row, but without the morbid name tag. David was trying to recruit Fingers to help him escape, but so far their talk had been anything but good.

"I'm sorry," David said, "but I lied to protect you. Listen, if I'd told you, what would you have done? Tried to escape, right?"

"Probably. So what?"

"My plan is crazy. There's hardly *any* chance it'll work. I'll likely end up dead."

"Then why bother?"

"What choice do I have? *You* have a choice, though. They're going to fry me in five months, but your sentence will be up in . . . what, six years?"

"Four, actually," said Fingers. The steam had gone out of his anger at the mention of his friend's date with the chair.

"There you go. That's why I didn't tell you. You have a life to live, but I don't. If I had any other choice, I wouldn't be trying this either. I need your help, my friend. There's no way out of here unless you help. What do you say?"

"Ah Christ, you know I will. I'd do anything for you. But tell me something. Why'd you do it? The warden? All our years together, I never once saw you get violent."

"You wouldn't understand, Fingers. I *didn't* kill the warden. Can't prove it or say anything to make you believe that, but it's true. I was framed again. I don't have time to tell the whole story. You'd probably laugh anyway. Guess you can believe me and help, or walk away. Which is it gonna be?"

Fingers looked hard into his best friend's haunted eyes, and in them he could see the truth, or at least enough of the truth to convince him. "I'm in. What do ya need?"

David smiled, digging a scrap of paper out of his pocket and handing it over. "Some of this stuff might seem strange, but don't ask. If you can't get *all* of them, forget the whole thing. What do you think?"

Fingers quietly studied the list. "A book on human anatomy? How the hell is that going to help you escape?"

"No questions. Can you get all that stuff?"

"Sure, except it'll take time. Don't know where I'll find that damn book."

"You'll get it, you always do. Besides if you can't, no big deal. Guess I'm just a dead man."

"Good," said Fingers, picking up on the joke, "least there's no pressure."

The two friends let the joke die as they looked sadly at each other. They'd been through a lot together, and it was awful, the way things were turning out. Neither talked for a minute, the silence saying far more than either of them could have.

"How long, Fingers? Not to rush you, but I'm on a tight schedule here."

"At least another month, maybe two. I'll do my best, Muddy. . . . Promise."

"I know you will. Thanks for helping, I'll never be able to repay you."

"You'll never need to. See ya."

Under his breath David whispered, "Soon, I hope."

Two months would be cutting it close. Real close.

It was June 7 before he met with his friend again. It had actually taken Fingers nearly three months to make an appearance, and David had been worried sick. He hadn't thought Fingers would abandon him, but that maybe something had happened to him, or he hadn't been able to find everything on the list.

"Where the hell have you been? I've been pulling my freakin' hair out."

"Take it easy, Muddy. I did the best I could."

"Please tell me you remembered the anatomy book."

"Relax. Got it out of our own pitiful library here at the pen. The librarian had one right on the shelf. Didn't even have to steal the bloody thing, I just signed it out."

"Good man. What about the rest of the stuff? Any trouble?"

"Nah. The key took some extra work, but they don't call me the best for nothing."

Fingers slid the small sack of supplies through the bars into David's hands. David scoured the contents, double-checking everything. "You did good, Fingers. Real good."

"Nothing to it, Muddy, but tell me, how are you getting out of this cell? There's nothing in that sack to cut through these bars."

"Don't worry about it. I don't want you to know anything. Get your ass out of here before you get in trouble."

"But when you gonna make your move? Maybe I can—"

"No, Fingers . . . no way."

"It'd at least be nice to know if you made it out. You know they'll never tell us."

"Don't worry, you'll know."

"How?"

"July 29, if the lights start dimming at midnight, I didn't pull it off."

Fingers soon left and David immediately began stashing his supplies throughout his cell. The only thing he didn't stash was the worn copy of *Mysteries of Human Anatomy*, by someone named Dr. Simon Adams. Taking the book over to his bed, he began poring through it. It only took a minute to find the chapter he was looking for.

For eight days, until June 15, he made plans and studied that chapter as if his life depended on it—and likely it did. He finally laid the book down, though, knowing he was stalling and that it was time for action. If he didn't go tonight, he'd probably still be sitting in his cell when they came to fry him.

He steeled his nerves and psyched himself up for what he was about to do. At 12:45 A.M., David gathered his supplies and was ready to go.

CHAPTER THIRTY-TWO

It ended up being another twenty minutes before he plunged the knife into his belly. To prepare himself, he had to strip down to his underwear to conceal his supplies beneath his clothing. He used the thick roll of black electrical tape Fingers had stolen, carefully attaching the things he was going to need to his legs. The hardest object to hide had been a large Phillips screwdriver, but luckily he was thin, and his prison-issued pants were big and baggy. When his pants were back on, he examined his handiwork and thought he'd pulled it off quite well. He didn't think anyone would notice any odd bulges. Notice or not, it was the best he could do.

He hoped the guard wouldn't be looking at his pants anyway. If things worked out as planned, the guard would be more interested in all the blood. That was where the short, wooden-handled knife and the anatomy book came into play. The book had never been intended to help during his escape. He'd wanted to learn where to stab himself, to cause a fair amount of bleeding, without accidentally killing himself in the process.

At first David had decided just to fake an injury in order to be taken out of his cell. Maybe he could scream he was having terrible stomach cramps. Something as simple as that might not work, though. He was a convicted murderer on death row and was regarded as dangerous. Chances were, the ruthless guards wouldn't risk coming into his cell for something as silly as stomach cramps. In fact, they would probably enjoy seeing him doubled over in pain.

He only had one chance to escape and couldn't risk blowing it before he even started. He needed a surefire method that would guarantee the guards would remove him from his cell, and stabbing himself would definitely get their attention. If they believed he was trying to commit suicide, they'd have to take him away.

The knife slid in surprisingly easy, much easier than he'd thought it would. He had aimed its point at the lower-right-hand section of his belly, just below the belt line. From the anatomy book, he'd decided this area was his safest bet. All the vital organs were located above this area, and most of the intestines coiled above and to the left of it. David was messing around dangerously close to the appendix, but his studies had reasonably confirmed he'd be okay. There would be lots of blood and some pain, but nothing crippling or fatal—he hoped.

He'd been right about the blood—there was much more than he'd imagined—but he'd been dead wrong about the little bit of pain. There was a great deal of pain. It hurt like a bastard. It was as if someone had started a small fire burning in his belly and was furiously fanning the flames to make it grow. And grow it did. The small slit of fire exploded throughout his entrails like quicksilver, searing everything in his lower abdomen. He started screaming in agony, no playacting required.

Thankfully, a burly looking guard David didn't recognize showed up, and within minutes he found himself lying on a table in the small hospital ward. The pain in his stomach had lessened somewhat or had at least gone numb enough that he couldn't feel it as much. It had been a painful, but bearable, trip from his cellblock. The best part was that the guard hadn't noticed the supplies hidden on his legs. He'd been too repulsed by the sight of the blood to notice anything. All he'd done was put David on the examining table, informed the doctor he had a suicide attempt, and ducked out the door to wait outside.

The doctor on duty was a wiry, nervous man in his mid-fifties. He looked like a younger version of Woody Allen, but had thick gray hair. Most of his nervousness probably came from the fact he thought David was a serial killer. His shifty green eyes kept glancing toward the doorway to confirm the guard was still within shouting distance.

Nervous or not, the man was a fine physician. He worked quickly and efficiently and soon had the wound cleaned and bandaged. David's lower abdomen still flared with a stabbing pain when he moved quickly, but he was confident he hadn't suffered any permanent injury. Studying the anatomy book had proved worth it after all.

The guard in the hallway peeked back into the examining room, and with David's wound bandaged up, now felt capable of returning to the room. "He gonna be all right, Doc?" the guard asked. He sounded much younger and frailer than he looked.

"Sure. Nothing more than a deep scratch, really," answered the doctor.

"Is he going to stay here tonight, or what?"

"Christ, no!" said the doctor, paling visibly at the very thought of spending the night with the infamous Ripper Killer. "Take him back to his cell now, if you want. He can rest there as well as here. I'll check on him in the morning."

This wasn't what David had in mind at all. He'd hoped to be kept in the hospital ward all night. Most prisoners probably would have been, but his reputation was obviously worse than his wounds.

The guard was closing in to drag him back to his cell. If he wanted to escape, he couldn't let that happen. A change in plan was called for, and he had only five seconds to come up with it. He buzzed through his limited options and made a quick decision. As if his body had been seized with convulsions, he lay on the examining table and began to shake. He let his eyes roll back as high as he could get them and gripped the edges of the table with clawed hands. His body continued to buck and writhe convulsively and to great effect. His abdomen began to ache again, but he didn't dare stop.

"What's happening?" asked the guard.

"Get over here and help me," shouted the doctor as he scrambled in his medicine cabinet for something. "He's having a seizure of some kind, maybe epileptic. I'm going to have to sedate him."

From the examining table, David could see the doctor removing a small, clear, liquid-filled bottle and a not-so-small syringe from the medicine cabinet. The doctor filled the syringe and hastily moved toward David. Behind the doctor, the guard was also closer, striding quickly to assist. The point of no return had arrived. Driven by desperation, David struck out at the approaching doctor just as he reached the table. He pounced on the surprised doctor, smashing his chin with a right. The vicious blow knocked the doctor's head back, crashing his jaws together hard enough to snap a few teeth off as they slammed shut. Out cold, the doctor slumped forward and crashed to the floor. On his way down, David grabbed for and miraculously came up with the sedative-filled syringe. The guard was more surprised than the doctor. David jammed the needle deep into the guard's upper arm and pressed down on the plunger before the guard realized what was happening. He tried to put up a fight, but it was too late. Whatever type of sedative was in the syringe, it was powerful, and almost immediately the guard slumped to the floor beside the unconscious doctor.

David could hardly believe his luck. He hastily refilled the syringe from the small bottle in the doctor's pocket and injected it into the doctor's arm to buy some extra time.

The beginning of his escape had been successful, but now David had to get to the gymnasium in order to implement the final stage of his plan. Doing that was somewhat problematic: The hospital ward wasn't far from the gym, but he couldn't just waltz down the hallway and walk through the gym doors. There would be prisoners' cells to walk by, and the inmates would surely make a racket if they saw him. Also, the guards would be patrolling the corridors.

Luckily, he had no intention of using the halls. He was going to reach the gymnasium via the heating ducts in the ceiling. Years ago, he'd been assigned to help some workmen do repairs on the ducts and knew they were large enough to crawl through. He also knew the hospital ward and the gymnasium were both located on the main heating system, with interconnecting ducts. That was why he'd needed to be brought to the hospital in the first place.

He positioned the examining table underneath the metal heating grate located above the medicine cabinet. Without a glance back, he was up and into the heating system and a small step closer to freedom. Inside, the duct was more cramped than he remembered, but still roomy enough to shuffle along on his belly. It only took a few minutes to reach the main heating shaft, which ran the length of the prison complex, and from which all other heating ducts branched. The main shaft was roomier, allowing him the maneuverability to crawl on his hands and knees.

He had brought along a tiny penlight, which was one of the items strapped to his legs. He had imagined it would be dark inside the shaft, but was pleasantly surprised to find a sufficient amount of light filtering through various heating grates from the rooms and corridors below. He was relieved at not having to fumble for the light.

A mild rumbling noise echoed along the air shaft, but David wasn't able to figure out if the source of the noise was in front of him or behind. It didn't really matter either way, so he ignored the noise and started moving toward the gym.

Crawling along on hands and knees, he could have traveled faster, but he took his time, inching slowly and carefully, trying to be as quiet as possible. The only time he felt at risk was when he crossed over a heating grate, which left him visible to anyone who might look up. The odds on that were slim, so he moved slowly but confidently toward the far end of the shaft and the gymnasium. He made it there without a problem.

The heating wasn't on at this time of the year, but it was still quite hot in the confined shaft. Sweat ran freely into his eyes, although not all of the sweat was caused by the heat. Tension, nervousness, and fear also played their part.

The rumbling noise was much louder now; obviously he was heading toward the source. It was a strange noise: sometimes loud, sometimes soft, at times rhythmic, at times broken and jumbled. The more David concentrated on the noise, the more it sounded as if it was coming from more than one source—not one noise, but many, all multilayered and overlapping each other.

What is that? At this time of night, nobody should be making that racket.

David shook his head, determined to concentrate on the business at hand. If he didn't get moving, the next noise would be the wail of the prison sirens and the approach of angry guards. He inhaled a deep breath and started moving again.

He came to the end of the east-west air shaft. The wall of the gymnasium was directly in front of him now, but from where David was, there was no access to the room. The heating ducts leading into the gym—or at least all of the ducts that he could fit through—were located on the ceiling. There were ground-floor heating vents, but they were all smaller, offshoot shafts. He was too big to squeeze into any of those. His only option was to go for the ceiling shafts.

The prisoners' gymnasium, being a tall three-story structure, presented a large problem for David. He was presently in the ceiling of the first floor, which meant he had to climb two full stories to get to the roof. That might not have been too bad, but taking into account the cramped quarters he was working in, the fact he had no handholds, the pressure of trying not to make noise, and the pain from his stab wound, things began to look tougher. To David, the climb looked impossible, but since the hot seat was being prepared for him downstairs, the climb had to be attempted—impossible or not.

His first attempt failed after three feet. His sweaty hands couldn't give him enough grip to support his weight. His second attempt failed too. Fear mingled with frustration, as images of the electric chair flashed through his mind. He leaned his back against the vertical wall of the shaft to ponder his predicament. The second his back touched the wall, the solution came to him. He'd been going about this climb all wrong. Instead of trying to support himself with his hands and feet, the answer was to use his body. The vertical shaft was small and constrictive enough to allow him to press his back against one side of the shaft as he wedged his legs up against the opposite side. By doing this, he found he could wedge himself without fear of falling, then use his hands and feet to slowly inch his way up. When he felt tired, he simply pressed back against the wall and rested for a moment. Within minutes, he'd reached the top.

Pain flared along David's side and belly from his knife wound. He touched his fingers to the bandage and felt them wet and sticky. It was too dark to see, but from the sticky feel he knew his wound had reopened. There was nothing to be done for his cut now; all he could do was move on.

The rumbling noise he'd been hearing since entering the shaft was much louder on this level. So loud, in fact, it was becoming rather deafening.

What's happening? This is crazy. It must be close to two o'clock in the morning.

The noise was coming through the large metal heat gratings above the gymnasium, thirty feet directly ahead. This close to the source of the racket, David was beginning to hear screams and yells and cheers filtering up to him. For a confused moment, he wondered if there was a prison riot in progress that he hadn't known about. A small bell rung nearby and the answer finally dawned on him, but he still didn't want to believe it.

No! Not tonight. It can't be happening tonight.

But David knew that it was: after one o'clock in the morning, cheering crowds below in the gymnasium, no guard whistles or sirens, and a bell being rung. Those things could only add up to one thing. They were playing the Game again.

There was nothing David could do except wait it out in the air shaft until everyone left. He started wondering about the doctor and the guard, and about how long the sedatives would last. If they regained consciousness before the Game was over, he would be in an awful lot of trouble.

If they'd started around the usual time, the Game had to be almost over. Curiosity started to get the best of him as the minutes ticked by. Soon he was wondering who was fighting. Memories of Mouse's last fight spun through his head, bringing with it all the intense anger he still felt over his brutally unnecessary death.

Is Shadowman fighting tonight?

A beautiful idea occurred to him: maybe this time, Shadowman might not make out as well. If David were to move to the grating, he'd be able to see the fight, and maybe have a chance to see that sick bastard buy his ticket to Hell. It was tempting, but also incredibly stupid. A hundred inmates and guards would be standing in the room below. He'd have to be a fool to risk being seen when he'd made it this far.

Fool or not, David couldn't help himself. If there was a chance to see Shadowman get his, he just had to take the risk. He inched along the shaft and nosed up to the edge of the metal grating. His eyes had barely crept over the lip when he almost screamed in panic. The gym floor was packed with inmates and guards, and every last one of them had their heads tilted, looking directly up at him.

No, wait a minute. They weren't looking at him. They were all looking up at the fight. Two huge men grappled silently on the thick hanging ropes not ten feet from David. One of them was indeed Shadowman, who looked infinitely happy as he drove a vicious uppercut into the chin of some dark-haired mutant David didn't recognize.

He let his glance slide away from the fight, up the rope, to the hinged trapdoor at the top of the ceiling that he was hoping to climb through. The trapdoor had been cut so that the two hanging ropes could be bolted and attached directly up through the ceiling into one of the main support beams of the roof. The trapdoor was no big secret to the inmates at the pen, since everyone from time to time had seen the hanging ropes changed or removed for basketball games or whatever. David's plan was to use the trapdoor and climb down one of the ropes to the gym floor below.

A scream of pain snapped his attention back to the fight. Shadowman and his opponent were back on the ground and to David's disappointment the scream hadn't come from his former cellmate. On the contrary, Shadowman looked as if he was having the time of his life. He was laughing and grinning like a schoolboy. David remembered that awful grin all too well, a chill running down his spine at the memory.

David had seen enough. Sliding back out of sight, he hoped it would come to an end soon—he was running out of time. A loud scream cut off abruptly by the crack of breaking bone told him the fight was over. A quick peek confirmed the unknown opponent's back had been snapped like a twig, probably over Shadowman's knee. The victor was now crossing the finish line.

Within ten minutes, the gymnasium was cleared and everyone was shuffled back to their cells. Having wasted enough time, David quickly crawled across the metal grating, slipped out of the trapdoor, and scampered down one of the hanging ropes.

It felt wonderful to stand on solid ground again. He wasn't terribly claustrophobic, but it felt nice to be out of that cramped, stuffy shaft. His side hurt, but all in all he felt okay. He was in the gymnasium and freedom was within reach.

David let his excitement get the better of him and threw caution to the wind. Instead of slowly sneaking around the gym behind the bleachers as planned, he rushed straight across the center of the gym on a direct path to the main entrance, a very bad and potentially fatal mistake. Halfway across the floor he realized his error. He wouldn't have anywhere to hide if one of the guards returned to the gym. No sooner had he thought about it, it happened. The door at the main entrance opened and a tall figure walked in. David stopped on a dime, but there was nowhere for him to go. He was frozen on the spot, as if someone had applied Krazy Glue to the bottom of his sneakers.

David damned himself for being so stupid. Why hadn't he followed his plan and stayed hidden? Why hadn't he been more patient? Why had he been such a damn fool? Frustrated and dispirited, he waited for the guard to come get him, but when the tall figure stepped out of the darkness into the light, it wasn't a guard at all.

It was Shadowman.

"Well, well, well. What have we got here?" Shadowman icily hissed, stopping fifteen feet away.

"Where did you . . . ? I mean how did you know . . . ?" David started to ask, but was abruptly cut off.

"I saw you. I was at the top of the ropes and I happened to look up into the grating. Something caught my eye. Silly me . . . I thought it might have been a rat. I saw someone crawling around, but it was too dark to see who. Funny, I was right on my first guess. It was a rat, after all."

"Did you tell the guards?" David asked, a part of him hoping a few guards would bust in at any moment, taking him away from this cold-eyed madman.

"Of course not. Why would I? We can have more fun on our own. I have an agreement that after each fight they leave me alone in the gym for an hour so I can unwind. I usually lift weights and stretch, but tonight's going to be different. Tonight's special. I never thought I'd see your pathetic little face again. I blew my first chance by underestimating you, but it won't happen again."

Shadowman began walking slowly toward David, unzipping his pants, his intentions crystal clear. "Now tell me, Diana, my pretty. Where were we last time . . . before we were so rudely interrupted?"

David found himself running. His body had reacted instinctively, but it was his brain that was going to have to get him out of this mess. What could he possibly do to escape this depraved lunatic a second time? Where was he going to go? The gymnasium wasn't that big, and the guards wouldn't be back for an hour.

The ropes, he decided. *Climb the ropes and get back into the air shaft.*

That might work. Shadowman would be too big to fit into the cramped shaft to follow him. It would almost certainly put an end to his escape plans, but at the moment, even the prospect of the electric chair seemed better than the alternative.

David looked over his shoulder to see how much of a lead he had. He was pleased to see Shadowman hadn't moved yet. Obviously the long-haired freak was thinking there was nowhere for him to go. He was laughing at David's futile attempt to avoid him. His laughter stopped abruptly once David made it to the hanging ropes and started climbing. Somewhere in his head it registered what David was trying to do. He looked up at the open trapdoor in the ceiling and immediately broke into a crazed sprint.

"Stop right now, bitch. You're not getting away this time."

David didn't stop. He climbed faster, now that he heard Shadowman's approach. His belly screamed in protest with every upward movement. It felt as if someone had replaced his intestines with white-hot coals. In a different situation, the pain would have been unbearable, but tonight he had no choice. Gritting his teeth, he climbed as fast as his weakening body would allow.

He was nearing the end of his climb when the crazed animal jumped for and grabbed hold of the rope, causing it to sway to the left suddenly. It shifted under Shadowman's weight, almost causing David to lose his already-weakening grip. Barely hanging on, he inched toward the trapdoor a few feet above.

He forced himself to stop looking up and to just concentrate on moving. Faster than he thought possible, his hand touched the trapdoor and he was moving up into the air shaft.

I'm gonna make it, he rejoiced, as a fresh batch of adrenaline coursed through him.

Then a powerful hand clamped like a steel trap around his ankle.

Shadowman was much stronger than David and calmly pulled his weary body backward out of the safety of the shaft. He'd been so close to getting away.

"Where do you think you're going, sweetheart?" the muscular freak whispered into David's ear. "I don't appreciate my girlfriends running away, understand? I said, do . . . you . . . *understand?*"

"Yeah," David said, frightened. The hatred and madness flowing off of this madman was almost a physical thing, and David recoiled from the blow.

"Good," he smiled. "That's a good girl. Now let me tell you what we're going to do. We're going back down to the floor, and then we're going to have us some fun over behind those bleachers. Understand?"

This time David was unable to find anything to say. Shadowman took his silence to mean agreement and smiled even more. He brought his black-toothed, disease-ridden mouth closer to David, and it wasn't until his foul breath caressed his cheek that David realized the brute was going to kiss him.

"*No!*" David screamed and drove his knee up into his assailant's aroused groin.

It happened more by accident than planning. He'd only

been trying to put some distance between them, but his knee connected solidly. Shadowman cried out, obviously hurt badly, his eyes rolling back slightly in his head. David was sure his attacker would lose his grip on the rope and fall, but that never happened. Instead, he clung tenaciously to the rope, digging his powerful fingers in like an animal using its claws.

David used the time he'd created to try and get away. He intended to climb up into the air shaft, but Shadowman was recovering quicker than anticipated. The powerful pervert reached for David, catching him around the waist. His grip was feeble and weak, but it sickened David to be touched by this groping madman. Escape into the shaft wasn't going to happen, and going down the rope was also out of the question. What could he do? David glanced over at the brass bell hanging on the far side of the grate. The small knife was still taped to it. Probably, neither fighter had had a chance to use it.

Shadowman was almost fully recovered, so David broke free of his weak grasp and headed out onto the grating, not looking back until he'd reached the bell and retrieved the small blade. When he did, Shadowman was smiling again.

"My, you're a feisty little bitch, aren't you? I *like* that in a woman."

David felt weak, but the knife he held in his teeth made him feel somewhat more powerful. Through clenched teeth, he said, "Fuck you, psycho. Come on over and see how much you like this knife."

Shadowman laughed, enjoying every minute of this.

"Why should I? How are your arms feeling? How about your fingers . . . or maybe that little boo-boo on your belly there?"

"I'm fine," David said, trying to sound convincing.

"Sure you are, Diana. No, what I think I'll do is stay right where I am and wait for you to come to me. I have a feeling you haven't got what it takes to make it back over to this rope. You're hanging by a thread of stubborn strength, and soon you might be headed for a long fall. What do you think?"

"I think you're an asshole." David was trying to act tough, but he knew the bastard was right. His belly was on fire and his body ached. Realistically, he wasn't going to be able to hang on much longer. Getting the knife had felt like the right thing to do, but obviously it had been a mistake. Now he was trapped out on the heating grate and losing strength, with a knife that was useless to him. He opened his mouth and watched the knife take the long fall he'd soon take himself. He was giving up.

"You want to know something?" David asked Shadowman, who was licking his lips in silent anticipation.

"What?"

"I'm looking forward to this fall. At least if I kill myself . . . it'll stop you from having your little fun behind the bleachers."

"Why? Just because you're dead, that's not going to stop . . . Hey, what the hell?"

Shadowman had been talking when the rope he was hanging onto dropped an inch. They looked up at the same time and were shocked to see someone hanging out of the trapdoor in the ceiling, rapidly cutting through the thick rope with a sharp knife. The rope cutter looked around at David and for the first time, David realized who it was.

"Fingers," he said, astonished. How on earth had Fingers ended up here? Fingers never paused to explain; he continued to cut, saw, and hack at the thick rope.

Shadowman recovered from his initial shock of seeing an unexpected third party enter the fray, and began climbing up to deal with the intruder. Before he'd moved a foot, the rope dropped again, as its thick strands began to unravel. Deciding against climbing farther and instinctively knowing he didn't have time to climb down, Shadowman tried to climb over to the other rope. He reached out and almost had his hand on it when his rope finally let go. The rope went slack and for the slightest moment, both he and the severed rope seemed to hang in midair, defying gravity. The madman spun around and locked eyes with David, and then he plummeted to the hard gym floor far below.

Shadowman never did scream, not even when he thudded onto the hardwood floor and lay broken and still. The entire fall he had locked eyes with David, hatred colder than ice shining in his dark eyes. Until the last moment he wore that cold, sneering smile.

"Muddy? Hey . . . you all right?"

For a heart-thumping second, David thought it was Shadowman talking from beyond the grave, but it was Fingers. He'd managed to wiggle out of the air shaft and onto the one remaining rope. David wanted to say something to his friend, who had just saved his life, but couldn't find the words.

Fingers tried again. "It's over, Muddy. Shadowman's dead. You still have to live, so get your ass over here and we'll climb down together."

"I can't, Fingers. I can't move or I'll fall too. I'm too weak to make it."

"Shut up and move. We're in this together now. I need you Muddy. . . . You're the best friend I ever had. Don't let me down now."

The power of friendship is something that is sometimes underestimated, because somewhere in his friend's words, David found the strength inside to carry on. His body throbbed and screamed and ached, but somehow he reached the rope and his friend. Together they helped each other down to the floor.

"How did you end up in that air shaft with a knife, Fingers?" David asked.

"Simple. I was in the gym for the fight tonight, and I heard one of the guards being told to go see why you were screaming. I'm not totally stupid. I knew you had to get out of your cell to try your escape, and I also knew time was running short. I put two and two together and figured tonight was the night. I thought maybe I could help, so I slipped out the gym and followed the guard.

"It took me a while to figure out what was going on in the hospital ward. I knew you were in there with the doctor and the guard, but it was so quiet in there. I waited a bit, then snuck in to see what was happening. The doc and the guard were out cold on the floor, and I thought you'd killed them, but then I noticed the needle and the sedative bottle. You left the grating for the ceiling duct open, so I knew where you went. I grabbed the knife off the table before I went into the shaft—the same knife I'd stolen for you."

He pointed to the spreading red stain on David's belly. "You stabbed yourself?"

"Yeah. I know it was stupid, but I had to get out of my cell. Don't worry . . . I'm fine. It just stings a bit."

"That's a lie, but let's drop it. What do you say we get out of this dump?"

"Oh no. Thanks for the help, but I'm not taking you with me. You've only got four years left on your sentence and you're out. I can't risk your future like that. You're going back to your cell."

"It's too late for that, Muddy. We're in this together. I can't go back."

"Sure you can. Nobody knows you're involved. You might get caught getting back to your cell, but at the most, you'll get a slap on the wrist."

"I'll get more than that. Something happened back in the hospital I haven't told you about. By the time I realized you'd gone into the heating duct, the guard was waking up. The doctor was still out like a light, but the guard—probably because he was so much bigger—was recovering from the sedative quicker. I had to kill him. I didn't want to do it, but what else could I do? I killed him with the knife and went into the shaft to follow you. My fingerprints are all over the place, Muddy. I can't go back. They'll be strapping me in that electric chair instead of you."

From the look of anguish and shame on his friend's face, David could see that Fingers was telling the truth. He decided it would be best to just drop the subject and say what Fingers had been waiting to hear. "Let's get the hell out of here, then."

Fingers's face brightened instantly, and he shook David's outstretched hand. "For sure, buddy . . . Let's go. What's the plan, anyway? We going over the wall?"

"No. We're going under it. Do you remember the guy they used to call the President? He sort of looked like Bill Clinton, except skinnier. Really thin guy."

"Yeah, I think so. He was the guy who tried to escape out through the sewers?"

"Try, my ass—he made it. I talked to him once, before his break. He told me how this place used to be medium security, until Kingston Pen became overcrowded. It had to get a facelift to make it ready for us hard-asses. They did a pretty thorough job too, beefing up the entire place, but they made a few mistakes.

"The President told me the sewers under this prison are really close to the main city lines. That means they're big and roomy, to handle the large volume of waste. If someone could get into them, he could get into the main branch of the sewer system easily, and from there he could take off in any direction without being followed. The point is, if we can get into the sewers—just like the President did—we're in the clear. They'll never find us."

"Great, Muddy, but how do we get into the sewers? If my memory is right, the President went through the drain in the prisoners' shower room."

"Yeah, that was one of the mistakes I was talking about. When they converted the prison over to max security, they left the prisoners' shower room exactly the way it was. In the middle of the floor was this large drain, and the floor angled down toward it. It was big so it could handle the massive amount of water flow from the showering convicts. A smaller drain wouldn't have been able to handle the job, so the drain was left unchanged. The trouble was, the drain was *too* big. Once the grille was removed, the pipe was big enough for any ambitious man, albeit a fairly thin ambitious man, to wiggle down into it and gain access to the much-larger sewer network beneath. That's what the President did, Fingers, and we're going to do the same thing."

"We can't. They changed it . . . the drain, I mean. They brought work crews in to tear up the shower floor and install a new one with four smaller drains in it. Hell, we'd be lucky to stick one leg down them, never mind the rest of us."

"I know. I was on the list of prisoners that volunteered to help the workers change the drain. You're right. There's no way we're getting into the sewers from the prisoners' shower room. We're going out through the *guards'*."

"How do you figure?"

"Think about it. This whole place was built at the same time. If the prisoners' shower room had a large drain in the floor, the guards' shower room did too. They changed the floor in the prisoners' shower, but not in the guards'. Why would they? No prisoners can get into their showers; they're always locked. The only people who can get into the guards' showers are the guards . . . or maybe a couple of smart convicts like us who just happen to have a spare key."

David dug down inside his pants and removed the key taped to his inner thigh. He held it up in triumph.

"The key," gasped Fingers, "I forgot about that. When I stole it, I didn't have a clue what you wanted it for. I though you were nuts, but you're not. . . . You're a genius."

"And you're the best damn thief on the planet, but let's not pat ourselves on the back too much. We're not out of here yet. Let's move."

David started to head for the exit again, but Fingers grabbed the back of his shirt.

"Do you think we ought to do something with him?" he asked, pointing over at the twisted, broken figure of Shadowman.

"Just leave the bastard. We'll be gone before the guards come looking for him."

They headed for the exit, but this time it was David who stopped. He walked back to the slumped body and without warning, kicked Shadowman with all the strength he could muster. He was already dead and gone, but David still smiled at the sound of some ribs fracturing. His frustration and anger gone, David rejoined his puzzled friend.

"What was that for?" Fingers asked.

David took one last look at Shadowman and then looked deep into his friend's eyes. "That, Fingers . . . was for Mouse. Let's go."

Together they made it to the gymnasium exit and out into the short hallway that led to the guards' shower room. Luck was on their side; no one was in sight. The key Fingers had somehow gotten his hot little hands on worked perfectly, and within seconds they were inside the shower room and closing the door silently behind them.

"We made it, Fingers. We're almost home free. All we have to do is . . . Hey, what's the matter?"

David had been prancing about, excited to be so close to freedom, but the look on Fingers's face stopped him cold. He followed his friend's sour look down to the floor and gasped. The drain had been changed. Instead of a large drain, big enough for them to wiggle through, there was a solid metal plate with an eight-inch drain in the middle of it.

"They changed this room too, Muddy. We're sunk."

Despair threatened to overwhelm David, but when he examined the drain closer, fresh hope surged through him. "Maybe not Fingers . . . look. I think the old drain is still here. I don't think they changed the pipe. This metal plate is just a cover screwed down on top of it. If we can get this off, I'll bet the original drainpipe's still there."

Fingers rushed to inspect the metal plate. "Did you say *screwed* down? What kind of screws? Phillips? They are, Muddy, look." Fingers slapped David happily on the back.

"That's what kind of screwdriver I snatched for you. We're not done yet!"

David withdrew the Phillips screwdriver from his pant leg and began removing the metal plate. It was going to take some time—there were forty screws. After fifteen, Fingers took over, giving David a break. For a man that had the quickest fingers around, he couldn't remove a screw for the life of him. After ten more screws, David grabbed the screwdriver back, unable to stand the slow pace.

"I guess these fingers weren't meant for honest labor," he said, giggling, as David went back to work.

The closer David got to the last screw, the more anxious they became. The tension was so thick in the room David wanted to scream. They were so close to freedom, they could taste it, and all that was in their way was a few damn screws. David tried not to rush, to clear his mind and concentrate on nothing but the screws in front of him.

"Almost there, Fingers, this is the last one. There, I got it. . . . I got it!"

He'd been concentrating so hard on removing the last few screws that he'd been ignoring his friend. He looked up and was shocked to see another disappointed look on his friend's face. "What's the matter?" David asked.

"That," Fingers said, pointing toward the door.

David turned slowly around. In the doorway, with a revolver pointed at them, was one of the night-shift guards. Before David could move, Fingers leapt by him and charged the guard. He thought the guard was going to shoot, but Fingers must have surprised him. He made it over and was trying to wrestle the gun out of the guard's hand. The guard was bigger and stronger, but Fingers had adrenaline and fear working on his side. David sat transfixed, unable to think of anything to do to help.

"Go, Muddy. Get out of here, you're free. Don't just sit there . . . *move*!"

His friend yelling got David moving, and he yanked off the metal floor plate, exposing the drainpipe beneath. Just as they'd hoped, the pipe was large enough to fit into. He dropped both legs in and prepared to escape, but hesitated, not sure what to do. He couldn't leave Fingers, could he?

"I said go, Muddy. I can't hold this bastard forever."

David was confused. The idea of leaving was tempting, but would he be able to live with himself afterward? If he tried to help Fingers and got caught, the hot seat would be waiting for him. On the other hand, if he left alone, it would be Fingers who would go to the chair for killing the guard in the doctor's office. David couldn't let that happen. After everything Fingers had done, there was no way he could run out on him now. He had to help.

He pulled back out of the pipe while the battle at the doorway raged on. David could see they were wrestling for possession of the gun. The guard still had a hold of it, but it looked as if Fingers was getting the upper hand. David ran across the room to help his friend. Together, they could overpower the guard and then both make their escape.

Suddenly, the gun went off with a loud bang.

He was just reaching to help Fingers when the shot fired. David said a quick prayer, hoping the guard had been the one shot, but instinctively he knew it had been Fingers. David reached out to catch his friend, and together they slumped to the floor.

The guard took a step back and pointed the gun at David, who knew the screw would shoot him if he made any attempt to move. Other guards could be heard running toward them from down the hall, drawn by the sound of gunfire. David's one chance to escape had passed him by, and he wouldn't get another.

"Muddy?" Fingers asked in a raspy, weak voice.

David cradled him in his arms, noticing the fading light in his friend's eyes.

"You should have went, Muddy. Now you'll never get out."

"I couldn't go without you. I wanted to set you free too."

"You have, Muddy . . . you have."

Three more armed guards rushed into the room, dragging

David away from Fingers, but not before he looked down to see that death had already freed his best friend.

Tears welled up in his eyes as the guards dragged him back to his cell. He wasn't crying for himself, he was thinking about what his friend had said with his last breath. The thought of Fingers free at last caused fresh tears to well in David's eyes.

He wasn't sad for his friend—he envied him.

CHAPTER THIRTY-THREE

Paula Lewis snapped to attention. She was exhausted and had briefly fallen asleep. Being exhausted was acceptable—she'd been working around the clock for weeks—but falling asleep was completely out of the question. How could she sleep when her client was only hours away from being executed for crimes she felt he hadn't committed?

July 29 had sneaked up on her and her client with frightening speed. She'd been working nonstop on Mr. Winter's case, and the last six weeks had flown by. It was now the night of his execution, and although she was getting close, she still didn't have any concrete evidence for a last-minute stay.

In the last two weeks, too many gaps and unanswered questions had been uncovered as she furiously interviewed and reinterviewed the relevant witnesses. Getting David off of death row tonight was impossible, but she continued to go over every scrap of paper, trying to find something that would buy some time and convince the premier of Ontario to grant her a stay of execution—a delay. Maybe then she'd be able to get him a new trial, or at least get his sentence reduced. Easier said than done. David Winter was a convicted killer from way back, and the evidence against him in the warden's murder was substantial. The fact that he'd tried to escape from prison the previous month wasn't going to help, either.

Paula was shuffling through her notes and was about to head to the premier's office with what little she had. She was reaching for the light when her eyes locked onto a single sheet of paper jutting out of the pile. It was the coroner's report on Warden Steele's body. She'd looked at the report before, but felt she was missing something. Something important.

Her eyes scanned the report with an intensity that could have burned the page. After an anxious minute of searching, she found it. Near the bottom of the page was a standard question asking the estimated time of death. Paula had never paid close attention to that part of the report, because it was generally inadmissible in court, due to its being speculative. Now she stared at it with wide, unbelieving eyes. She gathered up everything and dashed for the door, knocking her chair over in her rush. She had to get to the premier's office in Toronto . . . fast.

I can stop this execution, she thought. *Maybe not forever, but tonight . . . yeah. If I can get there on time.*

Paula glanced at her watch as she gunned the car out the driveway. She almost screamed. It was later than she'd thought. From Hamilton, it would take an hour to get to the premier's office in Toronto.

"Move your ass, Paula," she said as she pulled out onto the highway.

She glanced at her watch again. For every minute she thought went by, five actually disappeared. She was cutting it close. It was now 9:52.

David sat immobile on death row, his twenty-four-hour-a-day home since his attempted escape last month. The guards and prison officials were taking no chances. They'd upped the security on him, and he couldn't even piss without an audience now. David didn't care. His lawyer kept telling him she was still working to get him off, but he didn't take much stock in her enthusiasm. The creature had █████ him good this time, and there was no way out of this mess.

"The *creature*," David muttered, disgusted.

It wasn't enough that it had ruined his life and manipulated everything and everybody to the point of killing him. It had to keep taunting. It could have allowed him to live out his last month in relative peace, but no way, not the creature. It had been waiting in his cell on the night of his botched escape when the guards had roughly brought him back. It had been all laughs and jokes that night, true enjoyment of his suffering. Of course, the guards hadn't been able to see it; only David was allowed a glimpse of the creature's vast powers.

Since then, the creature had constantly been in his cell, laughing and making fun of him. The abuse seemed to drag on forever, slowly chipping away at David's deflated ego. He wanted to die. At least death would set him free, and perhaps lead to something better.

July 29 had finally arrived, and his execution was scheduled for midnight. That thought actually made him feel somewhat cheery. The creature had even left him alone for a while. "Final plans to take care of," the creature had said. David didn't care. He was enjoying the peace.

At 8:00 P.M., they brought David his last meal. He'd ordered a turkey dinner with all the trimmings. As the guards carried in his tray, David almost felt happy—until he lifted off the cover to discover his meal was gone. Only a few crumbs remained on the platter. At that moment, the creature returned, licking gravy off its black teeth. The bastard had even deprived him of a last meal. He could have called the guards back, but what could he have said? They would only have laughed. A feeling of gloom washed over him again as he sat in silent despair on his bed.

Around ten o'clock, a priest entered the cell to comfort him and, presumably, hear his confession. David hadn't felt much like talking, so he just sat and listened. Behind the priest, the creature danced and sang in total disrespect. He didn't really want to hear either of them, but ended up having to listen to both.

Later the new warden appeared, accompanied by six stone-faced guards. David felt as if he'd been hit in the stomach by the rock of Gibraltar. He knew there was only one reason for this gathering entourage.

"David Winter," Warden Brown said. "There's no easy way to do this . . . but as no reprieve is imminent, it's my unpleasant task to ready you for the sentence imposed by the court. Stand up please; it's time to go."

David tried to be strong, but his legs buckled. He'd been praying for this moment, but now that it was here, he was shocked to realize part of him wasn't ready to die. Part of him wanted to scream out about the injustice of it all. Part of him still wanted to live.

The guards rushed in to help him along. He tried to struggle and put up a fight, but it was an act of futility. Without much effort, they had him handcuffed and shackled, and dragged him unsympathetically from his cell. It was now 11:01.

Paula made decent time getting to Toronto, but traffic inside the city limits slowed her down. It was a few minutes past eleven by the time she charged into Premier Douglas Matthew's corner office at city hall. The premier was still there, staying near his phone until the execution was over. She could hear Premier Matthew on the phone through his closed private office door. His secretary, a prune-faced older lady, was sitting at her desk by the window.

The secretary scowled the minute she saw Paula enter the room. She'd been to see the premier many times in person and had bothered him on the phone a hundred times trying to plead her client's case. Every time, she'd had a run-in with his secretary, and tonight was no exception.

"What do you want this time, Miss Lewis? The premier has made it quite clear your client's case is a closed matter. Mr. Matthew doesn't have time to play games with some sassy lawyer."

"Shut the hell up," Paula said. She was too exhausted and nervous to listen to this old bag rattle on while her client's life ticked away.

"Really, Miss Lewis, that kind of language is quite unacceptable in this—"

"I need to see the premier," Paula said louder. "Right now!"

"Out of the question. He's in the middle of an important phone call. You're going to have to wait, whether you like it or not."

"Important call . . . from whom? He's supposed to keep that line free. Get him off the phone. Whoever he's talking to, it can't be *that* important."

"The premier happens to be talking to the prime minister. Mr. Page called here ten minutes ago. Now I know you're arrogant, but in my book the importance of the prime minister will always excede the importance of one of your little visits."

"What about the importance of the life of an innocent man about to be wrongly executed?"

"I haven't a clue what you're talking about, but if you'd come back tomorrow, I'm sure the premier will listen—"

"My client doesn't have a tomorrow. They'll fry him tonight if I don't get to see Mr. Matthew, so move your ass and get him off that bloody phone. *Now!*"

The urgency of the matter finally sunk into the secretary, and her thin veneer of confidence cracked under Paula's insistence. She rushed into the premier's office at a pace Paula had never seen her move before. Paula slumped into a chair, more nervous by the second. If the premier refused to see her, David Winter was as good as dead. It was now 11:06.

David was half dragged, half carried down the cement corridor. His strength to walk on his own was gone. If not for the guards, he'd have fallen flat on his face. He was ashamed of the way he was acting. He could see that the guards and the warden were looking at him with contempt. To them, he was nothing more than cowardly garbage. David didn't blame them; after all, that was how he felt about himself.

For the first time since leaving his cell, David noticed how quiet it was in the prison. There's no place quieter than death row on the night of an execution. The rest of the rats trapped in their cages weren't stirring, as usual. It was silent, except for the shuffling of heavy guard's boots and the mutterings from the priest following behind. Even the creature was oddly quiet, as if it didn't want to break the somber mood. It couldn't suppress its rotted grin, however, following behind everyone happy as could be.

David looked up to see that they were coming to the end of the hallway. *Fear* is far too weak a word to describe the feelings of terror and helplessness that raced through his body. How had things gotten this bad? He knew he'd been a screwup most of his life, but did he really deserve this? Hadn't he suffered enough?

Up ahead, there was a heavy, black steel door. Somewhere on the other side, Death was waiting to meet him. There was a small clock on the wall above the door. It was now 11:10.

"That's it," Paula said. "I'm not waiting another second."

Bursting into the premier's office uninvited to break up a conversation with the prime minister was definitely not going to win her or her client brownie points, but she didn't have a choice. Time was running, and she couldn't just sit back and do nothing. Fortunately, the premier's secretary came back out of the inner office before she had the opportunity to try kicking the door down.

"Okay, Miss Lewis, you win. Mr. Matthew will see you, but believe me . . . he's not in a good mood. Relax another few seconds and he'll be off the phone."

It ended up being closer to quarter after before Paula got to see the premier, and as his secretary had warned, he wasn't happy.

"What the hell do you want this time, Lewis?" Premier

Matthew yelled across his oak desk. "Do you realize who was on the phone?"

Above his bulging green eyes, a vein stood out on his otherwise-unwrinkled brow. The vein throbbed in time with his angry words. It was obvious to Paula she had best tread lightly with her argument or he would throw her out, pronto.

"First of all, I'm sorry about disturbing you tonight. I know you're busy and I appreciate your taking the time to see me." She was laying it on thick and it disgusted her, but anything was worth trying. She was relieved to see the vein in his head stop throbbing. She had softened his anger, a little. "To get right to the point, sir, my client, Mr. Winter, is an innocent man, and I'm here to ask you to stop his wrongful execution."

The words seemed to hang in the air above their heads as if in cartoon balloons. Finally, Mr. Matthew found a response. "You never give up, do you Paula? Although I find your tenacity admirable, I'm sick and tired of running around in circles. Get it through your head: David Winter is guilty. Period. Tonight at midnight he's going to pay for his crimes."

Paula dug out the coroner's report on the warden from her briefcase and slid it across the desk.

"The coroner's report . . . So? I've seen a copy of this document."

"I know, but take a closer look at the estimated time of Warden Steele's death."

"It says between seven and nine A.M. So? Obviously he died in the morning."

"Exactly my point, Mr. Matthew. He died sometime in the early morning hours of October 6. Agreed?"

"That's what it says."

"Okay. So tell me how it was possible for my client to have murdered the warden, when he wasn't even admitted to his office until well after two o'clock in the afternoon?"

The premier had been ready to shoot any of her questions

down, but this one momentarily silenced him. "It's a mistake, that's all. The coroner made a typing error."

Paula and the premier both knew he was reaching. They knew how meticulously this autopsy had been performed. The chance of a mistake this drastic was zero.

"They're very accurate at determining time of death these days. You know that as much as I do. It may be off a little, but it's close. That time of death isn't a mistake . . . it's a fact."

"I tend to agree, Miss Lewis, but it's an *impossible* fact. It can't be true."

"It can, sir, if someone else killed Warden Steele."

"That doesn't hold water, Lewis. The prison guard escorted Mr. Winter to the warden's office. The secretary even saw them talking to each other, and all that took place in the afternoon. How do you account for that?"

"Easily, Premier, they lied. I've been putting pressure on both of them lately. The guard, a Mr. Pearson, was on somewhat friendly terms with my client. He never escorted Mr. Winter to the warden's office. He only told him he was supposed to go. They met in the prison courtyard, and my client walked on his own to the meeting."

Paula paused to dig another sheet of paper out of her file. It was a signed letter by guard Pearson, stating exactly what she'd just told the premier. She let him look at it briefly before going on.

"As for the secretary," she said, pulling out another signed document, "she didn't quite tell the truth either. She only heard two people talking in the warden's office. *Heard*, not saw. Someone in the office called her and indicated that they weren't to be disturbed. She thought it was the warden, but now she's not sure. She seems to recall his voice sounded a little funny, and that maybe it could have been someone pretending to be the warden."

Mr. Matthews carefully examined both signed documents in front of him and then glanced again at the coroner's report.

"So you're saying someone killed Ben Steele in the morning, then hung around the warden's office all day just to frame your client. I agree this is all very unusual, but it's crazy. It can't justify canceling tonight's execution. This is all speculation."

"It's all fact! This new information brings up an awful lot of unanswered questions, and unanswered questions constitute reasonable doubt. You can't tell me you're still 100 percent sure my client did it—so you can't fry him. I'm not asking for the world here, sir, just some time. Let's call this off, temporarily, and see if we can find answers to those questions."

"I can't. The prime minister is on his way to witness the execution. That's what he called about. Every newspaper in Canada is here. It would be a big mistake to call it off now."

"I don't care if Santa Claus and the fucking jolly old elves have ringside seats. . . . It'll be a far bigger mistake to electrocute an innocent man. I want a stay of execution, Mr. Matthew, and I need it now. We're running out of time. David Winter is running out of time."

The premier sat back in his chair, unsure of what to do. The vein on his forehead had started throbbing again. His next decision could be one of the most important decisions of his life. To call the execution off now would almost certainly cause a nasty confrontation with the prime minister. The PM had clearly been pushing for this execution for a long time. But what if David Winter *was* innocent?

Paula Lewis sat rigid as a stone and awaited his decision. She had done all she could for her client. All she could do was wait. It was now 11:25.

David had been escorted through the steel doorway at the end of the hall. A chair waited for him in the small room on the other side of the door, but it wasn't the chair he'd expected to see. He'd forgotten about having to get prepared first. They'd instructed him that he would have to have parts of his body shaved in order for them to properly attach the various electrodes to his skin.

He was seated in the barber chair and had to listen to the creature teasing him that he should just ask for a "short, back and sides." The creature found this incredibly amusing, but David most certainly did not.

"Bastard," he said, and the barber thought David meant him. "Not you," he added. "Some other bastard."

The confused barber just shook his head and went to work. He had to completely shave David's head, and then parts of his arms and legs. He also removed David's shoes and socks and rolled up his pant legs. Within fifteen minutes, he was finished and hastily left the room. Apparently, governmentally approved murder wasn't his cup of tea.

Warden Brown bent down to David's level to speak in semiprivate. "Listen, David. The electric chair is through that next doorway. I'm not telling you this to scare or torment you. I'm just trying to prepare you. The sight of it can be unnerving if you're not ready for it. This will all be over before you know it. I promise not to let you suffer. Do you understand?"

David could only find the strength to nod his head. This was really going to happen. They were going to kill him for something he hadn't done. Tears started to stream down his cheeks and the warden clasped his shoulder in a show of sympathy.

"We have to wait here for a while, Winter. We don't leave until quarter to twelve. Just try and relax."

Relax? David thought. *Yeah right.*

It was now 11:29.

Paula paced restlessly around Premier Matthew's office waiting for his answer. He was still deep in thought. His secretary had popped her head in to inquire if either of them wanted a cup of coffee or tea, but had immediately noticed the tension in the air and disappeared without waiting for a reply.

"We can't wait any longer, sir," Paula said, breaking the

silence. She wanted him to make up his own mind, but he was taking too damn long. "You can't worry about who you're going to piss off. There will always be tomorrow to justify it to everybody. There is no tomorrow for David Winter. If there's any chance he might be innocent, you can't let him die. Sign the paper, Premier. Do the right thing and sign it now."

Premier Matthew looked into her eyes and took a deep breath. She was right and he knew it. He just couldn't sit back and let a possibly innocent man die. "Okay, Lewis, but for both our sakes, I hope you know what you're talking about. If I get hung for botching this, believe me, you'll swing with me."

"Fine with me," said Paula as she watched the premier fill out the stay-of-execution form.

"This stay will grant Mr. Winter a delay in his execution, Miss Lewis. A *delay* . . . not a pardon. If you can't come up with another potential killer and proof-positive evidence your client is innocent, he's going back to the chair. Understand?"

"Crystal clear. Can you make the call now? We cut this a bit close for my liking."

"I know what you mean," Matthew smiled back as he dialed the hotline number for the penitentiary. Someone would be waiting at the far end to immediately put a stop to the execution and return Mr. Winter to his cell.

The phone never rang at the prison.

"That's funny. Let me try it again."

"What's funny?" Paula asked, renewed tension in her voice.

"The phone," answered the premier. "When I dial the penitentiary, I don't get a ring at the other end. It's the same thing again this time. Nothing but static. I'd better check with Bell Telephone."

A few more precious minutes ticked by as the premier talked to the technician about the prison phones. From the ashen look on his face and the way his voice was trembling, Paula could tell the news wasn't good.

"I don't believe this. The tech doesn't know what's going on. She said that as far at the phone company is concerned, there doesn't appear to be anything wrong with their systems, but she couldn't get through either. In fact, every phone and fax within a mile radius of the prison isn't functioning. No reason for it . . . they just aren't working."

Paula listened, a cold chill inching up her back. If they couldn't get through to the prison, how were they going to stop the execution? "What the hell are we going to do?"

"Nothing we *can* do, Miss Lewis. We can't get word through to them. I hate to say this, but innocent or not, David Winter is going to die."

Paula shuddered. Had she really come this close to saving her client, just to be foiled by some stupid phone glitch? She'd never forgive herself if David died like this. That familiar stubborn feeling began to wash over her again. She couldn't give up now.

"I can still stop it, sir. I can deliver the stay of execution myself. We can't be more than ten minutes from the prison. I can still make it in my car if I hurry. Keep trying the bloody phone. Maybe it'll come back on while I'm driving over there."

She grabbed the signed document from the premier and was gone out the door before he could say another word. The premier tried dialing the hotline to the prison again, but it was still dead.

"Godspeed to you, young lady," he muttered under his breath. "Godspeed."

It was now 11:41.

David couldn't stop shaking. He feared death now. For a long time, he'd tricked himself into thinking death would be a good thing, but now that its stark reality was so imminent, he cringed at the thought of it.

A gentle hand falling lightly onto his left shoulder caused

David to jump. He looked up expecting to see the Grim Reaper towering over him with its arms open wide, but it was only the priest.

"Don't let it overcome you, my son," the clergyman began. "Death doesn't have to be feared. Ask the Lord for forgiveness and paradise awaits you. Your next world can be a much better place than this one, but to get there you must give your heart to the Lord. You must, my son. . . . It's the only way."

David considered the priest's words then shook his head in denial. "I can't father. My faith is considerably less than it should be. If there *is* a God watching from above, then how can he allow all these awful things to happen to me? I'm innocent of these crimes, father, and your God is still going to let them murder me."

"The Lord works in many strange ways. If what you say is true, and you really are innocent, believe me when I say God will know. If he allows you to die tonight, then he must have a purpose for it. We can't and don't understand everything. That, my son, is where faith comes in. Give yourself to him, David. I promise you he won't let you down. Besides, don't give up hope yet. The premier might still call this thing off."

"What do you mean?"

"The premier has the power to cancel this execution right up until the stroke of midnight. All it takes is a phone call. You never know my son. . . . Like I said, the Lord sometimes works in strange ways." The priest squeezed David's shoulder again and moved off to let him think.

Do I believe in God? David wondered. *Can I, after everything that's happened?*

The answer was yes—David did still believe. The creature had said it had escaped from Hell, and he believed it. *If there's a Hell, then it only stands to reason Heaven exists too. If there's a Devil, then God must also be there. God knows I'm innocent, so maybe he'll put a stop to this. Maybe the premier really will phone and cancel the execution. Maybe—*

"Still the same dreamer, aren't you David?" the creature said, cutting him off midthought. "Hate to burst your little bubble, but the premier isn't going to be calling here tonight. Nobody will be. I took care of the phone lines all over this area of the city. Trust me, nobody will be calling this party off. Tonight you're going to die so that I can live. Get used to the idea and stop boring me with all your meaningless thoughts."

David was about to shout back at the creature, which would really have made everyone in the room think he was insane, but another hand fell onto his shoulder, startling him again. This time, it was the warden.

"It's quarter to, David. We have to go through into the next room now. It's time."

Nothing but a low moan escaped from David's mouth in reply. The guards moved in to secure him, but he surprised them by standing under his own power and walking shakily over to the metal door on the opposite side of the room. The door slowly opened and he had his first look at the last place he would ever sit down. Ten feet directly in front of him, waiting with open arms, was the electric chair.

The warden had warned him the sight of the chair could be a bit unnerving. That was an understatement. The electric chair wasn't unnerving—it was horrifying. It wasn't the chair itself. It was more the feeling that came from it. The chair was nothing more than a large wooden high-backed seat, plainer than David had imagined it would be. The only distinguishing features that set it apart were the thick leather restraints on the arms and legs, and the series of multicolored wires and electrodes that trailed over to a power box on the far wall.

No, it wasn't the chair itself that instilled horror in David. It was the feeling that this chair was somehow alive. It was hard to describe, but he couldn't bring himself to think of it as an inanimate object made of wood, metal, and plastic. To David, the chair looked like some kind of large, hungry animal from some bizarre sci-fi movie, sitting waiting to be fed.

His newfound strength deserted him, and he collapsed in a heap. There was a loud gasp off to the left as he hit the ground. David looked, but all he saw was a large framed mirror hanging on the wall. It didn't take a genius to realize it was a two-way mirror, and that a crowd of spectators was obviously behind it watching his every move.

The guards hauled him to his feet. They dragged his limp body across the floor and sat him down unceremoniously in the hot seat. The creature danced his way into the room behind them and stood over against the wall in front of David. It wanted to look into his eyes when they threw the switch.

The chair itself was comfortable to sit in, which didn't in the least make David feel better. He was weeping openly and without shame. The warden leaned down to whisper to him while two guards begun to strap him down. "Listen, David . . . try and be strong. A lot of people are here from the media. The prime minister himself is also watching. You don't want them to see you go out bawling like this, do you?"

"Screw the prime minister, and screw the media. And screw you too," was all David could think to say. If he wanted to have a bloody good cry, who the hell were they to stop him?

The warden moved away and let the guards finish strapping him down. The electrodes were taped on and secured next. Last of all came the wire helmet, which fitted snugly and uncomfortably onto his head. The helmet held seven Vaseline-covered electrodes firmly against his recently shaved scalp. When everything was rechecked, the two guards disappeared from the room and the exit door closed.

The only people remaining in the execution chamber now were David, the warden, a guard stationed at a red telephone, a provincial official manning the power switch, and of course, the creature. The creature was holding what was left of its rotted stomach as it howled with laughter.

"If you could only see yourself, Davey. Do you think they're using enough electrodes? Jeez, you're gonna light up like a bloody Christmas tree."

David tried his best to ignore the creature and instead concentrated on the guard by the phone. Maybe the creature had been lying about tampering with the phones. Maybe the premier would still call before it was too late. There was nothing he could do but wait. It was now 11:53.

The Toronto Maximum Security Penitentiary was located on a busy street named Tucker Avenue. Simon Tucker had been one of the city's earliest settlers and had been renowned for his kindness and honesty. Why the city had chosen to name a street filled with nasty, dishonest criminals after him was anybody's guess.

Paula Lewis couldn't have cared less. The only thing she cared about Tucker Avenue was that it was still two stoplights away. The lights changed, and she gunned her car across the intersection. She had driven from the premier's office like a woman possessed, barely using the brakes unless absolutely necessary. Up ahead, she spotted her turnoff onto Tucker Avenue. From there, the prison was just on the right.

"Hold on, David. I'm coming."

Paula turned onto Tucker and ran straight into a traffic jam. She had to slam on the car's brakes with both feet to avoid rear-ending the car stopped in front of her. The road ahead was clogged for what looked like miles. Way up ahead, she could just barely make out the flashing lights of two police cars and an ambulance.

"No. Not a bloody accident on this street. Not tonight."

But there was, and all the denial in the world wasn't going to change anything. She tried honking to get people out of the way, but it was useless. Up ahead, the prison was lit up brightly against the dark night sky. Paula couldn't have been more than a quarter of a mile from it, but it may as well have been a thousand miles. With traffic bumper to bumper, her car wasn't going anywhere.

Frustration and anger welled up inside her and she pounded on the steering wheel until her hands ached. The answer popped into her head suddenly. *Run*. She still had time if she ran like a bat out of hell. Without waiting another heartbeat, Paula dashed from her car, leaving it running right in the middle of the street, and tore off toward the penitentiary, stay-of-execution order firmly in her fist. Her guts were already cramping, more from stress than exertion, but she ran harder, not letting pain get in the way. Less than a block and she'd be there.

"God, help me make it before it's too late," she screamed to the heavens above.

It was now 11:54.

Warden Brown walked past David without even glancing in his direction. David watched him check his watch and walk over to the guard stationed at the red telephone. The warden tried to keep his voice low, but in the silence of the quiet room, David could hear every word spoken between them.

"Any word from the premier yet?" the warden asked.

"No, sir. Nothing," the stone-faced guard answered.

"Let's get this over with, then."

Out of his inside suit pocket, Warden Brown produced a folded sheet of white paper. He took up a suitable position in the room in a spot that was visible both to David and to the room full of media spectators. He checked his watch again and then read aloud from the paper held in front of him.

"David Winter . . . It is by order of the court, that as a result of being found guilty by a jury of your peers for the murder of Benjamin J. Steele, you are to be sentenced to death. In accordance with the law of this country, electricity shall be passed through your body until you are dead. This judgment shall be carried out at midnight. Do you have any last words or requests?"

David listened to the warden, but the words didn't quite

register. It was as if the warden were speaking to him from miles away. David sat rigid in his chair, thinking about his old friend Johnny, who was sitting watching him from behind the two-way mirror. David had hated him for his involvement with the creature, but now he realized his onetime friend was also a victim. The creature had been playing in his mind for years and was now about to take over Johnny's body as soon as David died.

What was in store for the rest of the world after that? At least death would spare him those horrible details. The warden was staring hard at him, still waiting for his response. He couldn't think of a single thing to say. It was now 11:55.

Paula took the prison stairs two at a time and burst through the heavy double doors at the top. A startled guard rocketed up out of his chair at the reception desk to confront her. She was in no mood to be delayed by some flunky in a rent-a-cop costume.

"Get out of my way, mister. I'm under direct order of the premier of Ontario to stop the execution scheduled for tonight. Get in my way and it's your job . . . not to mention your ass." Paula thrust the signed stay of execution in his face and was surprised when he said that he'd help her.

"I can call from here. Hold on a second," the guard said, reaching for the phone.

"It won't do you any good. The phones are all down. The premier's been trying to get through for half an hour now."

"You're right. I guess I'll have to take you to Security Wing F and . . . Hey, wait."

But Paula was already gone. She'd visited the penitentiary enough to know how to find death row by herself. She was exhausted, but sprinted down the gray-painted corridors anyway. She had to hurry. It was now 11:57.

"Do you have any last words or requests, Mr. Winter, or should I proceed?"

The warden was aware of the scrutiny the media would

attach to this historic execution. He was determined to play it to the letter in every way possible, so that nothing bad could reflect back on him. The law stated the accused was entitled to a last word or reasonable request, and Mr. Brown intended to see that was exactly what he got.

The wheels inside David's mind were spinning at a blinding pace. An idea had formed in his head, and he almost let it out to the creature, who was still smiling happily over against the wall. From years of practice, he felt the creature gently brush across his mind trying to pick up his last thoughts, and he instantly tried to think about everything in the world at once in order to jumble the message the creature received.

The mad scramble of images relayed back to the creature was so distorted, it obviously thought David had slipped over the edge into madness. David continued to scramble his thoughts until the creature's mind probe slipped away.

Thank God, he thought, when he was sure his mind was his own again. What he was about to try could only work if the creature didn't know about it. He pretended to act unbalanced as he motioned with his head for the warden to come over to him.

The creature burst out laughing as David whispered some nonsense into the warden's ear. It was a bit confused when the warden left the execution chamber after talking to David. For a brief moment, the creature thought the warden had decided to call things off. It checked in with David's mind again to see if he knew what was going on, but the same helter-skelter of images flooded back. Obviously David wasn't going to be much help.

A minute passed and the creature began to worry, but then the warden returned. A smile started to stretch back across the creature's blackened, rotted skull, but the smile never fully formed. It froze, replaced by a look of sheer horror, when it saw what the warden was holding in his hand.

It was the ring of Power.

Somehow, the warden had gone out and taken the ring from Johnny's finger and was now placing it onto David's. It watched in stunned silence as David made a tight fist around it. The creature probed across his mind, expecting more confusion, but David's mind was clear as a bell and waiting for it.

I got you, you son of a bitch, David laughed at the creature. *For once in my life, I actually tricked you. Let's see you get yourself out of this mess.*

What mess? the creature wondered. Now it was confused. Stunned by what had happened, it hadn't had time to think things through. When it did realize what David was trying to do, it went berserk.

The spells were already cast and set to go as soon as David no longer lived. The moment of his death would signal the ring of Power to draw the creature into the body of the wearer. It was supposed to have been Johnny out in the media room, but David had somehow changed all that. Now David was wearing the ring and, from the look of his white knuckles, was holding onto it for dear life. If he were to be executed now, the creature would be drawn into his dead body—still strapped in the electric chair.

The creature let out a gut-wrenching howl of rage and ran toward David. He grabbed for and tugged at his hand, but David held tight.

The warden approached David when he noticed him thrashing uncontrollably in the chair. He couldn't see the battle being waged with the creature and mistook his flailing around as panic. He thought David was trying to break free of his bonds and get away. Nothing could have been further from the truth.

"Mr. Winter, calm down," the warden said. "Thanks to the graciousness of the prime minister, I honored your last request. Now what? Do you have any last words?"

"Yeah," David screamed. "Stop fucking around and pull the bloody switch, you idiot. Pull it *now!*"

The Warden looked at him as if he were from outer space. The people in the media room gasped at the comment and began scribbling in their notes. David continued to fight a battle none of them could see, much less ever hope to understand.

It was now 11:59.

Paula rounded one of the last corners a bit too fast and smashed to the ground, having fallen over a floor cleaner's mop and bucket. She sprawled across the floor amid a river of soapy warm water. The floor cleaner, a husky-voiced German lady, recovered enough from the fright Paula had given her to help her to her feet.

"So sorry . . . so sorry," was all the cleaning lady kept saying. She probably figured Paula would get her fired.

Paula wanted no part of the large woman's apology and dashed off again without even speaking. She only had a short distance to run now, and she'd be able to put a stop to this madness. She could almost picture the look of happiness spreading across her client's face when he found out she had delayed the execution. It was now only a few seconds before the stroke of midnight.

"Throw the goddamn switch!" David hollered at the top of his voice. He knew he couldn't fend off the creature much longer, and he'd never get another chance. His fear of death was gone. His only wish was to take the evil creature with him. He had never lived as a hero; maybe he could at least die as one.

The clock on the wall clicked over to twelve o'clock and the warden frantically signaled the official to turn on the juice. He badly wanted this whole affair over and done with. The official standing at the power switch reached up and grabbed the activating lever, pulling down hard, instantly sending thousands of powerful volts of electricity coursing along the wires to hammer unmercifully into David's body.

Unlike the warden's promise, the pain was excruciating while it lasted, but David savored every painful second. In the few blinding moments of agony before he drifted into oblivion, he knew for the first time in his life what it felt like to succeed. He'd finally beaten the creature, and that knowledge allowed him to smile as the deadly currents stopped his racing heart.

Although David had passed on, the electricity continued to convulse his body for another twenty seconds before the power switch was turned off. An unnerving silence settled on the execution chamber and media room. Nobody could find much of anything to say, so they all just watched the tiny swirls of steam leaking out of David's ears as his brain boiled inside his skull.

The creature had jumped back as soon as the power switch had been thrown. It hadn't even been able to watch as David had strained against the thick leather straps in his final moments before death claimed him. The creature was now cowering in the far corner of the room, terrified at what it knew was about to happen.

For a few precious seconds nothing did, but then it felt the inevitable and inescapable tugging by the Power in the ring. The feeling began in the core of its rotted guts and spread throughout whatever was left of its disgusting body. The ring was calling it home, and the spell would not be denied. It was as if a huge magnet had been turned on.

The creature's lower body began to slide across the floor toward David's slumped and waiting corpse. It tried to hold onto something to stop the slide, but there wasn't anything available to latch onto. Even if there had been, the creature knew deep down it couldn't overpower the strength of the ring.

The powerful pull increased as the creature drew nearer. It only had time for one last scream, and then its rotted body would fuse with the still-bound body. Five feet . . . four feet . . . three feet . . . two . . . one . . . *Fusion!*

The creature's mind swam in a cool pool of darkness for a moment before it began to reassert itself, getting used to its new and unfamiliar body. The creature would gladly have stayed in that cool shadow forever, because when it was finally fully aware again, it found itself sitting in the electric chair.

It tried to scream out and tell the warden to get him out of there, but David's tongue had burned and become stuck to the roof of his mouth in the initial power surge. His vocal cords had also fried in the electrical devastation. All the creature managed to do was squeak out a pathetic moan through its newly charred lips.

Warden Brown's heart nearly stopped when he thought he saw David's head rise up and heard a moan of agony issuing from his lips. He had no idea the real David Winter was already dead and gone. It was therefore quite natural for him to presume he was still alive and quickly order the power switch to be rethrown.

The provincial official was way ahead of him this time. The deadly surge of electricity coursed through the wires once again toward the still-steaming corpse. The creature screamed out in agony and fury at the mistake being made, but the electricity had no prejudices—its only job was to seek and destroy. Within seconds it had done its work, and the creature had joined David in oblivion.

Paula Lewis stormed into the media room screaming for the execution to be stopped, immediately realizing she was too late. She hadn't missed the mark by much, but everything she'd gone through had been for nothing. Her client was dead, and now she would never know if he'd really been innocent or not. She had arrived in time to see the final seconds of the creature's execution, and now that it was over, she balled up the stay of execution order and threw it into the garbage can on her way out.

A minute earlier and I could have stopped it, she thought. *One lousy minute!*

By the time Paula left the building, a terrible feeling of

uneasiness had settled over her. The feeling would stay with her for the rest of her life. It wasn't because she had failed to save her client—that wasn't it at all. The uneasiness came from the unshakable feeling that just before Mr. Winter had died, just for a single moment, she thought she had seen his eyes glowing an unnatural shade of crimson.

CHAPTER THIRTY-FOUR

The walls were starting to crumble—the walls inside Johnathan Page's mind, that is. Now that the creature was gone and no longer in control, there was no one left to hold the memory blocks in place. He sat in the back of the white stretch limousine heading away from the prison, as bits and pieces of memory began to return to him.

He was confused. He was also very scared. Johnny knew enough to know he was the prime minister of Canada, but for the life of him, he couldn't remember how he'd achieved such lofty heights. He remembered being on the debate team in high school, but that was about as far as his political memory stretched.

Fragments of other memories were also frightening. There was something swimming around in his mind about a huge man with strange glowing eyes. Who was that? And what was the bloody knife that kept slashing out of his subconscious? He kept seeing his childhood friends too. They were all down in some dark place made entirely of concrete. Something about foul-smelling water. What did these things mean? Too many questions and not one answer. His mind began to spin out of control. He sat in the brightly lit limo with his mind completely in the dark.

Lawrence Duncan sat beside the prime minister, confused as well. Lawrence was Johnny's public-relations man and had accompanied him to the execution tonight. His puzzlement stemmed from the way the prime minister was acting. Not just right now, but earlier, when they were back at the prison.

Mr. Page had always been in control in every situation. Lawrence held the PM in the highest regard. He'd thought Johnny was a virtual pillar of confidence and strength, but after tonight he wasn't so sure.

In the media room at the prison, Johnny just hadn't been himself. He'd been quiet and detached from the moment they sat down. When the warden had entered the media room, things had really gone downhill. Warden Brown had announced that he was trying to carry out the prisoner's last request. Mr. Winter had requested something be returned to him that he'd once possessed. Lawrence had nearly fainted when he'd found out it was the prime minister who was in possession of the desired object.

Apparently, the prisoner and the prime minister used to be childhood friends, and a ring that David Winter had once owned was now in Johnny's possession. The warden described the ring, and sure enough, it was on Johnny's left hand. The condemned man's last request was to have his beloved ring back, so he could die in peace.

The media had eaten it up, scribbling frantically in their notebooks. They could smell a great story about how the prime minister had helped execute his childhood friend. To top it off, the PM had just sat there, impassive as a rock. Not even a flicker of emotion had crossed his face.

Within seconds the pens had been flying again. Was the prime minister going to just sit there and keep Mr. Winter's ring? Was he really so cold that he would deny his old friend's dying request? From the way he was acting, the answer to those questions had been a big, fat, politically devastating yes!

Luckily, Lawrence had been there to save the day. Noticing the way Johnny was acting, he'd started making excuses that the prime minister wasn't feeling well. He'd lied, saying Johnny was simply overcome with sorrow at what was happening to his distant friend. "Of course Mr. Winter can have his ring back. It's the least the prime minister can do."

Lawrence had taken the ring off Johnny's finger himself. Thankfully, Johnny hadn't protested, and the execution had been carried out. The prime minister had certainly lost some face tonight in the public eye, but the damage was repairable. After all, when everything was said and done, the PM *had* granted the prisoner his request.

"Driver," Lawrence said, "get us to the hotel. The prime minister has had an exhausting night and we have an early flight back to Ottawa."

"Right away, sir. It shouldn't take—"

"No," Johnny said. "I need to go to Dunnville . . . to my mother's house. I want you to take me there."

"Dunnville?" Lawrence asked, frowning. "What do you want to go there for? Your mother's not even there. You said she's in Ottawa visiting you for a few weeks."

"She is . . . I think. It's not her I want to see. I'm confused about a lot of things right now, and something inside me thinks the answers I'm looking for can be found at my old house. Listen, Larry, don't argue. I don't want to go to Dunnville. . . . I feel like I *have* to."

Lawrence thought it was a bad idea, but Johnny was the man in charge of this show, so off they went back to the small town Johnny had grown up in. They didn't arrive until two thirty in the morning. The streets in Dunnville were completely deserted.

"I'm staying here by myself tonight, Larry," Johnny told his public-relations man, holding up his hand to stifle any protests. "This isn't up for debate. I'm staying here and you can get a room at one of the town hotels. Pick me up in the morning and we'll still make our flight. Okay?"

It wasn't, but Lawrence and the driver didn't have much say in the matter. Johnny was out of the car before anyone had a chance to argue.

"Something's definitely wrong with the PM tonight," Lawrence said as they drove off. "I don't know what, but if I didn't know better, I'd swear he isn't the same Johnny Page as the one I knew yesterday."

Lawrence Duncan was kidding, but he had no idea how close he'd come to hitting the nail on the head. Johnny most certainly wasn't the same man he'd been yesterday. The creature that had been Johnny was gone. All that was left was a child suddenly cast into an adult's body. Somewhere along the line, Johnny had lost twenty to thirty years. Fragments of those years existed, but the majority were gone. To Johnny, it felt as if he'd never even lived them, which was essentially the truth. Unknown to Johnny, the creature had lived them for him.

The limousine pulled away, leaving Johnny standing in the gravel driveway. All around him it was dark and silent. "The well out back is where all this started," he whispered and then wondered where that thought had come from. What had happened at the well? "Leeches"—the word came hurtling out of the darkness of his troubled mind. "Leeches all over me."

The memory of sitting on the edge of the well covered in bloodsuckers came back to him, and he was repulsed all over again. He could almost still feel them. "How could I have forgotten that? What's happening to me?"

He wanted to go look at the well, but was terrified of going near it. It wasn't just the thought of the leeches. That was a horrid memory, but there was something else. Something far more terrifying must have happened back by the well, because he just couldn't bring himself to take a look. He decided to go into the house instead.

Inside, more of his memory walls collapsed. Every object he looked at or touched jogged another long-forgotten image: his childhood, his mother, his friends, and his father.

My father?

What was that all about? He couldn't have memories about his father in this house. His father had left him and his mother when he was only a baby. The memory stirred inside him again. Someone had told him he was Johnny's father. Someone he'd been scared of. Somebody that . . .

The memory was gone again as fast as it had come, just

staying frustratingly out of Johnny's reach. "Christ. Maybe Larry's right. I should just go upstairs and climb into the . . . *basement*."

The most powerful memory yet crashed into his head, overpowering everything else. Something was in the basement, something very important that he felt was probably the main reason he'd returned to this house tonight. Fear squirmed in his belly like a nest full of snakes, the panic making him want to run away screaming, but also confirming he was right. Whatever he was supposed to see in the basement, Johnny was positive it was the key to unlocking the rest of his scattered memory. Going down the creaky basement stairs was one of the hardest things he could remember doing.

Now what? Johnny thought, once he'd reached bottom and was standing on the cold cement floor. *Where am I supposed to look?* He closed his eyes and tried to concentrate. Immediately, the memory fragment returned. It raced by quickly, but it was there long enough for him to know that what he was looking for was in the fruit cellar. He ran over to the door and hastily threw it open.

"It's buried in the floor."

The fruit cellar was the only part of the basement that had a dirt floor. Johnny let his memory guide him to a spot on the ground, and he dropped down on all fours to start digging. He still had no idea what he was searching for, but he'd know when he saw it.

Johnny pulled a wooden box wrapped in a plastic garbage bag from where it had been buried under eight inches of dirt. A feeling of dread overcame him the second his fingers touched the box. Multiple images of people covered in blood assaulted him, the memory of their screams ringing fresh in his ears. With shaking hands, he removed the cover.

His memory walls stopped crumbling. They simply evaporated—protecting him one moment, gone the next. Wave after wave of horrifying images hammered against Johnny's broken soul, memories so terrible his mind started to close like a Venus flytrap, his rational thoughts devoured within. Inside the box was a blood-encrusted filleting knife and a large pile of dried-up human ears.

He had done it. Johnny had killed all those people, not his friend David. The creature had been in control of his body at the time of the murders, and David and Tom had followed along in their dreams, but he'd been the one holding the knife in his hand. He had been the Ripper Killer!

The creature. The well. The ring. The knife—oh God, the knife! I killed them all. The creature killed Pete and Tom, but I killed the rest. Even . . . David.

Guilt raked through Johnny as he realized he had helped put David in jail for over twenty years, and tonight he'd been executed for a crime he hadn't committed. This was all too much for him. It probably would have been too much for anyone to handle, but especially Johnny. His mind and soul had been crushed by the creature for so long, he knew no other life. When the creature was destroyed, Johnny had been left with nothing more than an emotional shell. His soul felt empty. It was as if his soul had been released into a cavernous room so large that it stretched as far as the eye could see. Instead of rejoicing in its freedom, it was shivering in a corner trying to crawl back into the safety of its shell. Johnny was slipping over the edge into a dark abyss.

He welcomed the fall.

He reburied the box of severed ears where he'd found it, but he kept hold of the knife. He had other plans for it.

In the morning, Lawrence Duncan found Johnny dead in a hazy red pool of water in the upstairs bathtub. He had slit not only his wrists with the large filleting knife, but his throat as well. It appeared to Lawrence that Johnny had also been in the process of hacking off his right ear, but he'd died before fully completing the macabre task.

The media and general public were, of course, spared the details. They were informed that the prime minister had passed away due to a sudden heart attack. Government insiders and top-level officials believed the suicide was related to work overload and Johnny's increased job stress.

Everyone involved thought they had everything figured out—from the people who believed they had captured the correct Ripper Killer, to the ones who believed the right person had been executed for Warden Steele's murder, to the ones who thought they understood Johnny's suicide. They all thought they were right, but every last one of them was wrong. With Peter Myers, Tom Baker, David Winter, the creature, and now Johnny Page all dead, there was no one left in the world that knew the *real* truth.

Afterlude

Still Where They Buried Me

Well, that's just about everything I can tell you. There's not much else to say really, except to assure you that every word of what I just told you is the honest truth.

You want to know something that's ironic? I spent almost every waking minute of my precreature childhood with my head in the clouds. I was always daydreaming about being Superman or Batman or some other great superhero. I think I honestly believed some day I would save the world. The way that crazy ball of life ended up bouncing, I guess it's not too terribly arrogant of me to presume that I did. The only trouble is, now that I've finally realized my dream of saving the world (if that is in fact what I did), nobody has any idea I did it. Now that's irony.

It's also a crock of shit. I was nothing more than a lifelong coward that fate just happened to smile on at the right moment. I have to admit I'm proud of myself. I took a great deal of pride and joy in fucking up the creature's great master plan. Unfortunately, like everything else in my life, the creature still managed to get the last laugh. I was under the impression that once I died in the electric chair, that would be the end of it, and I would at last be at peace. Wrong again.

When I rode the electric highway into oblivion, I enjoyed about thirty seconds of blissful peace. That was how long it took for them to reexecute my old body and kill the creature. The big mistake I'd committed was that, by inviting the creature to join with my body, I had inadvertently invited it to join with my soul. When people die, their souls don't immediately vacate their bodies. Just as the creature had done a couple of times, my soul had to wait around to see which way the tugging sensation would take it. By that, I mean whether I was headed up or down. I guess your soul has to wait around until the decision is made.

There I was, waiting for my ticket to Heaven, when all of a sudden the creature is dead and inside me. When our bodies were fused by the Power in the creature's ring . . . our minds and souls were also blended together.

That was when the real problem started. I was no longer simply David Winter, and it was no longer just the creature. We were both parts of one joint soul, one previously unheard-of entity. Heaven wouldn't have anything to do with me, seeing as part of me was now so tainted with raging evil, and likewise with Hell. My contribution to this bastardized soul was way too goody-two-shoes for them. As a result we went . . . *nowhere.*

You might find this hard to swallow, but right now we're still occupying my slightly ripe corpse, which was buried unceremoniously the day after the execution.

I haven't told you the worst part. When they buried our body, they buried it with the ring of Power still wrapped around my finger. Our body's flesh is dead, but the Power in the ring still lives, slowing down the decaying process to a snail's pace so our body remains strong and intact. The creature has been trying to convince me we don't have to stay buried in this cold ground forever. It tells me that if we work together, we could use the Power in the ring to get someone to help us. It wants me to do exactly what the creature did before. It wants us to take over someone, and then we could live again.

When I first died, it was simple for me to shrug the creature off and tell it to go fuck itself. Now, to be perfectly honest, it's getting harder. Spending day after day, month after month, potentially year after year in this slowly rotting corpse will become intolerable. I don't think I'll be able to take it much longer. Certainly not forever, that's for sure.

I think another factor to consider here is that the more time I spend as part of the creature, the more I seem to be becoming like it. I find myself thinking the same bitter, evil thoughts. I think soon, very soon, the creature and I will be indistinguishable from one another, and the assimilation will be irreversible. That's why I need your help.

I don't have the strength to hold off the changes that are happening to me, and I can't resist the temptation to try using the Power. This is where you come in. We can never get out of this hole without someone else wearing the ring. To do that, you'd have to fall under our Power and be convinced to do a little grave robbing.

Before I lose all control to the evil in me, I want to ask you—no, beg you—to listen. If you ever find yourself walking along and you feel something powerful pulling at your senses, ignore it. Run away, sing a song, dance a jig, or do anything it takes to free your mind and get it back on other things.

Your best option would be to stay far away from graveyards. If you find that you must go into one, then by all means don't go alone. You don't know where my body is buried, but with a little bit of bad luck, you may just stumble on it.

I have no way of knowing whether you believe any of what I have been telling you, but I suppose that part is irrelevant. People have always done whatever they thought was best. If some crazy bastard out there chooses to seek me out and dig me up, what can I do about it except say that I warned you all beforehand.

One last message to all you people who might consider digging me up: don't do it. You wouldn't like what you saw.

I don't imagine I look very nice right about now. You see, I've been slowly rotting away for a while now, and my skin seems to have turned a rather nasty shade of green. Mind you, the green hue does agree nicely with the shade of my eyes, what with them beginning to glow red and all. . . .